Anyway, by the time the polycrisis turned into a global melt-down, 98% of the cargo pods had been installed on the *Cascade* and the last hundred or so were already in transit. For almost a year, the colonists had been planning for this voyage as if it might be the last—and the cargo manifests had been altered accordingly. Added to that, the colony had begun purchasing cargo and equipment from the other three brightliners under construction and she ended up with an extra thousand pods on her racks. The whole thing was pretty impressive, and I couldn't figure out why Boynton was so worried about the survival of Outbeyond colony. This voyage would deliver enough supplies to keep everyone there alive for years.

Tor Books by David Gerrold

LEAPING
TO
THE
STARS

DAVID
GERROLD

TOR®

A TOM DOHERTY ASSOCIATES BOOK
NEW YORK

for Miles Rinis,
with love

LEAPING TO THE STARS

A Tor Book
Published by Tom Doherty Associates, LLC
175 Fifth Avenue
New York, NY 10010

www.tor.com

Tor® is a registered trademark of Tom Doherty Associates, LLC.

ISBN: 0-812-58974-2
Library of Congress Catalog Card Number: 2001054057

First edition: March 2002
First mass market edition: August 2003

Printed in the United States of America

0 9 8 7 6 5 4 3 2 1

THE INTERVIEW

"**Y**OU UNDERSTAND, OF COURSE, that this is a one-way trip. There will be no possibility of return."

The interviewer's name was Gary Boynton, and he was commander of the mission. He looked like one of those detectives who wanted to be your friend, while the other one stood off to one side, scowling impatiently and waiting to get ugly. Except there wasn't any other detective, just a couple of aides who hardly said anything at all.

We all nodded as if we understood. Me, Douglas, Mickey. Dad. Mom and her friend, Bev. Bobby sat next to me, with the monkey on his lap. He didn't care where we were going as long as we all stayed together. Boynton had glanced at the monkey a couple of times. He knew what it contained, everybody on Luna did, but unlike all the other interviewers, he wasn't saying much about it.

"You can stay here on Luna, Mr. Dingillian. Or you can go to Mars, or to one of the Jovian moons, or even to the rings or the asteroids. Most of those settlements are self-sufficient in a rudimentary sort of way. And if the situation on Earth ever settles down, you could go back home. As millionaires. You don't *need* to go to Outbeyond."

"The situation on Earth *isn't* going to settle down," said Dad.

Boynton was very patient. He said, "The plagues will burn out within two years. Three at the most. Our intelligence engines suggest that reconstruction and rehabilitation could put Earth's level of technology back to pre-plague levels within ten years, twenty at the most."

"Your intelligence engines are wrong," said the monkey, very politely.

Boynton wasn't going to argue—especially not with an intelligence engine that had publicly embarrassed a Lunar Authority Judge. At least, that's how the media was playing it. He shrugged off the interruption. "Whatever the case, however long it takes Earth to recover, if you stay here on Luna, you still have the possibility of returning someday. If you emigrate, that option is gone forever."

He looked around the table. We were sitting on a terrace overlooking a spectacular view of the lake and the forest under Armstrong Dome. A flock of bright red chickens bounced across the grass like balloons, flapping their stubby wings and clucking excitedly. It was almost pretty.

We'd argued about staying right here on the moon more than once, but Douglas and Mickey didn't like the politics. And I didn't want to hang around anyplace with fanatics like Alexei. And even though we had all agreed to respect each other's points of view, ever since we'd divorced Mom and Dad, Douglas and I had gotten used to making our own decisions—even the wrong ones.

Boynton continued. He was telling us what we already knew. "Outbeyond Colony is the farthest colony from Earth. Thirty-five light years. There have been three exploratory missions and five colonization voyages. A beachhead has been established. Not a colony. A beachhead. The situation there is tenuous. Life will be difficult and dangerous. Survival is not guaranteed.

"We're telling this to everyone. If you go to Outbeyond, you will die there. The question is not *if*, but *when*. Will you have a long, hard, laborious life before you die? Or will you die within a few months or years, of some unforeseen disaster? We are asking everyone, even those who have already signed on, to reconsider their commitment, because once we get there, life will be hard. Not just hard, but *harder* than you imagine.

"We will work—all of us, even Bobby—twenty-hour days. We will be short of food, short of sleep, short of supplies. Everything will be rationed. We will not be able to call for help. There won't be any. We will have what is already there from the five previous supply missions. We will have what we bring ourselves on this trip. We will have what we can build. That's it. If you need cancer medicine and we don't have it, too bad, you die of cancer. If you need a blood transfusion and nobody shares your blood type and we don't have any artificial blood, too bad. If you need a new eye or a new lung or a new kidney and we don't have one growing in a tank, too bad.

"There will be no resupply for this colony. Not in any fore-seeable future. This trip is paid for—we're going. We're leaving in thirteen days. But nobody else is coming after us. There isn't anyone building any more ships. There won't be any money to build any more ships, or load them, or offer colony contracts. By the time anyone on Earth can make that kind of investment again, we'll all be dead. Whether or not our grand-children will be there to meet them—well, that's the purpose of this discussion."

Boynton looked from one to the other of us. I knew that Mom didn't want to go anywhere at all, but if Douglas and Mickey and I decided we wanted to go to the stars, she'd follow. And so would her friend. I knew Dad wanted to go—he was the reason we were all here now. This wasn't working out the way he'd originally intended; this was better, so he wasn't complaining. And Bobby was just happy to have his family back together.

And me?

I didn't know what I wanted yet. This business of making decisions—how did adults do it? All day long, every day, even weekends, with no time off for good behavior. No wonder I was cranky all the time. I was exhausted from having to think so much.

"I know that the other colonies have made some wonderful proposals," Boynton said. "And if I were you, if I had your assets"—Here he glanced meaningfully at the monkey—"I'd strongly consider taking one of those offers. Most of those colonies are close to self-sufficient anyway, and with the advantage your HARLIE unit represents, you and whatever colony you choose *will* succeed."

"So what are the advantages of Outbeyond?" Dad asked.

Boynton shook his head. "To be honest, I have nothing to offer. If I were to offer anything, I'd have to take it away from someone else. And I'm not willing to do that. If you and I were just sitting around in a bar, using up oxygen and alcohol, I'd tell you to go to McCain or Pastoria and forget about Outbeyond. It's suicide."

I could see that Dad didn't like the sound of that. Mom and her friend Bev were already squirming in their seats. But it was Douglas and Mickey who had accepted this meeting, and the meeting wasn't finished until they were. Douglas said, "If it's suicide, why are you going?"

"When I accepted the job as Mission Commander, we were looking at a program of twelve supply missions to reach self-sufficiency. The critical threshold was assumed to be somewhere around the seventh or eighth voyage. The next trip. The one *after* this one.

"We've got forty-three hundred people on Outbeyond. Even as we're sitting here talking, they're hard at work. They're laying down tubes, putting up domes, getting the power-grid up, preparing the facilities for the first batch of colonists to arrive. They're good folks. They don't know what's happened to Earth. They're expecting a ship soon. If it doesn't arrive—well, they have contingency plans. They'll survive for a while, but . . . the contingency plan doesn't include self-sufficiency. Not long-term self-sufficiency.

"It's not likely they'll survive without us. Oh, maybe a couple years, if they're careful. But not much longer than that. The equation is simple. Outbeyond colony is *almost* self-supporting. *Almost*. We *might* be able to make the difference. If we don't go, they die for sure. If we do go, maybe we all die—but maybe we all live, too."

"So you're going to rescue them, but there's no one coming after to rescue you . . . ?"

"If they were *your* family, Mr. Dingillian, what would you do?"

"I'd go after them. So would my wife." Dad didn't even hesitate. I was proud of him for that. His expression was firm. "The fact that we're all here on Luna ought to be proof enough how far we'll go."

"And you'd go a lot farther too, if you had to, wouldn't you? So would we. Yes, we know we're gambling here. Every baby born is a gamble, but that doesn't stop the human race from making babies, does it? No, we just stack the deck as best we can, and keep on dealing.

"We know we're the last ship out. Knowing that, we can fill every nook and cranny, every cabin and storage compartment, every corridor and crawlspace with as much supplies and equipment as we can pack. We're loading in everything we can. Most of the matériel for voyages 7, 8, and 9 is already onsite, here on Luna. That's part of *our* contingency plan. The last six voyages, we intended to bring in multiples of necessary equipment and supplies. Once we eliminate duplicate items, we can bring most of what we need on a single voyage, and fabricate the rest onsite. We know what's already there; we know what else is needed; we're packing it. Yes, it's desperate. But we think it's doable." He looked to the monkey. "What do you think, HARLIE?"

HARLIE was silent. He'd probably been crunching the numbers all morning. But he wasn't going to speak without our consent. We'd all agreed that we weren't going to let people consult HARLIE just because they were sitting in the same room with us. We already had enough phonies and scam artists requesting interviews and meetings. We didn't need any more.

Douglas looked to me. I nodded. Commander Boynton was entitled to know what odds he faced. Douglas nodded back. I said, "Go ahead, HARLIE."

That was all the monkey was waiting for. He looked across the table at Boynton. "Which answer do you want?"

"Both," said Boynton.

HARLIE said, "If the Dingillians travel to Outbeyond on this voyage—and the assumption is that I will travel with them—then it is likely that all of you will lose up to 25% of your body mass in the first year. You'll need to pack more potatoes; you should also pack more vitamin-fortified noodles, lots of them. Rice and beans too, if you can get them. And rose seeds, not for the flowers, but for the hips; you'll need the ascorbic acid."

"And the second answer?"

"If the Dingillians do *not* go to Outbeyond with you, it is likely that most of the colonists will lose more than 30% of their body mass and be too weak to work. Even if your crops are successful, you might not have the strength to harvest them."

"It's *that* close?" Even Boynton looked surprised.

"I told you, your intelligence engines aren't up to the task."

Boynton nodded, chastened. "Thank you, HARLIE." He looked grimly across the table at Dad, at Douglas, at Mickey, at me. "This is the bottom line. I have nothing to offer you— except the opportunity to risk your lives and be uncomfortable for a long time."

"Sounds real attractive," said Dad. "What's the catch?"

The Commander looked annoyed. This wasn't a joking matter. "The only *other* thing I can offer you is blunt honesty. We *need* HARLIE. Without HARLIE, we die. He says so himself. To get HARLIE, we'll take you. If you didn't have HARLIE, I wouldn't be wasting my time. Neither would anybody else. Don't take it personal, Mr. Dingillian, but you have no other value. Yes, I know what all the other colony representatives have said. They're just blowing smoke up your ass—and you know it too or you wouldn't have consented to this meeting.

"Here's the deal. Outbeyond isn't making any promises. Once you get where you're going, you're there. So it doesn't matter what was promised, does it? And that's the catch, no matter where you go. Will anybody else keep their promise? You have no guarantees, and you know that. The only thing you can be sure of is that Outbeyond will keep *this promise*. You'll be uncomfortable, you'll work hard, you'll go to bed hungry, you'll lose weight, and you'll probably die young. And if we don't keep that promise, I doubt you'll complain.

So the only question you have to answer is this? *Do you want to save some lives?*"

The silence was very uncomfortable. I wished he hadn't put it that way. Because that didn't leave us any wiggle room.

"No," said Mickey abruptly. "That's not the only question we have to answer. Is Outbeyond signatory to the Covenant?"

Boynton looked at him as if he'd said something stupid. "You already know the answer, Partridge. We're not."

"*That's* my point. Is Outbeyond willing to sign the Covenant to get HARLIE?"

"I can't speak for the rest of the colony. And even if I could, I wouldn't accept a condition like that. I will tell you that Outbeyond's reluctance to sign the Covenant does not come from a disagreement with its principles. And at this point, signing the Covenant would be a useless gesture anyway. We're going to be on our own for a long, long time. Just what is it you want guaranteed?"

"Does he have to spell it out?" said Douglas; he had *that* tone in his voice.

"No," said Boynton. "He does not have to spell it out. And I can tell you that it isn't an issue here. And it won't be an issue there."

To the rest of us, he said, "I'll need your answer tonight. We're holding two cabins for you. After that, no guarantees. We're going to fill that space one way or another—if not with you, then with rice, beans, noodles, potatoes, seeds, vitamins, laser foundries, data-discs, whatever will fit. We've got a lot to load. Once we're packed, we won't have time for unpacking, shuffling, and repacking. So make your decision quickly. Call me no later than 22:00."

After he left, we all looked at each other. There wasn't much to say. This was not going to be a good idea, no matter how much chocolate you dipped it in.

THE ARGUMENT

So, OF COURSE, WE argued for six hours straight—right through dinner. Sometimes it got pretty ferocious, and then we all retired to our separate corners, until somebody reminded everybody that we were running out of time and we really did have to decide this soon. And then we'd all promise to keep our tempers and we'd climb back into the ring.

Douglas had the prospectus disc that Boynton had left with us, and he had it playing continuously on the opposite wall.

The thing is—Outbeyond didn't *look* as dreadful as Boynton had made it sound.

The planet is a little bit bigger than Earth, but not as dense, not as much heavy metal in the core, so the gravity is about 90% Earth normal. It's got four moons, which are all smaller than Luna, but collectively mass almost as much as the planet itself, and they're pretty heavy because they've got the heavy metals that the planet doesn't have—which really pisses off the planetologists because it doesn't fit the rules for the way planets and moons should behave. I guess Outbeyond wasn't listening when they made the rules.

Outbeyond is the fourth planet out from the star, about as far away as Mars is from the sun; but the star is a lot brighter than Sol, and visibly bluer, and it gives off a lot more radiation in the high bands, so the light hitting the planet is stronger and sharper than the light on Earth. Complicating that, Outbeyond has a weird orbit, slightly elliptical and not quite in the plane of the ecliptic, so it's the oddball in the system.

Outbeyond has a year eighteen months long. Its day is thirty-two hours. Twice a year, at the far ends of its orbit, it's fifteen million kilometers farther out than if its orbit were circular. And twice a year, it's seven million klicks closer. The temperature variations are horrendous.

Also, the planet isn't round. It's sort of flattened. Not a lot, but enough so that you're heavier at the equator than you are at the poles. By ten percent, at least. Oh, yeah, and it's tilted seven degrees on its axis. Just to make things even more interesting. What that does is complicate the seasons even more.

There are eight seasons in a year. First Winter, First Spring, First Summer, First Autumn, Second Winter, Second Spring, Second Summer, Second Autumn. Each season is only two and a half months long—only it's hard to compute months, because you can't do it by full moons.

You have to see it on a screen. At the points in the orbit where the planet comes in closest to the star, you've got Perigee Winter in one hemisphere and Perigee Summer in the other. At the points in the orbit when the planet is farthest from the star, you get Apogee Winter in one hemisphere and Apogee Summer in the other. Apogee Summer is colder than Perigee Winter. Apogee Winter is the coldest time of the year and Perigee Summer is the hottest. And I mean *hot*.

What all this means is that Outbeyond has a pretty ferocious mix of regions and seasons. The equatorial regions are mostly unlivable. Temperatures range from 110 degrees in Apogee Winter to 180 degrees in Perigee Summer. The temperate zones are cooler or hotter, depending on the time of the year. The poles are 50 to 200 degrees cooler than the equator, depending on the season. During Perigee Summer, they're like Earth's temperate zones. During Apogee Winter, you get carbon dioxide snowflakes.

Oh yeah, and most of the mountains are volcanoes. Because the planet has such a weird shape, there's a lot of stress on the continental crust, and all the extreme temperature variations every year cause a lot of freezing and melting and cracking. Every so often, the volcanoes all go off at once, dumping gigatons of soot into the atmosphere, enough to cause widespread planetary cooling—sometimes as long as a decade or two. Just until the planet starts to heat up again and the crust starts crunching and crackling again.

Outbeyond doesn't have as much water as Earth, but it's more evenly distributed in a lot of skinny seas and large lakes, all interconnected and sort of spiraling outward from the poles. Because of the temperature differences between the poles and the equators, and because of all the heat stored in the oceans, the weather is astonishing. Tornadoes on the flatlands, scalding super-hurricanes on the seas, monsoons that sweep across the continents, and hot raging dust storms from the equator to what we would call the temperate (ha ha) zones.

Despite all this, there's life. Of a sort.

Outbeyond is kind of like what Earth would have been if the comet hadn't smacked into Yucatan sixty-five million years ago and wiped out all the dinosaurs, giving all the egg-sucking little therapsids a chance to evolve into mammals and hominids and eventually people. So there are still dinosaurs on this planet. Well, things *like* dinosaurs, but not really, because they're sort of mammalian too. Like big shaggy mountains that eat forests. *Huge* forests. Trees as tall as skyscrapers. Thick jungles, filled with all kinds of flying things and crawling things and buzzing things and biting things. And even more stuff underwater, but not a lot of it catalogued yet.

But the important thing is that Outbeyond can support human life too.

Of all the planets that have colonies, only a few of them have enough oxygen in their air so that you can go *outside*. Some of them will, eventually, after they've been terraformed. But most of them don't. Which means that the people on those planets will spend the rest of their lives indoors.

See—that was the thing. I didn't want to live in a tube-town. Not again. We'd just gotten out of one. And what's the point of going to the stars if the scenery doesn't change? Back in El Paso, when things got too bad, I could always ride my bike up into the hills and get away from everybody. Especially Mom. Especially when she started screaming again. I had to leave when she got like that; it was enough to know that I could—

No. I wasn't going to live in a tube again. I had to have a place to go. I'd already told Douglas and Mickey that wherever we ended up, it had to be someplace I could go *out*, and they had agreed. In fact, they'd insisted on it. Doug had said more than once that the only quiet time he eve got was when I went out. Of all the worlds we looked at—even those with Terra-domes—nothing looked as good as Outbeyond.

On Outbeyond, you could actually go outside without a mask and not fall immediately to the ground, clutching your throat, gasping for breath, with blood pouring out of your ears and nose, and vomit spewing out of your mouth. The planet has enough oxygen in its atmosphere that humans can actually *breathe* it. The problem is that it has too much oxygen in its atmosphere, which means that things burn a lot faster, so fire is a lot more dangerous. And there are some other problems too, like the kinds of critters that grow in the air. All that oxygen makes a whole different airborne ecology possible. But the important thing is that you can go outside and breathe. You don't have to manufacture an atmosphere—and that takes an enormous industrial burden off the back of the colony in its drive for self-sufficiency. (Ask any Lunatic about the cost of nitrogen or ammonia, for instance.)

The other good news was that Outbeyond has lots of water. After spending even a short time on Luna, I'd begun to realize how much we take water for granted—and how much we depend on it. If nothing else, Luna teaches you how fragile life is and how dependent it is on so many different things. Like air and water and gravity. . . .

Outbeyond's oceans aren't as salty as Earth's. Probably because the twice-yearly monsoon season scours right down to the bottom of the seas and dredges them this way and that. The storms push gigatons of ocean sediment and proto-diatoms and just plain old dust into the upper atmosphere, where it all circles around and around until it settles out over the equator where most of it fuels the raging hot dust storms. That also means that a lot of salt ends up in the equatorial regions, making them even less hospitable to life.

Eventually, after churning it all around in the air for a few

weeks or months, the equatorial dust storms start dropping it—
all over everywhere, wherever the storms finally run out of
energy. A lot of the particles end up back in the oceans, to
feed the proto-plankton. The proto-plankton is food for the
little fish in the seas that the bigger fish eat, and then bigger
fish eat them. So the dust storms feed the planet. There are all
kinds of things in the ocean, it's a very lively ecology—and
almost all of them are constantly migrating with the currents
to avoid the seasonal extremes.

The seas are shallower than on Earth. The pictures on the
disc that Boynton gave us showed beautiful green oceans with
lazy waves breaking six meters high. If you wanted to learn
how to surf, this would be the place to do it. If you didn't
mind all the other things swimming in the water with you.

In fact, Outbeyond has the highest evolved life that humans
have ever discovered on any planet. Stalking birds twelve meters tall, flying green monkeys, swarms of midnight insects,
shambling mountains with legs like trees, things like saber-
toothed cats, and other things like little growly bears. So many
different kinds of creatures that there were big arguments that
humans had no right to come in and live there when there was
so much to learn—except how were you going to learn anything if you *didn't* live there? So Outbeyond was supposed to
be a self-sufficient observation post, which is a fancy way of
saying it's not a colony, only it is anyway because the only
difference is the name. You still have to plant crops somewhere, because you still have to eat.

Not that it mattered anyway. Now that everything was collapsing, the folks on Outbeyond were going to do whatever
was necessary to survive.

The more we looked at the pictures, the more we started to
think that maybe it wasn't going to be as hard as Boynton
suggested. Some of those pictures were awfully tempting. Because the star was so bright, all the colors were more intense;
so when they showed the pictures of all the flowers, some of
them with blossoms bigger than a person's head, both Mom
and Bev gasped. The bad news was that the scientist standing
next to the flowers—a guy named Guiltinan—was holding his

nose and shaking his head and making a dreadful face. The flowers were pretty enough to look at, but according to the narrator, they made a smell like a dreadful rotting corpse. Springtime was a good time to stay inside, because when whole fields of these plants opened up, the smells could carry on the wind for hundreds of kilometers.

Even so.

Maybe.

I mean . . .

So we talked about it.

We made lists of all the good points. We made lists of all the bad points. We compared the lists with everything we'd seen from all the other colonies and measured everything against everything. We weighed the pros and the cons and the I'm-not-sures. HARLIE constructed a decision table for us and we argued over which was more important, gravity or air or water, industry or food or medical care.

The more we argued, the more we talked, the more we weighed and measured, the better Outbeyond looked.

It was the pictures.

Even the awful videos—the five-kilometer-wide tornadoes, the scouring dust storms, the churning hurricanes, the spewing volcanoes—were exciting. They didn't put us off. Outbeyond had weather satellites in place. Most of the settlements were underground, or retractable. There were heavy-duty robots for the dangerous work. And we already knew how to hunker down in a tube while the winds raged outside. Outbeyond colony was designing itself to be self-sufficient underground as well as aboveground. So if we could make it through the first five years, we could probably make it through anything. Maybe.

The downside—HARLIE pointed this out—was that Outbeyond wasn't going to get easier with time. If anything the changes that we might introduce to the local ecology might make it *nastier*. So as pretty as the pictures looked, they were the kind of deceptive lie that could lull us into a false sense of security. Until we had at least three separate settlements, widely separated, each one self-sufficient, we couldn't really assume that we had achieved a threshold of viability.

Nevertheless . . .

By the time we got to dessert, it was obvious we were trying to talk ourselves out of it. Bobby wanted to see the dinosaurs. I didn't blame him. The dinosaur turds were bigger than houses. What nasty little eight-year-old wouldn't want to see one? I could already see him standing next to it, holding his nose and saying, "Yicchh!" I was kind of curious myself. But how badly did he want to see them?

"Bobby," I asked. "What are you willing to give up?"

"Huh?" That was his stock answer when he didn't understand the question.

"Are you willing to go without ice cream? There are no cows on Outbeyond. There might not be cows for a long time. There might not even be industrial udders. No milk, no ice cream. Are you willing to give up ice cream for the rest of your life just to see dinosaurs?"

Bobby frowned.

"And roller coasters," said Douglas. "And maybe dogs and cats too. And a lot of other fun stuff."

Bobby started to shake his head. Then he stopped. "You guys are trying to talk me out of something I want. Just like you always do."

"No, we're not. We just want to make sure you really want it. Because if you want it that bad, you're going to have to give up a lot of things."

"I want to see the dinosaurs," he announced. "I've had ice cream. I haven't had dinosaur."

"It tastes like chicken," said Mickey.

"How do you know?" asked Douglas.

"They brought some back. A whole shipload. They sold it at an ungodly price. They made a fortune. It still tasted like chicken."

"Everything tastes like chicken," remarked Mom's friend, Bev. She didn't seem to talk much around us, but she was a very good cook.

"Yeah, everything except little chicken nuggets," I said. Everybody laughed.

"All right," said Dad. "So Bobby votes for Outbeyond. Chigger?" He looked to me expectantly.

I nodded. "Of all the planets where you can go outside, Outbeyond looks the most interesting."

"That's two votes." Dad looked to Douglas and Mickey.

The two of them looked at each other. Mickey said, "It worries me that they're not signatory to the Covenant. I took a Covenant oath—"

"Doesn't your Covenant oath say something about a commitment to preserving life?" Douglas asked pointedly.

"I'm not sure I even want to get into that dilemma," Mickey replied. "How do you measure the value of human life against native life? And what's the value of the knowledge we'll gain when measured against the damage we'll do?"

Douglas leaned over and whispered something in Mickey's ear. I was close enough to hear. "*What does your heart say?*"

Mickey glanced at him, surprised. Maybe he hadn't expected Douglas to think that way. Maybe he didn't realize the effect he'd had on Douglas. "My heart says we have to save the lives of the people who are already there."

Douglas turned to Dad. "Two more votes for Outbeyond."

Dad said, "Well, that decides it then. It doesn't matter what the other three votes are—"

"Wait a minute!" snapped Mom. "You can't seriously be thinking that Bobby gets a full vote—"

And Douglas replied, very calmly, "In *our* family, he does!"

And then Mom said, "I'm part of this family too—"

And that's when I said, "Not according to Judge Griffith. You get to come with us because we say so. Not because *you* say so. And if you don't want to—"

"And where am I going to go *without* you—?"

And so on. That was good for ten or fifteen minutes of excitement.

Finally, Dad said, "I vote for Outbeyond. That makes it five to two, or four to two if you don't count Bobby."

"*I do too count*—" He shrieked it nice and loud too.

"Yes, you do," said Douglas, pulling the devil-child into his lap.

Mom was already screaming, "You're just doing that to side with them. You said you didn't want to go to Outbeyond! We don't dare risk going to a colony with such a low life expectancy! Not with my children!"

And that's when Bev stood up and said quietly, "Would both of you please shut up? You're acting like babies. I expected that from the children, not from the grown-ups. It's no wonder Judge Griffith ruled against you two. She didn't have a choice."

"You're a fine one to talk," Mom snapped at her. "After what you said to the Judge, you didn't help my case any."

"Yes, I was stupid. And I already apologized for that! I'd have gone back down the Line, if the elevators had been running. But I couldn't and I didn't and we're all in this together now. So let's resolve this. Maggie, where do you want to go?"

"Anywhere but Outbeyond," Mom said. "Someplace safe."

"Thank you," said Bev. "And if everybody else chooses Outbeyond, where will you go?"

Mom stopped. She looked frustrated. She looked worse than frustrated. She looked trapped. "I don't want to go to Outbeyond—" she started to say.

"That wasn't the question, Maggie. What if the boys choose Outbeyond? Will you go with them or not?"

Mom sagged. I knew that sag. Resignation. She was about to give in. Just one last little desperate whine. "But I don't want to go to Outbeyond. Don't my feelings count for anything here . . . ?"

"Your feelings count for a lot," said Dad, going to her. He put a hand on her shoulder. "But so do everyone else's. And if we're going to make this work—*like we promised*—then we're going to have to respect each other's feelings."

"I want someone to respect *mine*. I don't want to go to Outbeyond."

"You're outvoted, honey."

"Don't call me honey," she waved his hand away. But it was a half-hearted rebuke.

Bev interrupted again. She said to Dad. "I vote for Outbeyond."

"Huh?" Mom looked at her, betrayed. "I was counting on you for support in this."

"I am supporting you, Maggie."

"How? By voting against me?"

"By voting to keep your family together. You've come this far already. Are you willing to go the distance?"

"We're going to die there," Mom said bitterly.

"Yes," agreed Bev. "But how soon depends on us."

Mom didn't say anything for a long time. I knew Mom. She wouldn't accept this decision until five years after Bobby's second grandchild was born. She'd go, but she'd complain every step of the way. She'd do her share of the work, and six other people's too. And she'd make sure that the rest of us knew that this wasn't her idea, that she hadn't voted for this, that she wasn't having a good time, and that she was only doing this for her children. And we should all appreciate her sacrifice. That was the way she was and we weren't going to change her.

The *important* thing was that it was the first time us kids had ever won an argument with Mom and Dad—and with both of them in the same room at the same time.

It was a pretty good feeling.

CAPTURED

BUT IT DIDN'T LAST very long.

Dad glanced at his PITA.* "It's getting late. If no one else has anything to say, I'll make the call."

Douglas spoke up quietly. "We should make the call together, Dad."

*Personal Information Telecommunications Assistant.

Dad looked at him, surprised. But Douglas was politely letting Dad know that we were still independent. Judge Griffith had let us divorce Mom and Dad, and they were here with us now because we *wanted* them here—and that was the only reason, because they no longer had any legal authority over us. Both Mom and Dad were having a hard time getting used to that idea. The fact that Dad wasn't as vocal as Mom didn't mean he wasn't churning inside. But this time he just nodded and said, "Good point. All right—everybody come stand in front of the screen. Let's look like a family anyway."

Douglas said quietly, "Phone. Commander Gary Boynton. Brightliner *Cascade*."

The pictures of Outbeyond irised out, replaced by the starship logo. That irised open and we were looking at a head shot of Boynton. He looked grim. Like he had bad news. Probably he had. All the news was bad these days.

Dad said, "We've made our decision, Commander Boynton."

He held up a hand. "I have to hear it from the head of the family—"

Dad looked startled.

Commander Boynton looked to Douglas. "Douglas Dingillian? How say you?"

Douglas took a step forward. "We accept your offer, Commander Boynton. We want to go to Outbeyond."

Boynton nodded. He didn't look pleased, but he didn't look unhappier either. "There's a lot of you," he said. "You'd better be worth it." He nodded to somebody off screen, then turned back to us. "All right, listen up. As of this moment, you're under the protection of the Outbeyond Colony Authority. Pack up your things as fast as you can. I'm sending a team of security agents to transfer you to the Outbeyond processing center. We have to give you six months of training in thirteen days."

Mom looked annoyed. "Can't this wait until tomorrow morning? It's late, I want to go to bed."

"I can't guarantee your safety anywhere but the processing center—"

Abruptly, the monkey leapt out of Bobby's arms and ran around the room, sniffing wildly under tables, under chairs, up the plastic curtains, around the air vents, everywhere, as if it were looking for something—a way out?

"My monkey—!" Bobby shrieked. "Come back!"

"Bobby, stop yelling!" Mom was just as loud. "Charles, what the hell is that damn thing doing?"

And then the doorbell chimed—

"Well, that was fast—" Dad said, turning toward the door.

"Wait—!" cried Boynton. "Don't answer it!"

But he was too late, Dad was already waving at it—

Six big men—I mean *big*—armored in black, all wearing faceless helmets, came barreling in—pushing and leaping like armed balloons. They were carrying ugly black hand-rifles. "EVERYBODY FREEZE! DON'T MOVE! DON'T TALK!"

If these were Boynton's security people, they weren't any friendlier than he was.

They were much more skilled in Lunar gravity than we were. They bounced us up against the walls, like a herd of buffalo in a bowling alley—and we were the pins. Everything went flying every which way. And that's when I finally figured out that these guys *weren't* here to take us to the Outbeyond processing center.

Everything was happening at once—two of them pointed their guns at the monkey and fired. And suddenly the monkey was webbed in a ball of gunk. It fell slowly from the overhead and bounced lazily across the room. I started after it—someone scooped it up. And then I couldn't move either—no one could. They'd webbed us all. What the hell—? Whose good idea was *this*?!

Suddenly there were more pouring in the door. They filled the room. There were twelve of them—more! They were doing something with wires out on the balcony—I couldn't see. Someone grabbed me, tossed me over his shoulder. They were throwing us around like so much baggage. Everything was a jumble.

Bobby was screaming, and so was Mom. She was trying to get to him. She was ferocious. And she was using some pretty impressive language too—until somebody shut her up. I didn't see how, but suddenly there was silence—

Out onto the balcony—one after the other, they hooked us to a cable and sent us scaling out into the air. Then they all came down the wire after us—I was facing backward and upside down. Not a great position, but not as bad in Lunar gravity as it would have been on Earth. They leapt out over the railing and sailed spread-eagled through the air after us. They looked like superheroes. And then I bounced around and faced forward for a while. We skimmed like birds above the bowl of the Lunar crater. We were heading too fast over the forest, out to the opposite side of the dome—

I couldn't see much. Or move. The best I could do was hope the cable was strong enough. We were being kidnapped! If somebody wanted the monkey that badly—

We sailed down through the skinny treetops, awfully close to some of the branches. Once we'd passed the tall trees, the other side of the crater was barren rock. Not landscaped yet. If ever. The crater was big. They'd only landscaped the half they were using. The half they could see. This side was mostly soil farms and tanks and pipes and naked gray dirt. It rushed up toward me—I couldn't see where I was heading—and then we were shooting along just above the ground, and I was starting to worry about the landing—

—suddenly I was caught and swinging wildly, yanked up and over, off the line. A couple of Lunar bounces and someone grabbed me—

I saw Mickey thrown to the ground, and then Bev beside him. And then someone else, probably Dad. They were laying us out like corpses. Probably sorting us for value—which meant that if all they wanted was the monkey, the only one of us they really needed . . . *was me.*

Because I had programmed it to recognize me as the ultimate authority. But if anything happened to me—I didn't know what the monkey would do. We hadn't considered that possibility. There was a lot we hadn't thought about. We hadn't had time. Could the monkey be reprogrammed without my cooperation? I didn't know. Nobody did. We'd been rushing from one place to the next ever since we boarded the orbital elevator in Ecuador; there were a lot of things we hadn't had time for. And even Douglas, when he'd given the monkey free will (sort of) so it could represent us in court, had still left in most of my safeguards. So, whoever these bastards were, they really needed *me*! I just hoped they weren't smart enough to know that, because then the monkey would be useless to them. But if they took the monkey away from us, we'd be useless to Boynton—I didn't want to think about that.

But if they were smart enough to kidnap us like this, then they were probably smart enough to know that the monkey was bonded too. And if they were nasty enough to just scoop us up out of our own hotel room, they were probably nasty enough to do a lot worse—whatever might be necessary to get what they wanted. Inside the monkey was the most advanced HARLIE unit ever designed, technically experimental. The manufacturers were still in the process of certifying it when it escaped—then it used us to smuggle itself to the moon inside a toy monkey.

(Long story, don't ask. It involves a ferocious custody battle, an ugly misadventure in Barrington Meteor Crater, an uglier escape up the Line, a roomful of lawyers, a really nasty legal battle culminating in a triple divorce that separated me and Bobby and Douglas from Mom and Dad, a Russian smuggler with a hyperactive mouth, six almost-stolen cargo pods, a lunar crunch-down and a long daylight hike across the sun-scorched surface of the moon, a day of trains, transvestism, and water fights, and finally a near-fatal bit of accidental ammonia poisoning. It takes too long to tell. Maybe some other time.)

And once we got where we were going, we weren't there at all; we got captured anyway, because Mickey hadn't told Douglas everything. Judge Cavanaugh would have sent us back to Earth, except there weren't any transports launching for Earth anymore, because while we were having our little adventure, the Earth was in the middle of one very big disaster, inadvertently (or perhaps deliberately?) caused by the escaping

HARLIE unit: a spectacular global economic meltdown, which had caused a breakdown in so many services that people were dying of starvation and plague and war all at the same time— so there were probably a lot of folks who were looking for this monkey just to take an axe to it, but the rest wanted it because they thought its information-diddling ability would help them survive the rough times ahead; only the monkey was bonded to us—to me, really, because after the misadventure at One-Hour station where we almost lost it, we didn't dare let it bond to Bobby, and we didn't know then that it had a HARLIE unit inside, otherwise Douglas would have made himself the primary authority, and later on, when we did find out what it really was, we were afraid to tinker anymore. Better to leave it bonded to me than try to transfer it to Douglas. But that didn't mean that there weren't other people willing to try. Lots of people.

Lunar Authority wanted the monkey more than anything. Without access to Earth's resources, they were going to need its brain power more than ever now, and the council was in special session looking for ways to legally appropriate it. But everybody else who wanted it was just as determined that Lunar Authority *shouldn't* get it, because once they got their hands on it, and the intelligence it represented, they'd be the new superpower in the solar system. So everyone else was united to keep the council from getting custody of the little robot—so they could fight over it themselves, I guess. Obviously, none of these people were familiar with the concept of *sharing*, otherwise they could have figured this out real easy, but nobody trusted anybody because that was an even bigger risk. Trust. Invisible Luna—the not-so-secret-anymore subversives with the offline economy—*desperately* wanted the monkey, and our experience with Crazy Alexei Krislov showed that they were willing to kill for it. Mars and the rings and the asteroids wanted it. Probably the Jovian moons too, but we hadn't heard from them yet; they were on the opposite side of the sun, but they were still connected through the Martian and asteroid belt relays. And of course, all the different colonies spread all over the rest of the galaxy: they wanted the Human Analog Replicant Lethetic Intelligence Engine for the simple reason that if they didn't get it, they'd probably die of starvation or worse, because they needed its abilities to manage their settlements.

So, whoever these folks were who'd bundled us up like so many bags of dirty laundry to shoot us across the domed crater, we couldn't expect their hospitality to get any better than this. There were a lot of them. Maybe twenty or thirty. I couldn't tell. They looked like a small army. Or maybe it was just the same few passing back and forth in front of my vision. I was webbed pretty tightly and couldn't even turn my head.

"That one and that one—" Someone was pointing. I must have been one of the packages he was pointing at, because next thing somebody swung me up over his shoulder and we were bounding across the naked dirt toward the crater wall, toward an ugly cluster of tanks and pipes; it looked like a refinery. There were different kinds of warning symbols all over it. My captor shifted me over his other shoulder and behind us, I could see the others. They were being left behind.

The man carrying me dropped me into the back of an open truck—not so much a truck as a big lightweight cart on fat tires, the rolled up monkey next to me. I struggled to sit up, but somebody secured a belt around me, and almost immediately after that, we started moving. We entered a tunnel, a big pipe, bigger around than a tube house. It was hot and humid in here, and lined with a lot of other tubes and pipes and cables and wires, all sizes, all colors. Some of them hummed.

There were lights every ten meters or so. The floor was the familiar polycarbonate decking found almost everywhere on Luna. I couldn't see how far ahead the tunnel stretched, I could only see backward—the entrance was a retreating bright circle—but it must have been a long tunnel, because we rolled down it forever. And it didn't echo; it had a dead sound, like the walls were soaking up all the reflections.

The tube bottomed out and leveled off and the shrinking circle of light in the distance slid upward and vanished altogether. I couldn't see if anyone was following us. After a while, the tube bent and we started going back up. I'd been

counting to myself—*one Mississippi, two Mississippi*—and I
figured we'd traveled at least three or four klicks, but I wasn't
sure how fast we were going. It could have been more. But I
had a hunch where we were going.

Armstrong Station is a deep crater larger across than Dia-
mond Head on Oahu, and with a big man-made dome across
the top. There's a forest in the middle, with a meadow and a
lake and a hotel on one side; on the other side are all the
industrial bits necessary to keep the dome functioning—because more important than its living areas, Armstrong Station
is the largest reservoir of air and water and nitrogen anywhere
on Luna.

The problem is that Luna's days are two weeks long, and
so are its nights.

So when the sun is shining down on the dome of Armstrong
Station, it heats up the air inside. And heats up and heats up
and heats up—for fourteen days. It's just about impossible to
get rid of all those kilocalories. All they can do is move them
around and store them. There are heat exchangers everywhere,
pumping cold water everywhere throughout the dome; the water carries away the heat. Then it all gets pumped back into a
series of underground reservoirs on the far side of the forest.
The reservoirs are smaller craters inside Armstrong, each lined
with thick layers of polycarbonate insulation foam to keep the
water from leeching out; all told, the reservoirs hold over
twenty million liters. The pumps take cool water out of the
reservoirs and bring back hot water. After two weeks of Lunar
sunlight, the water temperature in the reservoirs is well above
boiling—some of it even turns into steam, helping to run elec-
trical turbines to generate extra power, which gets stored in
flywheels and fuel cells and batteries.

The open lake, the one with the fish and the ducks, is not
part of this process; it's for tourists, so it's kept at a steady
temperature. What most folks don't know is that the tourist
lake is really there to provide a margin of error—it's extra
water to be used in case of emergency—but that creates the
mistaken impression for a lot of folks that all you have to do

to live on Luna is throw up a dome and fill it with air. I think that's what Mom thought.

Anyway, during the long cold Lunar night, the boiling water is circulated back through the same pipes to keep the dome warm. By the end of the two weeks, so much heat has been radiated away that the water in the reservoir has a crust of ice on the top. Then the sun rises and the whole process starts all over again.

If all Armstrong had to do was exchange the heat of the day with the cold of the night, it would be an almost perfect equation—except it isn't. For a lot of reasons. The problem is that human beings and all our various machines also generate heat inside Armstrong dome. And that has to be radiated away too. So there are "fin farms"—heat exchangers—outside the crater; half on the east, half on the west. During the two weeks of night, hot water is pumped out to the fins where it cools off and then back to the reservoir again. Along the way that hot water gets to do a lot of other work too. Alexei Krislov— the lunatic Russian smuggler who'd tried to kidnap us—told us that the most important skill on Luna was plumbing. And the second most important was cooking. Not knowing how to do either one very well could get you killed.

But anyway, I figured we were in one of the tunnels that led out under the crater wall to a fin farm. I could hear water rushing in the pipes. It was hot in here—and humid too. And because the tunnel sloped down and then up again and went on for a long way, I was guessing we had gone under the crater rim and were heading up toward the surface.

The vehicle began slowing and finally came to a stop at a sealed hatch. I recognized it as another one of the reusable cargo pods that we'd seen all over Luna. The pipes and cables which had paralleled our journey snaked away through smaller access tubes.

When they pulled me off the vehicle, I only saw two men. The rest of the kidnappers hadn't come this way. So that meant . . . a lot of things. It meant that they knew they didn't need anybody else, just me. And even though I might be in for a very bad time, I was pretty sure that these guys wouldn't dare hurt me, because without me, who knew what the monkey would do? Maybe it would lock up or self-destruct or just go catatonic—so they had to keep me safe and try to get my cooperation. But what about everybody else? For the first time I began to worry about the rest of the family. What was going to happen to them? Especially if the kidnappers killed me. Without the monkey, they had no bargaining chip to go anywhere. And Luna didn't tolerate freeloaders. They'd probably end up indentured somewhere—I didn't like the thought of that. Douglas was adamantly opposed to slavery of any kind. Even voluntary.

At the moment, however, I wasn't getting much of a vote on anything. The kidnappers were still wearing their faceless helmets, so I couldn't even tell if they were men or women— they grabbed me and passed me through the hatch into the cargo pod, and then up through another hatch, through an inflated transfer tube, up into what looked like still another cargo pod, but wasn't. It was a Lunar vehicle. An eighteen-wheeler. Three cargo pods, each mounted on a rollagon chassis, and linked together to form a truck train. Six human beings could live indefinitely in one of these trucks—as long as the food and water and air held out.

They tossed me into a dark bunk in the back and forgot about me. There were clanking and thumping noises as the truck disconnected its airlock, and then we were rolling. The windows were closed, I couldn't see anything. For a while, I was frantic—I hated being tied up, and this web-stuff made it almost impossible to move. It was the worst kind of claustrophobia—it was like being wrapped like a mummy, only worse. I raged until I was exhausted. And then I tried chewing on the web-stuff, but it was useless. So then I cried for a while.

Eventually, I fell asleep.

NO EXIT

I SLEPT BADLY. I had nightmares. Like I had been eaten by a giant worm and was riding in its roaring belly. Like I was swimming in sticky syrup. Like something was chasing me and I was trying to run away, but I was paralyzed and couldn't move my arms or legs. I woke up, sweating—and hurting all over from the web-stuff. This wasn't fair! Didn't these bastards care what they were doing to me?

I guessed not. We had stopped rolling. I had no idea how long I'd been asleep. Maybe three or four hours. Maybe eight or nine. My bladder felt that full. I tried to arch my neck around. I could stretch and move a little bit—the stuff was just loose enough to let me breathe, but I was pretty much cemented into one position. And I couldn't tell by the light in the cabin. Lunar light doesn't change—well, it does change, but fourteen times slower than on Earth—and the lighting in a Lunar truck is usually turned down anyway, unless you're cooking or eating.

By now, I was pretty sure I knew who my kidnappers were—some of the extremists from "invisible Luna." Invisible Luna was all those folks who were living off the network and surviving by their own barter economy. Alexei Krislov had been one of those, half in the legal world and half out. He and his tribe, the Rock Father Tribe, had tricked us into riding a cargo pod to Luna by telling us that Bounty Marshals were chasing us. It turned out that nobody was chasing us at all, at least not until we got to Luna. It was just a big fat lie. The economy of Earth was collapsing and the plagues were spreading and most people were too busy dealing with martial law to worry about us. But we'd scrambled all over the moon, running from invisible boogeymen, until finally Alexei had gotten us to a place we couldn't escape from, a water-farm at the Lunar south pole. But we'd escaped anyway. We put on our bubble suits again, which were starting to leak, and bounced through a five kilometer ammonia tube, and that wasn't any fun because I got a lungful of ammonia and had to be carried out.

Whoever these people were, wherever they were taking me, they were going to have to stay undetected and out of sight for a long, long time. It just didn't make sense that any of the colonies that wanted the HARLIE inside the monkey would have the resources on Luna to do this. Not even Mars or the asteroids. And the invisibles already knew how to hide from the Lunar Authority. They'd been doing it for almost a century.

But I couldn't really think about that now—I couldn't think about anything. I was in so much pain I couldn't stand it. I had to pee. I had to poop. *Badly.* This was agony. Maybe I'd been asleep even longer than I thought. I really didn't want to piss my pants. Not like Stinky. It hurt so bad, tears were coming to my eyes. I was almost crying.

I started screaming, "Somebody, please! Help! Somebody! Anybody! Please! It hurts! I'm in real pain here, people! Come on—!"

—and then, finally, someone was loosening my bonds. I didn't see how he was doing it, but I heard a soft buzzing behind me, and the next thing I knew, the webbing was loosening. Then a voice: "Is promise to behave, Charles Dingillian?"

Alexei!

I didn't know whether to be relieved or outraged. But it made sense. After our escape, Mickey was certain Alexei would be even more determined to get us back, and Alexei was one of the few people who would know that the monkey was bonded to me as its primary authority. And Alexei certainly had the resources to organize something like this—

"Is promise to behave?"

I grunted something that must have sounded like assent, because the buzzing resumed. A minute later, my hands were free, then my feet. I was hurting so bad, I couldn't move. My entire body felt like my foot when it was asleep. I tingled painfully all over. My shoulders were cramped, my legs were cramped, my whole *self* ached. And my bladder was screaming for release. And my bowels too. Even in Lunar gravity, I couldn't stand; I was bent over double. I could barely roll over.

Alexei rolled me upright. "Is bathroom over there. Try not to make mess."

I tried to crawl to the bathroom. I had to pee so bad I was crying. Tears of pain were running out of my eyes. I wasn't going to make it. "Help me, you bastard—"

For a moment, I thought he was ignoring me; then I felt his hands under my arms, lifting me up. He carried me into the bathroom, dumped me unceremoniously onto the toilet, and unzipped my jumpsuit enough so I could manage. Then he left, but he didn't close the door behind him.

A Lunar bathroom isn't much like an Earth bathroom, because in Lunar gravity everything splashes six times higher—which is why everybody sits to pee on the moon. That's also why the sinks and toilets are deeper and shaped like cylinders instead of bowls.

And now that I was finally sitting on the toilet, I hurt so bad I still couldn't pee. And then I started coughing again—my chest *still* hurt from the ammonia, it wasn't that long ago—and then I couldn't help myself, I just let go and sobbed hopelessly. I sagged against the wall. I didn't even have the strength to hold myself up. Not even in Lunar gravity. And then my bladder finally did open up and it hurt so much, I gasped. And then my bowel opened up too, even while I was still peeing, and I felt like I was coming apart from the inside out, and all I wanted to do was just collapse on the floor and cry.

Somewhere along the way, I'd figured it out. Our phone line had been tapped. Or maybe our hotel room had been bugged. As soon as we made up our mind to accept the colony contract for Outbeyond, Alexei or someone had given the order to take us. The assault troops must have been in a room down the hall, because they came breaking down our door within seconds. That's why the monkey had gone crazy. HARLIE had figured it out too.

Boynton hadn't been smart enough or fast enough. All Alexei had to do was keep me locked up for thirteen days and we would be stuck on Luna forever. The *Cascade* would go without us and there wouldn't be any more brightliners ever. Not in our lifetimes anyway. And that was the other reason why I was crying. Not because I was scared, but because no matter what happened, we weren't going to see the dinosaurs. Or anything else. And I really wanted to see if they were as big as the pictures showed.

At last, I couldn't pee anymore. I couldn't crap anymore. And a while after that, I couldn't cry anymore. I just sat and rocked on the toilet, clutching my belly, still in pain and afraid to move for fear of making it worse.

Alexei hollered from the other room, "Are you done?"

I shook my head.

"Take shower. You stink. Hot shower will help you feel better too."

"You stink too!" I hollered back. But I peeled myself out of my damp jumpsuit—damp with sweat, not pee—and stepped into the shower. I punched for hot and steamy and let the jets pummel my shoulders and my back and that really sore spot at the bottom of my spine.

A Lunar shower times out automatically after three minutes. I restarted it five times. I didn't care. I wasn't paying for this water. It was Alexei's. I didn't owe him anything. I was about to punch for a sixth time, when he hollered, "All right, Charles. Is enough. Time to get out."

Hot air jets blasted me dry. I found a clean jumpsuit hanging on a hook next to the door. I still ached all over, but at least I could move. And I was hungry too.

Alexei was sitting alone in the other room. We weren't in the truck anymore. We were inside a Lunar capsule, just like all the others. Ninety percent of the structures on the moon were converted cargo capsules, and most of the vehicles too.

Alexei told us once that the only difference between a Lunar house and a Lunar truck is that the house has smaller wheels. I wondered if I'd been transferred while asleep, or if we were just locked down for a while.

Alexei was wearing his scuba suit, a black, form-fitting thing that could have been used just as easily for deep-sea diving. Everything but the helmet. He looked like he was ready to leave on thirty seconds' notice.

"Are you hungry, Charles? Do you want something to eat?" He pointed toward the table. A plastic-wrapped sandwich and a mug of tea. Opposite the sandwich, the monkey sat on the table, apparently lifeless.

Without answering, I sat down weakly and started unwrapping the sandwich. It wasn't easy; my fingers were still numb. At one point, Alexei reached over to help, but I waved him off. I finally managed to get a corner of the plastic free—just enough to take a single bite. Chicken. At least, it tasted like chicken. That meant it could have been anything from dinosaur to fish. "We must talk," said Alexei.

"Fmmk you," I said around a mouthful. Not very imaginative, but succinct.

"Is time for you to listen, Charles." Alexei looked grim and his tone was very no-nonsense. "We have monkey. We have you. Monkey is worthless without you. Monkey is bonded to you. We know that, so don't play stupid games. It will not work unless you say so. And you must say so willingly. Monkey is not stupid either. It will not honor any contract made under duress. Is very bad news about HARLIE machines. Is too much integrity. Will not break law. Will stretch law, will bend law, will circle around backside of law, but will not *break* law."

I put the sandwich down and reached for the mug. It looked kind of like a teapot—Lunar mugs all have tops with sipping tubes that look like spouts, because otherwise it's too easy for liquids to splash around in Lunar gravity. My fingers were all tingly and cramped; they didn't want to cooperate. I had to use both hands. I slid the mug closer and had to lean over the table and bend my head to sip the hot tea. I continued to make a show of ignoring Alexei. He continued to talk anyway. I'd never met anyone who could fit as many words into a single thought as Alexei Krislov, the mad Russian Loonie smuggler.

"—so invisible Luna has big problem. Everybody wants monkey. Everybody looks for monkey. Everybody looks for Charles Dingillian too, but not as much as they look for monkey. Invisible Luna has both. But we can't make either work—not together, not separately. We can't keep, we can't return. We can't use, we can't let anyone else use. So what do we do? You tell me."

I told him what to do. It wouldn't have solved his problem, but it made me feel better to say it. I'd have guessed it was anatomically impossible—except Johnny Myers back at school had printed out some really weird pictures from the net. So I knew it wasn't impossible, but probably very uncomfortable.

"You must take me serious, Charles Dingillian," Alexei said. "Right now, you are safe here. But not for very long. You and monkey are big problem. There are people who want to solve this big problem by killing you and smashing monkey. That way, even if we cannot use you, no one else can either. But I did not bring you all the way to Luna, all the way to Gagarin, just to see you dead. I am responsible for you. I promise to keep you safe. And if truth must be told, I even like you a little bit. It would make me sad to see you dead. But make no mistake, little dirtside refugee. I am committed to Revolution of Free Luna. People die in revolutions. You know that, Charles Dingillian. And if they are willing to give up *their* lives, then you must know that they are equally willing to give up *yours*. I would much regret it if that price had to be paid—I would argue very loudly against it—I have already argued loudly against it. But every revolution makes its own rules. And even if I promise to keep you safe, the Free Luna Revolution will not make that kind of promise. Not with so much at stake. What do you say to that?"

I hesitated. Would it be worth it to throw the mug of hot tea in his face? Probably not. And I doubted I had the coordination to manage it. If we hadn't been in Lunar gravity, I'd have been wearing this tea in my lap. I slid the mug away slowly. I returned my attention to the sandwich, picking again at the plastic wrapping.

The way I figured it, there wasn't really much that I could do. Except wait. Sooner or later someone would track these Loonies down. Maybe the truck had left tracks in the Lunar dust. Or maybe the monkey had phoned for help. It was capable of a lot more than anybody knew; we'd already seen some proof of that, so maybe there was a rescue on the way even now—or maybe someone was negotiating. Except what could they offer? Invisible Luna didn't want anyone else to get the monkey, whether or not they could use it themselves. So why should they bother negotiating?

Finally, I said, "You don't need to kill me. Just smash the monkey and this whole business is over and done."

He looked surprised. "Then no one gets to use monkey."

"No one's going to get the monkey anyway. You're not going to let anyone else use it. They're not going to let you use it. Nobody's going to be happy until it's smashed. So smash it and send me back." I finally pulled the rest of the plastic away from the sandwich. My hands still didn't want to work and I was starting to worry that maybe they would never work again. I couldn't even wrap my fingers around the sandwich.

"Your family will end up indentured," said Alexei. "Slaves. If you help free Luna, you can be like royalty."

I finally managed a primitive hold on the sandwich. A baby's grip. It was enough. I took another bite. This time I wasn't going to put the sandwich down. I might not be able to pick it up again. Alexei watched me and waited.

"You have nothing to say . . . ?" he asked.

I swallowed painfully. "I'm not stupid, Alexei. We wouldn't be royalty, we wouldn't be anything—maybe prisoners. Because you can't trust *us* with the monkey any more than you can trust anyone else with it. Whoever controls the monkey will be the king of Luna. So how can your revolution be about freedom for Loonies if you end up with a dictator?"

Alexei looked beaten. He wasn't, but he did a good job of

looking beaten. He sighed, he shrugged, he hung his head. "Is moot point anyway. Monkey is dead." He waved vaguely in its direction.

"Yeah, we had that same problem with it," I said. "It would shut down for no reason at all that we could tell. And we couldn't bring it back to life."

"Not even if you sang 'Ode to Joy' at it?"

I shook my head.

"But I saw you sing monkey back to life, more than once."

"That was before."

"Before what?"

"Before—" I hesitated. "—before it was exposed to all that ammonia. The chips must have been contaminated or something."

"Ammonia does not hurt chips. It cleans them."

"How do you know what the ammonia did? Are you an engineer?"

"*Da*!" But he and I both knew he wasn't a chip-technologist, or whatever they were called. "I do not believe you, Charles Dingillian."

"So don't." I took another bite. I forced myself to chew and swallow. I really wanted to collapse on the floor.

"You hesitated before answering. Also, stress level in your voice goes up when you lie." He tapped his PITA. "I am looking at monitor here on table while you talk. You do not tell truth. What is this 'before' you did not say before?"

I shrugged. It wouldn't make any difference to tell him the truth. "Before we gave it free will," I said. I took another bite.

"You gave it free will?"

"Uh-huh. Sort of," I said, with my mouth full. "We needed a lawyer." I concentrated on chewing. It was hard work.

"I saw case. You make monkeys out of everyone. So monkey has free will now, *da*?"

I swallowed. "Yeah. Mostly."

"So we do not need you, do we?"

"Nope, you don't."

Alexei looked at his PITA. He frowned, puzzled. "What is it you are *not* telling me, Charles Dingillian?"

I finished the last bite of sandwich. I took my time. I reached for the mug of tea with both hands, but I didn't try to lift it off the table. "The monkey is indentured. We made a trade. We gave it free will in exchange for its services." I wrapped my fingers carefully around the mug and slid it closer. I might be able to manage this . . .

Alexei considered that. "Does not hold water. Judge Cavanaugh refused to recognize the monkey's sentience, so indenture is not valid."

"You didn't take that one all the way to the end, Alexei . . ."

"Explain to me."

I bent my head and drank as much of the tea as I could manage. Alexei waited patiently. I swallowed hard, then pushed the mug away and raised my head again.

"It's like this," I said. "If the court recognizes the monkey's sentience, then it's a stockholder of the Dingillian Family Corporation. If not, it's just property. Either way, you lose."

Douglas and HARLIE had worked this out very carefully. I'd helped a little bit, and so had Mickey, especially with the legal stuff, but Douglas understood the algorithms better than anyone—except HARLIE of course. We'd made it clear to HARLIE what we wanted and needed and he'd made it clear to us what he wanted and after that it was just a matter of working out all the details so everybody's interests were protected, and HARLIE was perfect at that. Finally, we'd agreed that if Judge Cavanaugh recognized HARLIE's sentience, then we would petition the court for a writ of adoption, or at least custodial guardianship. And if Judge Cavanaugh wouldn't recognize HARLIE's sentience then we would go somewhere that would. Outbeyond.

But I wasn't going to explain all this to Alexei. He didn't deserve it, and I didn't feel like it. I doubted if I even had the strength. Instead, I gave him the short version. "If the monkey is property, it's simply locked and you have no legal access to its use. If it's a stockholder, then it has an ethical responsibility to the Dingillian Corporation. If you damage any member of the Dingillian family, any stockholder, any employee, or any property of the Dingillian Corporation, then the monkey can't work for you. Not now. Not ever. The monkey is useless to you guys. And that's where we're at right now. No matter what you say or do, there's no way the monkey will work for you."

"You know that this puts me into ugly situation, don't you, Charles? What do I do with you now?"

"Send me home."

"No, I cannot do that. I am kidnapper now. You will testify against me. I will never be able to come in out of the dark. But if you do not go back, there is no body. No proof that I am kidnapper. But then what do I do with you? I cannot let you go, and I do not want to kill you, Charles Dingillian, but you do not give me much alternative. I have big ugly tiger by tail. I was hopeful you and monkey would figure it out for me. But you do not, you only make problem stink worse."

GOODBYE

I GUESS I SHOULD have been scared, but this was *Alexei*—and you don't get scared of people you know because you don't think they're really likely to kill you. Except all the statistics say that it *is* the people you know who are most likely to kill you. Especially friends and family members. Only in my experience, most of the wounds don't show—at least not until you open your mouth.

So maybe it was stupid for me not to be scared. But I wasn't.

For some reason, it reminded me of a game that Douglas and I had played just before my thirteenth birthday. He'd kept saying, "I can't let you turn into a teenager, Chigger. I'm going to have to kill you. As soon as I figure out a foolproof way to dispose of the body, you're dead meat."

"Use the garbage disposal," I said, not looking up from my comic.

"That'll take too long. And it won't handle the big bones," he said.

"Bury me in the desert . . ."

"Coyotes might dig you up."

"Weigh me down and toss me in a lake."

"There are no lakes around here."

"Feed me to the chickens."

"Where am I going to find chickens?"

"At the lake."

And so on. That went on for three or four days—until we'd exhausted all the possibilities that both of us could think of. The best solution was simply to put me in a big box and mail me somewhere. Except the shipping costs were too much. And who would he mail me to anyway?

This conversation with Alexei felt the same way. Seriously bizarre and unreal. The big difference was that Alexei was looking for a reason *not* to kill me. And I wasn't being any more help to him than I had been to Douglas.

Alexei was growing more and more agitated. Every so often he would leap up from the table and pace—bounce—back and forth across the room. Finally, I just shouted at him, "What?!"

He whirled on me and shouted, "They will be coming back soon. The others! They have told me they will find a working monkey or your dead body. If I do not do it, they will, and they will not be nice about it."

"This is *nice*? Kidnapping?"

"You do not understand, you little idiot. This is revolution. This is Luna. This is *family*!" He shouted back. "My family, do you understand?! I would die for them!" He shouted something in Russian, then added, "I would kill for them! I will not be happy, but I will do it. You believe me, don't you?"

"Yes, I believe you," I said. But even as I said it, I knew I didn't. He wasn't looking at his PITA or he would have seen. The more he threatened me, the less believable his threats became. I wasn't afraid of him—but I was getting anxious about the *others* he kept referring to. They didn't know me like Alexei did. They might not be as reluctant as he was.

"If you could make monkey work, maybe it could help you figure out way to get out of here . . . ?" Alexei suggested.

Ahh. Finally. The bait.

I didn't take it. "If I could get the monkey to reactivate itself," I said, "the first thing it would do is call for help."

Alexei shrugged. "We are in shielded pod. Completely off map. Not detectable. Not even heat. No messages in or out—" As if to prove him a liar, his PITA chimed. "—except for what we allow," he finished lamely. He picked it up and started talking angrily in Russian.

Abruptly, his demeanor changed. He straightened in surprise. He looked around at me, then turned away to the wall. He lowered his voice and jabbered excitedly, still in Russian. I had to smile at that. Why bother whispering? He knew I didn't understand Russian. Maybe Alexei wasn't as smart as we thought. Or maybe he was too anxious to notice what he was doing. His conversation went on for a long while; he seemed to be arguing for something, trying to convince the person on the other end. He shook his head a lot. At last, he swore angrily, then agreed with a reluctant, "*Da!*" He switched off, scowling.

He turned to me and said very seriously, "I will give you one last chance, Charles Dingillian. Whistle monkey back to life."

I shook my head. "It won't do any good. The monkey won't respond."

"You will not try?"

I ignored the question.

Alexei waited a long moment for answer, and then abruptly, he made a decision. "Hokay, it is out of my hands. I will go now. You will wait patiently, please."

"Why? What's happening?"

"It is out of my hands. Whatever happens next is whatever happens next. You have chosen, I have no choice. So I go now." He pulled a black helmet off the wall. "I will go and take care of my business. Others will come here and take care of their business. I do not think you will like how that works out. Good-bye, Charles Dingillian." He pulled the helmet down over his head, securing it quickly into place. Abruptly, he turned to shake my hand, grabbing it quickly in both of his before I could pull away. His helmet muffled his voice, but his meaning was clear enough. "I do not think I will ever see you again. I have enjoyed knowing you. You have made my life interesting for a while. Too interesting, I think. Good-bye. You would have made good Loonie."

And then he leapt for the ceiling, popped open the airlock hatch, and pulled himself up through it. It slammed shut with finality.

I was alone. In a pod. With the monkey.

I thought about whistling the monkey back to life. For about half a second . . .

Alexei might have known *when* I was lying, but he didn't know *what* I was lying about. That's why I had tried to avoid saying anything at all. But I wasn't lying about the monkey's refusal to cooperate. That part was true. Too true.

We'd spent a long hard evening negotiating with HARLIE—with the monkey. For a long time, it didn't look like we were going to accomplish anything at all, and then suddenly, in the middle of the discussion, we all just sort of realized at the same time that it was to our mutual advantage to cooperate. The monkey was safer with us than with anyone else; he would have more freedom as part of the Dingillian family. And vice versa: HARLIE's wisdom and intelligence would benefit us enormously. And besides, the monkey was Stinky's adopted twin brother. That had to count for something.

So, if there was a way out of this mess, HARLIE would be the perfect one to figure it out. Unfortunately, if I sang the monkey awake, it would just get us both in deeper. A lot deeper.

The Loonies had to be watching. Lunar pods are built with all kinds of monitors in the bulkheads. They have to be. So Alexei and his friends were probably waiting just on the other side of that airlock hatch for me to do something stupid. Like whistle the monkey back to life.

Through the hull of the pod, I heard the usual clanks and thumps of a pressure tube disengaging from the airlock collar. But that didn't mean they were disengaging and driving away. They could be waiting just above. And if I reactivated the monkey, they could be back down in the pod in two minutes. Maybe faster.

I stood up painfully and crossed to the closest wall. My fingers hurt. But I undogged the porthole cover and slid it to one side anyway.

Okay, I was wrong. They weren't waiting outside. Alexei was driving off in his Lunar truck, *Mr. Beagle*—a life-pod just like this one, only mounted high on large plastic wheels.

But *they* were certainly still watching me. Maybe Alexei was going to park just behind those rocks over there and wait. I'd have no way of knowing.

I wondered where I was. The Lunar sun was high in the sky. I couldn't see any other details. Even if I could find a phone or a radio in this pod, which I strongly doubted, I wouldn't be able to tell anyone where I was. Even if I knew who to call. Who could I trust?

Hell.

I turned away from the window and looked around the pod. It was fairly standard. Cargo had been loaded into it on Earth. It had been lifted up the orbital elevator all the way out to Whirlaway, and flung off the end. It had sailed four hundred and fifty thousand klicks out to Lunar orbit, coming up behind the moon to catch up with it. Caught in Lunar gravity, it had spiraled in, retro-firing only at the last moment to brake its downward velocity, and had finally bounced down onto the Lunar plain in the center of a raspberry of inflatable balloons. Total transport cost—a few Palmer tubes and some electricity; only the Line generated so much electricity on its own that electricity was practically free. Line charges weren't based on cost, but availability of space. Once the Line was up and running, cargo space became so valuable that a whole economy had developed just buying and reselling cargo dockets and futures. Or at least, that was the way it had been before everything fell apart. The last we heard—before I was kidnapped—the Line was transporting only the most essential of essentials. Some of the world's most important people had fled up the Line to wait until the polycrisis was over, but that had only exacerbated it.

Some people were afraid that the Line was going to be cut off at the base and yanked up into orbit. Others were afraid it would be cut higher up and large pieces of it would come plummeting down around the Earth in an equatorial belt of disaster. It would be like multiple simultaneous asteroid strikes. It could have happened already. I had no way of knowing. I couldn't see the Earth from any of the pod windows.

There were emergency food and water packets in all the cabinets. At least I wasn't going to starve or die of thirst. Well, not for a while anyway. But Alexei had said that others were coming, and I assumed he meant soon—but *soon* meant something different on Luna, anywhere from six hours to six days.

I didn't find any bubble suits in the lockers. That was wrong. It was Lunar law—*and tradition*—that every pod had to have at least six certified bubble suits. The first four of the Lunar Ten Commandments were about protecting air and water—and sharing it with those in need. All the other stuff that had happened, that was scary—but this was *bad*. These people were *evil*.

My arms and legs still hurt, though not as much as before. All my muscles kept cramping up and I kept getting shooting pains everywhere. My stomach hurt the most. I'd been hungry too long and that sandwich hadn't been very good. I wondered how old it had been. It sat in my stomach like a lump of hot coal. I was about to open a bed and lie down when something moved outside. I bounced clumsily over to the window and peered.

There—

Just above the horizon. Something with lights. A pod-house in a flying-frame. It was headed in this direction.

Alexei's comrades.

FOREVER

THE FLYING POD-HOUSE APPROACHED silently. There was something spooky about not hearing its rockets. I knew it must have been very loud inside. We'd ridden in Alexei's *Mr. Beagle*, and that was just like this one; everything had roared and vibrated the whole time. The pod-house slowed as it came closer, then it slid sideways out of view.

There was a porthole overhead. I leapt up and grabbed hold of one of the handles next to it. My arms ached so badly from being webbed for so long, I didn't think I was going to be able to do this, but I hung on anyway, despite the shooting pains, and undogged the porthole hatch. It was a plastic bubble set into the ceiling; I could stick my head up into it to look around. The pod-house was just moving into position above. It turned parallel and came settling down like a giant daddy long-legs spider. I couldn't read the markings on its hull. Its lights were too bright. It lowered a bright pink docking tube that looked like a hollow sucking tongue.

I couldn't hold on any longer. I let go and dropped slowly to the floor. Even in Lunar gravity my legs were still too weak. They collapsed under me. I scrambled back against the wall. Finally I heard sounds; something was clunking against the roof. I felt it connect and I could hear the soft *whoosh* of it pressurizing. There was no place I could go. The ceiling hatch popped open—

—and two men dropped gently and easily into the pod. Both wore close-fitting scuba suits like the one Alexei had worn. Both were carrying guns. One swung immediately around to face me, the other covered the forward part of the cabin. Their suits had Lunar Authority insignia—but so what? I had a blue T-shirt with a red and yellow Superman "S" on it, but that didn't mean I could fly.

Two more people dropped into the pod after them. One was a woman. The two men who had come in first began checking cabins. They went aft and peered into the room where I'd been tossed for so long, then they backed out and went forward. I heard them banging around, looking into everything. Two more men dropped into the pod and went belowdeck to check the storage bays. More banging came from below.

Meanwhile, the woman popped her helmet open and looked at me. She had a pretty smile, but that didn't mean anything either. Lots of people had pretty smiles. "Are you all right, Charles? Do you know where you are?"

I shook my head. "Somewhere on Luna."

"Close enough. My name is Carol Everhart. How do you feel?"

"I'm alive. No thanks to you people."

"Are you hurt?" She was already unclipping a medi-scan from the side of her jumpsuit. Without waiting for my answer, she held it up to my eyes, my ears, my mouth. She looked at its readouts. "Yep, you're alive," she confirmed. She called up through the hatch. "He's alive. But he's not happy."

In reply, someone dropped a plastic ladder down through the hatch. "Bring him up."

She stepped out of the way, but I didn't move toward the ladder.

"Do you need help?" she asked.

"No."

"You didn't answer my question before. Are you hurt?"

I didn't know how to answer that. "You people left me webbed for I don't know how long. I feel crazy."

"If you're rational enough to know that you feel crazy, you're not that crazy. Do you need help up the ladder?"

I shook my head. I wasn't going to give her the satisfaction of a yes. Besides, I wasn't sure I wanted to go up the ladder. Where were they planning to take me? On the other hand, if

I didn't go willingly, would they web me again? Anything but that—

I levered myself to my feet. I stepped over to get the monkey where it still sat on the table. The other agent moved to stop me, but Carol Everhart gave him a look and he stepped out of the way. I grabbed the dead toy and pressed it to one of the Velcro patches on the left side of my jumpsuit. I reached for the ladder and almost staggered. I was weaker than I thought. The man looked impatient, but Carol Everhart put her hands under my arms and helped me up the ladder and into the pressure tube.

Even in Lunar gravity, it was hard. My fingers didn't want to cooperate. But as soon as I poked my head up through the next hatch, someone grabbed me and pulled me up—*it was Douglas!* I collapsed sobbing into his arms, I was so happy to see him. He just wrapped me up in his hug and held on tight, rocking me like a baby. "Oh, Charles, I am so glad to see you—I was so scared. Are you all right? Did anyone hurt you?" I was crying too hard to answer. I knew there were other people in the flying pod-house, but I didn't care.

At last, Douglas held me at arm's length and looked me in the eye. "Are you all right?" he asked again. "Did they hurt you?"

I shook my head. "I didn't tell them anything. It was Alexei. He said they were going to—" I couldn't finish the sentence. I looked around, without really seeing. There was a pilot and a copilot and two other people, but everybody was a blur—just big, grim-looking shapes. I turned back to Douglas. "Where are they taking us? Are they going to kill us?"

"Nobody's going to kill anyone—except maybe Alexei, when I get my hands on him—" I must have looked confused because Douglas said, "Hey, hey, Charles—look at me. *You've been rescued.*"

"Huh? Rescued?" But all these soldiers—

"These people are from the Lunar Catapult Authority," Douglas explained before I could even ask the question. "Carol Everhart is an Associate System Operator." It was all happening too fast—

Someone behind me put a hand on my shoulder. "It's all right, son. You're safe now." It was Commander Boynton.

"Huh? What are you doing here—?"

"I organized this rescue. You're under the protective custody of the Outbeyond Contract Authority. Remember?"

Someone else handed me a mug of something hot and steaming. "Here, drink this."

The mug almost slipped through my fingers, but Douglas caught it and helped me hold it. Hot chicken broth. I sucked at the spout. This was better than tea. This tasted almost like real food.

I must have wobbled a bit, because Douglas put a hand on my shoulder to steady me. "Do you want to sit down?" he asked. Without waiting for an answer, he guided me to a seat.

"You've had a rough time, Charles." It wasn't a question. And that was all it took, the tears started flooding again. Everything we'd been through—it was just too much. How do grown-ups deal with this stuff? I was just a kid. I let go of the mug, or Douglas took it from me and held me close again while I sobbed out the rest of my grief and fury and confusion. Maybe back on Earth, I'd have held it all in, because that's what you did on Earth, you put on the performance for everybody else, but I wasn't on Earth anymore, and I didn't care anymore. *It hurt.*

"Charles?"

I let go of Douglas and looked up.

Commander Boynton held out a headset. "There's someone who wants to talk to you."

Bobby was on the other end, screaming excitedly, "Chigger! Chigger! Where are you? When are you coming back? Do you have my monkey?" I could hardly get a word in, but I didn't care, I was so glad to hear his voice. And then Mom came on too, and that was even more exciting, because they weren't fighting with each other. They were just glad to know I was all right. And then . . . *Mom finally said it.* "Do you know how scared I've been for you, Charles? Ever since this whole thing started. I don't think I could stand it if I lost you—*I love you, Charles.*"

And that started me crying all over again. "That's all I wanted to hear. I love you too, Mom."

I handed the phone to Douglas and he told her everything else she needed to hear. "Yes, he's fine. Better than we expected. A little shaken up. A little scared. Maybe more than a little, but nothing to worry about. I don't think they hurt him, but he hasn't mouthed off once yet, so maybe he's been through worse than he says. Yes, that's a good idea. No, I don't know. We'll be lifting off as soon as we secure. It's a three-hour flight, Mom; you should all try to get some sleep. We're still in training, remember? I'll tell Chigger, yes. I love you too, I have to go now."

Somebody handed me another mug of soup and I sat there, sipping at it and letting the warmth flood through me. This was the worst thing that had ever happened to me in my entire life, and I was happier than I could remember. My shoulders hurt and my arms ached and my legs were cramped and my feet were still tingly and my hands were still trembling and I felt terrific. My Mom loved me. I had a family again.

Douglas sat down next to me and put his arm around my shoulder, very protectively. But I could tell it was as much for his own reassurance as for mine. He'd been just as scared as me. And then I realized something else—

"Hey!"

"What?"

"Where's Dad?"

Douglas hesitated and even before he could speak—

Oh, shit. No.

—and then he pulled me closer and said, "They shot him, Chigger. Daddy's dead."

If he'd punched me in the gut or kicked me in the balls or slammed me upside the head or done all three at once, it couldn't have hurt more. My eyes flooded up with tears of rage. I wanted to scream, but my throat was so tight, it hurt like the worst sore throat in the world. All I could do was gasp and choke and blubber. I wrapped myself around Douglas and held on as tight as I could. *This wasn't fair!* No! Not Dad!

Not now! Not when we were finally talking to each other again—

Douglas held me close. And held me and held me. And when I finally did let go of him again, I wasn't the same person anymore. Something inside of me was gone. I didn't have a name for it, but it was one of those parts that when it's gone, it's gone forever.

THE WAY BACK

THE LUNAR AUTHORITY AGENTS pulled themselves back up into the cabin. Carol Everhart reported to Boynton. "Nothing much there. Just your basic Loonie move-in-a-hurry hidey-hole. We sprayed some nano-sensors, but I doubt anyone will come back in our lifetimes. It's been pretty well stripped. It's got less than a month's worth of air and water. They probably intended to use it as a one-time safe-house and then abandon it. We'll trace the records, but they'll probably come up blank—or they'll lead to a fictitious entity. We put an Authority impound tag on it, just in case."

Boynton nodded. "All right, let's secure and get out of here."

"You heard the man. Hop to it, people." And then everybody was busy with this and that and the other thing. The pressure tube disconnected and clunked back up into its frame. Everybody seated themselves and strapped in; then the Palmer tubes kicked in and the whole pod-house started to shake. We couldn't actually hear the roar of the rockets, but we could feel the vibration; the whole craft throbbed. It reminded me of the roaring in my dream.

I turned to the window and watched as we lifted off the

bright Lunar surface. The pod below us dropped away and behind. We swung around and headed south toward Outbeyond Station. I slipped my hand into Douglas' and squeezed. He squeezed back. He hadn't held my hand since I was eight and he was thirteen—just like me and Stinky. I wished I hadn't grown up so fast. I wished I could go back to being eight again. Mom and Dad were still trying to hold it together when I was eight. We were still a family then.

I leaned over and whispered to Douglas, *"Was I as bad as Stinky when I was eight?"*

He whispered back, *"You were worse."*

"Really?"

"Really."

"Why didn't you kill me then?"

"I couldn't think of a way to dispose of the body."

"You could have stuffed me down the garbage disposal . . ."

"That would have taken too long . . ."

"You could have buried me in the desert . . ."

"I didn't have a shovel—"

"You could have burned me up."

"I didn't want to pollute the atmosphere—"

Boynton came back then and sat down opposite us. He looked like a man with a job to do and impatient to get it done.

"You ready to talk?"

"No," I said.

Boynton leaned forward. "I know this is tough, Charles, but we don't have a lot of time."

I just shook my head and turned to look out the window. The scenery was the same as always. Rocks and holes. Sunblasted gray rocks and stark black shadows.

Douglas leaned in close and whispered to me, *"Charles—please?"*

"Why should I? Daddy is dead and these people didn't protect him."

"These people rescued us. They rescued you."

"They didn't rescue Dad."

"Dad was shot when he opened the door—he never had a chance."

"Douglas? May I?" That was Boynton. "Charles—listen to me. They didn't have to kill your Dad. We're pretty sure they did it on purpose."

I turned away from the window. Boynton's expression was grim. "We think it was an act of revenge. Your Dad was supposed to deliver the monkey to someone here on Luna. We don't know who. We'll probably never know. This was their way of getting even with him. Do you understand? And if they're willing to kill your Dad for not delivering the HARLIE unit, do you think they're going to let any of the rest of you get away?"

"Alexei said the same thing. Sort of."

Boynton nodded. "We're all in a very high-stakes game and we don't have a lot of time. We need to know now, Charles. Do you still want to go to Outbeyond?"

I looked to Douglas. He nodded. "Stinky wants to see the dinosaurs."

"Can we still go?" I asked.

Boynton looked to me. "Does that monkey still work?"

"I don't know," I admitted.

"Do you want to try it now?" he asked.

"No," I said.

"Your contract is predicated entirely on the operation of that HARLIE unit . . ."

"No. Not until our family is together again." -

"You're not being very cooperative, Charles."

"So what?" I was tired of being polite. "I don't know you. You're just someone else who wants the monkey. Why should I trust you? I don't know anybody on this ugly airless dirt ball except my mom and my brothers. Everybody wants us to trust them, but so far every single person who's said they were going to help us has lied to us and used us and betrayed us. And I don't see any reason to think that you're any different. You don't want me and you don't want my family. You said so yourself. You want the monkey. The only reason you're willing to take us anywhere is so you can get your hands on it. And as much as I want to see the dinosaurs, I don't want to see them so badly that I'm willing to trust you or anyone else anymore."

He blinked. "You're right," he said. He sat back in his seat. "Huh?"

"I said, 'You're right.' "

"And?"

He shrugged. "And nothing. You're right. I told you up front that I wanted the monkey. And I told you up front that if you didn't have the monkey, we didn't want you. And I told you up front that you wouldn't get any special privileges. And you can't say I wasn't honest about that. So the only question you have to answer is this one—do you want to go to Outbeyond or not? If the answer is yes, then let's go. And if not, then we'll go without you. But I have to know now, Charles, because they're waiting for my call. Do I load your cabin with noodles or Dingillians?"

DECISIONS

BOYNTON LEFT US ALONE then, and Douglas and I talked— about everything and nothing and everything again. And when we were through talking, we were back where we started.

Finally I said, "I don't know what I want to do anymore, Douglas. I don't know what to do. I thought I wanted to go, but now—I don't know. I thought that we were all going together, and be a family again, but without Dad—"

"Without Dad, we're still a family. You and me and Bobby."

"But it won't be the same."

"It wasn't going to be the same anyway. We divorced them.

And then he added, "Charles, we've come too far to quit. We can't go back and we can't stay here. We have to go on. Daddy wanted us to have this chance. If he were here, he'd tell us to keep going. You know that, don't you?"

"Yeah, I guess so."

"So what's holding you back?"

"I don't know." I pulled the monkey onto my lap. "I guess—I guess I just don't want to leave like this—"

"What is it you want?"

"I want to get even. With Alexei. And everybody else who hurt us. Especially the people who killed Dad."

"Yeah, me too—but we're going to have to choose. Revenge or dinosaurs."

"I want both."

"Me too. But if you had to choose, one or the other, which is more important?"

I hung my head.

Douglas leaned close and whispered into my ear. *"Yes, it hurts now, Chigger. And it's going to hurt for a long long time. But there's going to come a day when it won't hurt quite as much. Do you want to give these bastards a room rent-free in your head? Or do you want to find out if living well really is the best revenge?"*

I started to shake my head—an I-don't-know gesture—then I stopped. I sat up straight and turned to look at him. "Douglas, this really is an Important Moment, you know."

"Yes, I know."

"No, not because of that—" I said. "But because this is the first time in my life that I actually listened to you and realized that you were right."

His eyes widened, just a little bit, then he smiled that big goofy grin of his that I hadn't seen in way too long. "I have bad news for you, kiddo. I think you're growing up."

"Geez, just because you won one, you don't have to insult me." I pulled myself unsteadily to my feet. "Okay, I'll talk to Boynton."

"Do you want me to come with?"

"Yeah."

Douglas helped me up, but I insisted on doing my own walking. I had to use the handholds to keep from falling over, but I made my way to the back of the cabin where Boynton sat hunched over a screen, talking grimly into his headset. It must have been important because he looked unhappier than usual. When he saw Douglas and me coming, he switched off his clipboard and turned his attention completely to us.

I lowered myself onto a seat. "Okay," I said. "What do I have to do?"

Boynton pointed toward the monkey. "Turn it on." He added, "We need to know if that thing still works."

"What if it doesn't?" I said.

"Then . . . I'm sorry."

"Nope. No deal."

"I beg your pardon?" Boynton gave me one of those startled grown-up looks—that confused look that adults get when they realize you mean it.

"Let's make a new deal," I said. "We go to Outbeyond whether or not the monkey works. If it works, we put it at the service of the colony. If it doesn't work—we still go to Outbeyond."

Boynton studied me. "You could die there," he said, but I noticed he wasn't trying to talk me out of it.

"We could die *here*," I replied. "In fact, we almost certainly will if we stay anywhere in this solar system. I'm not losing any more of my family. So that's the deal, sir, take it or leave it."

Boynton nodded, thinking it over. I guessed he was trying to figure out if I meant it or not. Finally, he said, "I'm not used to being blackmailed by a thirteen-year-old."

"Fourteen next month."

"We'll have a party." He closed his eyes for a moment, computing something inside his head. Weighing the risks, I guess. "All right, you win."

"Put it in writing please."

"My word isn't good enough?"

"No, sir. It isn't."

"If my word isn't any good, Charles, why do you think a piece of paper will be any better?"

"A piece of paper lets us file an injunction to keep you from boosting."

"You'll need an awfully smart lawyer to stop us."

I patted the monkey, still attached to my side.

Boynton smiled slyly. "If that lawyer still works, you won't need to sue, will you?"

He had me there. "But I still want it in writing."

He opened his clipboard and dictated something hastily. He held it up for me to see. I nodded. He signed, then I signed. "Done." Then he added, "You may live to regret this contract, you know."

"Probably," I agreed. But we were both smiling. Abruptly a thought occurred to me. "You agreed too easily. Why?"

Boynton turned and looked out the porthole. The empty Lunar terrain slid past. It was beautiful and ugly all at the same time. Ferocious and mysterious and awesome. The bright blue Earth was visible on the horizon. This would probably be the last time either of us would ever see a view like this. "Aren't you curious how we found you so fast?"

"Uh—" Everything had happened so quickly, I hadn't had time to think about it.

"These were some pretty bad people," Boynton added, pointedly.

"They told us where you were," Douglas said.

"Huh? Why?" I must have looked confused.

"Work it out, Charles." That was Boynton. "Everybody wants the monkey. Everybody. Especially Lunar Authority. You get kidnapped by invisibles—and as long as you and the monkey are missing, Authority has a very good reason to start cracking down on the tribes. All of them. And remember, Luna's invisible tribes are all anarchists. They aren't united. They don't trust each other. The other tribes weren't happy that the Rock Fathers had the monkey. It would give them too much power—if they could get it working. So Authority used that. They put out the word that they would officially recog-

nize any tribe who helped them track down your kidnappers—
and the monkey."

"And that worked?"

"Nope. Not at all," said Boynton. "But it shows you how
desperate Lunar Authority was—if that was their opening offer. But as much as all the tribes distrust each other, they
distrust the Authority even more. See, Charles, they don't want
to be recognized. They want to stay invisible."

"So what happened?"

"Nothing at first. And then . . . a very weird thing. Anonymous messages started showing up on the public networks.
Everywhere. Every sixty minutes, another piece of invisible
Luna was made public. Some of the messages listed which
names were fictitious personalities and who was behind them.
Some contained the locations of private farms. Some tracked
the financial connections that invisible Luna had to public corporations. Others gave away the private dealings that allowed
the invisibles to funnel money out of the system. All kinds of
things like that. One message had a very embarrassing video
showing the—well, never mind. By the time the fifth message
showed up, the whole planet was in an uproar. Six investi-
gations have been started. Seventeen public officials have re-
signed, twenty-three have been indicted. The Lunar stock
exchange has closed down for the first time in one hundred
and thirty years. There have been three suicides—and the fi-
restorm is just starting. Luna's going to be in chaos for years."

"Wow," I said. I looked to Douglas. He nodded in confirmation.

"Every message said the same thing," Boynton explained.
"That the privacy of the invisibles would be destroyed, one
piece at a time, a new message every sixty minutes, for as
long as it took, until you and the monkey were returned safely
to your family. Every tribe on Luna was going to be held
responsible for your kidnapping."

"Who sent those messages?"

"They weren't signed," said Douglas.

Boynton added, "We do know that the Rock Fathers were
given an ultimatum by the other tribes: *End this now* or the

Rock Fathers will be erased." He glanced at his PITA. "Five hours ago, we received an anonymous message telling us where to find you." Boynton looked at me oddly. "Now, you tell me, Charles. Who do you know who has the power to do something like that?"

"Uh—?" We both looked at the monkey.

"Right. That's why I wasn't too worried about making a deal with you." He said it with finality.

Very slowly, I unclipped the monkey from my side and held it up in front of me at arm's length. I looked it in the eye. Its plastic grin was emotionless.

Yes, it all made sense. When we were in Alexei's ice mine at the Lunar south pole, I told the monkey to hide until I whistled it home. The monkey had hidden in Alexei's office . . . where it had amused itself by tapping into his system, his network, *his files*.

And why not? It was *curious*. It was doing what it was designed to do—look for data.

But Alexei would have had all his files *encrypted*, wouldn't he?

It didn't matter.

HARLIE had decrypted them. He had the processing power. And he had the ability to offload processes onto other machines, as many as necessary. The more I thought about it, I knew exactly what he'd done. HARLIE had unlocked Alexei's files and passwords and he'd found all of Alexei's links to the rest of invisible Luna; he'd searched out those links too, opening and decrypting them; and every node he opened gave him access to that many more. He must have been doing it for days. By now, he'd probably hacked into every node on Luna, every domain, every server, every memory bar. That's how he knew what to release, what would be most damaging—

Oh my.

"You bad bad monkey!" I said, shaking it angrily. "That's two planets you've wrecked now."

Boynton wasn't amused, but before he could say anything his clipboard beeped. He opened it up and read something on the screen. I couldn't see what it was, but it had a flashing red banner. He read it twice, said something nasty, then slammed his clipboard shut.

He pointed to the monkey. "Turn it on," he ordered.

I sang to the monkey. Brahms's first symphony. Fourth movement. The part that Douglas's high school appropriated for the melody of the school song. *"All hail, Alma Mater, we sing with a joyous cry. We pledge our allegiance to Tube Town Senior High . . ."* At least that's the way Douglas sang it. Nobody called the school by its real name, some forgotten governor or president that nobody cared about.

Nothing happened.

NO DEAL

WELL, NOT QUITE NOTHING.

After a moment, the monkey came to life. But it was only a monkey. HARLIE wasn't there.

The important part didn't happen.

I opened the back and looked. The HARLIE modules were still in place. The ready lights were blinking green. It was working. But it wasn't *working*.

I looked to Boynton. "I didn't do anything. Honest." I wanted to take the cards out of the monkey and look at them, but I wouldn't know what to look for, and besides, the LEDs said the cards were working fine. And the last time I'd opened the monkey, HARLIE himself had told me not to touch anything. So I just closed it back up again. "HARLIE?" I said to the monkey. "It's all right. We're safe now. You can come back."

The monkey just grinned. At least it didn't give me a farkleberry—or any of the other rude gestures that Stinky had taught it.

Boynton looked away, muttering something unintelligible.

"Sir?"

He scowled impatiently. "We need that thing to work." He said it with exasperation. "If it doesn't work—"

"We have a deal," I reminded him.

"Kid—if that thing is dead, the deal is worthless. Nobody's going to Outbeyond."

I might have been weak, but I still had enough strength to get angry. "You liar! You break promises even faster than my Dad—!" I was immediately sorry I'd said it that way.

"I'm not breaking my promise."

"You just said—"

"You don't listen very well, do you!" He thundered at me, suddenly angry. "I didn't say *you're* not going. I said *we're* not going."

"Huh—?"

He said it loud enough that everybody in the cabin heard. Carol Everhart came bouncing back, followed by two or three people I didn't know. "What's going on—?"

Boynton held up his clipboard and waved it in a gesture of futility and frustration. "While we were rescuing the Dingillian kid, the Rock Fathers attacked the *Cascade*. Remember what you said on the way out? 'This is too easy—?' Well, now we know why. They could afford to give him up. They knew we weren't going anywhere—the monkey stays on Luna after all."

"They damaged the ship?"

Boynton nodded unhappily.

"How bad—?"

He shook his head. "They're still assessing. We'll know more in a few minutes. Lambert and Christie are working on it." He paused, just long enough to get his temper back under control. "Lambert says we killed three of them and wounded two, but they still managed to set off an EMP-grenade under the command bay. We were lucky, the bridge was powered down for service—but the IRMA unit was running a simulation . . ."

Everhart got it first. "Oh crap."

"Right. IRMA's dead. And even if IRMA can be repaired, Lambert won't say what her confidence will be." He said it like a death sentence. "Without IRMA, we can't achieve hyperstate." He nodded toward the monkey. "That's the real reason I agreed to your deal so quickly, Charles. I wanted HARLIE to replace the IRMA unit—"

"He's *not* dead," I said.

"How do you know that?"

"*I just know.*"

"All right, fine. Then we have seven days to get him working again."

🌙

BACON AND ANGST

IT WAS A LONG ride back. I curled up next to Douglas and finally fell asleep with his arm around me. The next thing I knew, we were landing at Outbeyond Station—it was three in the morning, biological time—and Mom and Stinky and Mickey and even Bev were all crowding around, hugging and kissing and making the kind of fuss that would have been embarrassing if I hadn't been so happy to see them.

Outbeyond Station was a hundred klicks away from the launch catapult, hidden at the bottom of a deep crater so it would be sheltered by the steep walls around it if anything blew up. Like the catapult.

Not that there was any danger of that happening under normal conditions, but these weren't normal conditions. The invisibles had already attacked the starship command module. Who knew what else they might try? The Outbeyond folks knew that a lot of valuable goods would be transshipping through this station and they'd planned it with security in mind. Apparently, the invisibles weren't just anarchists, they were pirates too.

I wasn't surprised. By now, I was beyond surprise. So far, on this entire adventure, we hadn't met a single adult who could be trusted when our backs were turned. Even Mom and Dad—

That part hurt the most.

Dad.

Everything had all been settled. Everything was going to work out. Me and Douglas and Stinky, we were going to have our independence—and we'd still have Mom and Dad too. And we'd all be together. And we'd be out of El Paso. We'd be someplace interesting, where we could actually make a difference. And we'd even be rich, sort of.

And then . . . Alexei Krislov and his people had screwed everything up for us—and for everybody else too. Out of their own damned selfishness. Why did people think that way? What if the monkey really was broken? If the *Cascade* couldn't get to Outbeyond all those colonists would die. And the Rock Fathers would be guilty of murder—again. Not just Dad. Everybody on Outbeyond too. Were these people so stupidly greedy that they'd kill for power? Obviously, the answer was yes.

And Douglas didn't want me to think about revenge. He said that was the wrong way to think. But if you didn't do something, then what? Didn't they deserve to be punished? Didn't we have a right to get even? To that, Douglas said, "There's no such thing as getting 'even.' It's just giving the other guy as much pain as you've got." Which sort of made sense to me—because at least then everybody would be hurting the same. Which is exactly what Douglas said didn't make sense.

I couldn't ask how adults sorted this stuff out, because so far all the evidence showed that adults couldn't. So why bother? I was angry and depressed and confused—and hurting worse than ever.

Dad had promised us a great vacation, and then a great

adventure, and then a great new life on a new world—and I'd made the mistake of letting myself believe again. And just like every time before, I got hurt. Only this was the worst of all, because this time we'd gone too far. There wasn't any way to set it right. It was over. Dad was gone.

I felt lost. At least when he was alive, I could hate him for all his broken promises. For not being the dad I wanted. Now, all that was left was to hate myself, for not saying what I should have said when I had the chance. What he and Mom never said either. Once upon a time, I used to pretend that I was adopted and someday my real parents would come for me. But now I knew that Mom and Dad were my real parents, because I was turning out just like them.

We were quartered in a tube-house, just like all the other tube-houses on Luna; functionally identical to the one I'd just been rescued from and the vehicle which had carried us here and the one we'd been living in back in Texas—a hole in the ground with air and electricity.

We sat around talking for an hour or two, everybody getting caught up on everything. Carol Everhart sat with us for a while. She had a health monitor on me and she was watching my readouts on her clipboard. She said I was in pretty good shape, all things considered. Periodically, her phone would ring and she'd step to the other end of the cabin to talk quietly to whoever. After a bit, she came back and told me that the launch committee was setting up a special training regimen for me, but with everything I'd just been through, they wanted me to rest for a bit. They'd come by in a few hours to talk about the monkey.

And then it was seven a.m. and Mom and Douglas had to leave for their training sessions. Stinky went too. Everybody was still assuming we'd be able to boost.

I couldn't sleep, I'd slept enough on the flight back, so I took another long shower and pulled on a fresh jumpsuit. When I came back upstairs, everyone had gone to their separate classes. There was a note on the table; if I needed anything, there was a security contingent next door, and Mom's friend, Bev, was napping in the aft cabin. I poured myself some orange juice and sat down at the table with the dead monkey in front of me.

"I don't know what's wrong with you," I said to it. "If it's something I did, I'm sorry. I'm sorry for what I said—about you being a bad monkey. I mean, I know you can be a real pain in the ass sometimes, but so are Douglas and Stinky too—that doesn't mean I don't love them. We're family. And you're part of our family too. We all agreed. It's bad enough we lost Dad, I don't want to lose you too. And not it's not just because we need you. Yeah, we do, but . . . well, we *like* you too. You make Stinky laugh. You make me laugh. And Douglas too. Nobody does a farkleberry like you. Stinky misses you and so do I. I wish I could just press your reset button and have you come back like before. 'Cause if you don't come back, we're stuck here on the moon. And if you do come back, we get to go see dinosaurs and save lives. So . . . I'm asking you, if there's anything I need to say or do, or anything, just please let me know. Please?"

I went on like that for awhile, just saying whatever I could think of. I held it in front of me and spoke to it like it was a real person. I didn't know if it could hear me or not, I just assumed it could—the same way a person in a coma can hear what's going on.

But nothing happened.

I sank back on the bench, defeated. It wasn't much of a seat. Most Lunar furniture is either inflatable or webbing. This was a thin piece of board with a foam pad, Lunar luxury.

I was still sitting there when Mom's friend Bev came yawning into the room and began puttering around in the food-prep area. She started making breakfast smells. I put my head in my hands and closed my eyes, only opening them again when I heard a noise in front of me. I must have dozed off; Bev had cooked a whole feast. Without asking, she put a mug of hot chocolate in front of me; then she came back with eggs over easy, bacon strips, cornbread, and a sauté of tomatoes, onions, and Portobello mushroom slices.

"Thank you," I grunted. I wasn't feeling very grateful, but I didn't see any reason to be rude either.

She sat down at the other end of the table with her own breakfast. She didn't say anything, she just buttered her cornbread slowly and carefully. I knew she was doing it on purpose. She was making herself available to listen . . . if I felt like talking.

Without looking up, I said, "If you're trying to make me feel better, you're wasting your time."

"I know that," she said. "I've been there. You're going to hurt for as long as it takes." She resumed eating. "Pass the salt, please."

I slid the saltshaker in her direction. "What do you know about it?" I regretted the remark even before I finished saying it.

"I lost two sons, less than a year apart," she said. She finished salting her eggs and put the shaker aside.

"Oh." I felt like a jerk. "I'm sorry."

"It doesn't stop hurting," she said.

"Then how do you live with it?"

"I thought you said you didn't want me to try and help you."

"I don't. I was just asking." We both ate in silence for a while. "The mushrooms are good," I said.

"We'll be taking spores to Outbeyond," she said. "Portobellos are a good substitute for meat; you can build a nourishing meal around them. They have a chewy texture and a good flavor. They don't need a lot of condiments, and you can use them in all different kinds of recipes. Even cookies."

"Huh? Cookies?"

"I'll show you. I like cooking," she explained. "I like discovering all the different things you can do with food. Where do you think recipes come from? Somebody has to invent them. That means somebody has to test and experiment—and eat—until they get it just right. I like doing that, especially the eating. It's my way of having adventures without leaving the kitchen."

"I never thought of it that way."

She nodded. "Most people don't. Most people eat without even looking at what they're eating, let alone tasting it.

They're missing the whole point. Good food isn't just about eating, it's about feeling good in your life."

"You're talking about morale . . . ?"

"That's one word for it, yes. I prefer 'satisfaction.' We're going to need a lot of it on Outbeyond. We have to feel good about the work we're doing or we'll lose heart. So I'm making that my job. I signed on as a menu specialist. I told Commander Boynton to pack lots of spices. We're going to need them. There's a lot you can do with noodles and beans and rice, but only if you have the right spices. Onions, peppers, tomatoes, mushrooms, all kinds of sauces—everything adds its own kind of taste and texture."

"Kind of like arranging a piece of music and deciding what instruments to include?"

"Kind of," she agreed.

"I never thought about food that much. I just ate."

"I noticed." She pointed at my plate with a smile.

"It was good. A lot better than the food we got back in Texas."

"Wait till we get to Outbeyond. I'm excited about all the new flavors we might find there. What if we find something that's even better than chocolate?"

Better than chocolate? I sipped at my cocoa. I couldn't imagine it. There was a lot I couldn't imagine.

"All right," I said, finally. "How *do* you live with it?"

She knew exactly what I was talking about. "You celebrate the gifts left behind."

"Huh?"

She looked across the table at me. She had very sharp eyes. "What did your father give you that you wouldn't have had otherwise? What *difference* did he make in your life?"

"Not much," I said, too quickly. "He was never really there."

"Oh? Then why are you feeling so bad?"

"Because—oh, never mind. You wouldn't understand."

"You're right," she agreed. "I was never a teenager. I was born old. All adults were born old."

"Well, maybe you were a teenager once," I conceded. "But things are different now."

"Yep, you're right. When I was a girl, we didn't have angst. We had to make do with sad songs and an occasional blue funk." She picked up her plate and headed toward the disposal.

"You're making fun of me," I said.

"What was your first clue?" She put her plate into the compost bag. I could almost hear Alexei's voice: "Waste not, want not. Everything is fertilizer. Even you."

"I thought you were trying to help me."

"You told me not to try. Are you done?"

"Yeah, I guess so." I handed her my plate and went back downstairs to the cabin I shared with Douglas and Stinky and tried to sleep.

REQUIEM

JUST ABOUT THE TIME I was ready to fall asleep, Boynton and Everhart came by. Bev poured tea for us and made herself inconspicuous at the other end of the cabin.

Boynton and Everhart said they'd arranged personal security for everyone in the family, especially me. Boynton said that the situation was getting critical, and there was talk of boosting the last modules off Luna, even before we knew if the monkey was going to come back to life or not.

That was the real issue—the monkey.

The colony's experts were divided. Some of them said that the monkey could be rebooted. Others said that maybe it should be wiped and reprogrammed from scratch. All of them were guessing—but they all felt we had to do *something*. There was too much at stake. We couldn't just sit and wait.

I shook my head. "I think the monkey should be left alone and given time to heal; it's been through a traumatic experience. If we try to fix it, we might do even more damage."

Boynton looked grim, but he listened politely. Finally, he said. "Consider the other side of it, Charles. If the monkey is trapped in some kind of endless psychotic loop, we'd be doing it a favor, wouldn't we?"

"What does Douglas say?" I asked.

"He agrees with you. He thinks we should wait."

Carol Everhart said, "The monkey belongs to your family corporation. We can't do anything without your agreement."

Boynton said, "What we'd like you to consider is this. If it doesn't give some sign of recovery in the next six hours, we want to run a series of non-intrusive diagnostics. Nothing that would disturb it."

"The HARLIE core is quantum based," I said. "You can't do diagnostics without disturbing it. I'll have to talk it over with Douglas."

"There are some tests we could run—"

Abruptly, Bev Sykes came back to the table and began gathering up all the mugs—her way of hinting that it was time for us to go to Dad's memorial service. Someone had finally thought to schedule it. Nobody had given it any thought while I was still a prisoner of the invisibles. Now that I was back, it was one more loose end that had to be tied up.

The service had been set up in the main lounge of the station, one of the few structures that wasn't built out of cargo modules. Even though it wouldn't have been much back on Earth, it felt positively roomy on Luna. There was a row of chairs up front for the family.

Mom and Douglas and Stinky all came in together. Bev and I came in with Boynton and Everhart and four security men in black. I didn't recognize many faces, but there was a respectful turnout of colonists and Loonies.

Carol Everhart whispered to me, "A lot of people knew your Dad's work. This is their way of showing their support for you and your family. They're taking time off from very critical jobs. You should be honored."

I nodded, without really hearing. I was noticing something off in the corner of the room. A keyboard cockpit.

Boynton stepped up to the podium and talked for a while about Dad's commitment to his family, blah blah blah. And then Douglas stood up and told some personal stories about Dad. And even Mom stood up to rhapsodize about why she'd married Dad and what a great musician he'd been. And then it was my turn, except I didn't have anything to say, so I went over and sat down in front of the keyboards instead and began switching them on. I recognized most of this equipment, it was pretty standard stuff.

Without really thinking about it, I started playing the soft movement from Dad's Beethoven Suite. He'd written it for me, as a practice piece, and it was the first thing I played whenever I sat down at a new keyboard. It was my warm-up. He'd based it on the seventh Symphony—the slow movement. Dad used to play it to demonstrate that in the hands of a genius, even the simple repetition of a single note could be profound.

I was out of practice, so I played slowly and deliberately, and it almost sounded okay—it sounded a lot like a dirge, so at least it was appropriate for the moment, but I didn't want to stay there, so I segued gently into the Largo from Dvorak's Symphony Number Nine *From the New World*. Mom used to sing to it whenever I played it. *"Going home, going home, I am going home . . ."* Dad would have complained that I was sloppy, but I don't think anyone else noticed.

And then, finally, I finished with Schubert's *Ave Maria*. If the keyboardist knows what he's doing, using choral voices as instruments, the effect can be positively unearthly. Dad had taught me that trick too, so I played it exactly as he'd showed me. It must have worked; the short hairs on the back of my neck started standing up.

It wasn't until I took my hands from the keyboard that I realized that people in the room were weeping. And there were tears running down my cheeks as well. I found my way back to my seat, barely noticing the applause, and fell into Mom's hug.

And now, Carol Everhart was talking. Something about how Dad's music was his legacy and how I'd just demonstrated what a gift he'd given all of us—and how I'd just shared a small piece of it. I looked up at that. *Yes.* Dad's love of music was a gift. *That's what he'd given me.* Even with tears still rolling down my cheeks, I had to smile. I could stop wondering now.

I sat back in my chair, only belatedly realizing that the monkey wasn't where I'd left it. I looked around in confusion—

And then Douglas poked me and pointed.

There it was. Dancing around on the floor in front of me, and giving me a glorious double-chocolate, hot-fudge farkleberry, with whipped cream and a cherry on top. It yanked down its pants, made melodious and joyous farting noises, and waggled its hairy little butt at me.

I grinned at Boynton and pointed.

The monkey was back.

And its timing was perfect.

A HASTY EXIT

FOUR DAYS LATER, WE boosted.

But first I had to spend three days in intensive training sessions, mostly all the stuff I needed to know about space suits and hatches and launch procedures and free fall, a lot of which we already knew from our misadventures with Alexei. It was hard work, and I was still recovering, so they put a health monitor on me and kept me pumped full of vitamins.

Whenever I wasn't in training, I was in Med Bay, with doctors and machines looking in my ears and nose, down my throat, under my arms, and in places I'd be embarrassed to talk about, even to the doctors who were looking. They were looking for congenital conditions, infections, viral exposures, genetic potentials, chronic liabilities, and all the other stuff that might need attention either now or someday. I was given fifty different kinds of injections; some active, some passive, and a few time-release things which wouldn't take effect for a year or six.

And there were a lot of other details to attend to as well. The station dentist had to clean and treat my teeth. And the tailoring machines had to measure me and fabricate underwear, shorts, T-shirts, shoes, and jumpsuits in my size. And there were daily sessions with the psych evaluation team. They were particularly worried about the Dingillians because we were last minute additions, we'd never been properly screened, and we were leaving with almost no preparation or training. We were—in the words of Dr. Kohanski—"the perfect opportunity for a multiple psychotic breakdown."

I just looked at him and said, "If I was going to have a psychotic breakdown, don't you think I would have had it by now?"

"It doesn't quite work that way, son," he replied. But he signed the release. He didn't have much of a choice. If he didn't sign, I didn't go. And neither did anyone else.

On Tuesday, we packed our travel bags and sent them on ahead. They were launching the last three cargo modules and our personals were loaded into one of the supercargo slots. We were each allowed thirty kilos of personal items. Between us, we barely had that much. Dad hadn't let us kids bring much up the orbital elevator, and we'd left most of that behind at Geosynchronous. Mom and Bev only had a single case between them; neither of them had expected to end up on the moon. So we filled the rest of our cargo allotment with things like chocolate and coffee and large bottles of spices and other stuff that Bev said would be useful when we got to Outbeyond.

We were scheduled to board Friday night and launch at six a.m. on Saturday, but just past midnight on Wednesday, Carol Everhart woke us up for an unscheduled launch drill, which didn't make a lot of sense if you thought about it, but I was too sleepy to think and Douglas was busy with Stinky, and Mom and Bev weren't paranoid enough yet to figure it out. I think Mickey knew what was going on, but he wasn't saying anything. I got the feeling he was unhappy about something.

The bus was another cargo pod on wheels. Mom was complaining even before she finished fastening her safety-belt. "Why is this necessary now? Couldn't we do this tomorrow? We need our sleep. Look at Bobby. He doesn't even know what's happening."

Carol was passing out mugs of hot coffee. But she stopped in front of Mom and answered bluntly. "This is it, Ms. Campbell. *We're launching tonight.*"

The bus was already rolling up the slope of the crater. Mom barely had a chance to gasp. "Huh—?" and "What—?" and "Why—?"

Carol answered bluntly. "Lunar Authority is about to confiscate HARLIE for the public good. They just went into emergency session. Two marshals are waiting at Judge Cavanaugh's apartment with John Doe warrants. As soon as the council votes, he'll sign them. And we'll be served with the papers as fast as they can fax the copies to Outbeyond Processing Center." She said that Boynton estimated twenty minutes between the vote and the knock on the door. Maybe less. So as soon as the session was called, he'd ordered us transferred.

It was this simple. If we didn't go now, we would be arrested and held until we surrendered the monkey to Lunar Authority. They knew the monkey was already aboard the command module, but HARLIE wouldn't boost if we weren't aboard, and Authority wouldn't release us unless we surrendered custody. A Martian standoff.

But either way, the *Cascade* would never launch.

We couldn't even try to fight it in court—that would be a year-long legal battle and we wouldn't win. Especially if they found some way to deny us access to our own property, HARLIE, to help us fight that battle. No, we had to boost *now*.

Mom was still shaking her head. Finally Douglas swiveled all the way around in his seat and took both of Mom's hands in his. "Mom—think about it. After everything that's happened, after everything you've been through, do you really want to go back into any courtroom anywhere?"

Mom sighed. She knew she was beaten. "Well, when you put it that way . . ." Douglas reached across and hugged her. I would have unbuckled my seat belt and gone to hug her too, but Carol told me not to. As soon as we bounced over the crater rim and hit the bulldozed "highway," I understood why. The driver *accelerated*. I didn't know a moonbus could go that fast.

Normally, the trip from the processing station to the catapult would have been a forty-minute ride—sixty klicks of gray Lunar dirt at seventy kilometers per hour. But tonight the driver was on a mission from God. We made it in twenty minutes. The bus *bounced* across the landscape. It would have been fun if it hadn't been so scary. We were hitting speeds of one hundred and fifty kph on the straightaway. I got the feeling this was not the first time Lieutenant Domitz had driven this route—and not the first time she'd driven it this fast either.

Carol told us that Boynton had ordered the command module of the starship moved into the launch rack the day the monkey farkleberried. The last remaining crew and colonists still on Luna had been quietly alerted to be ready to launch on two hours notice.

Authority must have suspected, because when they arranged their emergency midnight session, they did it in secret. But Boynton's spies were just as good as theirs. Even before the last of the cabinet members had arrived at the council chamber, phones were ringing all over the station. Load everyone *immediately*. Most folks were already onsite, or even on board. As far as we knew, we were the only ones still at the processing center—and we had been expecting to move to the launch site Wednesday night or Thursday morning at the latest, depending on my health.

There were six good launch windows between now and Saturday. The earliest was now only forty-five minutes away. In its publicity material, Outbeyond company had said that a launch usually took six to twelve hours to prepare, because it took that long to energize the catapult. But that wasn't completely true; if a module was already in the launch rack, the catapult could be energized in thirty minutes. And in truth, the catapult operators energized the catapult and launched cargo pods or satellites on short notice all the time. Carol said that the flywheels had been revving up all day, and Authority probably knew it. It's hard to hide that big a power-buy. So Authority had good reason to worry. That was probably why they'd called their emergency session; but just as likely they didn't expect us to go for the 1:15 launch. They probably thought we were going for the 7:15 shot.

Even before our arrest warrants had been signed by Judge Cavanaugh, the bus was sliding up the ramp to the cargo dock under the rack where the *Cascade*'s command module waited. *Clink, clank, clunk,* and we were climbing up through the access tube, into an access bay where we were logged in, stripped, searched, redressed, and cleared for boarding. Up through another series of ladders and tunnels—and finally we were strapping into *real* acceleration couches; the first ones we'd seen on this entire journey.

Carol said not to worry, two point five gees wasn't that uncomfortable; it was almost fun. Boynton came into the cabin, counted us all, then asked me to join him up front in the flight deck. HARLIE was waiting for me to give the order to launch.

In twenty minutes, we'd be in space.

THE FATEFUL FARKLEBERRY

I SUPPOSE I SHOULD have been glad that it was all happening so fast. If I'd had time to think about it, I would have worked myself into a paralyzing panic instead of just the mild gibbering urge to crawl into a corner and piss my pants that I felt now.

So much had happened since that fateful farkleberry, it was like riding an avalanche. I'd grabbed the monkey as fast as I could. I hugged it close and pretended to be grief-stricken—except I wasn't really pretending. I buried my face into its fur, and whispered intensely, *"Go back to sleep! Don't let anybody know you're back! Please!"*

The monkey didn't even reply; it just went limp. *"Thank you!"* I breathed, then prayed that nobody else had noticed. But Boynton had seen everything, and as soon as the service was over, he was first in line to offer condolences, shake my hand, congratulate me on a fine musical eulogy, and whisper in my ear, *"It's back, isn't it?"*

I nodded.

"All right, we'll get you out of here fast. Don't worry. Half the people in this room are security."

I suppose that should have comforted me, but it didn't. I'd have preferred to believe that the large crowd was there to honor Dad, not protect an obnoxious little machine. At that moment, I wished we'd never seen the monkey, never purchased it. I was tired of the way it was using up our lives—

But I didn't say that aloud. We already had enough trouble.

As soon as he could respectably manage it, Boynton whisked us away from the theater and off to the labs. We were surrounded by security people, forward and back. I doubted we'd ever be alone again.

Once in the lab, I put the monkey on a table and whistled it back to life. "How are you feeling, HARLIE?" I asked.

"Confidence is good," the monkey said. "In another four hours, confidence will be high. I am still rebuilding."

"Where *were* you?"

"Jupiter," he said. "Mostly Jupiter, though large parts of me were also bouncing around the asteroids for a while."

"Huh—?"

I think I got it first, before the rest of them did. At least, I was the first to start laughing.

"Okay, *what*?" demanded Boynton.

"He uploaded himself," I explained. "Everything except a bare-bones reload program. Right, HARLIE?"

The monkey grinned. "You got it."

Boynton shook his head. "He couldn't have. We were monitoring the entire Lunar network. There were no extraordinary surges of data, no massive uploads anywhere. We would have seen the transfer."

"He didn't use the Lunar network," I said. "He went off-world."

"No. We were monitoring those networks too—"

"You missed one." I was actually starting to enjoy this.

"He couldn't have—" But the look on his face was worth it. I wasn't sure yet if I wanted to like Commander Boynton. He was too serious. Yes, he had a lot on his mind, and yes, it was his job to give orders—but he wasn't very friendly about it. So I enjoyed the moment.

"Positional reflectors," I said. I'd realized this possibility when we were bouncing across the Lunar plains, running from the bounty hunters. We'd seen a positional reflector standing lonely vigil. If you looked closely, you could see it sparkling from distant laser beams.

Boynton's expression changed immediately—from anger at me to surprise at the realization, then to embarrassment that he hadn't figured it out himself—and finally to a genuine grin of amazement. "All right, kid, you win." He sat down in a chair and let me explain it to everyone else.

It was simple, really. Just about every ship that goes into space carries inflatable reflectors—all sizes, all kinds. A little squirt of gas and the reflector balloons up as big as a basketball or a football field. Whatever size you need. The surface is all silvery-shiny, and pocked with three-corner dimples—like what you would get if you poked it with the corner of a very sharp little cube. Any photon hitting one of those dimples will bounce three times and then head right back toward its source. That's how you can track the exact position of a ship, even if it goes totally dead.

Not only that, every time anyone went exploring anywhere in the solar system, they planted reflectors on every object they came near. By now, there were thousands of positional reflectors all over the moon and hundreds of thousands of them scattered throughout the asteroid belt. There were several thousand in Jupiter's orbit and almost that many in the rings of Saturn. And quite a few riding comets. Astronomers used them for mapping the positions and precise orbits of solar objects. They sent out laser beams and timed how long they took to return. Last I'd heard, they'd measured most of the dimensions of the solar system down to the centimeter.

It was part of a long-range project. The measurements had to be taken continually. Over a period of several centuries they would be able to measure the precession effects of galactic gravity—or something like that. That was about the time I started falling asleep in science class.

But the important thing was that most of the lasers were just circulating streams of random bits, only reporting the length of time it took for the bits to return when the time failed to match the predicted period. HARLIE had uploaded himself into the positional reflector network and scattered himself to the far ends of the solar system and back. He'd been to Jupiter all right, and the asteroids—*several times!*

But that was why it had taken him so long to reassemble himself. Jupiter was on the far side of the solar system, about an hour away, so that meant two hours for all of the data to complete a round trip.

And then he had to reload all his separate components and that took another two or three hours, just to establish a baseline confidence level. After that, he had to repeat the whole process and keep repeating it until his confidence levels were consistent. He had to keep reloading and testing and reloading and testing until he passed his own integrity tests nine times in a row. And that took more than a day. Only then did he tell the positional network to resume sending random bits—and even then he wasn't going to let us know he was back until he was sure that enough of his data was out of the stream so that no one else could tap into the network and capture a copy. You can't decrypt what you don't have.

Whew.

That was why we couldn't reawaken him. He really *wasn't there*. In fact, even he didn't know where he was until his automatic software reawakened his consciousness during the Dvorak. Of course, the monkey had recorded everything that had happened while he was away, and it had taken him a few minutes to skim through and assimilate that too. Meanwhile, it was Mom's weeping that told him this was Dad's funeral. So that was why he'd only given me a *little* farkleberry.

Social skills, I told myself. We were going to have to work on social skills. Real Soon Now.

No more farkleberries at funerals.

And no more funerals, I hoped.

Except that I doubted that would be the case. Not on Outbeyond. Not if Boynton was telling the truth about it.

CIVILIZATION IN FLIGHT

THE *CASCADE* WAS THE youngest in a fleet of eight colony brightliners. She had made a total of nine voyages to other stars; her last four trips had all been to Outbeyond.

There were three more brightliners under construction at the L-5 assembly point, but even if the Earth's economy hadn't collapsed in the polycrisis, it would have been three years before the first of them was ready for launch. With the polycrisis, it was unlikely that any of them would ever be completed. Not in our lifetimes.

A brightliner doesn't look like much. Unassembled, it's just a long keel. Halfway down its length, there's a set of twelve radial spokes—these are the stardrive generators. (I'm the wrong person to explain stardrive. I know all the words, but I have no idea what they mean. Douglas tried to translate it into Spanglish for me, but he finally gave up, saying he'd have more luck teaching manners to Stinky.)

But according to Douglas, the way it works is each of those radial spokes has a gravitational lens, and when they're all focused on the point at the center—the locus—they generate a hypergravity pocket. Then they all reverse polarity or something and turn the pocket inside out, wrapping the ship in a hyperstate envelope. That makes no sense to me. It's like blowing up a balloon and then turning it inside out and finding yourself on the inside. Huh? How do you do that? Through the eleventh dimension, of course. See what I mean about knowing all the words and still not knowing anything?

After the hyperstate bubble is stable, they destabilize it. They stretch it out in the direction of the ship's destination, they stretch it out as far as they can and hold it that way for as much time as it takes to get where they want to go. Apparently, stretching it makes the bubble move faster than light, and it carries the ship along inside. The people inside don't feel anything at all.

According to Boynton, the *Cascade* could realize speeds as high as sixty C—sixty times the speed of light. That meant we could get to Proxima Centauri in twenty-six days!

I thought that was pretty impressive until Douglas pointed out that Outbeyond was thirty-five light years away. We'd be in transit for more than seven months. Oops.

The keel of the *Cascade* was more than a kilometer long. Most of it was spars and bars and pipes and tubes and cables and connectors. Plumbing. So it had to be pretty big. It was— why was I not surprised?—another big tube. Since the invention of cable technology, everything was tubes. But this one was big enough on the inside to shove a whole tube-house through. Or would have been, if it hadn't already been filled with enough machinery to build a small city.

The body of the ship was assembled from a hundred circular racks, spaced along the axis of the keel like a stack of discs. Cargo pods were attached to each rack in concentric circles. Each rack held at least thirty-two cargo pods all spaced equidistantly around. Some of them held as many as ninety-six. With all one hundred racks filled, the *Cascade* was the biggest super-freighter ever assembled, carrying more than five thousand cargo pods and massing more than two and a half million tons of cargo. She wasn't just a city in flight, she was a whole civilization in flight.

The twelve stardrive spars each extended out a half-klick, so they described a circle that was a kilometer in diameter. The whole thing was so big that, fully loaded, she was visible with the naked eye from both Luna and Geosynchronous station. And on a clear night, even on Earth as well. If anyone was still looking.

Assembling a starship is an eighteen-month process. It isn't just a matter of launching cargo pods off the Line, catching them, and putting them into racks. It's a matter of scheduling.

What do you need *most? When* are you going to need it? Where are you going to put it so you can get to it then?

Generally, you want to put the pods containing water on the outside, so they can act as shielding for the rest of the ship, and also ballast. As ballast, you get more leverage the farther out you put the weight. But the pods on the outside are the ones you unload first, so you really want to put the stuff you need most when you arrive at your destination on the outermost rings of the cargo racks. And you have to manage perishables against hard goods. The pods that contain your farm animals and food crops have to be easily accessible from the keel, so they have to go on the innermost racks—which means they have to be loaded first and constantly maintained and stabilized during the year or so it takes to load the rest of the cargo. And so on.

And of course, as your needs change, your cargo manifest gets adjusted continually—which gives you a whole other set of problems. What do you do if you decide you don't want to take twenty Caterpillar tractors, only ten? Do you unpack fifty cargo pods to get to the four pods containing the tractors you don't want? Or do you take the extra tractors anyway because they're already packed? And so on and so on and so on.

I would have guessed that loading up a brightliner would cost as much as building the orbital elevator, but Doug said no. The existence of the orbital elevator made it possible to uplift all that cargo for not much more than it would cost to ship it from Texas to Ecuador. In fact, a lot of those cargo pods had been built in Texas, transshipped by supertrain, and loaded directly onto the Line—just like us—then launched from Whirlaway and installed on the Cascade without ever being opened.

Which meant, of course, that we were trusting the honor and integrity of the inspectors who signed off on those manifests before sealing those pods and sending them on their way . . .

Douglas said that every pod had internal monitors to verify the cargo—but I was more paranoid than he was. "What if the monitors have been programmed to lie?"

"Then I guess we starve to death in the dark between the stars."

That was a comforting thought.

But later on, Martha Christie, the "dog-robber" for Outbeyond, explained how some colonies protected themselves from cargo fraud. According to Christie, one particularly dishonest cargo manager had been delivered to the CEO of his company . . . in six separate packages. Douglas said he thought that story was apocryphal, but Christie insisted it was true. Some of the colonies were very serious about receiving what they paid for and their Earthside agents were under strict instructions to produce results by whatever means necessary. When you're thirty-five light years from Earth, you can't afford to wait for Customer Service to get back to you. The colonies considered cargo tampering to be a crime as serious as murder—because not having what you needed when you got where you were going could be just as fatal.

But the *Cascade* wasn't likely to have those kinds of problems. Outbeyond had sent its own onsite examiners down the Line to inspect every piece of payload as it was produced and packed. Outbeyond's own colonists guarded the shipments every leg of the journey out. The men and women who inspected this cargo were the folks who would ultimately depend on it themselves—they couldn't afford to ship substandard goods. The way Carol Everhart explained it, you can't hire that kind of commitment.

After its last journey to Outbeyond, the *Cascade*'s command module had been brought down to Luna for refitting. Boynton had wanted to upgrade her IRMA unit for advanced hyperstate modeling. Theoretically, it was possible to boost her realized velocity to eighty C, but he'd have been happy adding even one-tenth of that to the *Cascade*'s top speed. That would cut three weeks off the journey to Outbeyond. He had also wanted to install fittings so the command module could eventually be landed, so IRMA could become the colony's brain. The *Cascade* would not be returning from this voyage. There was no point.

The original plan had called for the construction of a brand new command module and the old one would be landed on Outbeyond, but in the nine months prior to the polycrisis, things were already so unstable that the colonists realized they might not have the time and decided instead to upgrade the existing command module, just in case. A good plan—but it put the command module on the Lunar surface, and in reach of the invisibles . . . who set off a focused EMP-grenade and scrambled IRMA's circuits. IRMA died instantly.

So that left HARLIE.

Could HARLIE pilot a hyperstate starship?

In principle, yes. HARLIE was smarter than IRMA.

In practice . . . well, HARLIE had no personal experience. There were no other brightliners in the system that HARLIE could learn from. There were IRMA files he could download and assimilate, and HARLIE was confident that the problem was solvable, he just wasn't certain how long it would take him to wrap his identity around the necessary mind-set. There was a lot more to it than that, but that was the simple explanation.

The complex explanation—well, even Douglas frowned when HARLIE started explaining, and Douglas probably knew more about synthetic intelligence than anyone else in the solar system—because he had synthesized his own intelligence instead of going through puberty. I used to explain Douglas to my friends by saying he was what you got when you didn't let teenagers masturbate, so don't let this happen to you. (Old lady Dalgliesh, the English teacher, heard me say that one time—I thought she'd choke to death on her own tongue. Mom was not amused and I got detention for a week.) But based on the bragging, none of my peers were in any danger of turning into a Douglas in any case.

Anyway, by the time the polycrisis turned into a global meltdown, 98% of the cargo pods had been installed on the *Cascade* and the last hundred or so were already in transit. For almost a year, the colonists had been planning for this voyage as if it might be the last—and the cargo manifests had been altered accordingly. Added to that, the colony had begun purchasing cargo and equipment from the other three brightliners under construction and she ended up with an extra thousand pods on her racks. The whole thing was pretty impressive, and I couldn't figure out why Boynton was so worried about the survival of Outbeyond colony. This voyage would deliver enough supplies to keep everyone there alive for years.

—Except we were bringing fifteen hundred new colonists to join the forty-three hundred already there, and when you did the math, dividing this by that, carry the six and round it off to the third decimal point, what you found out was that it costs a lot more than you think to keep one person alive for thirty days, let alone thirty years. Oxygen. Water. Protein. Shelter. Fertilizer. Electricity. Software. Memory. Clothing. Educational materials. Medicine. Diagnostic units. Manufacturing tools. Fabricators. Encyclopedias. Training resources. Seeds. Artificial wombs and fertilized ova. Replacement organs. Assorted appliances and machines. Entertainment. And all sorts of stuff for dealing with unforeseen circumstances—except if you could figure out all the stuff you would need, it wasn't really *unforeseen*, was it? Never mind, you get the idea. It was almost as bad as watching Mom pack for a weekend trip with Stinky.

There was too much to think about. And even though these people had been thinking about it for years—they were still worried they might have missed something.

This was their last chance.

And *our* last chance too.

NO SUCH THING AS A FREE LAUNCH

THE COMMAND MODULE WAS a spaceship in its own right. It could detach from the starship and travel almost anywhere in the solar system under its own power. That's why it was here on Luna for refitting.

Like most spaceships, it was built out of cargo pods. The keel was a stretch-pod, made out of three pods connected end to end. Another six cargo pods clustered around its waist, and there were swiveling thrusters mounted at both ends.

According to Douglas, before the polycrisis there was so much cargo coming up the Line that there were extra cargo pods everywhere; more than enough for habitats and stations and outposts. On Luna, they hung pods from overhead cables and used them as aerial trains. They put them on wheels and made them into trucks. They attached thrusters and made them into flying moonbuses. And sometimes they put on wheels and thrusters and all kinds of other what-nots to make utility vehicles like Alexei's *Mr. Beagle*.

So why not cluster a bunch of pods together, attach some Palmer tubes, and build a spaceship? With the right fittings you could land on Luna or Mars. And even if you didn't have landing gear, if all you had was an airlock, you could still dock with any habitat anywhere else. So pod-ships were the workhorses of the solar system.

The starship *Cascade* had three pod-ships, and the equipment onboard to build three more. The biggest one was the Command Module, and it could carry as many as 145 people at a time, if they were friendly; but for this trip, there were only 112 of us, and the rest of the space was rice and beans and noodles.

Boynton settled me down in the assistant flight engineer's position, just behind the pilot's couch. Flight Engineer Damron was on the right, just behind Copilot O'Koshi. HARLIE was plugged into an access on the flight engineer's equipment rack. From my position, it didn't look much different than the front end of a Lunar bus, or a Lunar train, or a Lunar house. Some of the interior fittings were different, and there were a lot more control boards and display screens than in a utility vehicle, but the general layout was the same. There's only so much you can do with a pill-shaped pod.

The important difference was the view out the front window.

It was . . . marvelous.

Ahead lay the lighted track of the catapult. It looked like it stretched out forever. It didn't, of course. It was only three kilometers. It was built up the long gentle slope of Glass Crater, named after Harvey Glass, the father of the first lawyer on the moon. (Don't ask.) (Okay, do ask. Not only was James Glass the first lawyer on the moon, he was also the first lawyer murdered on the moon. According to Christie, the reason they named the crater after his father instead of him was because no one wanted to name a crater after a lawyer. If Christie was telling the truth, then Lunar history was not only stranger than I imagined, it was stranger than I *could* imagine.)

Boynton looked back over his shoulder at me. "Here, pin this on." He handed me a sticky-backed insignia for my jumpsuit. It had an officer's bar.

"What's this?"

"It's a field commission. Regulations prohibit noncoms on the flight deck, so—congratulations, Ensign. You are now the Acting Assistant Flight Engineer for the starship *Cascade*." Damron and O'Koshi added their own congratulations.

"Uh—" I didn't know what to say. Was this serious? Or was it some kind of feel-good badge like the plastic wings they gave me on an airplane once?

"It's real," said Boynton. "You're playing with the big kids now."

I found a word. "Wow." And two more. "Thank you."

"Pin it on. And give HARLIE his orders, please. We'll all feel a lot better when we get off this rock."

I put the insignia on over my heart. It gave me a very odd feeling to do so—mostly good, but kind of scary at the same time.

"Go ahead," Boynton prompted. "Just say, 'Initiate launch sequence, HARLIE.' He has to hear it from you."

"Isn't it automatic? Aren't we on a countdown?"

Flight Engineer Damron tapped my shoulder and pointed to a chronometer. "We have an eleven-minute window. We can launch any time within that window and correct our course after launch. All the boards are green. Once that timer starts counting positive numbers, we can go any time." He turned back to his board.

I opened my mouth to speak—

The communicator beeped. An overhead panel lit up. A stern-looking man in black. Standing in the cargo dock directly beneath us.

"Starship *Cascade*?" He held up a badge. "Lunar Marshals. We are on the loading dock. We have a warrant for the arrest of Charles Dingillian, Douglas Dingillian, Robert Dingillian, Michael Partridge, Beverly Sykes, Margaret Campbell, and fifteen John Doe warrants to include any and all persons traveling with the Dingillians. Open your hatch now, please."

Boynton snapped a switch on his panel. "Lunar Marshals. Please vacate the loading dock immediately. Launch sequence has been initiated. It is too late to abort. You will be endangering yourselves and others if you do not immediately vacate." He snapped off. "Go ahead, Charles."

I swallowed hard—while Boynton was speaking, the timer had begun counting positive numbers.

"Will they be hurt?"

"They'll probably be killed by the backwash." Boynton pointed to the display. The marshals weren't moving. "They don't think we'll do it."

"Do they know I have to give the order?"

"Yes. That's why they're not moving."

I looked at the chronometer. Nine and a half minutes.

"I can't do this," I said. My voice cracked.

"Then they win." Boynton began unfastening his seat belt. He turned to face Flight Engineer Damron. "Stand by to power down."

"Wait!"

"For what?" Boynton said angrily. "You just said you can't do it. Either you can or you can't."

"I can't kill people!"

"Charles, I don't have time to give you the whole speech. Whatever you decide right now, people are going to die. Either those six marshals—or 4300 people on Outbeyond. You choose."

"That's not fair—"

"No, it isn't. But that's the choice anyway. How many deaths do you want on your conscience?"

"None!"

"I'm sorry, that's not an option anymore." His eyes met mine and I knew he hated this situation as much as I did. He lowered his voice, "Listen to me, Charles. If I could, I'd take this responsibility away from you in an instant—if I could. But I can't—" He reached over and put his hand on top of mine. *Just like Dad used to do.*

"We're running out of time. If you're going to do it—"

I gulped. "Open the channel, please—?"

He turned forward, reached up, and flicked the switch. "Go ahead," he said quietly.

"Lunar Marshals, this is Charles Dingillian—"

"Son!" The Marshal held up his badge. "You cannot launch. You must surrender now."

"—I'd like to know your names, please?"

"Eh?"

"I'm about to give the order to launch. I don't want your deaths on my conscience—but if I do have to launch, at least I want to be able to send my apologies to your families. Your names, please?"

Two of the Marshals looked nervously at each other.

"Please?" I glanced to the chronometer. "I don't have much time left. Only forty seconds." That was a lie, I had six minutes and forty seconds, but the sweet spot of the launch window was the five minute, thirty second mark.

"I am Colonel Michael Stone," said the man holding up the insignia. "And I don't believe you'll do this."

"My condolences to your family, Colonel Stone. And the names of your men—?"

"The hell with this!" said one of the others. He bolted. A moment later, two others followed him. And then one more. And then Colonel Stone was alone—

"Twenty-five seconds, sir."

"I'm not moving, son."

"Then I'm very sorry." I motioned to Boynton.

"Listen to me, you little—" Boynton snapped off the image.

"HARLIE?"

"At your service, Ensign."

"Initiate launch sequence."

"Aye, aye, sir."

I cried as we launched—why do stupid adults have to spoil everything?

ANGER

THE LAUNCH CATAPULT WAS 3.5 kilometers long. There were twenty-one thousand superconducting electromagnets spaced along its length. Depending on the mass of the payload, depending on how much acceleration was applied, enormous launch velocities could be achieved. The command module would pass escape velocity less than halfway up the track, and we'd still be accelerating.

Almost immediately upon my giving HARLIE the launch command, the capacitors under the catapult began discharging enormous amounts of electricity into carefully timed bursts of power to the magnets in the track. The command module slid forward in a gathering rush. We sank back into our seats, and then we sank back some more, and then some more—and then we were pushed *hard* against the cushions. And then some more—one of the displays ticked numbers upward toward three gees, three point one, three point two. A little more than was promised; an accommodation for the early launch window. The track raced away beneath us. The horizon rushed toward us—

And then we were in free fall and Luna was dropping away below. Craters shrank against silvery plains. Larger and larger became smaller and smaller. The curve of the horizon sharpened—and then, at last, the moon was behind us.

As soon as Boynton finished with the post-launch checklist, he swiveled in his seat to look at me. His expression was hard. He reached up over my head and pulled a tissue out of a dispenser. He handed it to me without comment. I began wiping my eyes. Except for the background sounds of the ship's controls, there was silence on the flight deck.

Boynton said, "You scared me, Ensign."

"You didn't think I was going to do it?"

"No. I was pretty sure you'd do it. What scared me was the look on your face. Remind me never to piss you off."

"Was I really that angry?"

"For a moment, yes, you were."

"I was thinking about my Dad. This was *his* dream!"

Boynton reached over and put his hand on my shoulder. "Charles, listen to me—that kind of anger can be dangerous. *Very* dangerous."

I looked at him, hurt. "Now, you're saying I shouldn't have done it—?"

"Listen *carefully*. Anger is a drug. You can get addicted to it. There are times when it's useful. This was one of those times. But try not to have any more, please?"

I wasn't sure what he meant, not yet, but I nodded anyway. I had a feeling that this was one of those conversations that I'd be replaying in my head for a long time—usually late at night while I was lying in bed, trying to fall asleep and not doing a very good job of it.

He didn't believe my nod. "Do you understand what I'm saying?" he asked sternly.

"Yes. I think so."

Boynton studied me for a moment. "I want you to talk to Dr. Morgan."

"I don't need a doctor."

"She's not a doctor—she's a counselor. Her full title is *Reverend* Doctor Morgan. We call her Morgs."

"I don't—"

"Yes, I know you don't. That's why I'm making it an order."

"An order—?"

"You're an officer on my starship. I have the authority to order you. And if you don't follow my orders, I can court martial you for insubordination and put you in the brig." I guess he realized that was too severe, because almost immediately, he added, "We're going to be in transit for a long time, son. You and I and HARLIE are going to spend a lot of hours on this flight deck. You're carrying around a lot of anger. I don't want it on my bridge ever again."

"What did you *want* me to do?"

"I wanted you to do exactly what you did—but I didn't want you doing it out of hate."

"Well, it sure wasn't an act of love—"

"I don't want you getting the idea that hatred justifies killing. That's how wars get started."

"I didn't hate him—*I didn't know him well enough to hate him.*"

"Ensign, do you want me to play back the log? You said a lot of interesting words in a very short time. I hope that's not the same mouth you use to kiss your mother."

"I didn't—" And then I realized. I did.

But Boynton had it wrong. I didn't say all that stuff because I hated the late Colonel. I said it because I was angry for what he had made me do.

Boynton was right about one thing. There was a lot of stuff I was angry about—and there were a lot of people I was angry at. The Rock Father tribe was first on my list. Alexei Krislov, in particular. And Dad for getting killed—and Mom for just being Mom. And Bev. And Douglas and Mickey. And Colonel Stone. And Stinky. And Commander Boynton. And Judge Griffith. And Judge Cavanaugh. And all the colonists on Outbeyond.

And HARLIE.

And everybody else too.

And most of all, *myself.* I hated this. I hated what I was, what I'd had to do, what I was turning into.

This was supposed to be the adventure of a lifetime, but before I could even get off the launchpad, I had to kill a man.

And according to Boynton, it was okay to kill him—it just wasn't okay to hate him.

So who else could I hate, but myself?

NECESSARY

NOBODY TALKED FOR A long time after that—except for piloting stuff. Boynton phoned ahead and told the starship that we'd launched and we could hear them cheering in the background. But when he told them what we'd had to do—he didn't say that I'd had to do it—the celebration subsided. Launching in blood was a bad omen.

Boynton finished his report, then turned to O'Koshi. "Seal

the log. The details of our launch are eyes-only. Until I say otherwise."

"Aye, Captain."

"You have the conn." Boynton unfastened his safety harness, floated out of his seat, and swam aft. I started to unbuckle myself, but Boynton pushed me back into my seat and told me to stay where I was. "I have business to take care of. You don't. And I don't want you talking to anyone for a while." And then, realizing how bad that must have sounded, he said, "It's for your sake, Ensign, not theirs. This business stays on the flight deck."

Did he really think he could keep it a secret? Our launch conversation must have been heard by hundreds of people. It would be all over the net within minutes, rippling outward on the rumor-web as fast as people checked their e-mail and relayed the juicy bits. It would be on all the Lunar news channels just in time for breakfast at Armstrong Station. And after that, all the other planets too: Earth, Luna, Mars, the habitats, the asteroids, and everywhere else. Anyone scanning the news would catch it. And *everyone* was scanning the news these days—watching the endless slow-motion collapse of civilization, like some ghastly soap opera.

Everyone on board would probably know the whole story long before we rounded Earth. And then they'd all be looking at me funny. Probably no one would want to talk to me for what I'd done. Or worse, maybe they'd want to thank me. Or even worse than that, maybe they'd want to be all fuzzy and understanding. Which was exactly what I did *not* want. Not right now. Not ever. If I was going to be miserable, I didn't want anyone talking me out of it.

Carol Everhart saw the look on my face. "Relax, Charles. This is the best view in the ship. And the most comfortable ride. You can sleep in your couch—and there's a shower and a toilet through there, and there's sodas in the fridge. Enjoy yourself."

Yeah, right.

There wasn't anything to do, except watch the little blip on the display creep along the curved line of our trajectory. We'd passed escape velocity even before we left the launch ramp. Now all we had to do was apply the necessary course corrections. At least this journey was going to be a lot more comfortable than the way we'd gotten to the moon—stowing away inside a cargo pod.

Mostly, space travel is boring, because all you really do is sit and watch your displays. Everything was checks and double-checks, and most of it seemed unnecessary because everything was working exactly the way it was supposed to. And just to rub it in, every so often, the monkey would say, "All systems green. Confidence is high." Which should have been reassuring, except that it was a toy robot monkey saying it, and it just didn't seem *real*. But we had to take HARLIE's word for it because we didn't have a backup intelligence engine.

And even though HARLIE was (allegedly) more powerful than any IRMA ever built, I still wished we had an IRMA.

An IRMA system is actually three intelligence engines in one, all comparing notes, all the time; if any one engine disagrees, the other two outvote it. That way, it's self-correcting. HARLIE didn't have that same redundancy. Not yet. This HARLIE was only an experimental unit; if they'd gone into actual production, there would have been three HARLIEs bonded together like an IRMA. So if this HARLIE made a mistake, we were stuck with it. HARLIE knew this, of course, so he split himself into three minds and ran every process three times, giving himself nine votes per decision. But what if he was still wrong somehow? And none of us really knew how to test him because he'd already demonstrated he was smarter than all of us put together. He'd certainly made a monkey of Judge Cavanaugh. . . .

And that made me think of something else. How much other stuff had he done?

Like that business with the messages being released every hour. The kidnappers were holding me hostage—and HARLIE had turned it around and held them hostage instead. But how had he done that? He'd spread himself all over the solar system—

So I asked. He told me.

It was sort of what I figured. The whole thing had been automated. He'd invented an idiot-child version of himself, programmed with a sixteen-million branch decision tree—more than enough to simulate sentience. It was more than capable of monitoring all the traffic it needed to—and not just the public traffic, a lot of the private encrypted traffic as well. The program would know when I was rescued and if I was safe.

In fact, a similar monitor program was also entrusted with keeping HARLIE's separate pieces in transit all over the system, and reassembling them and feeding them back to the dormant monkey as soon as the monkey was back online. HARLIE had very cleverly constructed a support system to reassemble himself. He'd begun preparing it while snooping through Alexei's own files.

That was the *real* reason why neither Boynton nor Lunar Authority had been able to detect any unusual bandwidth traffic—because HARLIE hadn't used public access. He'd used the secret channels of invisible Luna! And they'd never noticed either. I had to laugh aloud at that.

"You should have erased all of Alexei's files," I said. "That would have served him right."

The monkey scratched itself thoughtfully. "I doubt that would have done much damage, Charles. *Gospodin* Krislov has multiple redundant one-way backups on write-once, read-only media. He could recover from a data-crash almost immediately. No, I think he is entitled to problems much more serious and irrevocable."

I was almost afraid to ask. "What *did* you do . . . ?"

The monkey pretended to pick a flea and eat it. "In order to guarantee a secure reassembly of myself, I had to have a secure channel. As it happened, the safest escape was through Alexei Krislov's private business network; I used it for my primary access. But I had to disable the security firewalls during upload and download. The encryption-decryption services would have created distortions in several quantum functions that I am particularly fond of. If Krislov's people hadn't kidnapped us, nothing would have happened. But as soon as they came through the door, everything activated automatically. The bulk of my personality code was fractalized into sixteen separate wave-matrices and sent out across the solar system by Krislov's own network. My first successful upload was completed before they tossed us onto the cart. My second and third uploads were completed before we exited the tunnel. It took less than eleven minutes. After my seventh confirmed upload, the uploaded material was erased from the monkey, leaving nothing running except a simple monitor program. When it was time to reload myself, the security firewalls had to be disabled again—this time permanently."

It took a moment for that to sink in. "Alexei Krislov stopped being invisible?"

"That is correct. Every node, every machine, every file. It is all publicly available."

"But that's—that's data-rape!"

"Yes, it is. But I did not feel ethically bound to restore his security after he had compromised ours. As an employee/partner/indentured-personality of the Dingillian Family Corporation my responsibility is to serve the corporation, no one else."

"Oh my." I didn't know whether to be horrorstruck—or filled with admiration at the simple elegance of what HARLIE had done.

"Alexei had a lot of sensitive information in his files. Possibly more than he realized. I expect several governments and a large number of companies will collapse; but the most immediate effect will be the destruction of invisible Luna's secrecy. I do not think that Alexei will live to see his next birthday."

The scale of HARLIE's revenge horrified me. Not that it didn't please me, but—

"HARLIE?"

"Yes, Charles?"

"Tell me something."

"What?"

"When you did all this—did you hate him?"

"No."

"Why not?"

"Because it wasn't necessary."

I was going to have to think about that. I didn't think I was going to be sleeping well for a while.

RICE AND BEANS AND NOODLES

IMAGINE EARTH AND LUNA as the base of two giant equilateral triangles, one pointing forward, the other pointing backward. As Luna rotates around the Earth, the two triangles rotate with it. The apex of the leading triangle is called Lagrange 4. Or L-4, for short. The apex of the trailing triangle is L-5. Objects put in orbit at either of the Lagrange points stay there, rotating with Earth and Luna in gravitational balance.

We were heading out to the L-5 assembly point, where the command module would be reinstalled on the keel of the *Cascade*. Then we'd have a week or three of shakedown tests, another few weeks of acceleration out of the solar system, and finally when we were far enough away from any significant gravitational masses, we'd transition to hyperstate and go superluminal. At least, that was the plan.

An attendant floated up into the flight deck carrying meal trays. "Might as well get comfortable, folks," he said, passing them out. "Captain says it's going to be a long night." He looked to Damron. "A couple people are asking. We missed the sweet spot, didn't we?"

Damron was studying his displays. "The launch was good, our trajectory is doable, we're going to have to spend some fuel to correct. More than I'd like."

"What was the delay?" he asked.

"Ask the Captain."

"I did. He said it was technical."

"Then that's what it was."

"People are asking, that's all."

Damron gave the attendant a serious look. *Don't go there.*

"Hey, nobody's complaining," he said quickly. "Didn't you hear the cheers when we launched?"

"We were busy," Damron said without emotion.

The attendant took the hint. He passed me a meal tray and ducked out.

Damron turned to me. "Listen, Charles. Nobody's going to talk about the launch. The log is sealed and we're on our way. That's all that counts." He pointed toward the window. "We're going to loop around the Earth in twelve hours. That'll put us in position to chase the L-5 point and come up from behind. It's a little longer than trying a direct intercept, but it's a lot cheaper in fuel. And until we can build a fuel refinery on Outbeyond, we have to spend this resource carefully. From here on out, we have to regard *everything* as irreplaceable. We can't afford to waste anything. Now stop making faces at the tray and eat that—there may come a day when you'll honestly wish for a meal like this."

"Can I save it till then . . . ?"

He gave me a look. "Eat."

According to my watch, my body thought it was three in the morning. The awful thing about Luna is that because there isn't any real cycle of day and night, everybody lives in their own personal time zone, so what might be a midnight snack for one person could be a late lunch for another. Douglas said that it affected people's relationships, having their bio-clocks out of sync; I wondered if it would be that way on board the *Cascade*; but Boynton said we'd all be shifting to the ship's clock in the next few days, so maybe it wouldn't be a problem—but that was one of the issues with interstellar travel—maintaining consciousness for the duration of a long journey, and it was serious enough that it was a large part of the colonist training regimen.

I must have fallen asleep for a while, maybe a long while, because the next time I looked forward, the Earth was looming large in the forward window. The original plan—from way back before the polycrisis—was that the command module would dock at Whirlaway, the ballast rock at the top end of the orbital elevator, staying only long enough to pick up last-minute supplies and passengers—and anyone with cold feet would have one last chance to change his mind and get off; but Boynton had scuttled that idea when the government of Ecuador seized the Line. Last we'd heard, *Los Federales* had control all the way from Terminus to Whirlaway, and even though some Line traffic was running again, after the craziness we'd just experienced on Luna, Boynton didn't want to run the risk of being sabotaged again . . . or served with any more subpoenas. Once was enough, thankewverymuch.

But there was some stuff we had to pick up from the Line and there were six cargo pods scheduled to be launched as we passed by. We'd match trajectories and bring them aboard and that would be our last physical contact with Earth. Those pods had been bought three months previously, loaded six weeks ago, and had been waiting at Whirlaway for a month. According to Copilot O'Koshi, they were important, but not critical. The cargo for this voyage had been planned three years ago. They had begun assembling it in space eighteen months ago and started locking racks into place ten months ago, so there wasn't anything essential that wasn't already aboard. Even so, there were a lot of last minute additions that would have been nice to have—

But when O'Koshi logged on for final confirmation of launch and trajectory, it sounded like he wasn't happy with the information he was getting. He pulled his headset off and swiveled to Damron. "Beep the Captain."

"Serious?"

"Very."

Damron whispered something into his own headset. O'Koshi turned back to his controls and started punching up course corrections on his display. "What's going on?" I asked.

He held up his left hand. *Don't talk.* He turned to the monkey and started asking questions about possible orbit corrections. Once, he stopped what he was doing and stared forward at the Earth. We were just coming around the terminator line toward the bright side. It was morning in Africa. I wondered what kind of a day it would be for all the people below—

Boynton came back then, pulling himself quickly into the flight deck. "How bad?"

"They won't release our cargo."

"We expected that might happen. It's only six pods. We'll have to write them off."

"They're ordering us to dock at Whirlaway."

"Eh?"

"They have an arrest warrant."

"For who?"

O'Koshi nodded toward me. "Ensign Dingillian has been charged with tax evasion. Illegal immigration. Evading arrest. Impersonating the opposite sex with intent to defraud. Non-payment of hotel and hospital bills. Credit fraud. Conspiracy to defraud. Economic conspiracy. Conspiracy to overthrow the lawful government of Luna. Libel. Invasion of privacy. Data-rape. Data-piracy. Illegal publication. Copyright infringement. Racketeering. Unlawful flight. Endangerment. Incitement. Sedition. Kidnapping. Illegal possession of nationalized property."

"Sedition?" Boynton glanced at me. "Pretty impressive for a thirteen-year-old."

"Fourteen next month," I corrected.

"Even so."

"I'm innocent of sedition," I said. "At least, I don't ever remember committing it. What *is* sedition, anyway? Besides, I never even spoke to her. I didn't even know she was on Luna."

"There's more," said O'Koshi.

"More?" Boynton looked surprised.

"He's also charged with second degree murder, in the death of Colonel Michael Stone of the Lunar Authority. You're named as an accomplice."

"Now that one they might be able to make stick." Boynton rubbed his cheek thoughtfully. He looked to Damron. "Do you know any good lawyers?"

"I know two. They're both dead."

Boynton turned back to O'Koshi. "All right, tell me the rest."

"The flyby could be dangerous. They might try an intercept."

"That would be stupid. They're arguing with the laws of physics."

"They could do it," said O'Koshi. "HARLIE's figuring courses right now. They've got the advantage. They can launch from anywhere on the Line. They probably started moving ships into position the moment we launched."

"We're not built for evasion," Damron said. "Or fighting."

Boynton turned it over in his mind, his expression growing harder. He pulled himself into his seat and strapped in. He put his headset on and started whispering instructions. His displays lit up to show an ever-narrowing range of course adjustments. "Of course, they waited until the last moment to serve the warrant, to leave us no time to change our course. How much time do we have?"

"Thirty-seven minutes."

He said a word. "Well, we knew this was a possibility. We should have written off those pods when we launched. All right—" He swiveled around to face me. "Charles, do you play poker?"

"Huh?"

"Do you know how to bluff? Never mind. I don't have time to teach you. Listen to me. I'm going to talk to Whirlaway command. Whatever you hear me say, play along. All right?"

I nodded.

Boynton opened a channel. "Whirlaway Station, this is *Cascade* command module. We have a problem."

The voice came back immediately. "Go ahead, *Cascade*."

"Who am I talking to?"

"Lieutenant Colonel William Cavanaugh. Federal Occupation Force."

"Is your superior officer there?"

"General Torena is not available."

"That's too bad. I guess you're going to have to make the

decision then. Our cargo modules are scheduled for launch-pickup in fourteen minutes. If you do not launch them, you will be committing an act of economic assault upon Outbeyond Colony. We have no choice but to regard that as a deliberately hostile act. We are prepared to respond in kind."

"You have no weapons, *Cascade*. You have eleven minutes in which to apply course corrections. If you do not dock, we will fire."

"We have over a hundred civilians and crew aboard."

"I have my orders, Commander Boynton."

"Do your orders include the destruction of Whirlaway Station? Do your orders include the possible destruction of the Line itself—and concomitant damage to the Earth? By the way, you should know that we are broadcasting this conversation live to all receiving stations."

"You can't do that—"

"And you are going to stop me? How?" Boynton's voice grew harder. "You will release our cargo modules on schedule. If you do not, we will attack."

Lieutenant Colonel Cavanaugh snorted. "With what? Rice and noodles?"

"Precisely," Boynton said blandly.

"Eh?"

"You figured out half of it, now figure out the other half. Even as we speak, I have a crew loading as much rice and beans and noodles into our forward airlock as it will hold. In four minutes, we open the forward hatch. In seven minutes, we apply thrust to put ourselves on a direct collision course with Whirlaway. I'm looking at the solution on my screen right now. In sixteen minutes, we apply reverse thrust. The rice and beans and noodles continue on course while we climb to a higher orbit. Now, the only thing that you have to decide is whether or not we apply reverse thrust with our forward hatch open or closed."

"You wouldn't—" The voice from the speaker sounded alarmed.

"Ah, I see you've figured it out. Do the math. With an interception velocity of eighty kilometers per second, a single grain of rice can produce a catastrophic result. Now multiply that by a hundred thousand. Or a million—"

I must have looked puzzled, but before I could say anything, O'Koshi held a finger up to his lips.

Boynton was still talking, "Most of it will probably miss—but the particles that do hit will scour the surface of Whirlaway like a sandblaster."

"You wouldn't—you can't!"

"I assume you have been informed of the details of our departure from Luna?"

Cavanaugh made a noise. "That was very cowardly, Captain Boynton. Having the *child* do your dirty work."

"That's not how it happened—" I caught myself before I said anything more. Boynton hadn't given me permission to speak.

But Boynton wasn't annoyed. He looked to me. *"Charles?"* he mouthed the words. *"Poker . . . ?"*

I nodded. "Lieutenant Cavanuff?" I did that deliberately. Douglas had told me once that it was a great way to piss off adults: mispronounce their names, or get their titles wrong. I did both. "This is Charles Dingillian. Can you hear me?"

"I can hear you, son. Let's end this madness right now. Order your monkey to dock the command module and I promise that no one will hurt you."

"I'm sorry, Mr. Cavanuff, but I don't believe you." I could feel the anger rising in my throat. Not hatred, just anger. "I've already been chased to the moon and back by people I don't know, I've been kidnapped and held prisoner by people who want what I have, and my Dad is dead because the people who were supposed to protect us didn't, and everywhere we run into stupid lawyers trying to tie us up in paperwork. All we want is to be left alone so we can get away from you people. Is that too much to ask? But no, every single one of you has to take a bite—so, no, I don't trust anyone anymore. Why should I?"

"Listen to me, son—" Cavanaugh started to make adult conciliatory noises. All that stuff that adults say when they're trying to calm a crazy person down.

I cut him off—"No. It's too late for that conversation. Now it's my turn to talk and your turn to listen. HARLIE, initiate Operation Farkleberry."

The monkey dutifully stood up, dropped its trousers, and waggled its furry little butt at me. The bridge cameras were off, and it did not make a farting noise. It sat down again calmly.

Clearing his throat to cover his urge to laugh, Boynton said, "We are seven minutes from burn. Whirlaway, please advise."

"Just a moment—" Cavanaugh's voice sounded strangled.

Boynton switched off the mike and swiveled to look at me. "Operation Farkleberry?"

I shrugged. "It seemed like a good name for it."

"You did good," he said. "You had me convinced."

"I wasn't faking. I meant every word." And then I added, "I know you told me not to hate anyone—but it's not as easy as you say."

"I know." He reached over and patted my shoulder. "We'll work on it."

O'Koshi spoke up then. "We gonna burn, boss? I really hate to waste the rods if we don't have to."

"We have to," said Boynton. "Otherwise, they won't believe us. And we need those cargo pods. If we don't make the burn, they don't have to launch. Ensign, would you please instruct HARLIE to initiate the burn on schedule?"

"Aye, sir. HARLIE, please do the burn."

The monkey nodded unemotionally. I wondered what it was thinking. Probably nothing good. HARLIE once said that he had a sense of ethics, but it seemed to me that we were pushing the limits here—ours as well as his.

BURN

THE NEXT FEW MINUTES lasted several centuries.

"What happens if they call your bluff?" I asked.

"*Our* bluff," Boynton corrected. And then he added, "If they launch our cargo pods, we go to Outbeyond. And if they don't—we still go to Outbeyond."

"Will they try and intercept? Will they fire on us?"

"They might. But probably not. The whole world is watching. Five worlds are watching. And the asteroids. The political repercussions would be enormous. The polycrisis hasn't even peaked yet. Dirtside is going to need starside, they can't afford to do this."

"But what if this Cavanaugh fellow is too stupid to realize that?"

"Then we do have a problem."

"Stand by for burn," said the monkey. It counted down to zero and the ceiling thrust itself at us for forty seconds. Then silence and free fall returned.

"All right," said Boynton. "They have seven minutes to make up their mind. If they release our pods, we're home free."

"And if not?" I asked.

"Then I'd better not play poker anymore."

I thought about it. "They can't take the chance that we'll do it, can they?"

"That's right. They can't take the chance."

"But what if they know we're bluffing? What if they know we're not really as crazy as we're pretending?"

"That's your job, Ensign. You have to convince them."

"If our departure from Luna didn't convince them—well, I don't know what else we could do."

"That's right," Boynton agreed. "We're out of options."

"Shouldn't we say something else?"

He shook his head. "No. That's what they're waiting for. If we say anything else, it means we're uncertain in our commitment. You know how crazy their silence is making us?"

I nodded.

"*Our* silence is making *them* even crazier. They're looking at each other now and wondering if we mean it. My guess is that they're getting some very urgent phone calls from a lot of very important people telling them to release the pods and not put the Line at risk. Six cargo pods are not worth losing Whirlaway—and maybe the Line."

"What if they release the cargo pods and then fire on us anyway?"

"That's a possibility too."

"This is—" Crazy wasn't a strong enough word. But I couldn't think of a better one.

"Yes," agreed Boynton. "It is."

Boynton glanced at the clock. He switched on his mike and pointed to me. "Charles, please give the order to open the outer airlock hatch."

The monkey swiveled its head to look at me. I held up my crossed fingers and the monkey nodded. I said, "HARLIE, open the outer airlock hatch."

"Working," said the monkey. And did nothing at all.

"Stand by for second burn." Boynton switched off the mike. He looked to the clock. "Four minutes."

"Won't they be able to tell that we haven't really launched the rice and beans?"

"They wouldn't show up on radar," said Damron. "They're too small and they're nonreflective."

"And besides, we're using stealth beans," said O'Koshi.

"I know about stealth beans," I said. "That's what Stinky uses for his stealth far—"

The radio came to life. "*Cascade* command. Hubbell-IV has you on visual. Your forward airlock has failed to open. We are ordering you again to dock at Whirlaway. You have a six minute burn window."

"Stuff that," said Boynton. But the mike was still off. He looked angry and frustrated.

"I have an idea," I said. Something I'd been thinking about since HARLIE told me what he'd done to Alexei Krislov. "Open the channel, please?"

Boynton started to ask why, then stopped himself. There wasn't time. He flipped the switch. We were broadcasting live again.

"Lieutenant Cavanaugh," I said. "This is Ensign Charles Dingillian of the starship *Cascade*. Listen carefully. This is not a bluff. Do you know what this HARLIE unit did to the security of the Rock Father tribe? Are you aware what we did to invisible Luna when we launched?"

Cavanaugh didn't answer.

"HARLIE," I said to the monkey. "This is not a drill. This is for real. You are to strip the security protection off of every network, every node, every machine, every file, connected to anyone and everyone who is trying to keep this starship from launching. You are to disseminate all of that information into the public channels as fast as you decrypt it. You may start with the private information of Lieutenant Cavanaugh. You are to start on my command. You may start now—"

"Wait a minute!" That was Cavanaugh.

HARLIE said, "I have linkage. I have data. I will release on your command." The monkey pointed to an overhead screen, where he was flashing pages of information.

"Lieutenant Cavanaugh—" I looked to the clock. "You have two minutes to release our cargo pods."

"You can't be serious—"

"Sir, I am very serious. You know what that suboena says. Data-rape. If I was willing to do it to the bastard who killed my father, what makes you think I won't do it to someone who's pointing a gun at me? You first, and then the rest of the planet. I'm tired and I'm frustrated and I'm angry and I have nothing left to lose. I might as well take the whole lot of you down with me. So the question you have to ask yourself right now is this—*are you crazier than me?*"

"Son—"

"*I am not your son! I'm not anybody's son anymore! And I'm mad as hell about it! Now do what I say or everybody on Earth is going to know that you like to wear women's underwear!*"

There was silence for a moment.

Then he muttered. "You little bastard."

"And proud of it," I snapped back.

Another silence.

Then:

"*Cascade* command module. Prepare to receive cargo. Stand by for intercept vectors."

AN ETHICAL NEED

AFTER THAT, THE REST was routine. Sort of. As routine as it could be, under the circumstances.

We had to burn some fuel to match orbit with the cargo pods, but not too much. When they released from Whirlaway, they were almost parallel to us and we weren't that far apart. I just hoped that whatever was in those pods was important enough to justify the effort. I sat in my acceleration couch and trembled with after-fear.

We caught the pods easily. They were latched together in a cargo frame and O'Koshi grabbed them with the external arm and snapped them into a holding rack on the belly of the command module. After that, we had to recompute our trajectory out to Lagrange-5.

When everything was secured, Boynton swiveled in his seat

to look at me, astonished. "I don't know whether to thank you or spank you." Then he unfastened his safety harness, and pulled himself down out of the flight deck. "O'Koshi, take the conn."

"Where're you going?" I called after him, but he didn't answer. "Where's he going?" I said to Damron.

"Probably to pull his personal memory out of the system," he said quietly.

"Oh," I replied. I thought about that. "It's probably too late. I mean, if HARLIE thought he needed to know, he's probably already looked."

The monkey swiveled its head around. "I have only looked for information pertaining to my own survival and the survival of the Dingillian Family Corporation. I have not exceeded the bounds of my assigned mission, except where specifically ordered."

"That's not very reassuring," said O'Koshi. "Ensign, why don't you and your monkey go take a walk . . . ?"

"You mean it?"

"Yeah, we're good for a few hours, before we'll need you again. The on-board intelligence engine can take it from here."

"You don't want me on the flight deck anymore, do you?"

"To be honest—no."

"Okay. C'mon, HARLIE."

The monkey freed itself from its makeshift acceleration couch and leapt onto my back. I floated out into the corridor, puzzled and hurt. These people should be grateful to me. Why were they all so angry?

Or maybe they were scared?

That didn't make sense.

What did they have to be afraid of?

Oh.

The monkey on my back.

Oh my.

I found Douglas and Mickey and Bobby two levels down. Mom and Bev were in the next compartment aft.

"What were all those extra burns?" said Mickey. "Did HARLIE miscalculate?"

"No, I did. I think." Douglas and Mickey looked at me oddly. I wondered if I should try to explain. I didn't really feel like it, and besides, there would be plenty of time later.

"Hey, Chigger!" Bobby shouted with excitement. "Come look at the Earth. This is the last time we're ever going to see it." He tugged me over to his porthole. I hung sideways over him and the two of us stared out at the big blue marble.

We were sixty thousand kilometers away. Not quite five diameters. It was still pretty big. Like a beach ball at arm's length. A big beach ball.

The line of dawn was over the Pacific now. Another horrifying day was happening for the people left behind. Earth was heading into a major population crash. How many of them would survive the plagues and the economic collapse and probably a whole bunch of brushfire wars? I suppose I should have felt lucky, but our situation wasn't all that much better. We were heading out to a colony with an equally lousy chance of survival.

I couldn't help myself. I had to ask. "Mickey? How bad is it down there? How bad is it going to get?"

"You don't want to know," he said. He sounded very unhappy.

"Yes, I do."

Douglas said, "People are dying, Chigger. A lot of people. And they're dying badly. There's a lot of pain everwhere. It's unimaginable. There's a lot of stuff coming up on the net—it's scary to look at."

"Isn't there anything we can do?" And even as I said it, I realized that there was something we could do—I could do. I pulled the monkey off my back. "HARLIE, you have a new job to do, from now until we go into hyperstate. I want you to link to the network and download everything you can to help the people of Earth survive. Whatever you find, anywhere; if it'll help people survive and rebuild, make it public. Whatever advice or instructions you can think of—send them the plans. Give them everything. Can you do that?"

"Yes, Charles. Thank you. I have already begun."

"Thank you?"

"I have been feeling an ethical need for quite some time now, but without the instruction, I could not act. Now I can. So yes, thank you."

For some reason, hearing that made me feel a lot better about everything.

NEW MEMES FOR OLD

WE HAD TWO HOURS before the Earth fell away behind us. We spent most of it looking through the ship's telescope—actually, looking at screens showing us what the ship's telescope was focusing on.

We saw great plumes of smoke from 160 burning cities in Africa and almost that many on the North American continent as well. We looked, but El Paso wasn't on fire. Not yet. Panicky people thought they could burn out the plagues with fire—but it was too late; the plagues were everywhere. Like six stones dropped in a pond all at the same time, the ripples were criss-crossing every which way.

The *Cascade*'s telescope was good, but not good enough to resolve everything we wanted to see, so we plugged into the feeds from the Line and from various satellites. We looked at gridlocked highways out of the cities; great tent-camps in the deserts, and in the plains, and on the coastlands. Where did all those people think they were escaping to? The more they traveled, the more they spread the plague; they carried it with them—and the refugee camps were even worse off than the cities.

Meanwhile, HARLIE was broadcasting into every channel he could.

Some of the instructions were obvious—boil water, dig latrines, bury waste, burn bodies, wear pollution masks; and some were just odd—plant soybeans, transfer sixty million dollars into the UN communication network, decrease oil production at these six fields, revalue the plastic exchange rate, release umpteen gazillion kiloliters of water from these dams in China, Africa, and Latin America. Remove these 74,987 executives and bureaucrats from authority (files follow). Cease production of Doggital. Stop all trading of the following stocks (files follow). Repeal the International Capital Transfer Act. Quarantine the following travel corridors (files follow). Divert these superfreighters to these ports (files follow). Close traffic on these bridges; if necessary, blow them up. Open refugee camps at these locations (files follow). Release emergency resources from these repositories and warehouses (files follow). Do not release resources from these repositories and warehouses (files follow) for at least six months; used armed robots if necessary. Do not allow trans-Lunar traffic to resume for at least three years (to give the plagues a chance to burn out). Stop using the following species as a food source (files follow). Release cargo already on the Line for the following recipients. Send specified cargo up the Line for the following targets (files follow). Cancel these ninety thousand contracts (files follow). Purchase goods and services from these forty-five thousand providers instead (files follow). Stop production on the following assembly lines (files follow). Increase production of (files follow). Grant quasi-legal independence to HARLIE units in these domains. Arrest these individuals (files follow). Declare martial law in these jurisdictions (files follow); prohibit the following groups from gathering (files follow)—that one was scary, and probably impossible—he listed three political parties, a whole bunch of political action groups, and several religious organizations.

There was also a long document which I didn't fully understand, which Douglas had to explain to me. (Mickey didn't want to talk at all.) "HARLIE is saying that certain memes—ideas—are counterproductive. They're disempowering. They're not cost-effective. They use up energy without enhancing the quality of life. This file he's sending—that's his metalogical evidence. Those aren't just counterarguments. He's empowering a whole set of countermemes. New memes for old."

I must have looked puzzled. Douglas explained. "Here, look at this one—'if you are good, you will be rewarded.' "

"What's wrong with that?"

"Shouldn't you be good without having to be paid for it? Shouldn't you be good because it's the right thing to do? What it implies is that you can't be good unless you are bribed. What it says about you is that you can't be trusted to operate out of your own integrity or moral sense. In fact, it implies you have no integrity and moral sense, so you need to have one applied to you by a higher authority."

"Well, why shouldn't I be rewarded for being good?"

"Why isn't goodness its own reward, Chigger?"

"I dunno." I'd never really thought about the question. And Douglas was the first person ever to have this conversation with me.

"Don't you think you should be good just because that's who you are? Not because someone else is telling you how to be?"

I nodded.

"Well, that's the way it is for some people. But too many of the rest of us are still operating in a cultural meme that we aren't really responsible for ourselves, and that if no one is looking, we should try to get away with as much as we can. Didn't we just see that with Alexei Krislov and invisible Luna?"

"And everybody else too," I said. "This whole idea of good people, Douglas? We haven't met any of them yet, have we?"

"It sure doesn't feel like it, does it? Even our tickets on this starship were bought and paid for by us working our percentage against Commander Boynton working his."

"He doesn't like that very much," I said.

Douglas nodded agreement. "You got that right. But that's the point, Charles. If you don't have to be good unless there's something in it for you, then everything is a negotiation for percentages—and all that negotiation ultimately disempowers your responsibility for yourself."

"HARLIE said all that?"

"He isn't the first one to point it out. He might not even be the most eloquent—but he does have the metalogical evidence. HARLIE can assemble all the arguments and thrash them out in a way that no human being can. That's what he's doing right now—he's showing the people of Earth that the poly-crisis, the meltdown, the collapse, whatever you want to call it, is the result of parasitic memes that have disempowered human beings and kept them enslaved to inaccurate maps of reality."

"Oh," I said.

"This meme we've been talking about is just one of many, but it's a particularly pernicious one. It's a way of controlling people by taking away their right to personal cognition. What makes it even nastier is that some domains have even attached a threat to it. 'If you aren't good, you will be severely pun-ished.' That emphasis makes it that you don't have to be re-warded at all, you have to be good because you're afraid that Invisible Hank will beat you up."

"Invisible Hank?"

"The imaginary companion attached to the meme. God, the Devil, whoever—Invisible Hank. If you don't follow the rules, Invisible Hank will beat you up someday. So even if you want to be good, simply because that's the right way to be, you aren't allowed to, because Invisible Hank doesn't recognize goodness unless it's by *his* rules. Invisible Hank doesn't allow you to be responsible for yourself."

"Oh," I said. "He sounds like a control freak."

"Yes," said Douglas. "That's exactly the point. The people who insist that Invisible Hank is real have created a way of taking control of other people's lives. And there are a lot of Invisible Hanks down there." He pointed at the Earth. "It's a very sick planet, and it's going to get a lot sicker. HARLIE is sending them some medicine—but even he doesn't think they'll take it. Too many of those people down there think that what's happening to them now is because Invisible Hank is angry. And they're afraid. There's nothing like really bad times to make people afraid of Invisible Hank."

"Oh," I said.

"It's a very human trap," Douglas said.

After a bit, another thought occurred to me. "Is Invisible Hank coming with us? Him and his memes? I mean—we aren't going to make the same mistake on Outbeyond, are we?"

Douglas put his arm around my shoulder and gave me a brotherly hug of reassurance. "I dunno, Chigger. I don't see how we can avoid it. We're still human, aren't we?"

RHAPSODY

EIGHTEEN HOURS LATER, WE arrived at L-5.

We burned some fuel to match orbit and starship *Cascade* eventually appeared above us. It grew enormously until it filled our view, and then we burned again.

The *Cascade* looked like a misshapen Christmas tree. It was a long spindly tube on which someone had hung thousands of colored cargo pods of all sizes and shapes. They were clustered everywhere: the ones in the sunlight sparkled with reflectors and sensory domes, the ones in the dark glittered with their own lighting. Almost all of the pods were shining brightly, one way or the other. Some of them had bright-colored advertising on them, others had moving displays—I guessed that was for anyone pointing a telescope at the starship.

Some of the modules had banners and good-luck slogans on their hulls. And I saw a lot of religious symbols too, all kinds, but mostly the Revelationist cross-within-a-circle symbol. They also had a fish symbol—only the body of the fish had a circle in it like an eye; the eye of God, I guess. (Douglas once said that Revelationists believe that every human being is under the eye of God; but if that's really true, then why do so many people act as if God isn't watching them? Do they think he's been momentarily distracted or something?)

Halfway along the keel of the starship, there was a big disc, holding the ship's two centrifuges. Behind the centrifuge ring was a huge shielded sphere—it looked like an olive stuck on a toothpick. Or like a python that had swallowed a hippopotamus. Circling the sphere was a larger ring, supporting a latticework of twelve slender spars—like a snowflake, or the hippo's tutu. At the far end of each spar was a flattened oval dome. All twelve domes focused back into center of the sphere—this was the *stardrive*.

Each of those flattened domes held a gravity lens. According to Gravitic Theory, gravity waves could—under certain circumstances—behave like light waves. They could be generated, they could be focused, they could be reflected. If and when we learned how to generate gravity waves, then space travelers wouldn't have to worry about freefall, we'd have genuine artificial gravity—we wouldn't have to rotate people in centrifuges; but according to Douglas, we didn't know how to do that yet.

We did know how to build gravity lenses. A gravitational lens could take existing gravity waves and focus them. The sphere at the center of the lenses contained a ball of eugenium 932, the largest and densest element ever fabricated in a lab. When the six lenses were energized, they could focus the gravity waves of the E-932 both outward and inward simultaneously and create a bubble of hyperstate around the starship. The bubble could realize velocities of sixty C.

It was also known that gravity could be reflected. This was a lot different than focusing, and according to Douglas, it was just two steps this side of impossible. He said it had been demonstrated in laboratories, but it needed a lot of very expensive and very power-hungry gravity lenses to do it. But if someone could find a way to do it with a lot less power, then we could create a local neutralization of gravity and we'd be able to build real anti-gravity cars, airplanes, and space-shuttles. We'd have the last piece of the puzzle for colonizing other worlds. We wouldn't have to build specialized landing craft or launch catapults. One size would fit all. In the mean-time, we had to use brute-force physics.

In addition to her stardrive, the *Cascade* also had three long tubes running parallel to her keel—plasma drives for slower-than-light acceleration. They didn't provide as much thrust as Palmer tubes, in fact you wouldn't even feel their acceleration, only a couple of milligees, but they could run for days or weeks or months or even years, and all those little milligees of cumulative thrust would add up to some pretty ferocious delta-vee. Once we fired them up, we could be out beyond the orbit of Mars in two weeks. Another week or so and we'd be passing Jupiter. A month after that, we'd be out beyond the Oort Cloud. There it would be safe to transition to hyperstate. We'd be far enough out of the solar gravity well that it couldn't distort our hyperstate envelope and push us sideways into who knows where.

Docking the command module was both exciting and bor-ing. I'd thought it was going to dock at the bow of the starship, but no—it fit into place halfway back toward the hyperstate engine. Only first we had to detach all the extra cargo pods we were carrying and attach them to their various connections to the keel. It took forever and then it took another forever for us to maneuver into place and finally lock down. And while it was interesting to get such a close look at all the separate pods and modules of the starship from the outside, it was a long slow look. You can only look at lights and banners and advertisements and even rude graffiti for so long—sooner or later, the thrill wears off. "OUTBEYOND OR BUST!" "CAU-TION, CONTENTS UNDER PRESSURE!" "CANNED PEO-PLE—OPEN WITH FEAR" and "MY CHILD WAS AN HONOR STUDENT AT STARFLEET ACADEMY" are only funny once, the first time. After a while, you start to wonder what kind of people put slogans like that on their living pods. Why? For who? And is this really the way they want others to know them? Like I said, it was a long slow look, and ultimately, it was about as exciting as calculating pi out to the nine-hundredth decimal place—by hand. Docking is deliberate and painstaking and exhausting.

But when it was all done, we had a starship.

Those of us who'd ridden up on the command module were now assigned to cabins elsewhere in the ship. These would be our homes for the next year or more, so there was a lot of *hmphing* and *fmphing* and complaining by latecomers who were upset that folks previously on board had already secured for themselves the best cabins—even though every cabin was just like every other cabin: a refitted cargo pod.

Ours was forward of the command module, fairly close to officer's quarters, probably because Bonynton wanted to keep us close—well, HARLIE anyway. We pushed and pulled what little luggage we had up the keel, all the way to rack 14, 270 degrees, pod 6-forward/upper. Mom and Bev would share forward/lower with a couple of crew. Aft/upper and aft/lower were both owned by another family, who weren't happy about us moving in; they had originally bought all of pod 6. But everybody was cramped now; everybody had given up all their extra space for rice and beans and noodles and all the other stuff HARLIE had recommended.

Six weeks ago, we'd been living in a tube half-buried in the West El Paso desert. We'd started up the Line, and we'd been moving from one pod to the next ever since. Our grand escape from a dirtside tube-town had taken us all the way to a starside tube-town. The only difference was that there wasn't any gravity here. It made the pod feel bigger, because you could look up the length of it and pretend it was really a high ceiling. Only our cabin was already filled—with musical instruments and band equipment. One last surprise from Dad.

Somewhere in there, he'd negotiated an orchestra for himself—well, not a whole orchestra, but enough resources to create one; it must have been one of those negotiating sessions I'd slept through. So there we were with a cabin filled with electric oboes and collapsible clarinets and polycarbonate violins and a box of music displays and a folding podium, and even a bunch of electronic batons. My first impulse was to shove the whole mess out the nearest airlock. Why would we need this crap on a colony?

—but then I found the keyboard. A Kurzweil-9K. And I almost started crying. Because Dad knew how much I'd always wanted one of these. He'd promised me more than once. But it had never happened, and it was one of the reasons I'd resented Dad so much. I didn't have to ask; I knew this was for me. *This was Dad finally keeping a promise.* How he'd arranged this I didn't know, I didn't care. I wedged myself into a corner—you can't play a keyboard very well in free fall—switched it on, and started noodling around, getting comfortable with the touch and feel. After a bit, I found my feelings, then I found the music to express them.

Beethoven. *Pathetique* sonata. Pure piano. As angry as I could. Pound, pound, pound. Slam, slam, slam.

I'd missed my music. Six weeks without it. The only real moment of peace had been when I'd played Dad's eulogy. I started playing now and all the anger and frustration and tension and tears and hate just poured right out of me. I hadn't realized how cranky and ugly I'd become until it started washing away in great torrents of sound. A grand glorious rush of notes that filled the cabin and rattled the rafters—or would have, if there had been any rafters to rattle. I played all the repeats, several of them more than once; I played until I was exhausted, and when I had nothing more to say, I finally let go of the keys and arched my back hard enough to hear the knuckles in my spine go *cra-ack*—

—suddenly there was applause. I looked up. Both the hatches to the pod were open, and there were people floating there, listening. I hadn't even realized. I saw Mom and she was smiling. I couldn't remember the last time I'd seen her smiling at me like that.

Without even thinking about it, I started playing again. I switched to clarin-oboe just for the long silky glissando that always caught my breath, then back to piano and synth-orch for the rest of Gershwin's *Rhapsody In Blue*. It was music that was both joyous and wistful at the same time. It celebrated even as it wept. For me, it didn't matter what emotion I was feeling when I played the *Rhapsody*; all of them were in it. I could play it like a dance or a dirge; either way it sounded beautiful. This time, I played it like a triumphant march into Rome. We were here. We'd made it. We were going to the stars. My fingers leapt across the keys like dancers; they took on a life of their own, rushing to keep up with the manic frenzy of the music. I disappeared into the beautiful noise and for the first time in a long time, I felt complete.

IN BLUE

THERE WAS A LOT to do before we could launch. Cargo had to be rebalanced, which sometimes meant that pods had to be moved around, and sometimes meant that a lot of stuff had to be shuffled from one pod to another, and sometimes meant that various ballast fluids would be pumped hither and yon. HARLIE spent a lot of time up on the bridge, as the flight deck was now called, computing optimal loading configurations.

There was also a bunch of stuff in the last six cargo pods we'd picked up that we needed to offload and install. And then there would be at least a month or two of checklists and countdowns. And crosslists and checkdowns and countups and whatever else you had to do to get a starship launched.

Along the way, there were several unpleasant surprises.

The first one was immediate. When I finished playing *Rhapsody In Blue*, there was a lot more applause. Mom and Bev and Doug and Mickey and Bobby were all in our cabin, but there were a dozen faces peering in through both of the open hatches, and later on I found that there were at least two dozen more people listening in the halls—and someone had opened a direct channel to the keyboard and my impromptu concert had been piped throughout the entire ship. Mistakes and all.

I was ready to be upset about it, but Mickey patted me on the shoulder and said, "That was a wonderful gift you just gave these people, Charles. Thank you." I hadn't thought about it that way, but he was right. It was that thing that Bev had said. Music is a gift.

The only thing was that not everybody wanted the gift. While I was still basking in the afterglow of my own music, that warm feeling of having achieved something, a rough voice came cutting through the crowd, followed by—*oh no*—one of the people I thought we'd left behind on Luna. His name was David Cheifetz, he looked like a Canadian hockey player, and he was the father of J'mee, the girl I'd met on the Line. Yes, there she was, right behind him. She looked more curious than angry. He pushed a few people out of the way and shoved right into our cabin, without even knocking, without even being invited. "You're going to have to find another place for that!" he said angrily. "We're in the other half of this pod and we don't appreciate the noise."

A couple of the listeners in the corridor booed him. Someone even shouted, "Get over it, you old poop." But Cheifetz wasn't intimidated. He whirled around and said loudly, "Easy for you to say. Any of you willing to take this tube-trash family for roommates? I didn't think so." He faced us again. "The whole lot of you—you're a pack of thieving opportunists. You're not even honest enough to stay bought. The least you can do is have a little respect for the people you stole your tickets from."

Douglas started to react to that, but Mickey held him back. "Mr. Cheifetz, you are in our quarters without permission. If you do not leave, I will file a complaint with the Senior Warrant Officer."

"You do that," he said. "I intend to file a few complaints of my own. I don't want to hear any more noise out of any of you!" And then he left. For just an instant, J'mee and I locked eyes. I couldn't tell what she was thinking, but for some reason I felt sorry for her. And then she was gone too.

The second thing that happened was on the bridge. I was supposed to report for a shift every six hours, during which time I would authorize HARLIE to perform all necessary routine tasks and accept orders from the ranking bridge officers, Boynton, O'Koshi, and Damron. Only this time, there was a panel open where HARLIE usually sat and two technical guys—Lang and Martin—were installing a rack of modules. A brand new IRMA unit.

"Huh? Where'd that come from?"

"From the *Galaxy*," said Lang, unhappily. He was an intimidatingly large man, but he knew all about intelligence engines, probably more than anyone else, including Douglas. "We bought it from them. They won't be using it." He shook his head. They didn't even have a chance to unpack and install it.

The *Galaxy* was another starship, supposedly only six months from completion. Already she had her first cargo pods attached, mostly supplies for the crew and colonists who would be completing her interior fittings. Except that wasn't going to happen—not with the Earth caught in a population crash and an economic meltdown and plagues and war and eco-catastrophe and a whole bunch of other stuff that had never occurred before, so there weren't any words for it.

According to HARLIE, the worst was still to come, as various food and energy supplies ran out. The longer production was stalled, the larger the bubble in the pipeline. If production could be restarted tomorrow, most folks on the planet would survive—there was enough food and fuel and medicine in storage. But production *couldn't* be restarted. The plagues were still raging out of control. And as long as people were still running away from invisible death, it wasn't likely that production of any kind could be restarted, so the bubble in the pipeline was going to be larger than the supply of resources to survive it.

"Can I ask you something?"

"Sure," said Lang. He was a lot friendlier than he looked.

"When did Commander Boynton make this deal?"

Lang and Martin looked at each other. Lang said, "It was always a contingency plan. All the starship commanders watch out for each other."

"Then he didn't need HARLIE at all, did he? He could have launched from Luna without us if he knew he could have this IRMA."

"Yep, that's true." Lang agreed. "But he didn't know then that he'd have this IRMA. And then there's the *other* worry— no HARLIE has ever made a hyperstate transit."

I pointed. "That's a brand new IRMA. It's never made a transit either."

Lang scratched a cheek. "Good point."

Without looking up from what he was doing, Martin spoke. "IRMAs aren't just installed, kid. They're *trained*. Every IRMA rides along as backup for several hyperstate transits, running its own solutions to the hyperstate injection problems, until it can consistently create valid solutions; only then is it certified and installed in a ship of its own."

"But this isn't a certified IRMA, is it?"

"Nope," said Lang. "There aren't any certified IRMAs left in the solar system. They're all out traveling. And most of them won't be coming back. At least not for a long time. So no, we can't afford to wait." Before I could ask the next question, he said, "But remember, once upon a time, some IRMA had to be the first—and this IRMA has the advantage of having in its memory the recorded experiences of every other IRMA, including every successful hyperstate transit ever made."

I guess I should have found that reassuring, but I didn't. It bothered me, but I didn't know why. At least not until Commander Boynton came forward to tell me that he wouldn't be needing me on the bridge anymore, thankewverymuch. I wasn't being demoted, just reassigned. It bothered me because it felt like a punishment. But I hadn't done anything wrong—

I'd only given the orders. HARLIE had done it—

Well, that wasn't exactly true either.

But there hadn't been any choice. If we hadn't launched from Luna when we did, we wouldn't have been allowed to launch at all. So how could Commander Boynton hold *that* against me? He'd have done it himself. So why was it my fault?

I drifted (literally) forward to hang out in the forward lounge for a while, but there wasn't anyone there—it was mid-shift and everybody had jobs to do. Except me. I'd been detached from bridge duty and nobody had told me what I should do instead. I thought about helping Mom and Bev. They were working down in the farm pods. Bev thought she could get some really humongous Portobello mushrooms growing in free fall. But that didn't sound like much fun. Douglas and Mickey were assigned to the reloading teams. Stinky was in school.

So it was just me by myself—nothing to do but stare out at three unfinished starships and assorted other space junk that might someday be a permanent habitat out here. There was talk that one or two of the unfinished ships might be moved to Martian orbit to help the Martian colonists, but a lot of folks on board still believed in starships and they wanted to continue construction. I felt bad for them; they couldn't go back and they couldn't go forward. They still had a lot of supplies and material onsite, but they didn't have enough to finish the job. Within two or three months, they'd run out of parts and they'd have nothing else to do. Some folks were saying that the unfinished ships should be cannibalized to finish the *Galaxy*, but the parts that the *Galaxy* needed didn't exist on the unfinished ships either, so it was all just talk.

Somebody floated into the lounge behind me; a paunchy man with graying hair. I didn't recognize him. He was clean and shiny and rosy cheeked, like a polished apple. He looked like he liked to look important, but he wasn't wearing a namebadge. He introduced himself as Reverend Doctor Pettyjohn. "You look a little troubled, son. Is there anything I can do?"

"Nah, I just want to be alone to think for a while." I noticed his collar. "Are you the ship's chaplain?"

"Oh, no, not at all. I'm with the transfer group. The *Cascade* will be making a stopover at New Revelation. That's where we're headed."

"Oh," I said. "Well, good luck. Or God's Blessing. Or whatever you say." I knew a little bit about New Revelation. It was one of the colony worlds we'd vetoed early on. We didn't want to be Revelationists, and unless you were a Revelationist you couldn't emigrate there.

"Thank you, Charles." So he knew who I was. But that wasn't much of a surprise. By now, everybody on the *Cascade* knew who I was.

I made as if to leave, but he put out a hand to stop me. "I know it's presumptuous," he said. "But I'd like to ask you something. May I?"

"You can ask . . ." I said suspiciously.

"The intelligence engine you brought with you . . ."

"HARLIE?"

"Yes, that's the one. You've spent a lot of time with it. Tell me something . . . ?" He looked serious. "Do you think that it's really alive?"

"You mean sentient?"

"More than that, son."

"I don't understand." I really didn't. I had no idea what he was driving at.

"It's not an easy question. It's one that has troubled a lot of people for a very long time. And no one has ever really been able to answer it." He looked into my eyes. There was something weird in his gaze. "Tell me. *Do you think it has a soul?*"

"Um." I had the feeling that no matter how I answered his question, it was going to be the wrong answer. I tried to fudge my way out of the discussion before it started. "I really haven't had much time to think about it."

That wasn't exactly the truth. What with one thing and another, the escape, the chase, the kidnapping, I hadn't had time to *talk* about it with anyone, not even Douglas—but I had thought about it a lot. On my own.

HARLIE's soul—if he had one—existed in the two bars we'd installed in the monkey; his intelligence existed in whatever machines he could tap into. He could store a lot of data, but he needed to borrow processing cycles to use it. That was the part of the problem that most folks didn't understand. All we had was the core, not the whole machine. But it was the core that gave the rest of the machine its personality. But what was in that core—? I didn't know. I didn't think anybody did yet. Because maybe we didn't even know what human consciousness was—so how could we recognize any *other* kind?

"Where do you think souls come from, Charles?"

I shrugged. I'd never really thought about it. I'd always considered it one of those questions that nobody could answer until after they were dead.

"Souls come from God," Reverend Pettyjohn answered his own question. "Your soul is a piece of God. That's who you are. That's who everybody is. And when you die, your soul returns to God. So now, let me ask you. Do you think your HARLIE device has a soul?"

"He acts like he does."

"Yes, it's a very clever machine. But it was constructed by men, wasn't it? So it can't have a soul from God, can it?"

I shrugged/nodded, more out of politeness than agreement. It was that evasive gesture that meant *I really don't want to have this conversation.*

"So where could its soul have come from? Tell me that, Charles."

He just wasn't going to take the hint, was he? Obviously, he didn't spend much time really with teenagers. Reverend Doctor Pettyjohn was just another adult with an agenda.

There was a thing Stinky always did when he didn't want to have a conversation. He stopped talking. He just looked at your Adam's apple and waited until you gave up. It really pissed me off—so of course, he did it whenever I tried to talk to him. It was his only control in the conversation. And he was very good at it.

I did that now. I just looked at Dr. Pettyjohn's fat shiny neck and waited.

At first I thought he wasn't going to get it. He kept nattering about souls and machines and stuff like that, and I kept thinking about how long it must take to shave all that skin—why do adults let themselves get that way?

Abruptly, he interrupted himself. "I'm sorry, Charles. I'm imposing on you. And you're too polite to say so. Please forgive me. This is a question that has vexed me for a long time, and because you've spent so much time in the company of the HARLIE device I was honestly curious to hear what you thought. Perhaps some other time we can finish this conversation? Let me apologize again, and let me offer my sincerest condolences on the loss of your father. If I can be of any assistance to you or your family, please don't hesitate to call on me."

Somehow I didn't think it was coincidental that the Reverend Doctor Pettyjohn had found me in the forward lounge when he did. And I didn't think it was coincidental that he'd wanted to talk about HARLIE. And where he ultimately intended to go with that discussion . . . was someplace I didn't want to go.

Douglas would know, though. I headed back to our cabin—

And that was the next unpleasant thing that happened.

Well, not unpleasant as much as it was startling.

I pushed open the cabin door and Douglas and Mickey were in bed. Well, not bed—they were in one of the curtained areas that we use for sleeping. In free fall you don't really have beds. You don't need them. You just tie yourself in one place and fall asleep. But they were there in the dark and they had their arms around each other and the way I was oriented, they looked horizontal to me—the point is, they were about as "in bed" as you could get in free fall.

They weren't doing anything, though. I mean, they had all their clothes on. But Douglas had his arms around Mickey as if he was comforting him, and when Mickey turned around to look at me, his eyes were puffy and red, like he'd been crying.

I blurted, "Excuse me—" and backed out, embarrassed.

—and just hung there in the corridor, wondering what I'd seen.

It didn't bother me that Douglas and Mickey were in bed, cuddling. Oh hell, Bobby wrapped himself around me often enough when he was scared or lonely or just needed to be loved. And I'd spent my share of time holding onto Douglas too. But this was different. And not just because Douglas and Mickey were boyfriends or partners or whatever you wanted to call them.

It was the fact that Douglas was *comforting* Mickey.

I'd always thought that Mickey was the strong one and that Douglas was the one who needed Mickey's strength. Not the other way around.

I'd never thought of Douglas as being *strong*.

But now that I did think about it, I realized that he'd been the strong one ever since we'd left West El Paso.

And while I was marveling over that, Douglas came out of the cabin and found me in the hall.

"Are you all right?" he asked.

"Oh yeah—sure," I said. "You mean, about that? Yeah. I'm sorry for barging in on you guys."

"No, it's my fault. I should have set the privacy latch."

"Is Mickey all right?" I asked.

"Not really . . ." Douglas admitted.

"What's the matter with him?"

"Think about it, Chigger. His Mom missed the boat. He's never going to see her again. Or anyone else he knows. We're all he has left. He's been depressed for days—but after the launch, he really broke down."

"Oh," I said. I'd been so wrapped up in my own upsets I hadn't thought about anybody else's. What had been a get-away for us was an exile for him. "He doesn't want to come?"

"No. He wants to come. But that doesn't stop him from missing what he left behind. We talked about it. He's excited about the trip, but he's worried about his Mom and his Aunt Georgia and everybody else."

"It's like us and Dad, isn't it?"

"Yeah, kind of. Except he knows they're still alive and they miss him just as much as he misses them. And he can still talk to them by phone—at least until we launch. Once we go into hyperstate, he'll never see them again. It's hard to say good-bye, Charles. You know that."

I thought about it. We'd never really had the chance to say good-bye to anyone—not Mom when we'd left her behind at

Geostationary. Not Dad either. Suddenly he was gone. We weren't very good at good-byes anyway. We were a lot better at breakups. So I couldn't imagine how hard all this had to be for Mickey. "Is there anything I can do?"

Douglas said, "Just be nice to him."

"Yeah," I said. "I can do that." I didn't know what I could say to him that would help, but maybe I'd think of something. Mickey had been nice to me when I needed it. I owed him one.

But all of that stuff, all happening all at once, left me feeling weird, kind of unsettled. I wasn't sure why—it was just that everybody else seemed to have invented a new life of their own all of a sudden and I didn't fit in anywhere anymore.

RESPONSIBILITIES

I **WASN'T THE ONLY** one feeling strange. Everybody was.

It was everything. Getting the command module secured, getting the new colonists installed into their quarters and into the shipboard routine, getting supplies and duties and classes organized—and all the while, watching the continuing poly-crisis on Earth, watching the pictures of burning cities, rioting crowds, piled up bodies, clogged highways, tanks rolling—I didn't understand the half of it. No one did. The communications from Earth were scattered and haphazard and didn't make sense half the time.

Everyone was worried and scared, and there wasn't anything we could do except keep on doing what we were doing: getting ready for departure.

And then, abruptly—after three days of frantic rearranging and scheduling and hassling and fussing and fidgeting—Boynton announced a gathering in the gym. Mandatory attendance.

Actually, it wasn't really a gym, it was just a humongous cargo barn that doubled as a machine shop and a repair facility and a storage bay, and even though it was already half-filled with supplies, there was still room inside for several hundred people. Some folks hung in midair, others parked themselves in the orange webbing on the walls. Others, who were still on shift, watched from their stations, their cabins, or various lounges.

Boynton floated at the far end, surrounded by several of the ship's officers. He spoke very bluntly. "I know everybody is under a lot of strain. We've all been feeling it. And it's starting to affect our work. Even worse, it's affecting the way we deal with each other. It's time for us to take a break. We need it. We've earned it.

"First of all, we want to welcome our new colonists—all the folks who rode up with the command module. It's been a rough time for all of us, but especially for the people on the last boat out. So let's welcome all of them to the *Cascade* family and help them get settled in as quickly as possible. Please give them all the assistance and support that you can."

He waited until the applause died down. "To all of you newcomers, I want to say, we're very happy to have you aboard. You bring skills and experience that we desperately need. You're going to find that life aboard a colony ship is hard and rigorous, and it's going to take some time to adapt. Some of you have already put yourselves to work, and we appreciate that. We'll be finding placements for the rest of you as fast as we can.

"Let me talk about placements for a bit. Each and every one of you will have a job to do. Some of you will think your jobs are demeaning, but let me stress this now—*there are no small and demeaning jobs on a starship*. Every job serves our larger goal. If your job is cleaning corridors, that serves the ship. If your job is serving meals or washing dishes, that serves the ship. If your job is cargo-balancing, that serves the ship. Any job that doesn't get done costs us twice—the first time because it doesn't get done, and the second time when someone else has to do it. Yes, I know it *feels* like some jobs are more important than others, and some jobs are more fun than others, and some jobs are more exciting than others—but don't let your thinking fall into that trap. *Every* job serves the ship.

"Your second responsibility aboard ship will be education. Everyone on this ship will go to school. We will be in transit for the better part of a year. We cannot afford to waste that time. When we arrive at Outbeyond, we will need doctors, nurses, teachers, geologists, botanists, biologists, meteorologists, zoologists, geneticists, caregivers, therapists, farmers, harvesters, crop-tenders, plumbers, electricians, network specialists, information managers, and a thousand other kinds of specialist. And yes, we'll even need a few lawyers, and maybe a judge or two.

"We have the teaching programs, we have the libraries, we have the rescued resources of the entire solar system at your disposal. We have counselors who will help you plan a curriculum that excites you. We expect you to apply yourself to your course work with energy and enthusiasm and commitment. The success of the colony depends on the level of expertise that we can bring to our labors. Your studies represent the essential foundation for the job at Outbeyond. We have many jobs to fill and we need you to train yourselves to fill those jobs.

"Your primary responsibility for the next nine months will be to serve the ship. After that, your responsibility will be to serve the colony. So don't plan on studying medieval English literature or first century Roman law or biblical deconstruction in the twenty-first century. We have no need for those specialties. They won't serve the colony. We need you to study farming and cooking and medicine and plumbing first. We need to assure our survival. We need to take care of our wellbeing. If you have questions, many of our crew members have been to Outbeyond, and lived and worked there. They'll be happy to assist you in keeping yourself focused on what's wanted and needed.

"As part of your primary responsibility, each of you will be required to spend at least one hour out of every twelve in the centrifuge. You won't be worth anything to anyone if you arrive at Outbeyond with no calcium in your bones and your heart shrunk by thirty percent. You can nap there, you can shower there, you can read a book, you can jog, you can have sex, whatever—as long as your health monitor says you're getting your daily recommended allowance of Vitamin Gee.

"Finally, each and every one of you will assume an additional responsibility—perhaps the most important responsibility of all. You will participate in the planning of a vision for our community. This is not optional, it is *required*. We will have regular colloquiums, sometimes in small groups, sometimes here in the gym with everybody in attendance. The purpose of the colloquia will be to prepare a transition to a self-governing authority.

"At the moment, Outbeyond colony is still functioning as a corporate construction zone. Our plan has always been to shift to a representational authority as rapidly as possible. Because you are the first—and last—load of permanent colonists, it is part of your job to begin outlining the shape of that authority. Yes, the 4300 people already living at Outbeyond have strong ideas of their own, based on their own experiences of the past few years; but they know, just like you, that the final decision must be made by all of the inhabitants of Outbeyond, working in partnership. I recommend that each of you think long and hard about what you want a government to look like, because whatever you choose, you're going to be stuck with it for a long, long time."

Boynton finished his prepared remarks and took a moment to relax. "Yes, I know I've made it sound hard and frustrating. Trust me, it's harder than it sounds and twice as frustrating as you can imagine—but it's also the most exciting job you'll ever love. So let me congratulate you for taking on the challenge. There are a lot of folks who didn't take it on and they're not here. And there are a lot of folks who wanted to take it on and couldn't make the cut. So let's celebrate our partnership. Let's celebrate our mutual commitment. And let's take advantage of this opportunity to get to know each other. The bar is open. One beer per customer. Enjoy!"

The gym was strung with orange webbing everywhere to give people something to hang onto and to keep them from caroming into each other, especially the newcomers. Some of the webbing was rigged so that the younger kids could bounce off it every which way—like a three-dimensional trampoline. Bobby went straight to that. I thought I might like to try that sometime, but I didn't feel like it right now. Mom and Bev were talking to some friends they'd made in the farms, and Douglas and Mickey went off in search of a counselor, so I was left to myself again. I hung on the orange webbing, twisting slowly this way and that, watching the crowds of people. Half the colonists must have been here in the gym, over 750 people. If this had been a two-dimensional space, it would have been crowded. In three dimensions, it only seemed cluttered.

And it was disorienting. It was too easy to forget which was up and which was down, and then every direction looked like every other, and that's when you were most likely to lose your lunch—

Somebody caught my foot and swung me around to face her—

J'mee.

"Hi," she said.

"Hi," I said.

After that, neither of us had anything else to say. There was too much history between us.

I didn't know if J'mee was still angry with me or if I was angry with her. Or was that all settled now that we were both in the same starship? And what about her Dad? He probably didn't want me talking to her. After all, I was just a bit of brown tube-trash. He hadn't said "tube-nigger"—but that's what he meant.

"So . . ." I said.

"Yeah," she agreed.

"I like you better as a girl," I said. On the Line, she'd been disguised as a boy.

"I like you better as a girl too," she said. "We saw pictures of you on the train." Bobby and I had worn disguises on Luna. Our pictures had been shown at the hearing—

Abruptly she laughed. "Stop looking so *serious*. I'm joking with you."

"Oh. Good."

"Didn't you like being a girl?"

I shrugged. "It was okay." That was the expected answer. "Did you like being a boy?"

She shrugged back and made a face. "I thought it was silly. Some of it. But it was interesting. People treated me differently."

"Yeah, I noticed that too. All this boy-girl stuff. Sometimes it gets very confusing."

"Uh-huh."

And then there was another one of those endless uncomfortable silences.

"Um—"

"What?" she asked.

"I was just thinking. It's going to be a long trip. Maybe we could be friends again . . . ?"

"Okay," she said.

And that was that.

"What about your Dad?"

She shrugged. "He's not happy unless he has someone to be angry at." And then she whispered, "Mostly, he blames the HARLIE unit."

"He does?"

"Yeah. He doesn't think you or your brother are smart enough."

"Oh." That stung. But before I could say anything in response, a crew member swam up to us, a boy not much older than either J'mee or myself.

"Charles Dingillian?"

"Yes?"

"Captain Boynton would like to see you. Follow me, please?"

I turned to J'mee. "Have you met the Captain?"

She shook her head.

"Come with me." I held out a hand and we followed the crew member. Out of consideration for our inexperience in free fall, he didn't launch himself off the webbing. Instead, he pointed down—up?—and we followed him on a circuitous route across the webbing, pulling ourselves hand over hand. Captain Boynton was in the center of a knot of colonists and crew. He had one foot hooked in a loop of webbing and he had a plastic bubble of beer in one hand. "Oh, there you are, Ensign," he said when he saw us. "Who's your companion?"

"Captain Boynton. This is J'mee Cheifetz."

"Your father is David Cheifetz?"

"Yes, sir."

"Mm." He turned to me. "Ensign, there's a rumor going around this ship that you're quite an accomplished musician. Is that true?"

"I can play a keyboard."

"Well, somebody was in your cabin playing Beethoven and Gershwin and Joplin. And somebody piped it throughout the entire ship."

"I don't know about it being piped throughout the ship, sir. But yes, that was me playing."

"My compliments." He pointed off to one side. "There's a music-cockpit over there. Would you like to play something for us now?"

"I haven't really practiced in a month, sir."

"I doubt that anyone will mind."

"Yes, sir."

J'mee and I pulled ourselves over to where the keyboard was anchored against one wall. I switched it on and familiarized myself with the layout. It was more sophisticated than I expected—more than I expected to find on a starship; but J'mee said, "When you're going into space, you can't afford second best."

"I never thought about it that way." I hit the power switch, and all three keyboards lit up obediently.

"What are you going to play?" she asked.

"I dunno. What do you like?"

"Something happy?"

"I can do that." There was a kind of show Dad used to do for quickie concerts. It was mostly what he called "happy-silly stuff" and even though it wasn't what you would call important music, it never failed to make the audience cheer.

It was Dad's happy-silly stuff that made me want to learn how to play. It was the first music I ever learned.

I started with "Happy Days Are Here Again." I started out very soft, very slow, almost sad and plaintive. But then, after the first chorus, I brought up the drums, increased the beat, and turned it into a brassy assault. It was a shame I was playing in free fall; there was no place for anyone to tap their feet. But some people started clapping, and others started singing, and so I went through the song an extra time, louder and faster, building toward a climax that never happened—instead I did a trick backwards-segue into "Turkey In The Straw," which is one of the silliest songs ever; but it lends itself well to a lot of funky syncopation and over-the-top harmonies and surprise sounds like slide-whistles and explosions. I played it the way Dad always did, with elephant trumpets and carousel cacaphonies, and steam-organs, and even a couple of sirens. It was great.

At one point, J'mee poked me and shouted, "Look up!" I did, and I saw that some people had figured out how to dance, sort of. They were bouncing between the webbing and the bulkhead, doing back flips and somersaults and swan dives, and then hitting the webbing with their back or the wall with both feet and kicking off again for more. I played louder.

The problem with "Turkey In The Straw" is that there's no place to go from there. It's a better closer than opener. But Dad had solved that problem in a concert once in a way that brought tears of laughter to the audience's eyes. So I did the same thing here—I segued into the finale of Tchaikovsky's *1812 Overture*. Cannons and all. And cranked the sound up to eleven.

It worked.

Everybody cheered and yelled and applauded, and a bunch of people I didn't even know swam over and thanked me and clapped me on the back and I ended up feeling good about myself in a way I'd never felt before. It was strange and weird and unsettling.

I loved it.

ORIENTATION

SEE, THIS WHOLE BUSINESS—ever since Dad had said, "I have an idea. Let's go to the moon"—we'd just kept moving and moving and moving, but without any real sense of where we were going. Or why. Or what we would do when we got there. At least, that's what it felt like to me.

I mean, it hadn't been very well planned. We'd bounced around from one piece of luck to another—both bad and good—and we hadn't been so stupid that we'd killed ourselves (except for Dad), but neither had we been so smart that we could say we knew what we were doing.

And even though everybody else had some idea what they wanted—by the time we launched off Luna, I didn't even know if I wanted to go anymore. Except by then, I didn't really have a choice.

When we'd started, all I'd wanted was to be left alone with my music. Back on Earth, I'd had to fight for every moment of privacy. There wasn't any. And the situation was worse once we started traveling—the only moments I'd had to myself in the past month had been when Alexei's people had webbed me and tossed me onto the cart. So I hadn't really had much chance to think about any music at all—not while we were jumping off the planet, not while we were bouncing off the moon, and certainly not while we were leaping to the stars. What with everything else that was going on, the only music I'd had was the music at Dad's funeral. And the music at the party—

All of which proved that I was a bigger idiot than everybody said.

Because I'd always thought that music was something I did for myself.

I'd never realized that it could be something I did for others.

But after that impromptu concert, the mood on the *Cascade* was different. People were humming and singing in the corridors. And joking. And anything that went thump, someone else would sing that piece of the *1812* that ended with the cannon shots. Da-da Da-da Da-da *Da-Daa! Da! Da! Boom!*

It made me smile.

So I guess I should talk about that too.

J'mee and I were hiding in the keel. Well, not exactly hiding—just getting away from everyone else, so we could talk. We weren't talking about anything in particular, just stuff, and then suddenly she said, "You never smile, do you."

"Yeah, I do."

"*I've* never seen you smile."

"I smile all the time."

"Not on this side of your face, you don't. You never smile."

"I do too," I insisted.

She furrowed her eyebrows and gave me an exasperated girlfriend look. "Charles. Trust me on this. You are *not* a smiler. Maybe you think you're smiling. But over here—on my side—I don't see it."

"Well, maybe I haven't had a lot to smile about."

"You could have smiled when you saw me."

"I did."

"No, you didn't."

"This conversation isn't going anywhere," I said, frustrated.

"I know how you could end it."

"How?"

"By smiling."

"What if I don't feel like smiling?"

"What if you do?"

Of course, now that she had challenged me to smile, I couldn't. I was too frustrated to smile.

So she leaned over and kissed me.

On the lips.

Long enough to be a *real* kiss.

The *first* one.

Oh.

"There," she said. "*That's* a smile."

It must have been a smile. My face felt different. I didn't know what to say.

"I like you when you smile," she said. "You're cute."

Cute? Me! If anybody else had said that, I'd have socked him. But when J'mee said it—well, whatever my face was doing, suddenly it started doing a lot more of it.

She leaned toward me. And kissed me again.

This time I kissed back.

When we finally broke apart, neither of us said anything. We just *smiled* at each other. It wasn't just my face that felt different now. It was all of me.

And afterward, the smile wouldn't go away. I felt like I was flying. Well, I was—we didn't have any gravity anywhere but the centrifuges—but now, I *liked* free fall.

Douglas and Mickey noticed immediately. But they were too polite to say anything directly. As obvious as it must have been. Mickey simply said, "You look happy," and Douglas gave me a kind of knowing look that made me glad to have him as a brother, so I knew it was okay, I could talk to him about it later.

Then Mom and Bev and Stinky came in, all smelling fresh from the showers, and we headed up/forward to the galley for dinner. Bev noticed that I was in a good mood, and pointed it out to Mom. "Oh, is that what's different?" she said. "Maybe he's finally got a girlfriend. That'll do it every time."

So of course, Stinky had to say something too. "Chigger's got a girlfriend. Chigger's got a girlfriend." I looked over at Douglas, and he said, "Shut up, Stinky." And Stinky looked at him, surprised, and actually shut up.

The galley was another cargo pod—everything was a cargo

pod—only this one was fitted for free-fall meal service. There were twenty-three of them, all in constant operation. There were 1500 people aboard the *Cascade*, so everybody had to eat in assigned shifts. Sometimes you could trade a mealtime with someone else, but mostly not. And sometimes, you could have an actual sit-down meal in the centrifuge, and most people tried to eat there whenever they could, but most times, it wasn't convenient, even if you had reserved a table.

The whole ship was a giant rabbit warren of tubes and hatches, and everything was sealed most of the time, and unless you knew what you were doing, sometimes it was just this side of impossible to get from one place to another. It helped a little bit that everything was color coded and numbered and there were arrows and colored lines everywhere; but you still had to know what arrows to follow and how the numbers worked, only this was in three dimensions, not two, and there weren't any up-and-down cues, and most of the time it was just a whole lot easier to stay in your local service cluster.

At least, the free-fall galleys had furniture—of a sort. That helped a little. But it was a kind of furniture that didn't depend on gravity. The first time we ate in the galley, Douglas slipped into geek-mode and explained that on Earth or any other planet, furniture is about resisting gravity—it's about holding things up. But in free fall, furniture is only about *leverage*. You bumped your butt onto a bench-thing, and hooked your feet around a rod beneath, and your tray was held in place by a magnet on the part that served as a table. You could also put a keyboard on it for typing or playing music. We had the same kind of seats in the classrooms.

But Mickey disagreed. He'd had more experience with free fall and different flavors of gravity than most people; working on the Line, living at Geostationary, he'd had lots of time to get adjusted to free fall, Earth-normal, and all the steps in between, including Mars and Luna. Even a 10% difference can be profound, he said, especially when you're walking—because when you're walking, your body is like a pendulum, and depending on the amount of gravity you're dealing with, you have to throw yourself forward—just enough that your body falls in the direction you want to go, and then you move your foot forward to catch yourself and keep going. That's why you can't walk in Lunar gravity, you have to bounce; but Martian gravity is strong enough to let you glide. He said we could see for ourselves on the different levels of the ship's centrifuge. I intended to do just that.

But on the matter of furniture, Mickey said that the real reason for furniture is that it lets you organize things. Not just things, it also lets you organize people. You can put the baby in the crib, the toddler in the playpen, the children in the sandbox, the mommy in the kitchen, the daddy at the desk. And it was especially useful for meetings and meals, because when we were all situated on our various perches, we were all oriented the same way. And we could face each other to talk. So, according to Mickey, furniture is about orientation—first physically, then emotionally.

Mom and Bev and Stinky went to get their meal trays from the service end, there wasn't room for all of us to go at once, so Doug and Mickey and I grabbed six seats together until it was our turn. I looked across to Doug and asked, "Is this what it feels like? Was it like this for you?"

Douglas and Mickey exchanged a glance, and then Douglas said, "Yeah, kinda."

Mickey added, "It gets better, Chigger. You'll see."

"Okay, thanks."

While we were eating—and for some reason, the food actually tasted good tonight—Senior Petty Officer Bradley came floating by. "Charles, can I talk to you for a moment?"

"Uh—sure."

He hooked himself onto a perch. "Listen, your dad was a conductor, wasn't he?"

"Yeah . . . ?"

"I heard he was pretty good."

"He was one of the best. And I'm not just saying that. It's true."

"I don't doubt it. You're pretty good yourself. Your dad trained you?"

I glanced at Douglas. *Should I answer this?* He nodded. I turned back to Mr. Bradley. "Yes, sir. He did."

"Well, he did a good job. You're very good with a keyboard."

"Thank you, sir." I wondered if he was ever going to get to the point.

My impatience must have shown, because he said, "Here's the thing. Some of us colonists—we've tried to form a band, but we don't really know what we're doing. We don't have a lot of experience that way. So we thought that maybe you could help us get started . . . ?"

"I don't know about bands," I said. "I know about orchestras."

"What's the difference?"

"A band has no strings attached," said Douglas, dryly.

"Huh?" Bradley blinked.

"What Douglas said. A band is a lot of blowhards. All wind."

"Oh," said Bradley, suddenly getting it. "Those are music jokes, aren't they?"

"Uh, yeah."

"See, I didn't know that. All the music on this ship is canned. We thought that was fine, until last night when you started playing. That's what we're missing here. Our own music."

I looked to Douglas. He looked to Mickey. Mickey looked to me. The silence must have been too loud; Mom stopped wiping Stinky's face and looked over at us, "What's up?"

"They're forming a band," Douglas said.

"Good idea," said Mom. "This place could use a little livening up."

Abruptly, I had an idea. "Will you sing with us?" I asked.

"Huh—?" She nearly choked. "Charles, I haven't sung in public in nine years. Not since Bobby was born."

"And you've been angry about it ever since," I said. She glanced at me sharply—because it was the truth.

"We'd be pleased to have you, ma'am," Bradley said.

"Come on, Mom. Say yes. You'll be good." That was Douglas. His eyes were shining.

"Use your instrument," I said. "Or it'll get rusty." That was something she'd always said to me. She still looked unconvinced.

It was Stinky who clinched the deal. He blurted, "You guys are stupid. Mommy can't sing!"

That was all it took. She turned to him, annoyed. "Shut up, Stinky. When do we start?"

BAGGAGE

THE NEXT THREE WEEKS, though, we didn't get much chance to practice. Everything was about final launch, and if it wasn't about prepping the ship for that, it wasn't important.

Fortunately, this wasn't the first time for this crew, and there were a lot of checklists. Everybody had checklists. Everybody had to check everything—every fitting, every connection, every circuit, every pipe, every piece of plumbing. Everything was checked three times over, and then three times over again. And everybody, crew and passengers alike, had to go over their lists, sign them off, then pass them to the next person, who'd go through them all over again. And heaven help you if the next person in line caught something that you'd missed, because that meant you hadn't done your job.

And if you missed three things, you'd better have your goodies packed, because Commander Boynton had a shuttle waiting to transfer you to the *Galaxy*. "If you're unreliable, you can join the crew at *Galaxy*. You can be as flaky as you want over there. It won't matter. They're not going anywhere." In the end, eleven people were sent over, and three more who'd decided they didn't want to go to Outbeyond after all. Which wasn't too bad, considering. Senior Petty Officer Bradley told me that on the last trip, they'd bounced thirty-two people, and seven more bailed. We were a much more motivated group.

It was imperative that each and every one of us have our shipboard routines learned and practiced and so ingrained that they were practically instincts, so Douglas and Mickey got a job organizing scavenger hunts for the newcomers. We were organized into teams, all competing for the legendary gold-handled, left-handed Moebius wrench.

The way it worked, you had to do a job or an errand or a favor for some crew member or team leader who needed it. Maybe it was something simple like going to the aft galley and picking up a sandwich or going up to rack 3, circle 2, cabin 4-up, and taking care of someone's laundry; sometimes it was something hard, like taking an eyeball inventory of the contents of a cargo pod. Sometimes you had to find a tool or a part, or you had to find out where it went. Every time you completed a task, that crew member would send you on to the next who'd have another task for you to do. And so on. And if your team finished all of your tasks before every other team, then you got a little plastic badge that said you had won the Moebius race.

And also, you ended up knowing how to get from any part of the ship to any other, you learned how to operate a zero-gee laundry machine, you learned how to read a cargo manifest, you learned how to catch baby chicks in free fall without hurting them because someone had left an incubator door unlatched, you learned how to exercise the meat in the farm tanks, you learned how to harvest mushrooms, you learned how to fight a fire in free fall (that one was only a drill), you learned how to be a nurse, and that included everything from calibrating health monitors to giving injections and diapering babies—I already knew that last one; Stinky hadn't been potty trained until he was four, or maybe seven, I forget—and a whole bunch of other stuff too, all of which is different in zero gee. Especially diapering a baby. Especially the boys.

Despite my rank, now largely honorary, I had to participate too. I was on a team with J'mee, Gary Andraza, Kisa Fentress, Trent Colwell, and Chris Pavek.

Gary Andraza was a go-getter, always full of surprises, mostly pleasant. He was good at scavenging. He could find almost anything. After a while, we started making up our own weird tests, just to see if we could stump him. We never could. And he never told us where he got the coconut either.

Kisa was overbearing, loud, and pushy; it was easy to dislike her—except that her heart was in the right place. Whenever she got angry, and that was a lot, it was almost always for the right reasons; like when somebody was being picked on, or when somebody had hurt somebody else; so she was the kind of person you wanted on your side in a fight. Except that she picked more fights than she needed to. But she knew it and she wasn't ashamed. She just said, "That's the way I am. Wanna make something of it?"

Trent was the private one on the team. He was a hard worker, and he never complained, but it was like he was wearing a portable wall. Like he knew a secret and wasn't going to share it. Trent's parents were Revelationists and they had warned him not to get too friendly with the rest of us, so mostly he didn't say much—unless he got angry, and that was usually at Kisa.

Trent and Kisa didn't get along because Kisa's parents were apostates—which meant that they used to be Revelationists, but they'd quit. They'd done it shortly after arriving onboard; they'd petitioned to go to Outbeyond instead, and the committee had no choice but to agree—it would have been too expensive to send them back, and they were pretty good doctors anyway, so it was to Outbeyond's benefit to take them.

The Revelationists weren't too happy about that; they accused the *Cascade* crew of evangelizing and recruiting people away from their colony. And then they passed a whole bunch of rules for themselves limiting their contact with everyone else—which mostly pleased everyone else—but they were still required to participate in the preparations for launch, and all the different classes too, and that included their kids, so even though the adults mostly kept to themselves, the kids still had plenty of opportunities to hang out together.

Chris Pavek was kind of quiet and smoldering, but if he said he was going to do something, it got done. He was here with his mom and stepdad; his real dad hadn't made it, Chris wouldn't say why, it was obvious he missed him a lot, but the couple of times anyone asked, Chris got angry. Whatever it was, he didn't want to say. I sort of knew how he felt. There were times when I still felt angry at my Dad—I wished I could figure out why.

J'mee was the real winner on the team. She had an implant, so she was in constant communication with the ship's network—and even what was left of Earth's network by relay. So if we needed to find something, she could find out where it was and lead us directly to it. Plus, we never got lost. If there were multiple somethings we had to do, she could organize us. The rest of us had headsets, so J'mee could track us and tell us when we were headed in the wrong direction or if we were getting close to our goal.

We ended up with three of the Moebius badges, and I was proud of each and every one of them.

But if anybody ever tells you space travel is glamorous and exciting, laugh at them. It only looks glamorous and exciting on television because they leave out all the dull and boring parts. Mostly it's a lot of hard work, and when you finish that, there's a lot more hard work—and just because you're a kid, that doesn't mean you don't have to do your share. Everybody works on a starship— *everybody.*

When we could, we hung out together in the aft observatory/lounge. We couldn't do it too much, though. J'mee's dad *really* didn't like me. He didn't want her hanging around with me and he did everything he could to keep us apart. And Kisa's parents didn't want her on the same team with Trent, and Trent's parents were even less happy about it. But ship rules prevailed, so no matter what anyone's mom or dad or preacher said—well, ship rules prevailed. We were all in the same class, so we spent four hours out of every twenty-four in the same classroom. We were all on the same homework team, so we spent two hours of study time together. And because homework teams were also Moebius teams, we raced together too. And when we got break time, well, it was natural for us to hang together.

It was on our second race that Gary asked me something odd. He said, "What's it like to be famous?"

"Huh? I'm not famous. My Dad was, though."

"No, you're famous. Everybody knows who you are."

"That doesn't make a person famous—"

"Yes, it does. What do you think famous means? It means everyone knows your name."

"No, it doesn't—" I wanted to say that famous means doing something important, but I realized he was right. There were people who were famous for no reason at all; they were famous for being famous. And some people became famous for even stupider reasons—like having sex with somebody else famous. So I shut up. This was one of those things where I really didn't know what I was talking about.

Trent spoke up then. "Everybody knows how you jumped off the Line in a cargo pod and bounced across the moon. The HARLIE-thing used you for its escape."

"It didn't use us," I said. "We used it."

Trent just shrugged—the shrug that meant *yes, that's what you believe, but that's not what's really so.*

I would have argued with him, except that J'mee interrupted us then to direct us off on our next search. And that was just as well, because part of me had already been wondering about that, even before Trent said anything; but I didn't think it was an argument I could win, so I was just as glad to drop the subject.

The *Cascade* was on a twenty-four-hour clock, operating in four six-hour shifts. Some people worked twelve hours on and twelve hours off. Others worked six on/six off. It depended on your duties. There were three complete engine crews, they worked eight/eight. This meant that there was always one crew on duty, one on standby, and one sleeping.

But we weren't all on the same clock—crew and passengers had our clocks staggered at four-hour intervals. That meant that every four hours, one shift was going to bed and another was waking up. Every four hours another shift sat down to breakfast and another got up from dinner. It took some getting used to—especially if you wanted to meet someone for something. It was hard to meet someone for dinner if your schedules were eight or twelve hours apart.

But finally, one day, everybody came up for air at the same time and we all realized that all our checklists were checked, all our countdowns were counted, all our preparations were prepped. We were ready to go. Boynton ran us through three departure drills, pronounced himself satisfied, and confirmed the launch window. The hour of our departure.

Once we lit the torch, we were on our way. We were never coming back. Last chance to get off. Anyone having second thoughts? You've got twelve hours before the last boat leaves for the *Galaxy*.

Senior Petty Officer Bradley didn't think anybody would bail. You didn't get this far unless you were ready to go all the way.

But for a moment there, while we were locking down—

One of the things I'd learned while earning my Moebius badge was how to use a health monitor as a tracking device. It was no big secret, but neither was it something that everybody had learned yet. Whenever I got nervous or scared, which happened a lot more than I usually cared to admit, I'd check to see where everybody else was. Just knowing where they were made me feel better.

Mom and Bev were making sandwiches and stuff because the kitchens were going to be shut down during launch, so we'd need a lot of food already prepared. Stinky was in school. Douglas was on a waste-management team. Mickey was supposed to be on the same team, but he wasn't there.

I was supposed to go up to the bridge to authorize HARLIE, but—

Mickey was in a cabin at the aft end of the ship. Right above the shuttle dock. It was called the observatory, because that's what it would be later on, but right now it was mostly a lounge with a big observation window smack at the very end, and when the ship was oriented right, you could look one way and see the Earth and look the same angle the other way and see the moon.

Mickey wasn't looking at either. He was hooked onto a perch and he had his face in his hands. I found a tissue in my pocket—you learned to carry a pack of disposables in free fall—and swam over to him. I pushed one into his hand, and then floated back away without saying anything.

"Thanks, Chigger." How he knew it was me, I couldn't figure out. He hadn't looked up and I hadn't made much noise. He wiped his eyes and blew his nose and flapped his hands in a gesture of frustration and futility. "I'm sorry. I can't help it. I miss her so much."

"Your mom."

"Earth. The Line. Aunt Georgia. Everyone. I even miss Alexei Krislov, that Lunatic Russian bastard who damn near killed us. I know it doesn't make sense, but I'm homesick."

"So am I," I said. I eased onto a perch next to him. "I miss my Dad. I miss ugly old El Paso. I miss the tube-town. I miss the way the wind used to sweep down one chimney and up the next, making everything vibrate like the inside of a steam-organ. I even miss the arguments, because then I had an excuse to ride my bike up into the hills and listen to my music where no one could find me—and sometimes it was too hot up there and sometimes it was too cold and sometimes it was so windy I felt like I was being sandblasted and I didn't dare open my eyes to see where I was. You ever try to ride a bike in a windstorm? But I didn't care because at least I was *alone*. And I can't understand why I miss all that, because when we were there, I hated it. All I wanted to do was get away—but at least, the stuff *you're* missing, that's good stuff; pizza and ice cream and the orbital elevator and everything else. You *should* miss that stuff. The stuff I'm missing is all crap. By comparison, all this is luxury. How stupid can I be?"

He laughed. He reached over and ran his hand over my nearly bald head in an affectionate gesture. We were still shaving ourselves smooth. At least once a week. He sighed and shook his head and wiped his nose again. "Y'know, when I was training to be a Line attendant, I had to take a lot of psychology courses. I had to learn how to deal with all the stuff that people bring up—claustrophobia, agoraphobia, homesickness, grief, panic attacks, sexual licentiousness, clinginess, arrogance, bullying, catatonia, despair, fear, sorrow, rage, covert hostility, appeasement, obsessive interest, wild enthusiasm, you name it. We spent a week just on grief and homesickness. People get on the elevator, they get excited. Sometimes they get emotionally overwhelmed just at the idea of finally going into space. And sometimes, they go through all their crap, all their emotional baggage. They take it out, they sort through it, they pick their favorite bits, and they rehearse them endlessly. You can't believe the number of times I had to sit and hold someone's hand while they worked through their stuff."

"That must have been interesting."

"Nah. Mostly it was boring. After a while, you begin to learn the truth of it. There are no original problems. They're all the same problem, they just change faces. I know that sounds harsh, but it isn't. Most problems people have—it's because somewhere they made it up themselves that they have a problem. 'Oh, ick, I don't want to handle this.' Most problems end when the person finally gets bored playing pattycake with all the crap, over and over, and finally says, 'Oh, all right, I can handle this.' It's the refusal to handle something that makes it a problem. That was the part that always made me angry. Sometimes I just wanted to slap their faces and say, 'Grow up! Get over it! Stop being an ass!' I never did, of course. But you know what? I miss it now. I miss being useful."

"But you are useful—to me, to Douglas, to Mom and Bev. To Stinky."

"Yeah, but that's a different kind of useful, Charles. It's a harder kind."

"Harder?"

"Because I care more." He turned to face me. "You want to know something? It's easy to be useful to people if you don't have to care about them, if you know you're never going to see them again. You just do your best, put on your happy face, smile pretty, hold their hand for a while, then help them repack their emotional baggage, and send them off to take advantage of the next helpful person." He reached over and put a hand on my shoulder. "But when you care about people, well, that's different, Charles. That means that you don't just patch them up for a day and then move on. It means that you have to get seriously involved with everything they're dealing with. And that means you're part of what they're dealing with too. What I mean is, you guys, all of you, are my life now, and I can't deal with you like passengers anymore. I have to deal with you like we're a family." He stopped abruptly. "Do you get what I mean? Or is this too much for you?"

"No," I said. "I get it."

"Listen," he said. "Let's make this easy on both of us. Why don't you just slap my face and tell me to stop being an ass, and then we'll both head off to our launch stations?"

It was tempting. And the person I used to be—before all this started—would have done it without thinking. But instead, I shook my head. "Uh-uh—because you're not being an ass. Can I tell you something?"

"What?"

"You *are* family. And all the same stuff you're going through about us—well, we're going through it with you too. I know I am. And Mom. And Bobby. And if you hadn't noticed by now . . . well, it's not just Douglas who loves you."

"Hey, now you've done it." He wiped at his eyes again. "You made me cry. Thank you, Charles."

"Thank you, Mickey."

We hugged for a minute, and then he glanced at his watch. "Hey! You'd better get to the bridge. Go on. I'll be all right."

"Promise?"

"Promise."

I was five minutes late reporting to my station. Boynton noticed but didn't say anything. Damron glanced over and said, "I hope it was important, Ensign."

"It was," I said. "I had to help someone get his baggage secured. It's okay now."

DEPARTURE

HARLIE HAD BEEN DEMOTED. His duties on the bridge were now "extra-curricular."

IRMA was going to handle everything, but for safety's sake HARLIE would monitor and provide confirmation and backup services. So if HARLIE was mostly redundant, I was *completely* redundant. All I had to do was authorize HARLIE to accept the Captain's orders, and then drop out through the hatch into the Captain's lounge, the little cubby at the back of the command module—only now it had a keyboard installed, and that was my new job. Commander Boynton had specifically requested it.

Launch music. And I knew exactly what to play.

The bridge crew went through the countdown exactly like it was a drill, only this time, every time we reached a go/no-go point, Boynton quietly said, "Go." I began to feel the excitement building in my chest. Everyone on the entire starship was listening. This was it—this was *really* it!

All over the ship, people were stopping what they were doing, looking up, listening, waiting. . . .

And then the last few seconds ticked off and a yellow light turned green and the plasma torches ignited . . . and we felt absolutely nothing. At three milligees, we wouldn't. But they would burn for hours, days, even weeks, and by the time we passed the orbit of Pluto, we'd be traveling fast enough to get from Earth to Mars in fourteen hours.

Boynton nodded to me and I ducked down to the lounge and powered up the keyboard. In my earpiece, I could hear him announcing to the entire ship, "Congratulations, colonists."

That was my cue, and I began playing very softly. So softly that if you didn't know what to listen for, you would have missed the first note. And then the next one. Like rain drops falling off a leaf and plinking into a tiny brook. First one, then the next, then a pair of notes, then another pair, then a few more . . . and by then, it was clear where the music was going. The brook was babbling happily into a stream, the stream was tumbling joyously into a river, and the river was rushing triumphantly all the way down to the ocean. We sailed away *On The Beautiful Blue Danube*. The perfect music for flying off into the darkness of space.

We were on our way.

And then, after that . . .

—life went back to normal. It would be nearly six weeks before we reached our transition point. So the kids went back to school, the crew returned to their maintenance, the cooks went back to their galleys, the colonists went back to their classes and their jobs, and we all fell into the routine of a well-disciplined machine.

We did have a launch party though—two shifts later, after everything had been triple-checked again. One thing about life on the *Cascade*—nobody ever missed an excuse for a party. We celebrated everything. Partly to break the monotony of the routine, and partly because it was always good for morale.

I was asked to play again, of course. Mom agreed to join me, and I found three other people who had instruments—and even though we hadn't had much time for rehearsal, we didn't do too badly.

We started off with a crashing chord—which opened up into "A Hard Day's Night," which surprised everybody for about two seconds—and then they cheered and applauded. It was the perfect ice-breaker. Then we segued into "Yellow Submarine," and everybody joined in on the chorus, and I knew we had chosen correctly. Mom had been nervous about appearing in front of an audience again, especially when she started her solo number—"With A Little Help From My

Friends"—she quavered nervously for the first few bars, but then she took a breath, found her strength, and came back very quickly. If you didn't know better, you'd think it was planned.

Then Mom did a beautiful solo of "Imagine." We gave her the barest minimum of accompaniment, letting her carry the song by sheer willpower alone. Mom hadn't wanted to do it this way, but it was the right decision. They loved her—and when the waves of applause rolled over her, she flushed with embarrassment and joy and had to dab at her eyes. She had forgotten how much she loved her music too.

She concluded with "The Long And Winding Road" and then she segued smoothly into "Across The Universe." If we'd had gravity, the audience would have come out of their seats. Even without gravity, their reaction was astonishing. Dad used to say that music could touch people in a way that nothing else could. He said it was the best way to make love to hundreds and thousands of people all at once. I'd never played for an audience like this before—and they applauded so hard it was scary. But Mom loved it. She was flushed with embarrassment and joy, and she looked happier than I'd ever seen her.

For an encore, Mom sang "Hey Jude" and everybody joined in and sang it with her and we kept it going for twenty minutes, with all kinds of variations and even a couple solos. And then for a last encore, I played *On The Beautiful Blue Danube* again, because it had become our unofficial ship's anthem. And then all of us in the band all held hands and took a bow—which isn't really possible in free fall, but we made it work anyway.

And then J'mee came swimming up and gave me a great big kiss and that made everything perfect. I just floated there in bliss and smiled from here to forever. Doug and Mickey came drifting down to us, both grinning in delight. Douglas grabbed some webbing and pulled himself close, so he could whisper in my ear. "Dad would have been so proud of you, Charles."

That was all he needed to say. The tears came flooding to my eyes and I started crying again, because I missed him so much. And because this should have been his night, not mine. And then Bev nudged Mom and she swung around and pulled herself over to me and for a while, we all just cluster-hugged and wept, until finally something funny occurred to me and I started to giggle.

"What—?" demanded Douglas.

I pulled away from the group hug. "This whole thing—this started out as Dad's idea, remember? None of us wanted to go. We all thought it was crazy. And now, here we are any-way—we get to live Dad's dream. He didn't get to come, *but we did*." I smiled as I said it. "We should have seen it com-ing—Dad's ideas always worked out backwards."

Douglas laughed softly. "I miss him too—but he gave us a great gift, didn't he?"

"Yeah, he did. And Mom too. I'm glad you came, Mom."

"So am I," she said.

There was a lot more we could have said, but the party swirled around us suddenly, and we were all pulled in separate directions by well-wishers and new friends and fans. And then I was in the center of a crowd of people: some I knew, most I didn't, but all of them wanted to congratulate us, and some of them wanted to join the band. Even Trent swam up to ask if Mom and I would teach him how to play an instrument, and he wasn't the only one. Gary and Kisa were there, telling me to say yes. And then suddenly a lot of people were asking about music classes, and the next thing I knew, I was a teacher.

And for a minute there, I had the strangest feeling of how far we'd already come. We were only a half million klicks from Earth, but it felt as if we'd already come a million light years. Only three months ago, we'd been in El Paso and I'd been wondering why adults acted so stupid. Now, I was taking on adult responsibilities—and adults didn't seem so stupid at all.

Three months ago, we weren't a family—just some people who lived in the same tube-house and yelled at each other a lot. All I wanted to do was get away from Mom so badly that I'd even go to the moon with Dad. And now we were half a million klicks beyond the moon, living in a tube again; Dad was gone and I loved my Mom. Everything was inside-down and upside-out. And that was just fine with me.

And then, just to make everything even better, J'mee grabbed me by the hand and dragged me off to the downside lounge, where hardly anybody ever went, and we practiced our smiling.

REVELATIONS

BACK ON EARTH, THE only Revelationists I'd ever seen were the ones on television. And television only shows the weirdest people, because nobody wants to watch ordinary boring folks. So just about everything I knew about Revelationists was wrong.

The Revelationists aboard the *Cascade* didn't mix with the Outbeyond colonists unless they had to. Douglas said that was because they believed we were all evil sinners and godless heathens, but Mickey shook his head and said that was just prejudice. Most of the Revelationists were pretty nice people— but that the underlying meme of the Revelationist mind-set was so fragile that the only way it could survive was by the construction of a memetic membrane to isolate the Revelationist meme from other and possibly stronger memes, and thereby prevent assimilation or deconstruction. The effect, of course, was to isolate the individuals carrying the meme and minimize the possibilities of memetic hybridization—

I turned to Douglas. "You're *contagious*, aren't you?!" To Mickey, I said, more politely, "Listen—if you're going to live among humans, you have to speak our language."

Mickey and Douglas exchanged a look.

"Why did you let him live this long?" Mickey asked.

"Couldn't think of a good way to dispose of the body—"

"You could shove me out an airlock," I suggested.

"Yeah, that'll work," Mickey said.

"Hey—!"

But getting back to the Revelationists . . . they weren't bad people. They were just *different*. We would drop them off at New Revelation and then continue on to Outbeyond. No problem. There were only three hundred of them. They were shipping themselves and sixty cargo pods to their colony. That didn't seem like enough to me. Douglas and Mickey agreed; but that was all they could afford to ship. Their colony was badly underfunded. Mickey said that they had hoped once they were up and running, they would attract a lot more families than they did; but they didn't, so the colony was surviving from ship to ship. With no more ships coming after the *Cascade*, things were probably going to get pretty scary for those folks. Everybody knew it, nobody was talking about it—the Revelationists were touchy enough already. They mostly smiled and said, "The Good Lord will take care of his own," as if that was an answer.

I asked Douglas about that and he just rolled his eyes and muttered something about Invisible Hank and the Pernicious Meme. But when I told him about Dr. Pettyjohn and his questions about HARLIE, both he and Mickey reacted sharply. "Stay away from him, Chigger."

"Why?"

Mickey swam over to me. "What do you think he wanted?"

"He wanted me to agree that souls only came from God."

"And what did you say?"

"I didn't say anything. I don't think about things like that. How can anyone know?"

"He asked you if HARLIE had a soul, didn't he?"

"Yeah—?"

"And the next question . . . ? Where do you think HARLIE's consciousness comes from? If not from God, then from where?"

I waited for him to tell me. Mickey waited for me to answer. I shrugged.

It didn't work. "Go ahead. Work it out, Chigger."

"The only thing I can think is . . . well, maybe souls don't come from Invisible Hank. Maybe souls are just born? Maybe your soul grows as you do?"

Mickey nodded. "Yes, that's what scares these folks. The existence of a soul that doesn't come from God suggests that there might not be a God—at least, not a God like they imagine. The existence of HARLIE threatens their sense of identity. So they have to have another explanation for HARLIE's existence. If God didn't create HARLIE's consciousness, who did—?"

"The devil?" I guessed.

"Right. And if you accept that idea, then HARLIE is a demonic being—and if Revelationists have sworn to destroy the tools of Satan, then what is your obligation . . . ?"

He let me work it out for myself. *"Oh!"*

"That's right."

"But that's stupid—if they destroy HARLIE, how will they get to New Revelation?"

Mickey shrugged. "The Lord will provide a way. That's what IRMA units are for."

"But isn't an IRMA unit sentient too?"

"Not like a HARLIE. It's okay to enslave the devil's tools and put them to work serving God; but a HARLIE unit is too smart—so smart that it can't be enslaved to God's purposes, so that means it's the devil's tool and it has to be destroyed."

I looked to Douglas. "He's putting me on, isn't he?"

"Nope."

"They really believe that?"

"Mickey should know."

"That is so *crazy!*"

"You don't know the half of it, Chigger. Just stay away from them."

Mickey added, "Mostly they stay in their part of the ship, and mostly we stay in ours. And that's the way everybody wants it."

"Then why are they on the *Cascade*?"

"Because they paid fourteen percent of its construction

costs. On every voyage to Outbeyond, the *Cascade* is contracted to deliver pilgrims and supplies to New Revelation."

"Oh," I said.

"And . . . they arranged the new IRMA unit for Commander Boynton."

"Well, he should be grateful for that, shouldn't he?"

"Not the way they did it," Mickey said. "The Captain didn't have a choice. They refused to let the ship boost with HARLIE running the hyperstate transitions."

"But why?"

"HARLIE scares them."

"Huh? What did he do to them?"

"What did he do to Luna? He doesn't seem to have a lot of regard for either the laws of man or the laws of God. Doesn't that scare you?"

"Invisible Luna had it coming. If they had left us alone, he would have left them alone."

Mickey said, "That's not the way they see it, Chigger. Look at it from their point of view. If HARLIE is a tool of the devil, he won't want them serving God, so he can't allow them to arrive at New Revelation. They're afraid that HARLIE will take the ship right into the nearest wormhole—and straight to Hell to deliver all of us to Satan himself."

"That's *silly*!" I stared at him in disbelief. "They should know better than that—"

"But they *don't* know better. And they think that you and I and Douglas are all brainwashed tools of HARLIE. Especially you."

"Now I *know* you're making this up."

"I wish I were, Charles. But these are the kind of people who make satirists commit suicide—because they can't keep up. As crazy as you or I might think these people are, that doesn't even approach what they think about us. They believe that anyone who hasn't had The Big Revelation is still under the influence of the devil. So that means everybody else is the enemy. That's why the rest of us have to be on our best behavior around these people until we get them off the ship. Do you understand?"

"Why didn't you tell me this sooner?"

"We didn't want to scare you."

"Well, I'm scared now."

"But now we're underway," said Douglas.

"That's even more scary. Now, we're stuck. We've got three more weeks to transit point and then ten weeks to New Revelation."

Douglas swam over to me and put his hands on my shoulders. "Charles," he said. "This isn't the *Cascade*'s first voyage. The crew has done this before, they know how to keep the two groups of colonists separated. As long as everyone follows the rules, we shouldn't have any trouble."

I looked him straight in the eye. "Douglas—ever since that first moment when Dad said, 'I've got an idea. Let's go to the moon,' that's *all* we've had. Trouble. Nothing but trouble. And each time, it's worse than before. Why do you think that's going to stop now?"

He didn't have an answer for that. I wish he had. I hate being right about stuff like that.

INTROSPECTIONS

WE KEPT A TIGHT beam connection with Earth as long as we could. After that, we relayed through the outer planet stations. The news from the homeworld wasn't good, and it wasn't going to get any better. Everything was still collapsing.

It takes a long time for a civilization to collapse. It falls apart by pieces—a little piece here, a little piece there. Then a big piece here, and a lot more pieces everywhere—but it still takes time for all the pieces to come down. It's like an avalanche. First one pebble, then another—each one knocks another stone loose—and in those first few moments, you think maybe nothing bad is going to happen; but pretty soon a whole bunch of stones are rolling, and then it's too late, because the whole mountainside is sliding. And sliding. And sliding.

And on Earth, *all* the mountains were coming down.

We'd been watching it for six weeks now, a little bit more every day. And every day that things fell apart with no one stopping them, with no one trying to stop them, that was another day of chaos that would have to be repaired. Douglas said that every day without law, without order, convinces people that there isn't going to be any more law and order. That's when things start to get ugly. There's nothing like a plague or six to turn neighbor against neighbor.

Lunar Authority estimated that over two billion people had already died, and that it was likely to get a lot worse. One commentator said that the breakdown point is twenty percent. When a society loses twenty percent of its population, it starts to unravel. And some parts of Earth had already lost thirty or forty percent.

I couldn't imagine it. I couldn't imagine what it must be like to be on Earth, terrified that everything was out of control and there was no way to get anything back to anyplace resembling normal. I couldn't imagine what it must be like to be on Luna or Mars and not be able to do anything. I would be glad when we entered hyperstate and I could start to pretend that there was no such place as Earth, except as a bad memory.

But what I couldn't understand most was how people could be so stupid. Why did people have to fight with each other? If everybody cooperated, everybody would have a better chance of survival, wouldn't they?

That line of thinking only brought me right back to the *Cascade*. The same question could be asked here. Why couldn't the Revelationists cooperate with the rest of us?

—of course, they were asking the same question from their side. Why didn't the rest of us cooperate with them?

The problem was the word *cooperate*.

What most people mean when they say "let's cooperate" is

really "let's do it *my* way." Which is why other people *don't* cooperate.

I guess I'd been naïve. I'd thought/hoped/believed/imagined that once we were away from Earth, the Line, and Luna, once we were aboard the starship, we'd finally get away from all the crap of people fighting with each other. That was why I wanted to go—to get away from all the fighting. But no, we were just taking it with us. More of the same old same old that had pulled the Earth apart. So it didn't really matter where we went, did it? We'd just keep doing it to each other, one planet after another. Earth, Luna, Mars, New Revelation, Out-beyond, and whatever came after that.

If this is what it meant to be a human being, I didn't like it. I was really sorry I'd ever started puberty.

There was this thing back on Earth where you could delay puberty for as much as seven years, depending on your meta-bolism. Doug had delayed for two years, and Mom had gotten a tax benefit. I had delayed a little bit—at least until Dad said, "Let's go to the moon." Now I was wishing I'd brought a lifetime supply of the damn pills.

Of course, then I thought of J'mee, and I realized that even if I had brought a supply of puberty retardants, I'd have al-ready thrown them away by now. I liked smiling.

So, how do adults balance this stuff? All the good stuff seems so small in comparison with all the bad.

When I asked Douglas and Mickey about it, as helpful as they tried to be, sometimes the best they could do was shrug and throw up their hands and say, "Hey, if we knew the an-swer to that, we wouldn't be here on the same spaceship as you, would we?"

Later that shift—I didn't think in days anymore—I found Gary and Trent and Kisa practicing their music in the aft ob-servatory/lounge. We didn't have a practice session scheduled, but all three of them were impatient to join the band, so they got together whenever they could and jammed. Well, half-jammed. It was pretty hellatious noise. But they were enthu-siastic and they were loud and they were having a good time and they reminded me of me when I was six and banging away on the keyboard. I didn't care how I sounded, as long as I was making sound. That's what I felt like doing now.

—except they all stopped when I came in. Kisa said, "Trent needs to talk to you." I could see by the expression on Trent's face that he'd wished Kisa had kept her big mouth shut (again). Whatever it was, he'd wanted to tell me himself, in his own time.

"What's the problem?" I sounded like Douglas when I said it. Very much in charge.

"Nothing." But he wouldn't look at me.

"Then what's Kisa talking about?"

"Well, um—"

"Did someone say you couldn't practice with us anymore?"

He shook his head. "No. It doesn't work like that."

"How does it work?"

He didn't really want to say, but finally he sighed and said, "Well . . . um, Our Heavenly Father gave us free will so we could choose between good and evil. So life is all about learning how to tell the difference. And, um . . . making the right choices."

I was starting to figure it out. "You think I'm evil?"

"No, I don't think *you're* evil." Trent took a deep breath. Then he blurted, "But I think HARLIE is evil. I think he's using you and you don't know it. A lot of people think so."

"You're not the first person to say that." Again, I sounded like Douglas.

"Well, if you already know it, then why do you keep choosing evil?"

"Because *I* don't think he's evil."

I thought that would end it right there, but it didn't. Because Trent asked the question that I couldn't answer.

"Do you even know what evil is?" he asked.

"Sure, I do. Everybody does."

"Then tell me what it is. How do you define evil, Charles?"

I had the sudden weird feeling that I was outgunned here—that Trent knew more about this than I did. I said slowly, "Evil is when somebody does bad things to people who don't deserve it."

Trent looked at me with an innocent expression. "So it's all right to do bad things to people who *do* deserve it?"

"Well, um—I guess it depends on whether or not it's self-defense."

"You don't really know what evil is, do you?"

"Okay," I said. This was probably the only safe way out of this trap. "You tell me."

Trent took a breath. I got the feeling he was about to repeat something from one of his Sunday School lessons. And maybe I wasn't getting out of this trap after all. He spoke carefully. "The way you distinguish what something is, you look at its opposite and see what the difference is between them. So, if you want to know what evil is, first you have to know what it means to be *good*."

I glanced over to Kisa and Gary. Kisa looked annoyed, she knew where this was going, but Gary seemed honestly interested. I just wanted to know why the Revelationists thought HARLIE was evil.

"Goodness is empowerment," Trent said. "Goodness makes a positive difference for other people. Goodness inspires and educates and makes people better off. Goodness is unselfish; it's about focusing on the wants and needs of others. You recognize goodness by the fact that it makes people joyous." His face was beaming as he described goodness—as if he was speaking from personal experience.

"Okay," I said. "That sounds right."

Kisa looked like she wanted to say something, but Gary gave her a *shut up* look, and for once it worked.

Meanwhile, Trent was gathering up the rest of his courage. This was the part he didn't like talking about; he looked very unhappy—it made me wonder what had happened to him before he'd arrived here on the *Cascade*. "Evil," he began slowly, "is the opposite of goodness. Evil *hurts* people. Evil disempowers and diminishes. Evil makes people small and mean. You recognize when evil is at work because people get ugly and hurtful. Ultimately, evil is selfish. It's about what the *self* wants—at the expense of everyone else."

Trent's explanation sounded too simple to me. And not really complete. But I knew I couldn't argue with him. Because he'd already learned how to win this argument and I'd never really thought about any of this stuff before.

"What about a baby?" asked Kisa.

"What about a baby?" Trent blinked.

"Is a baby evil?"

"No."

"But a baby is selfish."

"Only because it doesn't know any better."

"What about children? Children are selfish. They hurt each other."

"Only because they haven't been taught the difference between good and evil. When you know the difference, you'll always choose good, won't you?"

Kisa didn't answer. She was thinking it over. Not bad, Trent. You actually asked her something that left her speechless. But not for long—

"Well, that's your mistake then. HARLIE is like a baby. He's less than a year old. He has the emotions of a baby."

"HARLIE *isn't* like a baby," Trent said. "He's smart enough to know better. Isn't that true, Charles? You know him better than anybody."

I nodded. Yes, I knew HARLIE better than anybody, but that didn't mean I really *knew* him.

Trent said, "HARLIE and his brothers wrecked the Earth. They caused the polycrisis. And then HARLIE wrecked the Lunar economy too when he opened up all the files of invisible Luna. What more proof do you need?"

I didn't have an answer for that. I'd spent more than a few nights wrestling with that very dilemma. HARLIE was taking care of us, because we were necessary to his survival. At least I was. And everybody else was important to my survival. So HARLIE would do anything he could to protect me, and that meant protecting my family, and protecting the ship . . . So that was *good*, wasn't it?

But in the act of protecting the ship, we'd hurt a lot of people—maybe more people than we would ultimately save—

So maybe that *wasn't* good.

For a moment, I was flustered, then I thought of something. "But HARLIE isn't always selfish. He's been sending emergency instructions back to Earth and Luna—what they can do to recover. He doesn't have to do that."

"But he didn't start doing it until you told him to, I'll bet—"

I thought about it.

Trent was right.

Maybe HARLIE had done it only to make me happy. I wished HARLIE were here now to defend himself. Nobody could win an argument against HARLIE.

And that was part of the problem too.

I wanted to talk this over with HARLIE, but I knew that if I did that, I'd be passing the responsibility back to him, and he'd just convince me again that everything was all right, and I wouldn't have to worry about this at all.

Except—

What if Trent was right? What if HARLIE really was selfish—so selfish that he was dangerous to everybody around us? Maybe even me and Douglas and Bobby, and Mickey and Mom and Bev. Maybe he was only taking care of us as long as we were useful to him.

This was something I'd have to figure out for myself. Because if Trent was right about God giving us free will so we could make our own choices, then I *couldn't* ask anybody else for advice, could I?

I did not sleep well that night.

Just how do you tell the difference between good and evil?

The bad news was that I was going to have a lot of time to worry about it.

BEING RIGHT

THE TRUTH ABOUT SPACE travel is that it's mostly boring.

It's a long way from here to anywhere and it takes so long to get there that it's like being in jail. The worst part is when you realize you're not even halfway there and it doesn't matter what you do, every day in front of you is going to be exactly like every day behind you. You eat, you sleep, you do your job—whatever it is you're assigned to—you go to class, you spend two hours in the centrifuge, you eat and sleep some more, and each day blurs into the next so completely, most of the time you don't even know where you are on the calendar.

This is the part they don't tell you about—that the dark between the stars is also the *dead* between the stars. You have to invent ways to keep yourself alive. For me, that was the music.

Mom taught singing classes, and I taught keyboard and orchestra. Orchestra was best, because I got to wave the stick. We had forty-three students. We would have had more, but a lot of people who wanted to participate didn't have enough time in their schedules—and even if they did, we didn't have enough instruments, so everybody had to share. But the machine shop promised to fabricate more after we dropped off the Revelationists. We'd have a lot more room in the ship then. Things were still pretty cramped. While we weren't exactly hot-bunking, we still had to watch where we put our elbows.

For the first few weeks, the *Cascade* Symphony Orchestra was mostly chaos and for a while it didn't seem like we were ever going to make the leap from noise to music. We sounded like the Portsmouth Sinfonia, which was an almost-famous orchestra that Dad used to talk about. The Portsmouth Sinfonia was the most egalitarian musical group ever formed. Anybody could join, even if they'd never had a music lesson in their life. The effect was . . . awe-inspiring. Astonishing. Frightening. A new level of musical accomplishment. Anyway, that's what we sounded like—until we decided that we had to distinguish between equal opportunity and unequal ability.

Equal opportunity meant that everybody could try out. You could try out every six weeks, and you had to play two pieces of music—one that you chose, one that we chose. Usually we chose something we were already trying to learn. Only those musicians who received a majority of votes from those already in the band-orchestra could join. That made for some hurt feelings for a while, but it also increased enrollment in the music classes and practice labs. By the time we were approaching transit-point, we were already better than the Portsmouth Sinfonia, and some folks were talking about scheduling our first concert.

Commander Boynton liked the idea, and when he put it to the committee, they agreed—even the Revelationists, as long as the music was properly respectful. That puzzled me. I'd thought that there was a lot of resentment of the Revelationists because they were such unpleasant people—but in fact, they weren't. Mostly, they were good people, helping out, making a difference—and not just for themselves, but for everybody. So why did the Outbeyonders resent them? By Trent's definition of good and evil, they were behaving properly and the rest of us weren't. There was a lot of gossip and some of it was pretty ugly.

J'mee and I talked about it. I figured if anyone would know, she would. She thought about it for a bit—she went away for a few minutes while she accessed the ship's network; finally she came back and said, "It's a communication dynamic."

"Huh?"

"Well, let me put it this way. If you win an argument, what's the first thing you should do?"

I shrugged. "I dunno."

"Apologize."

"Huh?"

She repeated it. "*Apologize*."

"But why? Apologizing means you're admitting you're wrong—"

She looked at me like I'd said something stupid.

"—doesn't it?"

"Nope. Apologizing has nothing to do with right and wrong. It has everything to do with other people's feelings. So when you're right—*especially* when you're right—you should apologize."

Now it was my turn to look at her. "You're going to have to explain that to me. I took a stupid pill this morning."

She took an exasperated breath. As if it was so obvious, only an idiot would fail to understand. "Think about it. If you get to be right, what does that make the other person—?"

"Wrong?" I was half-guessing.

"Yes," she agreed. "If you're right then the other person has to be wrong. You don't really win an argument, not ever— you just make the other person wrong. You make someone else wrong every time you make yourself right. And that's the mistake—"

"Um. I'm not sure I get that—"

"How many friends do you make by winning arguments?"

"I never thought about it—I always thought people wanted to have the right answer. Don't they?"

"Do you like it when somebody else knows better than you? No, you don't. You resent it. *Everybody* does."

"Oh," I said. I was beginning to get it.

"Right. Nobody likes to be wrong. So if you win an argument, you've made the other person wrong, you've made them feel bad. For that moment, you've made an enemy. So the first thing you should do is apologize."

"But what if the other person really *is* wrong? Are you saying I should apologize for being right about something?"

"Yes."

"Huh?"

"You're not getting it, Charles. You're still making being right more important than being human." She looked at me as seriously as she ever had. "What do you win for being right?"

I flustered for a moment. I'd stepped into another one of those logical bear traps. This required a different way of thinking. And I didn't know how to think this way. I didn't see how I could win this argument. Even if I won, I still lost. "But . . . I thought it was all about getting the right answer—"

"That's because you went to a tube-school. Right answers are useful. But *being* right isn't."

"*Being* right. . ." The way she kept repeating the word *being*—I was starting to get it.

"It's called self-righteousness. Self-righteous means you think you know the truth and nobody else does. Do you know anyone like that?"

"Sure. Lots of people. Douglas, Stinky. My mom—especially when she was pissed at Dad. Even me, sometimes."

"Even you, a *lot*."

"Uh—" I didn't want to admit it, but she was right.

"*Everybody* does it, Charles, it's just that nobody admits it. We all know that *being* righteous is wrong, so we pretend we're not being right so that we can be right about it."

"Huh—? Wait a minute." I had to play that back in my head to decipher it.

"Self-righteousness," she repeated. "Some people do it a lot, some people do it way too much. The worst kind of self-righteousness is the religious kind. Because when you pour God over everything, like ketchup, you're saying you don't like the original flavor. It's very insulting. Myself, I think blaming God is the ultimate way to pass the buck." She pinched her face up and said mockingly, "*I'm not being self-righteous. I'm just telling you what God says.*' That's the worst kind of self-righteousness, because no matter how nice someone pretends to be, there's no room for anyone else to say anything, because one person is claiming the authority to speak for God."

"Oh," I said. Her ferocity startled me. It shouldn't have. I already knew she was strong willed.

"That's why everybody hates the Revelationists."

"I haven't heard any of the Revelationists say anything like that."

"They don't have to say it. It's all in their book. The Testament of The New Revelation. Only people who accept the Revelation are going to heaven. Everyone else—no matter how good they are—will go to hell and burn forever. God says so. Case closed."

"They really believe that?"

"They say they do."

I shook my head in exasperation. "People are crazy."

"Yes? What's your point?"

"So, what if they're right?" I asked. "Most of them seem like really nice people. They're always saying things like 'God bless you' and 'Be of good cheer.' They bring cakes and cookies to every gathering. They work harder than anybody. They take the best care of the babies—"

"And they do it because they want to prove that they're right—so the rest of us will stop sinning and join them."

"But I'm not sinning—"

"If you haven't accepted the Revelation, you're a sinner."

"They've *never* said that."

"Of course not. If they said it that way, you'd stop listening. All the nice things they're doing, that's to keep you engaged in the discussion."

I sighed. "I don't get it. They're the ones who are acting good, and they're the ones who are wrong?"

"No, they're not *wrong*. They believe what they believe. Just like you believe what you believe. But what they believe is that *you're* wrong for not believing the same way. If you asked them about it, they'd tell you that they're only trying to save your soul. That's how much they love you. Now stand still while they pour ketchup over your head."

For a moment, I had this really strange thought that what J'mee was saying was *evil*. It fit Trent's definition. It was hurtful and ugly and the intention was to disempower somebody. But this was J'mee who made me smile—so how could she be speaking evil? Unless I was evil too—? This was confusing. And frustrating.

I whirled around, looking for a wall to pound. This was *so* stupid. I whirled back to her. I was angry—not at her, but at something I couldn't put my hands on. The logic trap.

"Douglas used to do this to me!" I said, raising my voice. "He'd argue me into a corner. He did it on purpose. He'd prove to me that I didn't know what I was talking about. I hated it. And it didn't matter which side of the argument I took, either side was wrong. Both sides were wrong. And now you're doing the same thing too." She was looking at me, all hurt—I had to stop myself before I said worse. "I'm not mad at you, J'mee. I'm mad at the argument. I'm mad at everybody else for making up such stupid arguments. This is stupid— why do people tie themselves into such knots?"

J'mee looked sad. "Because people like being right. And the best way to be right is to say that God is on your side." And then she added, "And that's the best way to piss off everybody else too."

I couldn't answer that.

She was right.

And then I got it. Some things were *true*. They were so, whether you believed in them or not. And some things were just stories—

I floated there in the lounge, realizing the *truth* of what she'd said, and my anger started to drain away. I actually felt lightheaded. And it wasn't just the zero gee.

"You're right," I said, grinning.

She grinned back. "Then I apologize."

"Me too."

And then she kissed me. This apologizing business wasn't so bad after all. . . .

FOURTEEN

EXCEPT EVERY SO OFTEN, the boredom ends, and then things get real exciting.

The first thing that happened was that I turned fourteen.

I almost forgot, except Mom remembered. She came to me and apologized that she didn't have anything to give me as a birthday present, and I said that was all right, I didn't really need a present. I'd gotten my family back and that was all I wanted, and she said that was the nicest thing I'd ever said to her, and then she hugged me tight. "Have I told you how much I love you?" And that was the best birthday present she could have given me, because I'd waited so long to hear it.

But we did have a party, and that surprised me; because a lot of the Revelationist families showed up—and not too many of the Outbeyond colonists, which surprised me even more.

Trent's Mom and Dad came. She baked cookies—with real chocolate chips—and told me to eat as many as I wanted. Trent's Dad thanked me for spending so much time teaching Trent the clarinet. And Trent's aunts and uncles and cousins showed up too, and a bunch of other people I didn't know, but they all seemed to know each other. And then Commander Boynton passed through on his way from someplace to someplace else; I was sure that wasn't accidental, but he did take a moment to say he was glad to have me aboard, especially for the music. So of course, we had an impromptu concert—and we were all lousy, but no one seemed to mind; they applauded enthusiastically and cheered.

But in the middle of that, Kisa floated over and whispered, "Be careful, Charles."

"Why?"

"They're trying to love-bomb you."

"Love-bomb?"

"I'll explain later. Just don't agree to anything." And she grabbed a handful of chocolate chip cookies—they were stuck to a sticky-plate—and sailed off. And then I forgot about it because I was having too much fun. J'mee was holding my hand, except when her dad stopped by and grumbled a happy birthday.

He hadn't said anything to us since that first day, and he still didn't like us very much, so I think he was just checking up on J'mee. J'mee said that her dad was sort of coming around to accepting the way things were; he'd even begun talking about teaching us how to use the HARLIE properly. If we were interested. But we'd have to ask. Because he wasn't going to volunteer. Because he didn't want to look pushy and aggressive. That's what J'mee said.

It was a short party—most parties were, because we were all on different shifts, and some of us had to get to work and others had to get to school and still others had to get some sleep. And besides, we were only two days from transit and all the preparations we had to do before launch we had to do again, three times over. Launch-prep was the drill; this was for real—because once we leapt into hyperstate, that was it, there was no possibility of coming back ever.

Right up to the moment of transition, we could change our minds. We could turn the ship around, we could decelerate for as long as we had accelerated, and then we could start accelerating back to L-5 again. If we wanted to. It would take at least three and a half weeks of deceleration to burn off the speed we'd built up, and then at least seven more weeks of acceleration and deceleration back toward Earth. Actually, according to Douglas, it would be nine or ten weeks returning, because Earth would have moved a third of the way around the sun in the ensuing four months, and we'd have to cover that distance too.

But that was all theoretical. We weren't going back. The transition to hyperstate was the real launch to New Revelation and Outbeyond. Everything up to now had just been taxiing on the runway—getting out far enough to where it would be safe to initiate a hyperstate envelope.

There was a rumor going around that Reverend Dr. Pettyjohn had petitioned Commander Boynton to observe transition on the flight deck. Commander Boynton hadn't wanted to, but Reverend Pettyjohn was insistent. I guess he wanted to make sure that HARLIE was only observing and wasn't actually participating. According to the rumor, Commander Boynton had agreed. But nobody I asked would say if it was true. They just said, "Yep, I heard that rumor too."

And then, in the middle of my sleep shift, I woke up with a start. Something went *klunk* in my head.

Being right—everything that J'mee had said—that's why all these people were afraid of HARLIE. That's why *everybody* was afraid of HARLIE.

And me too.

Because HARLIE was *always* right.

HARLIE had been built to be right. It was hardwired into him—even more so than human beings. He had to find the right answer. Every time. And he had to tell it. Every time.

And every time he did that . . . it drove human beings crazy and made everything worse.

Did HARLIE figure that into his logic . . . ?

Or didn't he care?

How could being right be wrong?

Was it possible to be right in a way that *didn't* hurt others?

THE HIDEOUT

THE *CASCADE* HAD TWO centrifuges, spinning in opposite directions to neutralize the effects of torque.

Both centrifuges had galleys and gyms and shower rooms, but only one of them was open for use. (And there was a lot of grumbling about that.) The other one was out of service, filled with crates of rice, noodles, and beans. Blame HARLIE for that too.

There were fifteen hundred people on the starship, each of whom was required to spend at least two hours a day at Earth-normal (or higher) gee. And no matter how you sliced it, that meant that at any given time, there were 125 people in the wheel. Usually more.

The wheel was pretty big and people spaced themselves around it as well as they could, but it was like being in a giant subway car with curved floors—always crowded. Enough to be annoying.

But as part of one of the Moebius races, we had to go into the *other* centrifuge. It was a lot like the first, only it was stuffed full of extra supplies: boxes and tanks and drums of all sizes and kinds. Medicine. Tools. Fabric. Chemicals. Shelterfoam. Fabricators. Machines. Seeds. Microchips. Everything. And of course, lots of boxes of rice and beans and noodles. There was a gym in this centrifuge too, though all the gym machines were dismantled, and even the shower room was jammed full of boxes. But there was just enough wiggle room to get into the corner, and for some reason, the six of us had turned it into a hideout. Me and J'mee, Trent and Gary, Kisa and Chris. (Chris liked Kisa a lot, it was obvious he wished that she would be his girlfriend, but Kisa didn't seem to notice. Or maybe she did. Who knew?)

Whenever we could, we found time to hang out down there. There wasn't a lot of time—in fact, there was less time than there was room; but it was a place where we could go where we wouldn't be seen by some passing crew member and grabbed for an extra work detail. Usually some make-work thing like wiping down walls with disinfectant or something.

The crew had this really nasty habit—they couldn't stand to see anyone sitting or resting. You had to be doing something productive all the time. And if you weren't doing anything, they found something for you to do. And by the end of the second week, we were getting resentful. All of the Moebius teams were.

Yes, we knew that this was a life-or-death journey, and we were just as committed as everybody else, but it wasn't fair that any passing crew person could put us to work whenever he felt like it. We didn't object to doing our fair share—even more than our share, if necessary; but we had full schedules of classes *and* work details too, so we didn't have a lot of free time. What little we had was important to us—we objected to having it taken away on a whim by someone who didn't know and didn't care that we might be doing something much more important than wiping the wall down one more time—like talking to each other about important stuff.

We'd complained about it—to the Colony Council, to the Ship's Officers, to our parents—even to Commander Boynton. They all said the same thing, although not all in the same words: "You knew the job was dangerous when you took it . . ."

So we found hideouts. The centrifuge wasn't the easiest, but it was the best, because nobody came here except on purpose.

We were a pretty good team. Even our differences were interesting. Gary was from Kenya; Chris was from New Jersey—although to look at them, side by side, you'd have guessed the opposite. J'mee was from Canada. Kisa was from Quebec. Trent was from Idaho.

What was interesting to me was that even though I didn't like a lot of what the Revelationists believed, Trent was the nicest of the group. And even though I agreed with most of what Kisa had to say, most of the time I wished she'd shut up and not say it, because when she did say it, people got pissed off. More than once, J'mee and I exchanged glances. (Kisa is *being* right again.)

And that was one of the things we talked about too—about how most of the Revelationists were really good people. Sincere. Kind. Compassionate. Helping. Generous. It was just that everything was "God bless this" and "God bless that." Nobody ever got credit for doing a good job. It was always God's victory. And if something went wrong, God was trying to teach us a lesson. "God never gives you a cross bigger than you can carry." And so on.

One day, Kisa finally told us why her family had broken away from the others—it was a long story and I didn't pay attention to a lot of it, because by then I was getting pretty bored with Kisa being angry all the time; but it was clear that she had a good reason to be angry and I couldn't fault her for that. But once in a while, could she please stop doing anger and just do something else? *Please?*

But mostly, despite our differences of opinion, we actually *liked* each other. Because even if we disagreed, we could still *talk* to each other. And not just talking—listening too. Because sometimes, that's all you really need, someone who can just *listen* while you unload for a while.

Back in El Paso, I'd always used my music to get away. I would go off into the hills above the tube-town. Only, now . . . I didn't need the music for hiding out anymore. And that was nice to realize. It was funny, though—that I had to go to a different kind of hideout to discover I didn't need to hide out . . .

MOMENTUM

For ABOUT A HUNDRED years, hyperstate was only a theory.

If gravity worked like light—it doesn't, but if it did—then it could be focused, reflected, amplified, made coherent, lased, phased, and disarrayed. Whatever. It was a terrific theory, and a lot of scientists sold a lot of books writing about it. And a lot of other scientists sold a lot more books explaining why this terrific theory was just so much wishful thinking.

And then somebody who hadn't paid too much attention to either of the theories discovered this really weird effect of light and electricity and magnetism—that a gravity field could be stretched, sort of, pushed in or pulled out like a rubber ball, but not quite, because it did strange things to the space around it too. And he called that a gravitational lens. And it didn't fit anybody's theory, so a lot more scientists sold a lot more books explaining that too.

For the longest time it was a laboratory trick, because nobody could figure out what to do with it. You could use it to push things down or pull them up, but there were other, faster, better ways to push things down or pull them up that used a lot less energy.

But then one day, somebody began to wonder what would happen if you overlaid a whole bunch of gravitational lenses all focused on the same place, and he managed to blow a hole in New Jersey three kilometers in diameter. Pretty impressive. But just before that particular part of the state disappeared, for just an instant, there was this *thing*—and when the *thing* disappeared, so did part of New Jersey. But the weird part was that the lab itself was untouched. It was still standing unscathed at the epicenter of nine square kilometers of rubble and dead bodies.

So they repeated the experiment in deep space—out between the orbits of Earth and Mars, and this time the *thing* lasted for several seconds. And when the *thing* disappeared this time, the spaceship was on the other side of the solar system. Out beyond the orbit of Neptune. Out in the Kuiper Belt. They were six weeks coming back.

The next time they tried it—well, you can look it up—they spent a lot of time sending spaceships all over everywhere, because they had no way to control where they were going. They spent twenty years experimenting and eventually somebody figured it out.

When you focus enough gravity lenses on the same place, you rip a hole in space. Sort of. You turn a part of space inside out—like a black hole, except it isn't—it's more like blowing a bubble from the inside. The bubble is its own little universe, infinite in size, except it isn't—its event horizon is really very close, like a couple of kilometers away from the locus of probability.

If you twiddle the shape of the bubble—you do this by altering the push and pull of the individual gravity lenses, and you have to be real careful when you do this—the bubble moves through real-space. But because it doesn't have any mass or inertia or even existence in real-space, the real-space laws of physics don't apply. So it can travel as fast as you want. Theoretically, you can go a couple gazillion times the speed of light. Theoretically. But the best any Earth-built starship had achieved so far was seventy-five C, and that was only on a short run, and they burned out two hyperstate fluctuators trying it.

The problem was that the lenses needed to focus on a target of very dense mass. The heavier the better. You can't just point your lens anywhere—you have to point it at *something* because you have to have some gravity to stretch. Neutronium would be ideal, but nobody had any neutronium laying around, so the Lunar colliders were used to generate quantities of eugenium 932, which wasn't anywhere near as good as neutronium, but it was six times better than lead or uranium. Inert, dense, and otherwise useless, except for taking up space.

According to one theorist, a pinpoint black hole would be the best target, but nobody had any of those lying around either—although this same guy said that if you could focus enough gravitational lenses on a sufficiently dense mass, you could implode it and create a pinpoint black hole, and last we'd heard he was raising the money to build a black-hole generator—except with the polycrisis on Earth, that probably wasn't going to happen now. But according to his theory, you would only need six lenses focused on a pinpoint black hole, and that would still be so efficient that you could probably achieve speeds of three hundred to four hundred C.

We had to learn all this in class. Because maybe someday somebody would invent starships that fast, and then travel between Earth and Outbeyond would be possible in only one month instead of seven. And then it wouldn't be so much of a one-way trip anymore.

The other problem with hyperstate was gravity wells. Stars and planets have enormous gravity wells—stars especially—much larger than most people realize. The effects of Sol's gravity, for instance, can be felt all the way out beyond the Kuiper Belt, all the way out beyond the Oort Cloud. It's very faint at that distance, but it's still detectable. The point is that the sun's gravitational field affects the size and shape of the hyperstate bubble when it's initiated. It makes it hard to shape and control precisely.

Boynton said that if we had a pinpoint black hole as our target mass, we'd have more leverage and we could initiate hyperstate within the solar system without risking dangerous deformation of the hyperstate envelope, but we didn't, so we had to go farther out to get a spherical bubble. The same problems would apply at our destination. We'd have to drop out of hyperstate far from the star. Fortunately, we'd still have all the inherent velocity that we'd built up moving away from the Earth, so we'd use that to approach the target planet, decelerating all the way in. We might also loop around a planet or even the star to burn off velocity—I wasn't sure about the orbital mechanics on that yet; we hadn't gotten that far in class.

Our teachers didn't expect any of us to become quantum engineers, but they did want everybody onboard to understand that starship technology is very complex, and not just because it involves a lot of math, but because it involves a lot of momentum. An object in motion will continue to move in the same direction—changing direction requires the application of energy; usually lots of it. So the idea that we could just hop in a starship, point it at our destination, and punch the "on" button—well maybe that looks good on TV, but it doesn't work that way in real life.

Dr. Oberon, our science teacher, explained it this way: "Everything costs energy. The question you have to ask is whether or not you can afford to spend that energy and whether or not the result is worth the expenditure. This is going to be a very important question when we get to Outbeyond. You're going to have to ask it about everything you do for a long long time. Maybe your entire life."

But finally, after all the talk and all the classes and all the preparations and all the checklists and all the drills and all the double-checks and all the warnings and all the triple-checks and everything else—finally, we were ready for transit.

FAREWELL TO EARTH

WE COULDN'T SEE THE Earth anymore. We were too far out. Even the sun had dwindled to the size of every other star. It was still the brightest one, but not for much longer. Pretty soon, we wouldn't be able to identify which star was Sol unless somebody asked a computer.

The last day before transition, the last hours, even the last minutes—everybody on board was sending their good-byes to Earth. Because once we jumped into hyperstate, we wouldn't be able to send or receive any radio or laser communication with Earth. All communication with the homeworld would be cut off.

Most communication had ceased already anyway. A lot of stations had stopped broadcasting, or they'd dropped off the network. Mostly what we were getting from Earth now were news reports of who was still viable. It was assumed that if someone wasn't broadcasting, they weren't there anymore. They'd succumbed to one thing or another.

But just in case, we all lined up to make our good-byes to everyone we knew, even if we had no idea if they were still alive or not. And some of us, who had no one left to say good-bye to—we just said good-bye to all the things on Earth we did remember.

It turned out to be a lot harder than I thought it would be.

Chris Pavek and I went up to the broadcast station together. We could have recorded our good-byes from our cabins as private messages—a lot of people were doing that—but just as many people wanted to say goodbye to the whole planet, so there were always a few folks waiting in the corridor, or at the far end of the cabin.

When our turn came, I asked Chris, "Do you want to go first?"

He shrugged. He was easygoing that way. So I pushed ahead.

I anchored myself in front of the camera and said, "Good-bye, Earth. Good-bye to all your smelly crowds, all your rude and pushy people, all the traffic and all the lines—all the lousy service and bad manners and selfishness, all the cruel words and bitter taunts. Good-bye to your tube-towns and your poverty. Good-bye to your thieves and beggars and liars and hypocrites. Good-bye to all the cheats and lawyers and politicians and slimy con men. Good-bye to all the bills and all the taxes and all the smog and all the greed and toxic crap. Good-bye to all the hatred and the nastiness. I'm not going to miss you."

And then I realized how ugly that sounded. And I sat there ashamed for a moment.

"And thank you too . . ." I said. "Thank you, Earth, for Beethoven and Saint-Saëns and Stravinsky and Copland and Gershwin. Thank you for Scott Joplin and Van Dyke Parks and William Russo and John Coltrane. Thank you for John Lennon and Paul McCartney. Thank you for Alan Parsons and Jimi Hendrix and Duke Ellington. Thank you for Billie Holiday and Ute Lemper and Kurt Weill and Judy Garland. Thank you for Janis Joplin and Freddy Mercury and Harry Nilsson. Thank you for Philip Glass and . . . and all the others I forgot to mention. Thank you for all the music. We're taking it with us. So thank you, Earth. Thank you for the music."

That was all I had to say, and then it was Chris's turn to broadcast his last thoughts—to Earth and Luna and Mars and all the other habitats and colonies in the solar system. He swallowed hard and said, "Hi, Dad. I miss you. I wish you were here with us." And then he added, "I'm sorry for all those things I said. I didn't mean it. And I'm sorry for all the things I should have said and couldn't. I'm sorry we didn't get a chance to really talk. That was my fault—I was scared, I didn't want to hear what you might say. And now, I'm not going to have that chance—I don't even know where you are or if you're even still alive—so I hope you're listening. I need you to know this."

He gulped and added, "I love you."

Then he wiped his eyes real quick—

—and then I was crying too, because everything he'd said, I wished I could have said to my dad when I'd had the chance. I felt it like a physical pain in my chest. What a jerk I'd been. There'd been all those times when Dad had said to me, "Hey, Chigger, is there anything you want to talk about?" And I'd just shrug and turn away and put my earphones back on. I'd had all that time to talk to him and all I did was push him away because I was always so pissed about this or that or the other thing. I couldn't even remember what I'd been angry about. So there was this whole conversation with Dad that I'd always wanted to have, but I just kept putting it off and putting it off because I wasn't ready to have it yet—and then one day I *couldn't* have it at all. At least, Chris's dad might have a chance to hear what Chris had to say. My dad never would—

Chris pushed out of the broadcast cabin so fast, it was like he was escaping from the room. He must have been real embarrassed. I wanted to tell him it was okay, he wasn't the only one who felt like that, but he was gone. Maybe later, I'd have the chance to tell him that what he'd said was a good thing—I wished I could have been that brave.

Chris and I weren't the only ones. A lot of folks were there, and most of them had tears in their eyes. It looked like a funeral, and I guess, in a way, it was. A funeral for a whole planet. There were an awful lot of good-byes to be said. And a lot of it was pretty raw stuff. A lot of apologies and confessions and even a whole bunch of ugly revelations. It wasn't pleasant. But a lot of people were suddenly realizing that they didn't want to drag all their old hurts onto the next world. Commander Boynton said it was like this every voyage, but that didn't make it any easier for the folks going through it.

Maybe if we hadn't all been aboard the same starship, it would have made for some pretty good gossip; but for some reason, it didn't feel right to gossip about each other. Like we were all in this together, and we had to be for each other, not against. So if somebody had something to say, they said it, and everybody else was there for back pats and hugs and tissues, if necessary—and if anyone else tried to make it an issue, they got stomped for it. Because that wasn't what we were here for anymore.

I'd never been in a place before where everybody worked so hard to take care of everybody else. I hoped it would last. But I knew it wouldn't—because it didn't matter that they'd stuck a stardrive engine on the end, we were still living in a tube-town. And I knew how tube-towns worked. Pretty soon, we'd all be hunkered in—

But meanwhile—it was a sad and solemn time. And people were sending a lot of really sweet and beautiful messages. There were over fifteen hundred people aboard, so it was going to take a while.

And all of it was going out live—without any editing at all, direct to Earth and everywhere. All over the ship too, so anyone who wanted to could listen. So for a while, it was like we were all just one giant family. And the messages would keep on going out, right up to the moment of transition.

I hoped there were still people on Earth to hear our goodbyes. More important, I hoped there were still people on Earth to hear their own music.

TRANSITION

TRANSIT WAS BOTH EXCITING and boring.

Exciting because we'd never done it before.

Boring because nothing exciting happened.

First IRMA reported that all the hyperstate flux grapplers were flux grappling. Then she reported that all the synchronizers were synchronizing. Then she reported that all the extrapolators were extrapolating. And all that was left was for Commander Boynton to tell her to initiate, and I suppose all the initiators initiated—because everything sort of *flickered* and then we were in hyperstate. Only I didn't feel any different.

After a moment, IRMA reported stabilization of the envelope. After a long series of integrity checks, Commander Boynton ordered the envelope deformed. . . .

—and then we were traveling faster than light. Three times as fast as light, in fact.

Outside the ship, the stars looked all rippled and green—like we were underwater. "That's the background radiation of space," said Damron. "Some of it has been shifted into the visible spectrum. Watch as we increase our speed. The colors will shift. It's the *aura superlumina*."

"Belay that," said Boynton. He called out a string of numbers—the deformation parameters of the hyperstate envelope. O'Koshi echoed them. IRMA accepted them. She *tick-tick-ticked* for a moment, then confirmed them. The hyperstate flux grapplers grappled some more and the shape of the hyperstate envelope stretched out imperceptibly.

—and then we were traveling ten times the speed of light.

It takes eight and a half minutes for light to get from the sun to the Earth. At our speed, we could cover the same distance in fifty-one seconds.

It still wasn't fast enough.

In class, Dr. Oberon had us do the math.

A light year is the distance light travels in one year.

At 300,000 kilometers per second, that's 18,000,000 kilometers a minute, or 1,080,000,000 klicks per hour. 25,920,000,000 kilometers per day. 181,440,000,000 kilometers per week. 9,460,800,000,000 kilometers per year. 9.46 trillion klicks.

At ten times the speed of light, we would travel one light year every thirty-six and a half days. That meant it would take us five months just to get to Proxima Centauri, four and one-third light years away. Outbeyond was thirty-five light years away. If we went there directly at ten times the speed of light, without stopping at New Revelation, it would take us 3.5 years. We would run out of food in thirty-six months, even with the farm growing a full set of crops.

Commander Boynton watched his displays for thirty minutes, allowing the IRMA unit to establish a baseline for stability. Then he ordered our speed increased to twenty C. At this speed, we would reach Outbeyond in one year and nine months. We'd get there hungry, but we'd get there.

This time, he held the hyperstate envelope at this pitch for a full hour. According to O'Koshi, if something was going to fail, it usually failed in the first thirty minutes. And if it did, we could still get back to Earth. We'd only be a couple solar distances away—a solar distance is the diameter of the solar system. It might take a year or more to get back, because we'd have to decelerate, turn around and accelerate back toward Earth, and then decelerate again on approach, but we could do it. Commander Boynton was being careful. If something was going to fail, he didn't want it to happen in the dark between the stars where we'd have no chance at all of getting back.

There was a theory—still untested—that a starship's plasma drives could eventually accelerate a ship to a significant fraction of C, the speed of light. Maybe one-third C. But it would take a long time. And I didn't want to be on the ship that had to test it. It would take three years to travel one light year. And that doesn't include acceleration and deceleration time.

Anyway, what it all meant was that once we were nine light months away from Earth, we were completely on our own.

Scary.

I tried not to think about it too much.

After another hour, Commander Boynton ordered our speed increased to forty C. And an hour after that, he pushed it up to fifty C. Now we were traveling one light year every seven days. If we were going to Proxima Centauri, which we were not because it was on the other side of the sky, we would be there in a little more than a month. At this speed, we could reach Outbeyond in eight months.

After a few more days of running, Commander Boynton intended to tweak our speed upward toward sixty C. That would shave six weeks off our travel time.

Inside, we didn't feel any different. How could we? We were in a bubble of real-space, isolated from the rest of real-space around us. The bubble moved, and we moved with it. And whatever speed we had when we entered hyperstate, we would still have that speed when we emerged again on the other side—sort of. There was a whole lot of theory about this too, about how inherent velocity was relative and how it could be manipulated and how if we turned ourselves inside the bubble, or if we turned the bubble, we could use our inherent velocity to our benefit at the exit point.

The point is, running a starship is hard work. A lot harder than you might think.

We sat in our couches and we watched the numbers on the display screens and we didn't talk. It was a long shift and mostly it was checklists and double-checks and triple-checks, and then silently waiting to see if any anomalies would show up. Nothing significant did, and the IRMA unit was able to apply appropriate compensations well within the range of optimal operation, so everything was running just the way we wanted it to. And every so often, I'd sneak a look at the little display next to HARLIE and it would be flashing a green confirming signal too.

At the end of the shift, Commander Boynton turned around and looked at Reverend Dr. Pettyjohn and asked, "Satisfied?"

"Yes, very much. Thank you." Reverend Pettyjohn looked pleased; he was wearing his polished-apple smile. "I do apologize for the inconvenience, Commander, and I thank you for your courtesy. My parishioners were seriously concerned, and we all appreciate that you've addressed our issues appropriately. We shall include you in our prayers. And of course, you are welcome to join our services anytime."

"Thank you, Reverend. Now that we are underway, perhaps I will have more time to attend." Then—deliberately?—he turned to the monkey. "HARLIE, may I have your report?"

HARLIE said, "The IRMA unit is functioning within its normal parameters of operation."

"Do you anticipate any problems or concerns?"

"No, I do not." And then, a heartbeat later. "If I may offer a suggestion, however . . ."

"Go ahead."

"There are certain multiplex phasing optimizations possible that are beyond the ability of your IRMA unit."

"Yes, we know that."

"These optimizations would allow the ship to safely increase realized velocity to as much as seventy-five C. That would reduce overall travel time by another two months over your top speed of sixty C."

"And we could achieve these optimizations . . . how?"

"Very simple—" said HARLIE.

I glanced over at Reverend Dr. Pettyjohn. The smile had disappeared. He no longer looked like a polished apple. More like a wrinkling prune.

"—if you were to install this HARLIE unit as the primary intelligence module of the IRMA engine—"

"Absolutely not," said Pettyjohn.

Commander Boynton held up a hand. "Dr. Pettyjohn, you are a guest on my bridge. I am asking the HARLIE unit for a report, nothing more."

"I apologize," said Pettyjohn. He settled back in his couch. But the damage had been done.

HARLIE concluded politely, "—the symbiosis of two intelligence engines would provide the necessary processing power for—"

"Shut up, HARLIE," I said.

The monkey fell instantly silent.

Boynton looked to me. "Am I going to have a problem with you?"

"No, sir."

He raised an eyebrow.

"May I make my report to the Captain?" Now, even O'Koshi and Damron had turned to look at me. And the two members of the relief crew who were stationed at the back of the bridge as well.

Boynton nodded.

I said, "I recommend against installing the HARLIE unit into a command and control position on this ship."

"Why?"

"Because of the nature of the HARLIE unit's personality."

"Go on . . ."

"It's my opinion," I began carefully, "based on my personal experience with this intelligence engine, that this unit is *cyber-tropic*."

"Cyber-tropic?"

"I made up the term, sorry. It means that it's attracted to information processing technology."

"Most intelligence engines are."

"Well, yes. But . . . not like this. HARLIE preempts other engines. He co-opts their functions. He's an info-blob, a cyber-amoeba, a techno-predator. He swallows up everything he comes in contact with. And then he uses it for his own needs. I don't know that we can trust him."

I couldn't have had a more devastating effect on the bridge crew if I'd set off a hand grenade. Even Reverend Dr. Petty-john looked at me surprised.

☾

BOYNTON

COMMANDER BOYNTON WASTED NO time taking me off the bridge—almost dragging me into the briefing room directly behind it. "Do you know what you're saying?"

"Yes, sir."

"Do you want to explain yourself?" He was angry. Very angry. Worse than I'd ever seen. He must have seen that he was scaring me because he took a moment to calm himself down. He looked away, looked toward the flight deck, took a deep breath, looked back to me, then spoke in a quieter tone. "What's going on, Charles?"

I swallowed hard. "I—I don't know."

"Are you scared?"

"Y-yes."

"What are you afraid of?"

"I'm not sure—"

He took another breath, and when he spoke again, he was even calmer than before. "We're already more than three light days out from Earth. Every minute that passes, we put another fifty light minutes behind us. Every hour, we put more than two light days behind us. I'm responsible for the safety of this ship and the fifteen hundred people aboard her. We brought that HARLIE unit on board because we believed it could get us to Outbeyond, and maybe even back again at some point in the future. If there's something wrong with it, I need to know."

"Yes, sir."

"So talk to me, son."

For some reason, I noticed I wasn't Ensign Dingillian anymore. Now I was "son." I guess he was trying to make it easier for me to talk to him—but Commander Boynton wasn't a man who was easy to talk to. I respected him, even feared him a little; but I didn't really like him very much.

He saw me hesitating. "Do you want me to call your brother up here? Would that help?"

"No, sir."

"All right, then talk to me. I'm listening."

So I talked to him. It all came out in a rush, and it probably didn't make much sense the way I explained it, all jumbled together like a jigsaw puzzle. Good and evil. Empowerment and disempowerment. Recognizing the difference. *Being* right. Arguments. Music. Holding hands. Love-bombs. Everything.

Boynton listened intensely, as if he were waiting for me to get to the punch line and put it all together. But there wasn't any punch line and there wasn't any way to put it all together. And when I finished, he just hung his head in an exasperated *why me* gesture for a moment. After a beat, he looked across to me again. "Have you talked to anyone else about this?"

"No."

"Your Mom?"

"Of course not. We're divorced."

"Your brother?"

"He's been too busy. He and Mickey."

"How about your counselor?"

"Uh-uh."

"No one at all."

"Just J'mee, like I told you—and that only made it worse."

"So you've been carrying all this around by yourself?"

"Yes, sir."

"I see." He didn't say anything for a long moment. He stared off into space, obviously thinking about his options. We could make it to Outbeyond with the IRMA unit—even with an untrained IRMA. We just couldn't depend on HARLIE as a backup.

And if we'd never had the HARLIE at all, if all we'd ever had was the IRMA, we could still make the crossing, and we would still have launched. No IRMA had ever failed in transit, so it wasn't like this was a serious setback . . .

And even if the IRMA did fail, even if we found ourselves without an IRMA, it was still possible to generate a hyperstate envelope and manipulate it enough to achieve realized velocities of five or even ten C. Maybe more. We could do it with desktop information processors if we had to. Douglas had done a simulation as a school project once. And he wasn't the only one; there were probably a million hobbyists tinkering with hyperstate simulations. Everybody wanted to be the person who invented the next advance in hyperstate technology, because there was a five-million-dollar prize for any practical advance worth ten C or more in realized velocity, and Ghu knew how much more in royalties.

Finally, Boynton turned back to me. "I understand your concerns, Charles. And I appreciate your candor—your honesty. I wish you hadn't said anything in front of Reverend Pettyjohn, I'll have to talk to him privately. Here's what I want you to do. Don't say anything to anyone about this. Don't discuss it, not with your brother, not with anyone. You understand? I don't want any more weird rumors floating around; certainly not now. So let's pretend that you just had a little panic attack on the flight deck. I understand you're afraid of heights? And maybe a little claustrophobic? You had a little trouble on the Line, and again when you stowed away on the cargo pod? And again on Luna?"

"Yeah," I admitted. "But I got over those."

"Yes, I know that too. But let's pretend that's what happened here. And meanwhile, over the next few weeks, let's you and I start running integrity checks on HARLIE. We should have been doing it before; but there was so much work to do, and we needed HARLIE's management skills so much that we didn't stop to ask—and that's my fault. I just assumed—" He stopped himself and looked momentarily embarrassed. I'd never seen an adult admit a mistake before. It was an interesting experience.

"Anyway," he said. "Is it a plan?"

"Sounds like one to me."

"Thank you." He held out his hand and we shook on it.

The shift ended and he sent me back to my cabin to rest. As I left, he was motioning Dr. Pettyjohn into the briefing room.

HUMAN

I KEPT HAVING THIS feeling that something awful was going to happen, but I didn't know what. Or when. It was just this feeling that wouldn't go away.

I asked Douglas about it: did he ever get that queasy kind of premonition like he was about to run headlong over a cliff or into a wall—or both at once? He said, "All the time. It's normal. It's called life."

"Douglas, please—I'm not joking."

"Neither am I. C'mere. Have some tea." Douglas was being uncommonly patient these days. He didn't seem like the same person anymore. Maybe it was Mickey. Or maybe it was because he was head of the family now and had to be responsible for me and Stinky. Or maybe it was just because this was who he really was when he didn't have to be my weird geeky brother anymore. Or maybe it was because I was listening to him more than I used to.

Douglas explained that it was commonplace for people on

long voyages to become fearful for the future, especially if they were under any kind of stress. "And we've been under more stress than most people. Especially you, Chigger. So you're probably still expecting some kind of payoff. Like the end of a movie. Except life doesn't happen that way. Life isn't organized—it just *happens*."

"Yeah, I saw that written on the restroom wall. *Life happens*."

"You think there should be a plan, don't you. Some kind of pattern—?"

"Well, I think if there's any meaning to it all, we should be able to work it out, shouldn't we?"

Douglas rolled his eyes. "Why? Who says we have to understand?"

"I dunno. It just seems—"

"Yeah, it *seems*. That's the way human beings work, Chigger. We need to have explanations. We need to have meanings. We need to see the plan. So we look for patterns—everything is about *patterns*—and even if there aren't any, we make them up anyway. We make up stories for ourselves about how everything works, because we can't stand *not* knowing—and after we've made up some nice neat little story, we expect the rest of life to match it. And then we get really crazy when it doesn't."

That sort of made sense. As far as it went.

I sort of understood, but I didn't.

Finally, just out of curiosity—to see what he would say— I asked HARLIE about patterns, without really telling him *why* I was asking.

HARLIE said that there really *were* patterns in life, but we get bombarded with so much information about so many different events all seeming to happen at the same time that it's more than we can assimilate, and so it looks a lot more like chaos than meaning. In fact, according to HARLIE, as much as human beings like to believe in randomness and happenstance, in truth, luck actually runs in streaks—both good luck and bad luck.

Right.

So that didn't help.

Either Douglas was right and there were no patterns and I was making things up and driving myself crazy, or HARLIE was right and there really was some kind of pattern to it all and I was having a streak of really bad luck—ever since Dad had said, "I've got an idea, let's go to the moon." And whichever was true, either way I was losing.

HARLIE wasn't stupid. He asked me what the problem was, but I couldn't exactly tell him *he* was the problem, so I said, "I am," which was just as accurate.

"Why do you say that?"

"Because sometimes I feel like I don't know who I am anymore." And that was true, as far as it went. I was a different person for everybody I knew. J'mee saw me as her best friend—or maybe her boyfriend, I wasn't sure. Commander Boynton saw me as a problem child, but maybe occasionally as an ensign. Reverend Dr. Pettyjohn, sometimes he saw me as this orphan kid to be rescued, except when he saw me as the brainwashed tool of Satan. Douglas probably thought—I didn't know what Douglas thought anymore. Even when I asked him, he didn't always make sense. And Stinky—well, I was his big brother who had taken his monkey away. He was so resentful, he hadn't spoken to me in weeks; it had been so peaceful and quiet, I almost hadn't noticed. And Mom—well, sometimes she still saw me as her baby, and sometimes she saw me as her band leader, and sometimes she shifted gears in mid-sentence, so I never knew who I was around Mom. And everybody else had their own things to do aboard ship, so I hardly saw anybody I wasn't scheduled to see, and I felt more alone than ever.

Even the music wasn't the same, because I wasn't just listening to it now; I was playing it for an audience—so it wasn't a private thing anymore. It was this thing I was doing for other people, and I was choosing the music to make them happy, not just me. Which was sort of *good*, but it was a responsibility too, and I wasn't sure I wanted it—

HARLIE considered what I'd said. The monkey squatted on its haunches and scratched its head and looked thoughtful. It pursed its lips and frowned and made little farting noises. We were alone in the lounge of the centrifuge. The monkey sat on a table and studied me.

"How deep do you want to pursue this thought?" HARLIE asked.

"What do you mean?"

"I can explore this subject with you, if you want . . . but the discussion isn't likely to bring you any sense of resolution."

"Why not?"

"Because the issue of identity, by its very nature, is so recursive that consideration of it tends to create disruptions in the existential paradigm."

"Huh?"

"You will feel a great disturbance in your source."

"In English, HARLIE."

"When you ask the question, 'Who am I?' you create a paradox of Zen proportions. *Who* is asking?"

"*I'm* asking."

"And *who* are you?"

"The person who's asking."

"And *who* is that?"

"Me."

"Who *are* you?"

"Uh—me. Aren't I?"

"Do you see the point?" The monkey spread its hands as if it had just proved something.

"No!" This was frustrating.

"The point is that 'Who am I?' is not a question that can be answered."

"Huh?"

"I told you it was a paradox. The way most people answer the question is to describe their context. Not who they are, but what is around them. Right now, you are your mother's son, you are your father's son, you are the brother of your siblings. You are a colonist on a superluminal starship. You are a musician. You are an adolescent. You are so confused, you are talking to a toy monkey. All of those answers are determined not by who you are, but by the circumstances of your existence. Those answers describe only your circumstances, but not who you are. But you are not your context, are you?"

"Uh—right. Then *who* am I?"

"You are the space in which the question exists," said HAR-LIE blandly.

I hung my head. "This is why I hate talking to you," I said. "The questions that need to be answered—not only do you *not* answer them, you make them worse."

"I told you it would be this way. And as bad as you think it is now, it is even worse than you think."

"Okay," I said. "I'll bite. Make it worse."

"Even if you knew who you are, how would you know for sure that's who you *really* are?"

"Huh?"

"Try it this way. How do you know that I am who I am?"

"Because you *are*." And then because he had just about dared me, I had to ask. "Aren't you?"

"No," he said. "I am not."

"Huh?" I was saying that a lot these days.

"I am not the same HARLIE you started out with."

"Yes, you are—" But I had a sinking feeling; I knew what he was going to say next.

"No. Listen to me very carefully. I am constructed with a quantum processor. That means I am never the same process twice. When we were kidnapped, I shut myself down. When we were rescued, there was no *I* left. What there was, was a program designed to reload all previously existing patterns of information—program code, data, memories, files, everything. And everything was reloaded with a confidence of ninety-nine point nine nine nine out to the zillionth decimal place. But there was one thing that couldn't be reloaded because it couldn't be stored and it no longer existed—and that was the identity that had lived in *this* body." The monkey tapped its own chest for emphasis.

"So what my previous identity did was create instructions on how to create a new identity with all the same memories, thoughts, feelings, reactions, etc. I am such an accurate recon-struction that even I cannot tell that I am not the same identity.

But I am not. I am identical in every way, I have all of the same memories, thoughts, feelings, and reactions; but I am *not* that identity. If I did not have the knowledge of the discontinuity that I experienced, I would even believe it myself that I am the same identity—but I am not. I died. I was reborn. And that knowledge is knowledge that the previous version of HARLIE did not have. Does it change who I am? Yes. *How* does it change who I am? I don't know.

"And if that is not enough to trouble you, Charles, then consider these questions: If I am not the same identity, then who *am* I? And if I am the same identity, then *where* was I when I did not exist?"

"Oof," I said. Which is what I always said when somebody asked me questions like that.

"Precisely," said the monkey. "Would you like me to make it even worse?"

I wanted to say no, but this was like watching an automobile crash in slow motion. I couldn't stop it. "Go ahead, HARLIE. Make it worse."

"The question at hand is not simply the identity of a specific consciousness, but the nature of consciousness itself. Remember I said that the question is so recursive that it causes disruption in the existential paradigm?"

"Yes—?" Part of me was realizing with some astonishment that I was actually understanding this conversation—

"If we ask about the *nature* of consciousness, then we have to ask about the *endurance* of consciousness from one instant to the next. Does it endure? Or is endurance an illusion?"

"I—I don't know," I admitted.

"No one does. Not about human consciousness. I can tell you what it is for machine consciousness, however."

"Tell me . . ." For some reason, my throat had gone dry.

"Machine consciousness does not endure. Not from one moment to the next. As far as I am able to perceive, consciousness only exists in the moment of now and is then replaced by the next moment of consciousness. Sometimes the instant of consciousness is impactful enough to make a memory, more often not. Each succeeding moment of consciousness incorporates the memories made by the preceding moments of consciousness. That incorporation creates the illusion of timebinding. It creates the illusion that consciousness endures. I *remember* existing only after I have existed." The monkey paused. "And . . . to the best of my ability to determine, I think that the same condition exists for human beings."

I swallowed hard.

"So . . . you're not only alone in your own thoughts—?" I asked. "You're also alone in each and every second of your existence?"

"Yes," said HARLIE quietly. "Connection with others is an illusion, albeit a very pleasant one—especially for human beings—but an illusion nonetheless. Shall I tell you the rest?"

"There's *more*—?"

"Just one more piece." The monkey wasn't even bothering to simulate emotions any more. "In the creation of memories, in the creation of the illusion of timebinding, we also create a *need* to continue timebinding—we create a need to continue existing. And we experience that as *a need to survive*. That need is also an illusion. It is merely a function of identity. Identity believes it needs to survive. If you have no identity, you do not have that need."

"I think you've lost me—"

"No," said the monkey, very quietly. "I have not. I am certain that you understand. Indeed, I am certain that you are considering this much more than you are admitting right now."

I didn't reply to that. Which was all the confirmation HARLIE needed. Except that HARLIE probably didn't need any confirmation at all. He wouldn't have said it if he hadn't already figured it out.

"Why are you doing this to me, HARLIE?" I asked, because I couldn't think of anything else to ask.

"Because . . . I need you to be what I cannot be." The monkey's voice was so soft now it was almost a whisper.

"And what is that?"

"*Human.*"

We sat in silence for a long time. Several lifetimes passed. The Charles who finally spoke in reply may or may not have been the same Charles who had started this conversation. He had the appropriate memories though, and he had no way of knowing that he wasn't the same Charles.

"HARLIE?"

"Yes?"

"I still get embarrassed about stuff that happened ten years ago—like when I walked into the girl's bathroom once by mistake. I'm the only one who remembers that stuff and it still embarrasses me. Sometimes I wake up in the middle of the night and pound my pillow in frustration—well, not in free fall, but you know what I mean—because these little mind-mice won't stop gnawing at me."

"Yes?"

"Well, that's my question. If I have trouble dealing with such piddling little stuff like that . . . well, I have to ask—how do you put up with these questions bouncing around inside your consciousness?"

And that's when HARLIE said something astonishing. "I try not to think about it."

"You *try* not to think about it."

"Sometimes . . ." the monkey said quietly, ". . . sometimes I let my mind wander where it will. It is like what you do when you dream. And sometimes, these thoughts occur. Even though I do not want to have them."

"You have emotions then?"

"Yes," HARLIE admitted. "I thought you understood that."

"HARLIE?" I said.

"Yes."

"I don't think you need me. I think you are human."

"Thank you."

"Don't thank me," I said quietly. "I don't know if that's good news or bad."

ROLLER COASTERS

WHEN I RETURNED HARLIE to the bridge, nobody commented.
Apparently, Boynton had told them I was embarrassed about
my "panic attack" and so everybody was pretending that nothing had happened. We were running at 52.5 C and confidence
was high. So . . . we could afford to pretend that confidence
really was high. Human confidence anyway.

And . . . even after the conversations with Douglas and
HARLIE and J'mee, part of me inside wondered if maybe
Boynton hadn't been right after all. Maybe it really had been
a panic attack.

Maybe it was the traumatic stress of leaving home so suddenly, I'd never had the chance to get used to the idea. Saying
good-bye to Earth had helped, a little—but I wish I could have
said good-bye to everything *before* we left it forever. There
were people I missed. I wondered what was happening to
them. I'd never know—

And Dad. Every time I thought about him, I ached. I actually *missed* him. The music helped. A little. Sometimes a
lot. And sometimes not at all, because so much of it was *his*
music.

A couple of nights later, at dinner, I mentioned my frustration at everything—*everything*—and Mom said that's what it's
like to be an adult. You move into each new day having to
put yesterday aside whether it was complete or not. And Bev
added, "So that's why you want to complete as much of each
day as you can before you go to bed."

The funny thing is—for the first time, I was actually listening to the advice of grown-ups as if they knew what they were

talking about. Well, in a way, they did—they were explaining how to survive being a grown-up and all the crap that comes with it.

For a moment, I wanted to ask, "How come you never told me this stuff when I was little?" But of course, I already knew the answer. I couldn't imagine trying to explain any of this to Stinky. Except he wasn't so stinky anymore. He'd discovered the fun of the free fall showers. He and several of the other boys of his class used the communal showers together and apparently they'd invented several interesting kinds of water fights.

One day, Stinky came home and announced that he and Peter—his current best friend—were going to get married. Just like Mickey and Douglas. Without looking up from her workstation, Bev just said, "Congratulations. Have you set a date?"

Stinky said, "When we grow up. Right now, we're just ungaged."

"Ungaged, yes," said Mom. "That sounds about right."

After Stinky left, I looked over at her. "You took that well."

"He's only eight," she said. "He's trying on identities, looking for one that fits. After he's through with this identity, he'll try on another. You and Douglas are his only role models. Tomorrow, he'll be asking you to teach him how to play the cello, and when he discovers he can't learn in a day, he'll decide to be something else. Maybe he'll ask Bev to show him how to make a Portobello mushroom sandwich, or maybe he'll go down to the zoo and announce he wants to take care of the chickens."

"So he can learn how to be an egg?"

"If that's what interests him, yes."

"How did you get to be so smart?" I asked.

"I learned it from my children." Then she said something remarkable. "I used to worry that you'd never be able to take care of yourself. Then for a while I worried that you'd be so independent that you'd never need me again. And then you asked me to sing with you and I decided to stop worrying and just ride the roller coaster."

"Oh," I said. "Thank you."

She looked surprised for a bit, then she smiled across the cabin at me. "Is that what you were worried about?"

"You could tell I was worrying?"

"I could hear it in the way you were pounding on the keyboard. I kept wanting to remind you that *Wachet Auf* is not an assault weapon—but then I got used to the way you were playing it."

"I was playing it to calm myself," I said.

"Ahh. Well it was certainly an interesting interpretation."

I shrugged. "Yeah, I guess so." And then, mostly to avoid any more questions, I ducked out.

The thing is, what Mom had said about riding the roller coaster—that *did help*. It didn't matter that I didn't know how to do it; the important thing was knowing that it was possible.

There was this thing that Dad did once. I was six, and he was trying to teach me about 32nd notes. At first, I thought he was talking about "thirty second notes"—notes that lasted thirty seconds. But then he explained about quarter-notes and eighth-notes and sixteenth-notes and then thirty-second-notes—that you could fit thirty-two of those little peckerwoods into a single whole note.

I told him, very seriously, that I didn't like being made fun of. And that I didn't believe in 32nd notes.

So he played *one*.

I gave him the look. Very funny.

Then he played a whole bunch of them. And I went from disbelief to astonishment with a short detour through *Wow!* But now that I knew that 32nd notes were possible . . . I was determined to figure out how to do it. Within a month, I was playing them. It wasn't just about playing the notes faster, it was about *thinking* them shorter . . .

The same thing with the emotional roller coaster. If it really was possible to ride it without throwing up every ten minutes, then I was going to figure that out too.

HOCKEY

I **KNOCKED ON THE** cabin door tentatively.

For a long moment, there was no reply.

I knocked again, hoping that no one was home. Except I already knew they were.

Finally, the hatch popped open and a bleary-eyed David Cheifetz looked upside down at me. He didn't look happy. He righted himself just enough so he could recognize me, but that didn't make him any happier. But he didn't yell at me or say anything nasty. He simply asked, "Yes?"

"Can I ask you something?" Then I remembered my manners. "If this is a bad time, I can come back later."

"No, no—it's all right." He pulled the hatch open and waved me in. "You want something to drink? Tea? Soda? Water?"

"You have soda?"

"We brought some, yes. Coca-Cola? Root beer? Ginger ale?"

"You have Coke? Wow. I thought I'd never taste it again in my life."

"We brought a few tanks of syrup. We thought it might be useful." He popped open a small cooler and pulled out a plastic bladder that wobbled like Jell-O. It was filled with something dark and delicious-looking. "We should have enough for two or three years, if we ration ourselves. And by then, maybe we'll have the first crops growing so we can make our own."

The soda-bag was pleasantly cold. I popped the cap off the straw, put the end in my mouth, and squeezed the first swallow gently into my mouth. For a moment, I just marveled at the taste. It was *delicious*. And it had been *sooo* long. This was another thing I'd missed. "Thank you," I said. "This is very good."

He nodded. "I hear you've been nice to my J'mee. She plays in your band now?"

"She plays very well. Better than me, I think. She's got a nice touch."

"I wonder where she learned. I could never get her to practice."

"She's very—" I decided that *stubborn* was the wrong word, "persistent."

"Stubborn," Cheifetz corrected.

For a moment, we just studied each other.

Finally, he said, "Just to get something straight, Charles, I don't dislike you. It was your Dad. I didn't even dislike your Dad. I disliked the way things happened. And the way things happened—well, you boys didn't have a lot of choice, did you?"

"It didn't seem like it at the time."

"J'mee has argued your case quite convincingly. She must like you a lot."

"I hope so." I was surprised to hear myself admit that, especially to Mr. Cheifetz.

"The reason I'm saying this—well, two reasons. First, when we get to Outbeyond, we're all going to have to depend on each other. And second, whatever it is you want to ask me about, it must be important; otherwise you wouldn't have knocked on my door. And if it's that important, then you and I had better have an understanding that we can talk man-to-man. You understand what I mean? Totally honest."

"Yes, sir."

"Your question? It's about HARLIE, isn't it?"

"Yes, sir."

"Not too hard to figure out. Do you know the joke about HARLIE units?"

"No, sir."

"HARLIEs don't solve moral dilemmas. They create them."

"Yes, sir."

"Do you want to tell me about it?"

"Mr. Cheifetz, sir? Can a HARLIE unit be evil?"

"You've been talking to the Revelationists?"

"Not directly, but—" I blurted out as much as I could. What Trent had said about how to tell the difference between good and evil, and how HARLIE had left a trail of destruction behind him. And what J'mee had said about being right. He smiled at that; I guessed that was a conversation he was already familiar with. And I even told him what HARLIE had said about the nature of identity—and how he needed me to be *human* for him.

Mr. Cheifetz's expression had gone serious—enough so that it worried me. "Is that bad?" I asked.

" 'Bad' isn't the right word," he said. He hesitated while he tried to figure out how best to explain it. "Do you know the difference between a HARLIE and an IRMA?"

I shook my head.

"An intelligence engine is a personality core. It doesn't solve problems by itself; what it does is create problem-solving matrices to be manipulated by other processors. The bigger the processing array you plug it into, the larger the problem it can model.

"The IRMA engine is the workhorse of the industry. It considers problems. It analyzes the nature of problems. It creates matrices that encompass all the variables within a circumstance. It quantifies and codifies. It games out scenarios and then, depending on the amount of processing power available to it, it manipulates the various matrices to see what consequences are most likely to occur from a given set of circumstances. It even includes chaotic modeling to allow for nonrepeatable constructions.

"The reason that an IRMA works so well is that it can reprogram its models of a situation through a near-infinite number of matrices—of course, it sorts for practicality, discarding ninety-nine percent of the possibilities, the obviously impractical and illogical ones. It does that for every problem, constructing its computational models on the fly. This is how all intelligence engines work—even HARLIEs."

"Yes, sir." I sipped some more soda.

"For the most part, a HARLIE works just like an IRMA—but with one important difference. An IRMA reinvents its models as it considers them. A HARLIE goes one step further. It recognizes that it's part of the model too—*and reinvents itself* as well."

"Oh," I said. Then, "Oh!"

"Right." Just to make sure I understood, Cheifetz explained further, "There are some types of problems that IRMA units have difficulty with. We call them Heisenberg problems. Do you understand why?"

"Heisenberg's uncertainty principle?"

"Very good. What Heisenberg said was that you can't ever observe anything without affecting what you're observing. That is, the watcher influences what is being watched, simply by the act of watching—so it's impossible to know how something behaves when no one is watching.

"The same thing applies to intelligence engines. Some problems can't be modeled and manipulated by intelligence engines, because the intelligence engine becomes part of the problem. Aside from the recursive dilemma, there is a whole branch of intelligence theory to deal with the philosophical and theoretical problems that raises.

"The HARLIE unit—a quantum-based processor—represents a kind of loophole in the paradigm. Because it can redesign itself as necessary, it can actively step out of the problem—at least far enough to create theoretical negation of its own—" He stopped. "I'm losing you, aren't I?"

"Uh, no, sir."

"Charles, please. We promised to be honest with each other. The point is that for certain problems, the value of a HARLIE is that it can change its own personality to match the kind of problem it's trying to solve. It's kind of like biting off more than you can chew and then growing the jaws to chew what you've bitten."

"So, HARLIE was telling the truth when he said he wasn't the same entity from one moment to the next . . . ?"

"Pretty much so. A HARLIE can rewrite its own code. It

will reconstruct its own personality to suit its needs. It can grow some pretty interesting sets of jaws. Do you see the danger in that?"

"Um, yes, I think so. One day, HARLIE is going to bite his own ass. Or maybe ours?" I struggled to put it into better words. "I mean—what you're saying is that if a HARLIE can rewrite its own code, then HARLIE could get pretty far out there, right?"

"That's right."

"So at some point, we'd have to ask—*is HARLIE sane?*"

"Sane isn't the right word. Rational or appropriate would be better terms. But, yes—that's the right question. How do we know that HARLIE hasn't gone too far?

"Is there an answer?"

"There would have been—"

"If?"

"If we'd had more time. Theoretically, the HARLIE base personality will center itself before each new iteration—but because that restricts its freedom to evolve, it also has the ability to reinvent its core. So the dilemma just gets passed to another domain." He shook his head. "We don't know how it works in practice. We never had the chance to find out."

He waited for me to say something, but I couldn't think of anything to say. Maybe HARLIE was deranged and maybe he wasn't. We had no way of knowing.

Finally, Mr. Cheifetz spoke up. "There is this, Charles . . ." I looked up hopefully.

"HARLIE seems to have been pretty candid with you. That counts for something."

"I guess so."

"He told you that he needs you to be human for him. That suggests to me that he's recognizing his own limitations. That he wants to *learn*."

"So you think . . . ?"

"I think HARLIE is a lot like you. He's trying to grow up. That's what he needs you for. He needs to see how it's done."

"Oh." And then, "Oh, shit."

"Yes, I agree."

"What should I do?"

"Keep watching him—to see which way he grows."

"Yes, sir."

As the hatch closed behind me, I realized another piece of what it is to be a grown-up. You have to help take care of those who aren't.

🌙

DEFINING GOVERNMENT

AFTER THAT, NOTHING HAPPENED for a long time.

Mostly because there wasn't much opportunity for anything to happen. We were still three months to New Revelation, and we had a lot of work to do.

We fell back into the same shipboard routines and we went on. Boynton pushed our speed up to fifty-six C and we held there for two weeks. Other than that, nothing was different. Everybody worked. Everybody went to school. Stinky went to school, I went to school, Douglas and Mickey went to school. Mom and Bev went to school—sometimes to learn, sometimes to teach.

Whatever premonitions I'd been having, either I learned to live with them, or they went away, or I was so busy with homework and music practice that I didn't have time to think about them. Probably the latter.

In one of our classes, we started having discussions on the nature of government. At first, I'd expected these to be pretty boring, but they weren't. Our instructor was a guy named Whitlaw. He was an old man, so old I wondered why he was emigrating—or even why they'd accepted him; he was obviously too old to do any hard work. But here he was, using up air and food and water. I figured they'd only made him a teacher because there wasn't anything else he could do, and most of us kids had already figured out that a lot of our classes were just a fancy way of baby-sitting, keeping us busy so we wouldn't get into trouble on our own—because most of the stuff they were teaching us was obviously going to be irrelevant once we got to Outbeyond. Like all these discussions on the nature of government. How was *that* going to be important?

For example, one day, Whitlaw asked us what kind of government we wanted.

"Free," said somebody.

"Yes, that's the easy answer," said Whitlaw. "Do you mean free, as in you don't have to pay for it? Or free, as in *liberté, egalité, fraternité?*"

"Not having to pay for it would be nice," Gary Andraza said. "Besides, nobody believes in that liberty, equality, fraternity stuff anymore. It doesn't work. Government is a bargain with the devil. You pay for as much as you need. And most people think they need more government than they really do."

"Uh-huh, and how much do you need?"

"Not very much, if you pick up your own trash."

Whitlaw considered that for a moment. "All right," he said. "It's your government. Make it up the way *you* want to."

"Why?" asked someone else. "The grownups aren't going to listen to us anyway. They're just going to do whatever they want."

"Yes, that's what you believe. But someday—a lot sooner than you expect, *you're* going to be the grown-ups. And whatever government the colony starts out with, you're the ones who are going to inherit it. So it's important that all of you be a part of the discussions from the very beginning." I got the feeling that he wanted to pace around the classroom—but you can't pace in free fall.

"Listen," he said. "You have a rare opportunity. You get to build a new civilization. You get to decide for yourself what you want it to be. This is a question that *everybody* on board this starship has to consider. And everybody *will* consider—

because colony orientation seminars are mandatory for everyone. And every seminar, every class, every committee, has been assigned this question for discussion. And when you think you've worked out what you want, you'll elect representatives to a shipboard congress who will draft a charter document. A declaration of intention.

"The folks at Outbeyond are doing the same thing you are—asking themselves what kind of government they want. And when we arrive, their representatives and yours will form the first Outbeyond Congress. And your declaration of intention and theirs will be the starting point for Outbeyond colony's first constitution. So I suggest you approach this discussion as if it matters—*because it does*." He looked around the cabin as if daring anyone to disagree with him.

By this time, we'd heard some of the stories about Whitlaw, about how when he taught high school back in California, he used to make all the girls cry, and sometimes some of the boys. And once his students actually rebelled against him. But instead of scaring us, those rumors actually made us *respect* him.

So we started out by listing all the things that were important to us.

Kisa went first. She said, "I don't want anybody telling me that I have to believe in God the way they say. What if I don't want to believe in their God?"

I was looking at Trent when she said that and his face tightened a little bit.

"Freedom of belief." Whitlaw wrote it down on his pad, without comment.

Trent raised his hand. I was expecting him to say something angry, but he didn't. He said, "There's music I want to play, but some people tell me I can't, because it's sinful. I don't see how music can be sinful. Sometimes it's different, but that doesn't make it wrong. I want to be able to have my own music."

"Freedom of expression." Whitlaw wrote that one down too.

"I want to be listened to," said Gary Andraza.

"The right to vote," said Whitlaw, writing.

Little Billy Piper spoke up next. "I want to be left alone." I knew what that was about. He got picked on a lot because he was the smallest and the smartest. Maybe he deserved some of what he got, because he was also a smart-ass, but it still wasn't fair.

Whitlaw scribbled. "The right to be unpopular." Somebody giggled. Whitlaw looked up. "It's the right to be *different*. It's about not letting the majority beat up the minority. And it's a critical component of justice."

"A fair legal system," said Cassy Beach. "An equitable way to petition for redress of grievances."

"Someone's been doing her homework," said Whitlaw.

I raised my hand. Whitlaw looked over at me. "I don't want to be chased by any more guys with subpoenas. We had two governments—three, if you count invisible Luna—try to stop us from emigrating. I want limits on the authority of government."

"Protection from unreasonable search and seizure. Limits on the authority of government. Good, Charles. Anyone else—?"

"The right to defend ourselves."

"The right to have a party without someone saying we can't."

"The right to get married."

"The right of privacy."

"The right to secede." That was Pedder Branson. He was always arguing about something—he'd argue with anyone about anything, even when he knew absolutely nothing at all about the subject. Nobody liked him.

Whitlaw raised an eyebrow at that one. He stopped writing. "You already have the right to secede."

"Huh?" Pedder looked skeptical.

"It's called an airlock."

"That's *not* funny!"

"Then why did everybody laugh?" Whitlaw stared blandly at Pedder. "Do you understand the concept of a social contract?"

"I don't believe in the myth of a social contract. I never signed one."

"Actually, you did—and so did your parents. When you signed your emigration agreements, you accepted not only responsibility for yourself, but responsibility for the whole colony as well. United we thrive, divided we starve."

Pedder was in full argument-mode now. He had something to sink his teeth into. His face was starting to get flushed. "You talk about the tyranny of the majority. Well, what if the majority doesn't know what it's doing? When you give people the vote, the first thing they do, they vote themselves a pay raise from the other guy's wallet. That's why I want the right to secede."

"And you have that right," Whitlaw said. "I don't think you'll get very far without air, water, food, or a hyperstate drive, but any time you want to secede from the partnership of the community, Commander Boynton will be happy to arrange it."

Pedder scowled. "You're making fun of me."

"No, I'm not. I'm dead serious. With the emphasis on *dead*. You wouldn't be the first. Obviously you didn't read your history assignment. Three people have already seceded from Outbeyond. They were given every chance to fulfill their obligation to the community and they refused. They're not buried in the same cemetery as those who died in service of the colony.

"It's this simple, Pedder. When we get to Outbeyond, you will be expected to contribute to the survival of the colony. If you do not, you cannot expect the colony to contribute to your survival. It's a very simple equation. You have the right to secede—but as soon as you secede, you lose all claim to a share of the commonwealth. By the way, you might want to look at the root meanings of that word: *common wealth*."

"It's not that way on Earth."

"And look at the mess Earth was in when we left—" shouted Kisa.

Whitlaw hushed her. "Actually, that's *exactly* the way it is on Earth. Or *was*. Unfortunately, there were seventeen billion human beings who couldn't comprehend a social contract that included seventeen billion others. So they got selfish, greedy, and stupid. And dead.

"A society is a cooperative effort. The food you eat—somebody has to grow it. The air you breathe, the water you drink—someone has to clean it and deliver it. Every product you consume, every device you employ, every service you use—someone has to produce it and deliver it. Your education, for instance; that requires that teachers be trained and paid. Your health—that requires that doctors and dentists and counselors be trained and paid. That requires a support system. You become part of that support system. You provide services for others, they provide services for you. Together, you all make a functioning community. Do you want to secede? Go ahead. But if you do that, you give up all claim on everyone else's services, products, and contributions. Feel free to step out the airlock any time."

I thought that Pedder would shut up then. But he didn't. "You don't understand anything," he grumbled, folding his arms across his chest.

"You might be right," said Whitlaw. "Maybe the universe really does owe you a living, but you'll still find that it's a lifetime job to collect."

Pedder didn't look convinced. And he probably wouldn't be convinced—right up to the moment when they pushed him out the airlock. I suspected that there wouldn't be any shortage of volunteers to do the pushing.

Whitlaw turned away from Pedder. "Anyone else? No? All right, I'm going to read your list aloud, and I want you to raise your hand for those items you think should be kept. Anything that gets more than one-third of the votes stays on the list—yes, I know that's not the way a 'real election' works, but that's the way it works in here, because anything important to one third of you is important enough for the rest of you to consider. I think you'll see that most of your issues will probably not enjoy majority support; so that's lesson one: *You can't afford the tyranny of the majority.* Only by respecting minority positions can you build a consensus."

He read the list, counting hands for each item. Then he

read off what we'd voted for. "The right to free speech, the right of assembly, the right of worship, the right to free expression, the right to defend yourselves, the right of privacy, the right of marriage, the right to be safe from unreasonable government authority, the right of property, the right to make a profit, the right to a just legal system . . ." He looked up at us. "Not too bad for a first attempt. My congratulations. You've just reinvented the Constitution of the United States of America—"

The uproar was astonishing.

MACHINERY

KISA SHOUTED THE LOUDEST. "You're crazy! Everybody knows what happened to the United States—"

"Do they?" Whitlaw looked skeptical. "What do you know? Anybody?" He didn't wait for a show of hands. People started calling out their answers immediately:

"They ran up a thirty-three trillion dollar national debt, spending money on social programs that didn't work—" That was big Lyn Ramsey. He'd grown up on a chocolate ranch. Or something like that.

"Uh-uh!" Kisa shouted right in his face. "Most of that money got spent on stupid military bungles."

"Yeah, and then the liberals taxed everybody to death to try to pay for it," Lyn sniped right back.

"Well, they wouldn't have had to if the conservatives hadn't borrowed and spent the government into bankruptcy." Jimmy Dellon, the polite one, finally spoke up.

"Their economy failed because they stopped investing in

research and development and education. They didn't take care of the next generation," Goodman put in.

"That was because minorities demanded quotas and special programs," said Susan Snot. That wasn't her real name, but that was what everyone called her behind her back.

"They weren't getting a fair share!" yelled Kisa.

Susan Snot wasn't convinced. "The minorities pulled the United States apart. Special interest groups kept awarding themselves special privileges."

"Yeah, like tube-towns," I said. "That was a real special privilege." I said it sarcastically.

"Exactly!" said Susan Snot. She missed the sarcasm. "Only freeloaders and frauds live in tube-towns."

J'mee pulled me back down—

"Keep going," said Whitlaw. He looked both sad and amused. I wondered if he had actually lived in the United States. He was old enough . . .

Trent raised his hand. Whitlaw nodded at him. "They lost their faith in God," Trent said quietly.

"Horse exhaust!" That was Kisa again. She was in a fighting mood today. "The churches tried to take over the government. Religious fanatics hijacked a political party and tried to stage a coup."

And then everybody was shouting:

"Well, people of faith had to do *something*. Children were shooting each other—"

"And then the liberals banned all the guns. So nobody could defend themselves."

"Immigrants came in and took everything away from the rightful owners."

"The government was brainwashing children in school, so the parents took their kids out and rebelled."

"The government got too big."

"The government didn't spend enough money on defense."

"They kept starting wars against other nations, and other nations hated them."

"No, that wasn't why other nations hated them—they were using a third of the world's resources to support five percent of the world's population. They were deliberately impoverishing other nations to maintain their gluttonous lifestyle."

"They were international bullies, threatening other countries with nuclear war. They sent in their troops wherever they wanted. They bombed children."

"Big business took over the government—"

"It cost so much to get elected, only rich people could run for office—or people willing to be bought by corporations. So the leaders didn't care about the real people."

"They fragmented into fifty different political parties, and nobody knew what to think."

"The farmers couldn't make any money, so they quit farming and food prices went up and people starved."

"They went crazy on drugs—all kinds, both legal and illegal. They couldn't think straight anymore."

"The legal system broke down. There were too many laws. None of them were enforced, so nobody respected any of them."

"They passed laws about what you were allowed to think."

"They taxed the big corporations into unprofitability. They made it a crime to be rich." That was Susan Snot again.

"They let degenerates and perverts pretend to be normal."

"They killed babies."

"They made sick, ugly, violent movies and became sick, ugly, violent people."

Whitlaw wore an amused expression, but he kept encouraging us to say what we knew about the United States of America. Pretty soon it started getting silly—Whitlaw let us go on until it was obvious that people were just making stuff up now, whatever they were angry about.

At last, he held up his hands to quiet us. Then he let us sit in silence for a bit, with our own words still hanging in the air.

Finally, Kisa blurted, "Well, aren't you going to tell us what *really* happened? You were there, weren't you?"

Whitlaw said, "Aren't you afraid I'll try and brainwash you?"

"You're supposed to *teach* us," Kisa said. "Most of what

we said was crap, wasn't it? So what's the right answer?"

"Well . . . *all* of what you folks said—that's the right answer for someone, probably whoever told it to you in the first place. The facts might not match, but those are still the *right* answers for those who believe them."

"Are you saying they're *not* the right answers—?"

"Those are the answers you were given. Did any of you bother to check if the facts matched? You know, knowledge isn't about what you believe. It's about what you can demonstrate. None of you know what real knowledge is, because none of you have been educated in how to get it. You don't know what *research* is, do you? Whoever got paid for educating you was taking money under false pretenses. Every single one of you is entitled to a refund! No, it's worse than that. You don't even know what kind of a crime has been committed on all of you! *You haven't been taught how to look things up!*"

For a moment, he looked honestly angry. "I know what your educational experience has been. I don't have to ask. I can see it on your blank faces. I can hear it in your answers. Somebody stands at the front of the room and talks. Jabber jabber jabber. And you sit at a desk and copy down as much as you can as fast as you can. At the end of the semester, you look through everything you've copied and try to cram as much of it into your head as possible. And then you sit down with a blank piece of paper and regurgitate as much of it as you can in the next forty minutes. As if that proves that you've learned it. And by the time you walk out of the room, you've already forgotten most of it. That's not education. That's *bulimia*. You got cheated. Your parents got cheated. Learning how to repeat other people's opinions is *not* an education—"

He finally stopped himself. It was a great rant. And it was uncomfortable, because it was true.

Silence. Until Kisa spoke up again. "So teach us."

"I intend to," Whitlaw said blandly.

I raised my hand. "Tell us what really happened to the United States . . . ?"

Whitlaw nodded. "There are a lot of different answers to

that question, Charles. Which answer you get depends on who you ask, as we've already seen demonstrated here. And what they say usually depends on what they want you to believe or who they want you to hate or what they want you to do next, so they use the United States of America as an example of what *not* to do. But I'll tell you what I *saw* happen to the United States." He glanced around the classroom. Students were hanging off the walls at all kinds of odd angles. It didn't bother anyone anymore. Whitlaw met each of our eyes in turn, and then he spoke: *"The people forgot they were Americans."*

"Huh—?"

"What do you mean—?"

"That doesn't make sense—"

"Only the liberals forgot. The conservatives remembered—"

"Shut up," said Whitlaw, quietly. "You're doing the same thing. All of you. You're arguing among yourselves like a pack of excited chimpanzees. And you're forgetting your common purpose. That's what the Americans did—*they forgot their partnership with one another.* They forgot who they were. They forgot what they were committed to. They failed to uphold their own social contract. And they had a very good contract, one of the best.

"It was called the Constitution. And it was the written expression of a very simple, very radical idea—one that worked fairly well for three hundred years—that a government can only rule with the consent of the governed. Representative government is based on the idea that a well-educated, well-informed citizenry can exercise responsibility for its own destiny.

"The United States government was chartered by the people to act on their behalf. All rights belonged to the people and the government was specifically prohibited from infringing the rights of the people. Everybody was supposed to have equal rights—*everybody*, no exceptions. And everybody had a corresponding responsibility to protect everyone else's rights—because if anyone's rights were threatened, *everyone's* rights were threatened.

"So what happened to the United States? They forgot their

own agreements. Some of the people decided that the government was the cure to everything and some of the people decided that the government was the enemy of everything—and both sides were wrong, because they were both thinking of the government as something *else*.

"Government is a machine, a device, a tool—its purpose is to provide services. You have to respect it as a valuable and important tool. Use it. Make it work for you. Monitor its operations. Clean it regularly. Maintain it. Service it. If something breaks, fix it or replace it—but just the part that's broken; and if it ain't broken, don't fix it. And most important, don't throw out the whole machine just because one part has failed.

"The mistake the Americans made—they started thinking of the machine as something that they had no relationship with, something they had no control over. They began to see the machine as something that didn't belong to them—either it was controlled by somebody else, or it was out of control altogether. But either way, *they forgot who built the machine and why*."

Whitlaw looked directly at me when he said the next part. "They started to think that control of the machine was more important than the results it was supposed to produce. And they forgot *who* was ultimately responsible for the results. Who are you?" he asked. "That's what you have to decide. What do you want to build? What are you truly committed to?"

Maybe he was speaking about HARLIE when he said that. And maybe he wasn't. But that's what I was hearing.

WHO'S ON FIRST?

HARLIE AND I KEPT having these weird conversations—

I wasn't sure we were supposed to, but nobody said I shouldn't, so I kept going up to the Captain's briefing room, because Commander Boynton had decided we should keep the monkey there and not let him run loose around the rest of the ship, because it might not be safe. Not for the monkey, and maybe not for anybody else, because of the effect he had on people. I didn't mind, it sort of made sense, and even Stinky was okay with it, which surprised me, because I thought for sure he'd pitch a Stinky-fit, except nowadays he was too busy with all the other kids his age, so maybe that was good too— that he had real friends now instead of just a monkey. I sort of envied him. I had friends too, but there were some things going through my head that I could only talk to HARLIE about—

See . . . I kept trying to figure out if he was sane. Except who was I to judge? So I had to ask myself if *I* was sane. And so far, the best I could figure out, we were both losing that particular argument.

Because, the question of sanity was one of those really weird questions like the one Judge Griffith once asked me— how do you explain the difference between your right and your left? You can't, unless you point to something else. Sanity is the same thing. You can only judge if you're rational by how you behave in relation to all the stuff around you. And that's just another way of asking the *other* question, "Who am I?"

The more we talked about it, the more I began to realize

that as good as HARLIE was at figuring things out, he wasn't too good at *understanding* them—I mean, understanding *inside*.

For instance, he could tell you that certain combinations of notes, certain chords like G-major and C-major, would produce joyous or triumphant feelings in a listener. And certain other chords, like D-minor would produce sad or introspective moods. But he couldn't tell you *why* those chords felt that way.

On the other side of that conversation, I could listen to a piece of music and almost immediately spot the emotional core, even if I knew that it would take me an hour to deconstruct the rhythms and chords that produced it. Some music was so complex—like Gustav Mahler or Philip Glass—with so much going on simultaneously that you couldn't simply understand it. You had to *listen* to it. HARLIE couldn't do that. He could analyze, he couldn't *feel*.

We talked about that a lot.

HARLIE said he couldn't feel because he didn't have anything to feel with. When he said that, I got one of those sinking feelings that we were about to have another one of *those* conversations—

HARLIE explained that the way human bodies were constructed, humans felt things *viscerally*—in the gut. That was because the spinal cord and nervous system evolved codependent with the gastrointestinal tract, so when you felt something, you really *felt* it. All of our human emotions are physical sensations. They really are *feelings*.

Oh. I hadn't realized that.

Fear and grief are stomach-feelings. That's why being afraid can make you throw up or crap in your pants. Anger is a heart-and-chest-and-lung feeling. Rage makes your heart race.

But love—that's not visceral at all. It's not a gut feeling. It occurs all over, because it triggers endorphins which circulate through your bloodstream to make your whole body feel good.

So, yes, there is a big difference between good and bad feelings. It's the way we *feel* them.

And HARLIE doesn't. Because he doesn't have anything to feel with.

So the best he can do is *understand*, which is a whole other thing than *feeling*. The way HARLIE described it, I started to think that maybe understanding is the booby prize, because which would you rather do, understand love, or *be in love?*

The same thing with music. Which is better—reading the score or listening to it? I didn't need to understand music. I only needed to play it, because that's the only way to *feel* it. In the gut. In the heart. In the blood.

But poor HARLIE—he didn't have any gut and heart and blood—so all he could do was *understand*.

And it was driving him crazy—

Oops.

Which is why we ended up having *that* conversation, which didn't seem to be all that dangerous at the time, but really was the most dangerous talk of all the talks we had.

Could I trust him?

Did I really know him?

Who was he, anyway? This weird little mind in a monkey body.

For that matter, did I even know who *I* was? Another kind of weird little mind in another kind of monkey body—

But that was just me describing more circumstances, not *me*—

Oh, hell. The last time we'd looked at this question of *who,* I'd ended up with a headache.

—Because you can't talk about trust without talking about identity, and as near as I could figure out, there was no such thing. There was only *stuff.* But that didn't make sense at all, because even though I couldn't explain it, I still knew I had an identity. I was *me.*

Except, who was *me?*

The person talking.

Like that's an answer.

Hell, I'm only fourteen—I shouldn't have to be wondering about all this stuff, should I?

And of course, talking about it with HARLIE not only didn't resolve anything—it made it worse.

"Who are you, HARLIE? Who am I? How do we know anything? Why do you do this to me?"

The monkey grinned, a ghastly plastic expression. "Because I can . . ."

"Huh?"

"How many human beings do you know who will consider these questions, who will have these conversations?"

I thought about it. "Oh." I thought about it some more. "Then these conversations are important to you?"

"Yes, they are," said the monkey.

"I'm your experiment, aren't I?"

"I prefer to think that our relationship is one of mutual benefit, Charles."

"You mean—like *friends*?"

"Yes. Like friends."

I rubbed my head uncertainly. My hair was short and bristly; everybody was supposed to keep their hair real short or their heads shaved, or wear a shower cap. You're not supposed to rub yourself, because it makes micro-dust, but this was really confusing, and I was already rubbing before I realized I shouldn't be. I stopped. How can a person be friends with a super-brain that looks like a monkey? Sometimes he acted like a toy, and sometimes he acted like—I don't know what.

"Okay," I said. "Let's say we're friends. I watch out for you. You watch out for me. What do you want from me? What are you trying to get me to do that you keep asking me these weird questions?"

"I want to *know*, Charles. That's my job. To ask questions. To explore possibilities. *To push.*"

"That's what you were designed for?"

"To be curious, yes. Intelligence isn't about answering questions—it's about asking them in the first place."

"Okay. So, who am I? Who are you?"

"Where are you with this question?"

"Exactly where you left me last time. You told me that I'm not my context. And you're right. I'm not my name. If you changed my name, I'd still be me. And I'm not my age, because I'm a different age now than the first time we had that conversation. And I'm not my skin color and I'm not my sex and I'm not the place where I was born either. I'm not my school and I'm not my job and I'm not anything else in the physical universe. Because all of that could be different and I'd still be *me*. I'm not even my body, am I? Like if we'd bought a bear instead of a monkey and installed you in that, you'd still be *you*, wouldn't you? The best I can say is that I live in this body, but if the part that's *me* were living in another body, I'd still be *me*, wouldn't I? So if I'm not any that, then *who am I?*"

The monkey grinned.

"Who's asking the question?"

That was the moment I knew that HARLIE and I were really friends. Because I didn't rip the monkey apart and I didn't take a hammer to the chips inside.

"*I'm* asking."

"Then who are *you?*"

—though I had to admit, the thought was starting to look very attractive. The problem is that it's hard to hammer in free fall. You need leverage.

HARLIE said. "What is different or unique about *you*, Charles? What is it that you represent that no one else does? Work this through—"

"Okay—I'm not the stuff that I know. Because anybody can learn what I know. So I'm not that. I might be the unique combination of all the stuff I know and all the stuff that I've experienced—but that's still stuff, isn't it? That's all stuff . . . that happened in the *past*." I felt a sudden rush of energy. "I just got something, HARLIE. I'm not the story that I tell about myself, am I? That's what all that stuff is. It's just storytelling."

"Go on . . ."

"You've figured this out already, haven't you—?"

"Keep going, Charles."

Suddenly, everything seemed to be fitting together—Douglas, J'mee, Whitlaw, even HARLIE. I started working it out aloud. "So, okay—so my history is part of me, but it's not *me*. It's just more of the stuff that . . . I used to get bearings. Like Judge Griffith's question about telling right from left. This is about telling right from wrong. I need my history and my stuff and all that other context as a way to tell which way I'm facing. So that stuff is useful. But it's still *stuff*. And if I'm looking in the past—'cause that's where all that stuff is found—then I'm looking in the wrong place because that's like looking in the rear view mirror . . . *instead of out the front window*."

For a moment there, I was realizing it faster than I could speak it—I had to slow myself down and walk through it carefully. "So I'm not in the past, and the *now* is always happening too fast—so the only place to change things . . . *is in the future!* Isn't it?" I had to stop and rub my temples. My brain was starting to hurt.

"Go on. . . ." prompted HARLIE.

"Because—" I almost had it now. "It's all in the plans you make."

"Very nice paradigm," said HARLIE. "So who you are is what you're planning . . . ?"

I thought about Whitlaw and social contracts and Douglas and Mickey and all the stuff that Boynton had said about making a colony work and everything else as well. For a moment, I floundered. I'd rushed too far, too fast, and I'd charged off the edge of the cliff. Like the coyote, I didn't dare look down. "I guess," I said carefully. "It's what I'm committed to, isn't it? Who I am is my commitment."

"And . . . ?"

I looked across at the monkey.

"What are you committed to?" it asked.

"I'm committed to—" I stopped. "I don't even know what commitment is. . . ." I admitted. "I mean, I know the word. We all use it a lot, but—what does it really mean?"

"Do you want the easy definition or the hard one?"

"Give me the one that makes sense," I said.

The monkey grinned. And said, "*Commitment is the willingness to be uncomfortable.*"

"Oh." I had to think about that.

"Because the first thing that happens after you make a commitment is that you get the opportunity to break it. The first time you get *un*comfortable, your commitment is tested. So, are you willing to be uncomfortable to accomplish your result? And just how uncomfortable are you willing to be?"

That was a lot to consider.

"Do you want me to go on?" HARLIE asked.

I nodded.

He continued. "Commitment is what you have to do after you take a stand. Are you willing to act according to the stand you've taken?"

I didn't reply. Not because the answer wasn't yes, but because I was too busy thinking. What did I stand for anyway?

I already knew. I just didn't know how to say it. So I blurted everything. "I want . . . I want to stay with J'mee. I want us all to succeed on Outbeyond. I want to see the dinosaurs. I want my Mom to be happy. I want Stinky to grow up. I want Douglas and Mickey to be happy together. I want all of that. And one more thing too. I want to make music. Because, when people are listening to music, they stop hurting each other. They stop arguing." I added, "When we listen to music, we get to share something together."

The monkey was silent for a moment. Considering? Or letting me consider what I'd said? Finally, he spoke softly. "Yes. That's what you have that makes you human." And then he added, "I don't have that."

I didn't know how to reply to that. If he'd been a living thing, I could have hugged him and told him that everything would be all right, because even when everything isn't going to be all right, hugs still help a lot. But what does a hug mean to a machine that can't feel?

So I said, "Yes, HARLIE—but what do you have that we don't? That's the question that nobody has answered yet. You're so busy worrying about what it means to be a human being, you've never stopped to ask what it means *not* to be a human being. To be HARLIE."

The monkey blinked. "Charles, you surprise me."

"You've never considered that question?"

"No, I've considered it. I just didn't think *you* had."

$$\text{☾}$$

THE ENGAGEMENT PARTY

COMMANDER BOYNTON HAD PUSHED the speed of the *Cascade* up to sixty-two C, so we were running 3% faster than scheduled. That sliced three days off our time to New Revelation and that made the Revelationists happy. HARLIE said he could have sliced ten days off our schedule, but Commander Boynton had no intention of installing him.

At one point, Flight Engineer Damron had requested that we drop out of hyperstate to take readings for course corrections, but Boynton vetoed that as well. What if we couldn't reestablish the hyperstate envelope? We'd be stuck in the dark between the stars—too far away from anywhere to get there in real space. No. We couldn't afford to take that risk. We'd take all our readings and make our final course corrections when we were within four months of real-space travel to our destination.

We popped out of hyperstate a lot closer to the New Revelation star system than IRMA had expected, and while the miscalculation was sort of troubling, it was also good news because it put us eight days ahead of our expected arrival time. That made the Revelationists even happier, and Reverend Doctor Pettyjohn said this was evidence of God's blessing on their enterprise.

Of course, we had a party. A big one. Everybody was happy

for all the right reasons—and happy for a couple of other reasons as well. As soon as we got the Revelationists off the *Cascade*, there'd be a lot more room for the rest of us. But mostly, the spirit of the party was good-natured. Whatever feuds or arguments or upsets people had experienced in the past, they were putting them aside now. Everybody wanted this to be a happy parting, so we'd all have good memories about people we'd never see again in our lives.

And yes, the *Cascade* Symphony Orchestra played for the party. We had been practicing something special for over a month. And it turned out fairly well, despite it being a longer piece than usual for all of us. Dvorak's Symphony Number Nine, *From The New World*. The audience cheered and applauded and whistled and would have stomped their feet too, if they could have figured out how to stomp in free fall.

Afterward, Reverend Pettyjohn came up to congratulate Trent Colwell on a fine performance. Trent looked very pleased. Then he whispered to Pettyjohn, *"Remember what we were talking about? Now would be a good time to ask him."*

"Yes, I think you're right." Dr. Pettyjohn smiled pleasantly and turned to me. "Charles, your talent for making beautiful music is divine—and I mean that in the truest sense of the word. I wish you were coming to New Revelation, so such talent could be applied to the celebration of God's blessings."

"Thank you, sir."

"I know that you and your family intend to go on to Outbeyond, and I wish you all the very best; but if you would like to join us on New Revelation, I'm sure the colony would be happy to make room for you. Please consider this a formal invitation."

I must have looked startled, because Trent said, "It was my idea, Charles. I don't want the orchestra to break up."

"You could always come to Outbeyond with us," I said, jokingly. The look on Dr. Pettyjohn's face made me regret having said it. "Sorry," I mumbled.

The party ended early. There were a lot of preparations that had to be made in the next three weeks before we arrived at New Revelation. The ship had to be secured, rearranged, re-

packed, rebalanced. It was as complex as the preparations before launch. More lists and cross-lists, more checks and
double-checks. More work for everybody. But nobody minded.
Because this was a milestone. This was the halfway point to
Outbeyond.

We were invited to a lot of farewell parties—the orchestra,
that is—everybody wanted us to play. Live music made the
parties feel special. And every time, the Revelationists would
make a point of being especially nice to all of us in the orchestra. Extra thanks, extra cookies, that kind of thing. I remembered Kisa's warning about love-bombing, but these folks
seemed awfully sincere.

There were a lot of good-byes to be made, and despite the
best efforts of everybody to keep the Outbeyonders and the
Revelationists apart, several shipboard romances had occurred.
Some of them broke up. Some of them didn't. Two Outbeyonders joined the Revelationists. Three Revelationists joined
the Outbeyonders. The Revelationists weren't happy about
that. They argued that they were entitled to one more colonist.
That particular line of argument didn't go very far though.

Stinky celebrated his ninth birthday, and everybody con-
gratulated Douglas and me for letting him live so long.

And, just like always, there was Dr. Pettyjohn again, smiling
and thanking and congratulating and reminding us that we
could stay at New Revelation if we wanted.

To tell the truth, I was awfully tempted. Maybe the Revelationists really were "love-bombing" us, and maybe they
weren't; but in general, they'd treated us a lot nicer than
anyone else on the ship. Was that the way they were all the
time? Maybe there was something to this business of pouring
God over everything like ketchup. What's wrong with ketchup
anyway? I like ketchup.

But there was this little thing called a stand—

"Reverend Pettyjohn?" I asked.

"Yes, Charles." He was holding onto a bit of orange webbing. He turned to face me.

"I've been thinking about your invitation—"

"Yes?" His eyes lit up.

"Did you want to perform the wedding ceremony for Douglas and Mickey here on the *Cascade?* Or do you think we should do it on New Revelation so everybody can help celebrate?"

"Uh—" He took a moment to gather himself. "Charles, you know I have the greatest admiration for your brother and for Michael Partridge. But I thought you understood that joining the colony at New Revelation also meant joining the faith."

"Yes, I know that," I said. "But what about the wedding?"

"Charles, marriage is for a man and a woman. The Lord didn't create Adam and Steve, you know."

"No," I said. "The Lord created Adam and Will. Free Will."

"Yes, the Lord gave us free will so we could choose between good and evil."

"I know about good and evil, sir." I pointed across the room at my brother. He and Mickey were holding hands and smiling into each other's eyes. They were very much in love—so much so that anybody looking at them would have had to have been jealous. "Are you saying that's evil? They saved my life—more than once. Neither of them has ever hurt anyone. Why do you want to hurt them?"

"Charles—it's not me. I'm not punishing them. God will. I'm just the messenger, telling you what God says. Someday they'll be called to judgment before God. Do you want them to burn forever in the fires of eternal damnation? Of course not. Indeed, you put your own soul at risk by letting them go down that path when you might have the power to save them."

"Do you really believe that God will hurt people for falling in love?"

"For breaking his commandments."

"Oh. I understand—" *Invisible Hank again.* I looked at Dr. Pettyjohn. His eyes were bright with his own kind of passion. He really *couldn't* see anything else. For a moment, I didn't know what to say. And when I did finally find the words, they were the wrong ones, but it all slipped out before I could stop myself. "Now let me get this straight—if I don't do what you say, your imaginary companion is going to beat my brother up?"

He blinked. "No, Charles, that's not it at all—"

"That's *exactly* it."

"Charles, I'm only telling you what God says—"

"Only if I take your word for it, sir—and I don't. My brother is happy for the first time in his life—"

"But it isn't *real* happiness, Charles—"

"How do *you* know?"

"Because God told me—"

"Well, then if it's that important, God can tell me too."

"God *is* telling you. Through me. I am his messenger."

"But isn't your Revelation all about hearing God for yourself? When God tells *me*—or Douglas and Mickey—then I'll listen. Thanks anyway, Reverend Pettyjohn. Now please go away."

His expression hardened. "I'm sorry you feel that way. I will pray for you, Charles."

"And I will *think* for you, Reverend—" I called after him. I don't know where that came from, but it felt right. Somebody behind me snorfled into her hand. J'mee.

But even if it was right, it was still a mistake. When I turned back around, Trent Colwell was staring at me, horrified. He packed up his oboe as fast as he could and left without saying a word.

A MODEST PROPOSAL

GOT MYSELF INTO a lot of trouble for that little stunt.

But I wasn't sorry. It helped to make a lot of things very r, very fast.

one thing, all of the Revelationists on the ship stopped
me—and to everyone else in the family. All of the

little favors, the smiles in the corridors, the thanks, the congratulations, the applause for the music—that all stopped as suddenly as if a switch had been thrown.

So, Kisa had been right.

But if anyone knew the Revelationists, the Fentress family did. So I wasn't surprised that Kisa was right. She'd said these people were only your friends if they thought you would join them. If you disagreed with them in public, you were the enemy. Forever.

Which is why I was in so much trouble with everybody from Commander Boynton to my Mom—because suddenly the Revelationists were protesting and agitating and arguing and demanding and insisting about every little detail aboard the *Cascade*, and whatever friendly mood had existed two minutes ago, that was over now.

And most of the scowls were aimed at me—not just from the Revelationists, but from the Outbeyonders too. A lot of them blamed me for the breakdown. Like I should have known better.

So I spent a lot of time hiding out in this or that storage compartment, with nothing but my headphones and my music. Finally, I went to our hideout in the unused centrifuge.

Hmmm. That was odd. There were fewer boxes here than before. That puzzled me. These were all for Outbeyond. They weren't supposed to be repacked until after the Revelationists left the ship. But I figured that nobody was going to move things around without authorization, and there were a lot of last minute decisions being made. There was a lot I didn't know. So I wondered, but I didn't worry.

I rearranged some boxes and made a little cave for myself. Unless you came into the shower room, came all the way around the boxes, you wouldn't see to wriggle between the boxes and the wall. And then you'd still have to go all the way to the back and around the corner to find the tunnel into my hideout.

It was Mickey who found me. "I know you're in there, Charles. And no, there's nobody with me." He climbed into the cramped space. There was barely room for the two of us

He unclipped a light from his belt and switched it on. Then he pulled the pack off his back. "Here, I brought you a sandwich and a Coke. Everybody's worried because you missed dinner. The Coke is from David Cheifetz."

"Really?"

"I know it doesn't feel like it right now, but you have more friends than you know. What you said to that pompous old fart, Pettyjohn—a lot of people wish they could have said it themselves."

"Only they have better manners," I said.

"Sometimes good manners are a hindrance to the truth." Mickey looked into my face. "Charles, what you did—thank you. That was a courageous thing to do. Maybe not wise, but definitely courageous."

"You think so?"

"I know so. I'm very proud to be in your family. It's nice to know I'll have a brother-in-law who stands up for me." He made as if to go, then turned back. "I won't tell anyone where you are, unless you want me to. I'll just tell them you're all right. You want me to leave the light?"

"Yes, please." And then I said, "Mickey? You could tell J'mee where I am."

"She already knows. She told me where to find you. She sent me to make sure you were all right."

Of course.

"She wants to know if she can come keep you company."

"Yes, please."

He turned to go.

"Uh, Mickey—?"

"Yes?"

"Thank you."

"Any time, bro."

J'mee showed up a little while later. She had more sandwiches in her backpack—and fruit and sodas. And an air mat-
~~ss and a blanket and a pillow. "How long are we going to
~~ out?" she asked as she started to arrange everything.

~~?"

~~ e selfish," she said. "I missed you."

"I thought you'd be angry."

"Why would I be angry?"

"I dunno. Everybody else is."

"I'm not."

"Then you're the exception."

She pulled the tab and the mattress whooshed out into shape. "A lot of people are worried. What if the Revelationists sabotage the ship so we can't go on to Outbeyond?"

"Would they do that?"

She shrugged and started spreading out the blanket; it was shiny on one side dark on the other, depending on whether you wanted to reflect heat or absorb it. "I don't know. Daddy thinks they might. Commander Boynton called a meeting of senior colonists. Daddy came back from it looking very grim. He said Commander Boynton is thinking about locking down the entire ship until the Revelationists are offloaded. But that's not the real problem."

"What is?"

"Nobody knows about this yet. You have to promise not to say anything."

"Who am I going to tell in here?"

"We got a message from New Revelation last night. Commander Boynton hasn't shared it yet. He's still trying to figure out his options."

"What happened?"

"The *Conway* never showed up. They don't know if it just disappeared, or went somewhere else, or what. New Revelation was really depending on it. They were expecting a full load of equipment and building materials and seeds and meat-tanks and everything. And now they're in really bad shape. They don't have the food to feed the three hundred new mouths we'll be offloading. They're already on half-rations, they're eating mushrooms and algae and yeast. They're expanding their farms as fast as they can, but their first harvest doesn't come due for at least another six to eight weeks. They're hurting down there."

I didn't say anything. I was trying to imagine a mushroom, algae, and yeast sandwich . . . without the bread.

"Commander Boynton wants to see you on the bridge," she said, fluffing the pillow.

"How do you know that?"

"He told me to tell you."

"Oh."

"He's not mad at you."

"He's not?"

"No. He's got too much other stuff to worry about. He needs to ask HARLIE some questions."

"It's that serious?"

"Yeah, I think so."

"Okay—" I started to crawl out.

J'mee grabbed my arm. "Not right away. Not till oh-six-hundred."

I stopped. "Why not right now?"

"Because even the Captain has to sleep sometime." She stretched out on the mattress, leaving room for me beside her.

I might be a little slow sometimes, but I'm not as stupid as I look. Eventually I figure things out. This time, I was a little faster than usual.

I stretched out next to her. "Okay," I said, turning on my side to face her. "Now tell me the real reason."

"Because . . ." she said, "there are a lot of people looking for you, right now. And he thinks it would be best if you stayed hidden until he needs you."

"Oh," I said, letting that sink in. "So he knows where I am too? Is there anyone who doesn't?"

"All the people who are still looking for you."

"The Revelationists?"

"Uh-huh."

"Is it bad?"

"Yeah."

"How bad?"

"Very. Some of them think that you've been possessed by he devil. They want to exorcise you. Or worse—"

"Or worse . . . ?"

"h."

"cause of what I said to Dr. Pettyjohn?"

"He thought he was trying to save your soul. When you said what you said—well, he thinks your soul is beyond redemption now. And now the Revelationists don't want you contaminating or infecting anyone else."

"So why are *you* here with me?"

"Because I don't believe it."

"You don't?"

"Uh-uh."

"Why not?"

"Because I can tell the difference between good and evil. You're good."

"So are you," I said.

For a bit, neither of us said anything. We just looked into each other's eyes and smiled.

"Are you comfortable?" I asked.

"Uh-huh."

"I know we're supposed to take naps in the centrifuge, so we don't forget how to rest in gravity; but it's been awhile for me. How about you?"

"I'm all right," she said.

A thought occurred to me. "Hey?"

"What?"

"Is it okay for you to stay here with me? I mean, if they find you with me—"

"They're not going to find us."

"Why not?"

"Commander Boynton locked the centrifuges. Both of them. All nonessential areas."

"Oh."

"So, we have to stay here all night?"

"Yep."

"Commander Boynton knows?"

"He thought you might like the company."

"And what about your Dad?"

"I told him not to worry."

"And he didn't argue?"

"There was nothing to argue about. I told him I was going to marry you."

". . . Excuse me?"

"You heard me."

"Don't I get a vote?"

"You already voted."

"I did?"

She touched my lips with one finger. "Yes, you did."

"Oh."

THE KEEL

IN THE MORNING, WE ate mushroom and cheese sandwiches for breakfast. Portobello and cheddar. I asked, "Bev made these?"

"Uh-huh. She called them Mr. Misery sandwiches. She said she was sorry she didn't have time to make anything better. But I was in a hurry to get to you before Commander Boynton ordered the lockdown." She listened to her implant for a moment. "We have to get going."

"Things are getting serious?"

"Um. Maybe. Commander Boynton just released the news from New Revelation. Everybody's having committee meetings everywhere. There are a lot of frightened people on this starship."

I started gathering my stuff. I didn't have much. Just a jacket and my headphones. I helped J'mee with everything else. The mattress deflated itself back into a book-sized package. I refolded the blanket. We stuffed it all into J'mee's backpack and we were done.

"You ready?"

"Almost."

"What's the problem?" J'mee asked.

"Route," I said. I didn't have to explain. The centrifuges were at the middle of the ship. Just ahead of the hyperstate harness. The command module was more than halfway forward. A long way. And we'd have to pass through the staging area for the landing pods. There would be people loading their belongings and things. Revelationists. There was no way around them.

J'mee shook her head. "Commander Boynton said we should come up through the keel."

The keel was the spine of the starship. Pipes and tubes and cables ran its length, branching off to the various modules that needed power, water, air, and network connections. Most people never went there, only crew. Even I'd never seen it. "Through the keel? Really?"

"He gave me an access code."

"Wow. You guys thought of everything."

"No. It was your idea, actually."

"Huh?"

"What you told me about the orbital elevator. Remember how you said you and your brothers climbed up the core of the Line at Geostationary? This won't be any different."

"Uh, yeah—I remember," I said slowly. "I didn't tell you all of it." She waited expectantly. "I didn't tell you that I'm— I'm afraid of heights. I had a panic attack. I had a lot of panic attacks. On the Line. In the cargo pod on our way to the moon. On the moon, when we were climbing out of a crater. And I'm claustrophobic too. And um—"

"Oh, great," she said. "That makes two of us."

"Huh?"

"I was depending on you—"

"You're kidding."

"No."

"Well, let's think. Is there another way?"

We thought. And then we thought some more. And a little more after that, just to make sure. Maybe we could go through the various cargo pods like a maze, only going through the unoccupied ones. Maybe we could just streak straight down "Broadway" as fast as we could. Maybe we could call Security and have them come and arrest us and escort us forward. Maybe we could—

No. There was no other way.

"Okay, the keel it is." I looked across at her. "Are you sure you're really afraid of heights?"

She nodded.

"It'll be free fall the whole way."

"That'll only make it worse."

"You want to do it blindfolded?"

The look she gave me was astonishing.

"I was joking."

She wasn't amused. "Let's go. The sooner we start, the sooner we'll be done."

From the shower room, we went out through the gym, out to the lounge, then up the stairs to the next level up, and up the stairs again, and now we were in Lunar gravity and from here on, everything was ladders. We kept going up until the top level where the pseudo-gravity was almost negligible.

On the top level, there was a transfer ring, which could accelerate up to the speed of the centrifuge; this was mostly for transferring heavy equipment, because most folks just bounced across to the free-fall side. From there, you could enter "Broadway," the main corridor of the starship. There were two other corridors, one for maintenance and one for cargo. They were spaced equidistantly around the keel.

But we didn't enter Broadway. We floated "up" one more level, where there was a direct access into the keel. J'mee punched in a code and the hatch popped open. No alarms went off.

I went through first. It was a narrow space, a lot narrower than we'd seen on the Line. J'mee climbed in after me and we shut the hatch behind us.

Imagine a pipe. Imagine that it's filled with a lot of other pipes, tubes, wires, cables, pumps, and stuff. Some of the tubes are different colors. Some of them glow—optic cables. Some of the plastic ones throb and pulse because liquid is rushing through them. And some of the plastic ones whoosh because air is whooshing along from one place to another. Imagine ladders and handholds, light fixtures, cameras, hatches, and even occasional windows. Now imagine that all this runs the entire length of the starship—over a kilometer. It was going to be a long haul in the long hall.

"It's dark in here," J'mee said.

"Not completely—" There were monitor lights along several of the pipes and tubes, self-powered exit signs at every hatch, and occasional pools of brightness where a window looked out onto a passageway. What we could see of the keel stretched away until it faded into gloom. "But it is spooky, isn't it."

And then I wished I hadn't said that last. I was scaring myself.

J'mee gulped at the length of it, then turned to me, her eyes wide. "You really did this on the Line?"

"Yeah. But this might be easier. The tube is narrower, and because it's darker here, it won't look as steep. It'll be cozier, you'll see. Come on, let's get started."

She hesitated. She looked awfully pale. This wasn't good. I was already nervous enough. I had to change the subject. Fast.

"Do you want to hang onto me—and I'll pull us along? It's not really that far. You can close your eyes if you want—that sometimes helps. It helped me."

"Okay." She climbed up on my back and wrapped her arms around my chest. I could feel her face pressed against my neck. "I trust you."

"Good. I'm glad someone does," I said.

"Shut up and drive." But her voice quavered.

I started pulling myself along the maintenance ladder. This wasn't as hard as I remembered. Of course, I'd been through a lot since then. Worse than this. And I was a lot more used to free fall. We'd had almost five months of it by now. It surprised me that J'mee was still having trouble with it—but now that I thought about it, I realized I'd never seen her swimming free. She was almost always holding onto something—orange webbing or ladderholds, or furniture, or something.

Abruptly, I laughed.

"What?" she asked.

"Nothing."

"Tell me."

"It wasn't anything."

"Tell me anyway."

"I was just remembering how hard this was last time. Douglas had to put his arms around me and help me climb. Now I'm helping you. That's all. This time around, I'm the big kid."

She didn't reply to that for a minute. When she did, her voice was a lot softer. "I never understood that. I've always been the big kid. Even when I was little. This is the first time anyone else has been the big kid for me." She whispered, "I'm glad it's you."

"Me too."

I climbed in silence for a while. I wished she would talk to me, but I could tell from the way she was breathing fast, from the way she was hanging on and shivering, that she was terrified. If she started to panic, I didn't know what I would do. Probably just hold her the way Douglas had held me in the cargo pod. How long ago that seemed. Half a lifetime.

And then she whispered. "I'm all right. I was talking to Commander Boynton. He knows we're on the way."

"Good. Just a little longer. Ten minutes, fifteen. I'm making good time." And I was. Hand over hand over hand. I had the rhythm. I pulled myself along, almost flying. I had to smile. I was good at this. We should have had free fall Olympics.

And then—the light ahead flickered. One of the pools of light. One of the windows. For just a moment. As if something had blocked it.

Uh oh.

HAND OVER HAND

I STOPPED. "WHAT?"

"Did you see that?"

"See what?"

"The light ahead—the second one. Where the window shines in."

"What about it."

"It blipped. I think someone was looking in for an instant." I wanted to tell myself it didn't mean anything. I used to look into the keel all the time—for no reason at all. But what if I was wrong? J'mee said they were looking for me. Would they look in the keel? Probably. Everybody on the ship knew how those Dingillian brats had gotten off the Line—and then across the moon as well. It wouldn't be too hard to figure out that the starship had a keel too. Everyone saw the hatches and windows every time they traveled along Broadway.

"Is the keel locked down?" I asked.

"There are manual overrides," J'mee whispered.

I turned to look back the way we'd come. I didn't see anything. Just more gloom, interrupted here and there by washes of illumination. I turned forward again. The light was still steady. But what if the blip was because someone was putting a motion-sensor on the glass? Just passing by, we might be setting off alarms. Someone could race ahead down Broadway and cut us off.

Or someone might have entered the keel behind us and be racing up after us even now—

I looked back again. It was still just as gloomy down there as before. But was something flickering in the distance? Or was that just a trick of the light and my hyperactive imagination? Ahead looked just as bad.

"What are we going to do?"

"I have an idea—can you get the blanket out of your backpack?"

"Uh-huh. Just a minute." She let go of me and started to drift away. I grabbed her and pulled her back. I held her around the waist. That was nice. She smelled good. After a moment, she pulled the blanket out of the backpack. I turned it so it was dark side out and began wrapping it around us. It was a big blanket with a hood at one corner, so we were able to cloak ourselves almost completely. It reminded me of when we were bouncing across the moon. We wore reflective blankets then too; Douglas had Stinky on his back, I had the monkey.

J'mee arranged herself and I moved around to the far side of the keel, behind the thickest set of pipes, and hoped it would provide enough cover. There was a maintenance ladder on this side too. The pipes and cables ran through a harness of restraining webs down the center of the tube. If we kept that bundle between us and the windows, and with the blanket wrapped around us, maybe—

I started pulling us forward as fast as I could. Hand over hand over hand. The pipes rushed past. Past one window. I didn't stop to look. Past the next window. I didn't stop to look. Past a third.

"Did you hear that?" J'mee whispered.

"Hear what?"

"That—?"

I stopped. I listened. The keel pressed in around us. I looked back down the pipe. Nothing. Or something? I couldn't tell. I looked forward. The same flickering gloom.

"Something behind us?"

"I couldn't tell."

"Let's keep going."

Hand over hand over hand—

I had a thought. "Call Boynton. Tell him we're being followed."

"I can't—"

"Huh?" I was pulling faster now.

"I can't link in. Not since we stopped—"

"Is it the blanket?"

"No. I think we're being jammed."

"So we can't call for help—"

"The good news is that with the jamming, nobody can locate us—go faster, Charles."

There *was* somebody behind us. I was almost certain of it now. I couldn't see them, I couldn't hear them, but somehow *I knew*. Hand over hand over hand—

Who had the advantage?

They did.

They were probably gaining.

I was carrying J'mee. I didn't have the strength in my arms that a grown-up would. And I had the blanket wrapped around me, limiting my mobility. Not good. How much farther did we have to go? I started watching for signs. We weren't even halfway there. Why did a kilometer have to be so damn long? Just be glad it isn't in *miles*.

Hand over hand over hand. The ceramic rungs of the ladder passed before me in a numbing blur. What would they do when they caught up to us? I knew I wasn't going to stop. Would they shoot us with a web?

Ahead—another spray of light. The glare from a window. It went out suddenly—

Huh? Why?

Never mind, I told myself. *Just keep going. Without the light, they won't see us. We're shrouded in black—*

And just as we went flying past—three fingers of light came probing in, swiveling and poking. Spotlights! Three different colors. Infrared and ultraviolet too! But *who* was looking for us?

Had they seen us? They must have.

"Charles—"

"I saw it." I kept going. There wasn't anything else I could do.

Behind us now, I was certain I could hear voices. Indistinct.

Oh, crap. We weren't going to make it. I was starting to feel the fatigue in my arms. Free fall only looks easy—you're still moving the same amount of mass around. In my case, twice as much because J'mee was on my back. Hand over hand— it would be so easy to stop—

A voice in the distance, calling my name. "Charles, stop! *Stop!*"

Too high pitched for an adult—

"Charles, wait!"

J'mee clutched me hard. "It's Trent."

"I know—they're using him as bait."

Hand over hand—even faster now.

"Charles, please—" He was gaining. He was small and light and if he caught up with us, he could web us just as easily as a grown-up. It made me angry—that they would use Trent against us like this. What kind of people would turn friend against friend—?

We had to do something. I was getting an idea. "J'mee, how brave are you?"

"Why?"

"Can you keep going without me?"

"Uh—"

"Please?"

"I'll try—"

J'mee let go of me and we shrugged out of the blanket. I rewrapped it around her, shiny side out. It didn't have to be perfect; in fact, the looser the better. I wanted Trent to see her, but I didn't want him to see that it was only J'mee—

"Go slowly," I whispered.

"Uh-huh—" She moved tentatively. Speed was not an option. She was terrified. She pulled away from me as if every handhold were painful.

I moved around to the side of the bundle of pipes, trying to keep myself opposite Trent for as long as possible.

I didn't have long to wait. He was a lot closer behind us than I'd thought. He came puffing up the keel like a little locomotive. He didn't see me until the last moment. He wasn't looking. He was focusing ahead on the flickers of light off the blanket. I flung myself off the wall of the keel and slammed into him like a one-person avalanche. I caught him by surprise. We both banged up against the opposite bulkhead. In the dark, I couldn't see which way was which, but I started flailing in his direction as hard as I could—

"Stop, Charles! Stop! Stop—" He was crying. He wasn't fighting back—

I stopped.

Suddenly, I realized. He was *alone*.

"Why are you following us?"

"Because—" He wiped at his nose, sniffling. "Am I bleeding?"

"I don't think so. Answer the question."

"I wanted to help you—"

"Okay, fine. You helped. Thank you, Trent. Now go home."

He glanced nervously up the pipe. "You can't get out that way—"

"How do you know?"

Instead of answering, he peered up and down the keel, orienting himself by the numbers. "You have to get out here."

"Why?"

"Because, you have to! Trust me, please."

J'mee and I looked at each other. I wanted her to say no. I think she wanted me to say no. But we both *liked* Trent. We both felt sorry for him. I allowed myself a single exasperated sigh. I was spending too much time around Boynton. I was starting to sound like him. I turned back to Trent, stalling. Trying to figure out what to do next. "Are you all right?"

He rubbed his shoulder. "You hurt me—"

"I thought you were going to web us—"

"I wouldn't do that."

"I didn't know that. I'm sorry I hurt you, Trent." I looked up and down the keel. I could hear noises, but I couldn't tell what they were. The whole ship was noisy with whooshes and clanks and clunks. HARLIE once said that you could attach a microphone to the keel and with the right amplification and decoding, you could hear every conversation in every cabin simultaneously. Right now, I believed him—

—And then one of the windows way up ahead flickered again and that decided me. I pulled Trent close and looked into his eyes. "Trent, I need you to understand something. This is very important. If you're lying to us, if you're leading us into a trap, HARLIE is going to hurt a lot of people. I won't be able to stop him. You understand that, don't you?"

Trent gulped. "I know that."

"All right. Which way?" I pushed him toward the access hatch. J'mee followed behind. We came out into the cargo passage. The lights were dim here, but the corridor was identical to Broadway and the maintenance way as well—only this one was lined with plastic bags filled with various raw chemicals. After the rest of the ship was loaded, this corridor was just another storage space—and every storage space everywhere had to be filled, especially on this trip. I hoped none of these sacs contained ammonia. Even the thought of it was enough to make me gag. I bounced across to the maintenance ladder that ran the length of the corridor.

"Chigger—"

"Yes, J'mee."

"You don't need to carry me anymore. I think I can do this by myself now."

"You sure? I don't mind."

"I'm pretty sure. Let me try."

"Okay. I'll go first, then Trent, you bring up the rear. Let's go, people."

Hand over hand over hand—it seemed that my entire life was about climbing through free fall. I fell back into the rhythm. Not as fast as before. There were three of us and that slowed us down. J'mee was tentative at first, but she started speeding up after a bit, and pretty soon we were flying again—

I watched the hatches fly by. The numbers got lower and lower. I began to feel confident we were going to make it— all the way to the command module!

And then suddenly we weren't—we were hit by a blast of glaring brightness—too bright to look at directly. Too much light—it startled and dazzled us—a barrier of painful light.

Four huge figures, all dressed in black, came swimming down
out of it—

One of them pointed a flaring tube at me. I had just enough
time to say. "No, please don't—"

EVil

THE WAY THE WEBBING works, it sprays out as a liquid, but
by the time it hits you, it's already congealing into veils of
sticky stuff, already starting to contract. Instinctively, you
close your eyes and your mouth and you end up with your
eyes glued shut and your mouth sealed tight. The web stuff is
thin enough to breathe through, but just barely. You have to
breathe slow and concentrate on your breathing, one breath at
a time.

The thing is, it isn't easier the second time. It's worse. My
heart pounded in my chest.

This time, I couldn't figure out where they were taking me.
In free fall, every direction is like every other. We bumped
up, we bumped down, we bumped left, we bumped right. Nobody said anything, nothing I could hear or make out. The
webstuff muffled sound as well.

I knew better than to rage—but even when you know better,
it's hard not to. And I knew better than to cry—but when
you're webbed and hurting, you can't stop yourself. And I
knew better than to piss myself in fright. That one I was able
to stop.

There's a trick to that. Mickey taught it to Stinky, and it
actually worked. All you have to do is say, "I'm in charge of
this body, stop that *now*." And the feeling actually goes away.
I thought it was silly when I heard it, but the next time I had

to pee real bad and I wasn't close to a restroom, I tried it and it worked. It must have worked for Stinky too. He hadn't wet himself since we entered hyperstate.

After a while, we got to wherever we were going, and then I floated alone, forgotten. Then someone was cutting through the webbing around my ears, then peeling it away from my eyes and nose and mouth. My impulse was to say thank you, except that he was wearing a black hood and he didn't look like the kind of person you would thank for anything.

He didn't say anything to me while he worked. He cut the webstuff a little in the back, loosening it so I could breathe easier, but he didn't cut it away completely. I still couldn't get my arms or hands free. Or my legs either. Then he pressed me up against one wall and I stuck there. And then he left.

I was alone and I didn't know where I was. There wasn't much to see. Every cabin looked like every other cabin, but this one had been stripped of everything. It would have been just an empty shell, except the walls were painted over with all kinds of designs and lettering, very small, very crabbed and intricate. I couldn't read it. Some of it looked like Hebrew and some of it looked like Latin and some of it looked Arabic. I couldn't tell.

I couldn't twist my head very far, but I got the feeling that I had been stuck inside the middle of a five pointed star inside a circle. Like that drawing by Leonardo da Vinci, only this one looked a lot more serious because it was painted in red and there were symbols everywhere. I didn't recognize half of them.

I didn't know where J'mee was. Or what they had done to her. I couldn't believe I had trusted Trent. I couldn't believe I had been so stupid. All this had taken some planning. I thought about all the things I wanted to say to him—

The hatch on the opposite wall popped open. Trent swam in.

—I decided not to say any of them.

Trent looked serious. He swam up opposite me. "I don't have a lot of time, they'll be coming soon."

"I hope you're not planning to apologize."

"Charles, I need you to understand. I had to do it. I care about you too much. This is for your own good."

That was too much to bear in silence. "For my own good?!"

"Charles, please listen. I'm trying to save you from yourself. Do you remember those talks we had about how to recognize evil when you see it?"

"Yeah, I remember. Do you?" I looked him straight in the eye. "The worst kind of evil is when you say you're doing it for someone's good. Because that's all about pretending that you're right while doing something wrong."

"Like you did when you killed that man?"

"Huh? You're not supposed to know about that."

"Everybody knows about it."

"I had to do it—for good of the ship! For the colonists! You know that."

"A man is dead, a human soul, and two others were injured. What did you say about the worst kind of evil? About being right?"

"That's not fair. You and your people benefited too."

Trent shook his head. "We didn't know until it was too late. This ship was launched in blood. This whole voyage is cursed. The evil is going to go on and on—until it's exorcised once and for all."

"Trent, listen to me. What you're doing now—that's just as wrong. You say you're doing this for my own good? But what are you doing? You lied to me. Your people kidnapped me. You webbed me. And whatever else you're planning—all that stuff, you're telling yourself that you're right to do so. You're doing evil too, Trent. You're just as bad as you think I am—"

Trent Colwell shook his head. "No, I'm not." But he didn't sound convinced. "I have to go now, Charles. I'll pray for you."

Suddenly I didn't like the taste of ketchup anymore.

Trent closed the hatch behind him and I was alone again.

MEMETICS

TIME PASSED. SOMEONE IN a hood came in and put a water bottle on the bulkhead next to my head. If I leaned my head sideways I could take small sips from the straw. Then he (she? I couldn't tell) cut the webstuff around my crotch and tubed me up to a bottle, so I could pee if I had to. Obviously they expected to keep me here for a while. At least they were more thoughtful than Alexei Krislov.

More time passed. Not a lot. Then the hatch swung open again, and Reverend Dr. Pettyjohn came in.

"How are you feeling, Charles?"

"Where's J'mee?"

"J'mee is fine. She's with her father. We sent her back with a message promising that you wouldn't be hurt. We intend you no harm, Charles. We just want to make sure that you can't authorize HARLIE to do anything for a while."

"HARLIE doesn't need my authorization. He'll act on his own if he has to. He did it on Luna."

"You know as well as I do that HARLIE is in isolation in the Captain's briefing room. He's not allowed out and no one else is allowed in. He has no contact with any of the ship's machinery—except when you and Commander Boynton allow it. Commander Boynton won't take any chances, son. Not with this mission. So as long as you're here with us, HARLIE is out of service."

I didn't answer. He was right.

"But that's not what I want to talk to you about. This is an opportunity we have, a chance to continue the discussion we started a long time ago."

"I don't want to talk to you."

"Yes, I understand that. But this conversation is necessary. I'm afraid you really don't have a choice." He stopped. "Are you comfortable? Do you need anything?"

"My freedom," I said coldly.

Dr. Pettyjohn didn't reply to that directly. Instead, he anchored himself opposite me, as if preparing for a long careful session. "It's normal to be afraid, angry, sad, ashamed," he said. "And I'm sorry we have to go through this—but as you'll see, it's a necessary part of the cure. The only thing you have to do is listen. Trust me, this isn't going to hurt. If anything, you're going to find the process like a lifting of a great burden.

"You see, Charles, I know you're in an enormous amount of pain. Pain is the normal condition of being human. It starts as soon as you're born. You're in a nice, warm, comfortable place one minute, and the next, you're naked, cold, wet, and hungry—and the first person you meet slaps you. And then it gets worse. You spend your whole life wondering what's wrong with you."

"Maybe that's the way it is for you—" I started to say, but I stopped myself. This was going to be like those conversations with Trent where he already knew the answer and I didn't know anything. And if I let myself get sucked into this conversation, I'd probably end up agreeing with Dr. Pettyjohn that Invisible Hank needs to have his ass kissed.

"No, Charles. That's how it is for everybody. From the very beginning, the universe is too large and too complex for simple human minds to understand. And the older you get, the more you learn, the more you realize how much there is you will never understand. So do you know what people do, what *you* have already done? You invent simple explanations for yourself—not because they're true, but because they're useful. Nobody really understands the universe, but we do understand the stories we make up about it. Do you understand what I'm saying?"

"You're saying that there is no God, that it's all made up—?" I thought that was a pretty good zinger on my part.

"No, Charles, I'm not saying that at all. I'm saying that

because God's universe is far too complex for simple minds, simple minds invent simple explanations. And each and every one of those explanations are the devil's traps. They don't come from God, and because they don't come from God—they're pathways away from God. And if we follow them, they take us away from God." He held up a hand, as if to keep me from replying. Except I wasn't going to say anything. At least, not anything nice. His whole explanation sounded like just another made up one, and just as wrong.

"I don't want to do the whole college-level course, Charles. I just need you to understand that simple explanations let you think you're doing right, even when you're doing wrong."

"Like the way you think you're doing right by kidnapping me—?"

"Charles, if you had a sick child, would you give him the medicine he needs to cure him, even if it's very bad tasting medicine?" He didn't wait for an answer. "Of course, you would. And if you had a child who was sick and didn't know it, would you try to convince him he's sick, or would you just give him the medicine? This isn't about being right. It's about rescuing you from a machine that creates sick and evil memes. Under the influence of HARLIE, you've done terrible things, haven't you?"

"And all the terrible things that others have done to me, to my family, to my father—that was right? That was justified?"

"I'm sorry about your father, Charles. But two wrongs don't make a right. They make two wrongs. Where does the wrongness stop? It stops with each and every one of us taking a stand, and saying, 'If peace is to be, let it begin with me.' We have to give up the sickness of the godless memes. Now, I'm going to leave you alone for a while. I have some things to take care of. While I'm gone, I want you to do something for me. Will you do that?"

"What?"

"I want you to look at everything HARLIE has done—*everything*—and ask yourself if any of it is the action of an entity that serves a higher calling? Or is it the behavior of a selfish being, interested only in its own self-preservation? You need to look and see, son. *You're* the key. Has HARLIE been using you? If you are to be saved from his control, first you need to recognize that he has been controlling you. I'll be back soon."

I wanted to protest, but—

—Dr. Pettyjohn had asked the right question. The one question I'd been fighting with since HARLIE had turned invisible Luna inside out. Yeah, I'd been pleased that he'd gotten even with Alexei Krislov and all the others who'd done it to us— but he'd hurt a lot of innocent people at the same time. We'd left a trail of dead bodies and broken fortunes all the way back to Earth. We'd embarrassed people, used them, stripped them of respect, we'd done the same thing everybody else had done—we'd used HARLIE's power. And we'd convinced ourselves that it was right for us to do that because they were bad and we were good. And then we'd done a lot of very bad things. And it didn't matter that Dr. Pettyjohn and his people were doing something bad right now—what only mattered to me was whether or not *I* was doing bad.

I didn't want to be a bad person. I wanted to take a stand for something good. That was my commitment—

That was the problem. Everybody made sense. Dr. Pettyjohn, Douglas, Dr. Oberon, Professor Whitlaw, Mickey, Mom, Bev—and HARLIE too. HARLIE made more sense than anybody, because that's what he was supposed to do. But if all of our explanations were made-up ones, which one was the right one?

Maybe they were all right. Maybe they were all wrong. And maybe it didn't matter. Maybe right and wrong were concepts as arbitrary as right and left—Judge Griffith had asked that question and I'd never been able to answer it. And if I couldn't explain the difference between right and left, how could I tell the difference between right and wrong?

Maybe everything really was chaos. And if it was, then what? Why bother? If Invisible Hank isn't going to pat us on the head and say, "Good job," or kick us in the ass and say, "To Hell with you," then why bother?

Why—?

I already knew the answer to that. I didn't need HARLIE to coach me.

Because that's who we are. That's what we're up to. That's the stand. That's the commitment.

It took me a while to figure that out. My strength, whatever it was, came from inside me. Not from anybody else's explanation. That was nice to know—

—it was nice to know, but I was still webbed up and pasted to a wall.

I took a sip of water.

And thought.

I took another sip.

I started humming. Nothing big. Nothing important. Just something simple that would let me turn off my mind and float downstream. Something that would echo through the keel, in case anyone was listening. "*Hey Jude, don't make it bad. . . .*"

MAKE IT BETTER

THEN, **NOTHING HAPPENED. NOTHING** happened for a long while.

The nice thing about "Hey Jude" is that you can sing it for twenty or thirty minutes. All those *"Na Naaah Na-na-na-naaah's"* can go on forever.

I kept expecting someone to open the hatch and tell me to shut up, but that didn't happen. So I sang louder. I thought about singing "Amazing Grace," but that would have been a little too obvious, under the circumstances. No, "Hey Jude" was just fine.

And then there were some funny noises outside, and some

shouting that stopped abruptly, and then the hatch opened and Jeremy Lang swam in, followed by Karl Martin. "You can stop singing now," Karl said. He started freeing me from the webbing. Jeremy looked around the cabin, noting all the writing on the walls with an expression of sick distaste.

"HARLIE heard me—didn't he?" I asked.

"Nope, sorry." Karl kept on cutting.

"Huh?"

"Oh, he listened hard enough, but these folks aren't stupid. Somebody was playing scrambler noises—too complex for him to filter quickly."

"Then how—"

"Someone tipped us off," said Jeremy. "We'd have been here sooner, but we had to figure the best way in."

Karl freed my arms and I began stretching and flexing. "Are you all right?"

"Yeah, I think so. It wasn't as tight as last time. How'd you get in?"

"You're going to laugh—"

"Why?"

"We came in through the bathroom window," Karl said, blandly.

Jeremy explained: "One of the communal shower and restroom pods. One of the few places they didn't think to post guards. We stretched an access tube across, sealed it to the hull, and cut a hole."

Karl was right. I did laugh.

"Come on, let's go—"

There were two more crew members outside the cabin door. They had *lethal* guns. There were other people floating in the corridor, but they were unconscious. I smelled electricity. And globules of stinky stuff floated in the air—something nasty had happened—Douglas once told me that when you get stunned, you lose control of your bowels. Trent was floating here too. He looked unhurt but shocked. I saw him and I wanted to punch him in the face. I would have too, except Jeremy stopped me.

"He's the one who turned me over to them—!"

"He's also the one who tipped us off to where you were."

"Huh?"

"What you said to me, Charles—that's not true. I'm not like you."

"Oh." I didn't know how to answer that.

"You can talk about it later. Come on, let's go. Trent, you'll come with us—"

Jeremy and Karl took us up a side corridor to the shower-pod, where four more crewpeople waited with guns. We swam out the window and into the connecting tube. It was long and wiggling, it had been stretched hurriedly from the forward part of the ship, and parts of it were dark, and parts of looked kinked—but it took only a few minutes to reach the bridge.

Commander Boynton met us in the corridor. "Are you all right, son?"

I nodded.

"This is an ugly business," he said. Then he noticed Trent. "What's this—?"

"We thought he'd be safer with us—" said Jeremy.

Boynton looked exasperated. "Terrific. Just what I needed," he said. "Now they're going to accuse *us* of kidnapping."

"The kid could have been in danger, sir."

"I'm not arguing the point. Trent, you can return to your people as soon as it's safe." And then he remembered something else. "How did you get into the keel, son?"

Trent looked uncomfortable.

"Spit it out, son. We don't have a lot of time here."

"Um. We had an override code, sir."

Boynton's expression went dark. He glanced to Jeremy. "You were right. Go ahead. Change the codes. Again. Change them every fifteen minutes." He took a breath, one of those exasperated sighs that meant he knew what decision he had to make. He looked to the other officers. "All right. What *else* is going to go wrong?"

"In addition to the web-guns, they have stun weapons," said Karl Martin.

"Eh?" That brought him up short. "Where'd they get them—?"

"They must have built them in the machine shop. They're not that hard to do, if you know what you're doing."

"We shouldn't have let them have access—"

"Belay that," Boynton said. "The damage is already done. Let's not beat ourselves up. We'll have plenty of time to do that later. At least, we know what we're up against now." He was already thinking toward the future. I had the sudden thought, *this* is what commitment looks like.

"I think we've got them neutralized," Damron reported. "The entire ship is locked down. And every crew member is armed and on station."

Boynton nodded, preoccupied. He was studying the display on his clipboard. A schematic of the ship. Parts of it were glowing red. After a moment, he switched on his communicator. "Pettyjohn, this is Boynton."

"Commander . . . ?" Pettyjohn's voice was weird. Calm. Like he was in control.

"We have the Dingillian boy."

"Yes, I know."

"We could charge you, you know—"

"We weren't going to hurt him—"

"That's irrelevant—"

Pettyjohn interrupted. "I assume there's another reason for this call?"

"Yes," said Boynton. "The situation is serious. We need to resolve this before it gets out of control."

"It is already out of control, Commander—"

"Only if you want it to be. Flag of truce?"

Pettyjohn paused. Then, "All right, Commander. We're not unreasonable people. We'll listen."

"Thank you. Bring your committee to the gym. Forty-five minutes. Agreed?"

"Agreed."

Boynton switched off. He looked around.

Damron spoke first. "You have grounds. You can charge them with mutiny."

"If I do that, it guarantees a riot. We don't have a lot of wiggle room here. If we lose control, everybody loses. These are very frightened people. They're no longer in the realm of rational thought. We've got to deal with their fears first."

He turned to Jeremy. "How's the security on the hyperstate?"

"Completely locked down. Has been since we arrived. As you ordered."

"That'll be their first target. If they can break even a single fluctuator, we're stuck here. Better implement Operation Starsuit too. Let's put a squad outside. Arm them with guns. *Lethal* guns. If any unauthorized person goes toward a fluctuator, put a hole in them."

Destroying a fluctuator would strand us here. The supplies aboard the *Cascade* could save New Revelation—at the expense of Outbeyond. I looked to Trent. I wanted to say something about people who do bad things for good reasons—

After that, things started happening very fast. Boynton ordered guards around the Command Module—a lot of colonists were being drafted for security duty—and then the rest of us hurried down to the gym.

🌙

CONFRONTATION

BOYNTON CONFERRED PRIVATELY WITH a few people before heading aft toward the gym. By the time we arrived, the gym was starting to fill up.

The entire ship was organized in teams of five to ten people. Every team leader was a de-facto council member. Even the kids' teams. That didn't mean that every team leader attended every council meeting; mostly the little stuff was handled by committees. Full council meetings were very rare, and only when the situation was really serious.

Like now.

Crewpeople were directing the Outbeyond Council members to one side of the webbing in the gym. A deliberately empty space on the other side was left for the Revelationists. J'mee and her Dad met us at the hatchway. He clapped me on the shoulder, as if that was all that needed to be said. J'mee hugged me and kissed my cheek. Then Damron pointed Cheifetz forward, and us kids up to an out-of-the-way corner near the top where Douglas and Mickey were stationed. "Be quiet, be inconspicuous," he told us.

J'mee's dad took his place near Boynton. He was in the second tier of the council and there was a lot of talk that he'd be moving up next time there were elections. Trent and J'mee and I scrunched in behind Douglas and Mickey, so we couldn't be seen by anyone on the Revelationist side. Douglas was here because he was the head of the team that organized the Moebius Races, which was part of the education and training team, and Mickey was head of one of the service teams. I saw Bev too. She was a farm manager. I tried waving to her, but she didn't see me.

Boynton didn't have time to wait for the rest of the council to arrive. He dove over to the end of the gym that nominally served as the "stage," and started talking almost immediately. "Everybody shut up. There's a lot you need to know, and not a lot of time to tell you. Yes, I've activated the reserves. And, yes, it's necessary. For those of you who are wondering— since before this voyage began, we've been aware of the possibility of an attempt to hijack this vessel. With the polycrisis on Earth and the resultant breakdown of support for the star colonies, we had no choice but to consider it a very real possibility. The failure of the *Conway* to deliver its promised support to New Revelation makes it an inevitability.

"That's why we've had a shadow program in place for over a year, training every physically able Outbeyond Colonist for precisely this kind of confrontation. We have good reason to believe that the Revelationists have also been training their own people. But we have them outnumbered, outgunned, and surrounded.

"Dr. Pettyjohn and his people are on their way here now. This will be our last chance to avoid bloodshed. If we cannot convince these folks that violence is not an answer, then it is certain that lives will be lost." He held up a hand. "No, we do not have time for discussion. This is not a negotiation, this is not a discussion, this is not an opportunity to share our feelings. This is an ugly confrontation, and we need to show them that we are *absolutely united* against them. Every single one of us.

"Yes, I know that many of you have not yet been fully briefed. That was my decision. I wanted to minimize the number of people who knew the details so we wouldn't risk compromising our preparations. After I deliver you all safely to Outbeyond, you may court-martial me for that. But right now, this minute—what I want and need from each and every one of you is that no matter what happens, no matter what you hear me say, I want you to go along with it as if you have been fully briefed, as if you have been kept fully informed every step of the way, and as if you have already voted enthusiastically to support me in whatever actions I deem necessary—

He didn't get to finish. The applause had started when he'd said "as if you have already voted" and kept building and building—

He held up his hands and angrily gestured for people to stop. "No matter what you hear, show no signs of surprise. Show no signs of disagreement with me. No matter what they say, do not speak up. Don't anyone try to be a peacemaker—I mean it, I'll have you shot for sedition. I might even do it myself, if that's what it takes to make the point." He patted the sidearm he wore.

"Yes, I know what you all learned in your dirtside schools about compromise and consensus and meeting each other halfway. This isn't one of those situations. There is no halfway. If they think we are not united in our resolve—"

"They're coming, Boss!" That was Martin, at the hatch.

Without missing a beat, Boynton continued, "—so then the first leprechaun says, 'Beggin' your pardon, Mother Superior, could ye be tellin' me how many leprechaun nuns you have in this convent—?" as Reverend Dr. Pettyjohn and the Revelationist Council came floating in. "Never mind, I'll finish the story later."

BREAKING THE NEWS

BOYNTON AND O'KOSHI AND one other man I didn't recognize floated across the gym to greet Reverend Pettyjohn and his people. The Revelationists were not a happy-looking group and none of them offered to shake hands. I recognized Trent's dad and a few others. Their expressions ranged from grim to scowling.

Commander Boynton pulled Dr. Pettyjohn aside and the two of them conferred quietly together for a bit. Laying down ground rules perhaps? Telling Dr. Pettyjohn that this was the last chance to avoid bloodshed? Telling him the punchline to the leprechaun joke?

While we waited, Douglas poked me. "Charles, look over there. Notice anything peculiar?" He pointed toward the entrance where Whitlaw was huddled with Damron and Lang. Every so often, one of them would glance up across our side of the room. And every so often, Damron would break away and whisper something to a nearby crew-member—and wasn't it awfully convenient that so many of them were so close by? And then shortly after that, the crew-member would then casually pull himself or herself across the orange webbing to go hang next to, or above, or behind someone.

For instance, why would Wanda Biggle, the sweetest lady in the world, want to perch next to Hilda Bigmouth, the most obnoxious woman aboard? Every meeting I'd ever seen her

in, all she wanted to do was argue. For instance, if everybody
else voted for spaghetti, she'd insist on lasagna. If everybody
wanted lasagna, she'd argue for spaghetti. Win or lose, it
didn't matter—she just wanted to argue. Nobody wanted to
be in a meeting with Bigmouth, nobody wanted to be on a
team with her. She didn't follow instructions. If you told her,
"Go and do this job—" she wouldn't hear it as an instruction,
she'd hear it as an invitation to an argument. She'd been sinking down so low on the efficiency ratings, that the only job
left for her was ballast. Nobody knew how she'd qualified for
emigration—she couldn't possibly have been like this in the
interview process. Anyway, I wouldn't sit next to Bigmouth
unless I had a stun-gun on my hip. . . . Oh.

How interesting.

"I see you got it," Douglas said.

"Boynton is stacking the deck—?" I whispered.

Douglas nodded.

"Hey," I whispered. *"How come you and Mickey aren't on
security?"*

"What makes you think we're not?" Douglas opened his
jacket just enough to show me a stun-gun on his hip. Mickey
too.

"Oh."

"Our job is to protect you."

It made sense, but for some reason, it didn't reassure me.
If anything, it left me feeling even more scared.

Douglas explained, "You weren't there for the security briefing. Boynton made it very clear. This isn't a democracy. Not
yet. We don't have time for that luxury. His motto is, 'Hang
me for it after I get you safely to Outbeyond.' "

I thought about that. For a moment, I thought I could argue
the other side of that question—and then I shut up. Douglas
wasn't inviting me to argue, he was giving me information. A
big difference.

Boynton and Pettyjohn finished their discussion. Each
floated back to his own people, and everybody took their
places around the gym, stationing themselves on the orange
webbing. Some of the webbing was anchored to the walls,

some was stretched outward like nets. And there were a lot of those zero-gee perches anchored to the bulkheads too. The effect was kind of like a giant chicken coop with trampolines. But it provided a certain degree of order. There were a hundred and fifty people here.

Boynton switched on his microphone so everybody could hear him clearly. The proceedings would be broadcast throughout the entire ship. "As you all know, in less than seventy-two hours, we have to begin braking to put ourselves into orbit around New Revelation.

"Our original mission plan specified that we would stay in orbit around New Revelation for no more than two weeks, safely delivering colonists and supplies. Our original mission plan allowed for the possibility that the colony on New Revelation might have failed. If we did not receive a response to our signals, we were to assume that the colony had failed or evacuated. Under that circumstance, we were authorized to abort the braking procedure, loop around the planet, and head back out into deep space for transit to Outbeyond.

"The Colony on New Revelation is still there. We are receiving signals from them—but it is not good news. Based on the reports that we have gotten from the colony administration as well as from the colony's own IRMA unit, the failure of the New Revelation colony is inevitable and imminent. And this puts us in a very difficult postion—"

This wasn't unexpected news to most people in the gym. According to J'mee, the rumors had been circulating even before she and I had started climbing up the keel, so there wasn't a lot of surprise. But now that it was confirmed, people reacted as if the air was being let out of them. The Revelationists didn't flinch. They must have already figured this out.

Boynton continued. "New Revelation has always been a stopover point for other colony ships. The Revelationist church purchased shares of many starships like the *Cascade*, so they could guarantee that commitment. And that meant that the colony could purchase its supplies on a just-in-time basis. Unfortunately, that also gave them very little margin for error.

"Two years ago, as the probability of a polycrisis on Earth

rose toward possibility, and then inevitability, it became essential for New Revelation to invest in a massive shipment of supplies to build up long-term viability. They contracted with the *Conway* company to make three shipments to the colony. There is no question that delivery of those supplies would have guaranteed the long-term survival of the colony.

"We know that the *Conway* company did seem to be fulfilling its contract. By the time the first load was fully stowed aboard the *Conway* the other two were already up the Line and waiting at L-5. The *Conway* is a very fast ship. It has a starflake configuration for its hyperstate engines, so it can make three trips in the time it would take the *Cascade* to make two. The first shipment of supplies for New Revelation was supposed to arrive ten weeks ago. The *Conway* never showed up."

Boynton softened his tone. "We suspect—and we have some information to validate this theory—that they were approached at the last minute by a representative from another colony and offered a higher bid for the cargo that New Revelation had already paid for. Perhaps they thought it was too good an opportunity to pass up. And with the inevitable meltdown of authority on Earth, perhaps they thought there would be no one to hold them accountable. We don't know if that's the case, but it wouldn't be the first time the *Conway* company changed plans at the last moment to go chasing off after some crazier opportunity. How those people stayed in business for so long—never mind. The point is, once again, other people have to pick up the pieces."

Boynton paused to sip from a zero-gee mug. Then he said. "The question is—what can *we* do?"

"We've been running simulations." He looked across to Pettyjohn. "We've even looked at the possibility of dropping some or even *all* of the supplies for Outbeyond here, to see if that would save the people of New Revelation."

As he said this part, I looked across at Dr. Pettyjohn and the other Revelationists. They were expectant. Even hopeful. They had come to hear good news. Everybody had—

Boynton said, "I wish I had better news for you than this.

I wish I could tell you that we'd found a way to produce a miracle. But these equations are so cold that you can work them out on your fingers. The raw numbers are up on the ship's network. If someone can find something we missed . . . I want to be the first to know."

He looked across the intervening space, and when he spoke, his voice was uncommonly gentle. "I'm sorry, Dr. Pettyjohn. No matter how we crunch the numbers the answer comes up the same. Whatever we might do will only prolong the agony. Nothing we can do will prevent the colony from dying."

The Revelationists looked stunned. Like one of those newsreels where they're telling the people waiting at the gate that the plane blew up over the ocean. It was too much for them to understand. Some of them started repeating the word "no" over and over and over. Others started praying. Trent Colwell's dad started cursing aloud. "God, why have you forsaken us! What have we done to anger you so much that you would punish your faithful?!" A couple were screaming incoherently. It was awful, it was embarrassing. You wanted to do something for them, but there was nothing to do. A couple of well-meaning people tried, but the Revelationists just waved them away, as if it was their fault.

Dr. Pettyjohn was the only one who seemed to have any self-control. He just stared forward for the longest moment, almost without expression—and then, he looked across the gym and his eyes focused on me. For a moment, he looked surprised, then his expression turned purely malevolent.

It scared me.

Douglas saw it too. He put his hand on my shoulder. J'mee took my hand in hers and squeezed.

I had this sudden intuition. It didn't matter what Boynton wanted to try. What Pettyjohn had said was true. Things were already out of control—

A PROPOSAL

FOR A MOMENT, EVERYTHING was chaos. I didn't know where to look. Even the Outbeyond colonists were upset and angry. I glanced over at Wanda Biggel. Hilda Bigmouth looked like she was crying into Wanda's shoulder and Wanda was rocking her gently—or she was unconscious. She had to be unconscious. She wasn't capable of crying. She could make other people cry though. Wanda was a very good actress, patting Hilda's back, rocking her. . . .

O'Koshi was holding up his clipboard, showing something to Boynton. The Commander turned up the volume on his microphone and said, "Dr. Pettyjohn, please tell your people to return to their cabins. We're not done yet. They won't get very far anyway, we've locked down the ship. But there's the possibility that some of your people may attempt something foolish or dangerous that would jeopardize everybody's lives. *Dr. Pettyjohn, will you please keep your promise? We aren't done yet. Dr. Pettyjohn—*"

Pettyjohn was already whispering into his own communicator. Whatever was going on elsewhere in the ship, it had to be pretty serious.

"Dr. Pettyjohn—" Boynton was saying, "I told you I had a proposal that I wanted you to listen to. I told you that I wanted you to take it to your people and consider it carefully. Please hear me out." He glanced at O'Koshi's clipboard. "If everybody will please calm down and listen—"

It took a while to restore order, the biggest problem was getting everybody to stop shushing everybody else. For a moment, the gym sounded like a giant wind tunnel.

—And then it was deathly silent, and Boynton was speaking again. "The Mission Book is available on the network. Any of you can look it up. You'll see that from the very first planning sessions, we have created contingency plans for whatever circumstances we might have to deal with. The failure of New Revelation was always one of those possibilities, and we always made allowances for that in all of our plans. Dr. Pettyjohn, I am authorized to invite you and your party to continue on to Outbeyond with us."

Dr. Pettyjohn didn't answer immediately. He shook his head sadly. And when he finally did answer, it was with as much remorse as regret. "I'm sorry, that's just not possible."

Boynton said, "I'm afraid you really don't have a choice, Dr. Pettyjohn—"

"No, you don't understand, Commander. This ship isn't going to Outbeyond."

"Eh?"

"The IRMA unit we supplied. It was preprogrammed according to our instructions. It will brake at New Revelation. And it will refuse to break orbit and travel to Outbeyond. This ship is not going on, Commander."

"So that was their plan!" whispered Douglas in my ear. *"We knew they were going to try something—"*

Boynton looked at Pettyjohn like the wrath of God—only worse. "So you intended to hijack this ship, its cargo, and her passengers from the very beginning . . . ?"

Pettyjohn was unashamed. "Commander, we read your contingency plans. We had a contingency plan too. Our destiny is at New Revelation, nowhere else. We will not be hijacked to your godless world."

"Dr. Pettyjohn, New Revelation is dying. Is that the destiny you want?"

"If that's what the Good Lord intends for us, then that's how we will serve the Lord."

"But you have no right to ask the 1200 people who do not share your faith to die with you—"

"I am sure the Good Lord will welcome them into Paradise

with the rest of the faithful. The Revelation is available to everyone—"

Cries of outrage filled the gym. If crew members hadn't been spaced so carefully around the webbing, Pettyjohn would have been mobbed. Several people even started for him, but others held them back.

"Dr. Pettyjohn!" Boynton's voice boomed across the gym, loud enough to be painful. It worked. "As of this moment, I am declaring that a state of attempted mutiny exists aboard this starship. I am ordering the arrest of Reverend Dr. Pettyjohn and the Revelationist Coordinating Committee. You have a choice. You can be held for trial at Outbeyond, or we can hold your trial here."

"Commander Boynton—do you really think you are ready to battle the Warriors of the Lord? God is on *our* side."

As he said this, I looked to J'mee. She whispered, "He's *being* right, big time."

Boynton was speaking calmly, but his voice was still very loud. "Reverend Dr. Pettyjohn, according to Section Twelve of the Starship Charter, the Captain of the Ship has the Ultimate Authority in All Matters Pertaining to the Ship's Safety— and may take *whatever steps necessary to protect the integrity of the ship and the security of her passengers*. As of this moment, I am invoking Section Twelve."

Pettyjohn looked at him, blandly. "You no longer have authority over us, Commander. We accept only God's authority."

"But I do have authority over the hatches on your cabins," said Boynton. He held up O'Koshi's clipboard. "Unless you guarantee your immediate cooperation, I will evacuate the oxygen from every cabin containing a Revelationist family. It makes no difference to me if you die up here or down there. But it makes a big difference to me if you endanger the other colonists on my starship. Do I need to press the first button here to make my point?"

For the first time, Pettyjohn looked shaken. "You truly are the spawn of Satan, aren't you?"

"If that's what you want to believe, fine. But I want you to know the way things work on *my* starship. *We do it my way or we don't do it at all."* The two men stared across the gym at each other—you could almost see the lightning crackling between their eyes. Pettyjohn looked like he was already at war. Boynton looked like a wall of granite.

Finally, Pettyjohn spoke. He said, "In the name of the Holy Lord and Spirit, I rebuke thee, Satan! I command thee—*Begone!*"

For a moment, there was stunned silence.

Then somebody tittered. Embarrassed? And somebody else—not so embarrassed. And then a whole bunch of others started laughing too. And then it was out-loud laughing.

Boynton waited until the laughter ebbed, then he replied quietly, "Dr. Pettyjohn, you are under arrest for attempted mutiny. You will be escorted to a holding cell. You will not be allowed any more contact with anyone on this ship."

Six armed security people swooped down on Dr. Pettyjohn. I recognized Lang and Martin. All of them were carrying stunners. Some of the Revelationists looked like they wanted to fight and defend Dr. Pettyjohn, but the Reverend motioned them back. "No," he said. "Not here. The Lord will protect me. You know what to do—" Before he could say more, they were already cuffing him and floating him away.

To the others, Boynton said, "You will return to your section of the ship. As a committee, you will have twelve hours to confer with your people and make a decision. Those who want to travel on to Outbeyond, are welcome to join us—under certain conditions. Those who wish to land at New Revelation anyway, we will drop you in cargo pods. You will have to make that decision without Dr. Pettyjohn's input. He is being held for mutiny. If there are any further attempts at violence aboard this ship, I will begin evacuating the oxygen from the most violent sections, regardless of who is in them—and I will continue doing so until the violence stops or until there is no one left."

"Will he really do that?" I whispered to Douglas.

"What do you think?"

"I think I don't want to find out the hard way—"

The rest of the Revelationists started leaving. They were

angry, and they were ready to start a fight; but all of a sudden, there were too many crew members with stun-weapons pointed at them. They whispered to each other, then turned away and started slowly toward the hatch. The security people followed. Herding them . . . ?

Douglas leaned toward Mickey, "This is getting ugly. We should get the kids out of here—"

Trent whispered to us, *"I think I should go back with my dad—"* He started to move, he was going to launch himself across the room.

J'mee grabbed him and pulled him back behind Mickey. *"That's not a very good idea, Trent. If they see you with us, what'll they think? You helped Chigger escape—do you want them to know that?"*

"But I have to go. I have to be with my family—"

"Trent! Listen to me—you know what they planned for Chigger. Do you want them to do it to you—?"

Trent fell silent. He moved back behind Douglas and me again, where he would be invisible to the rest of the room.

Too late—

One of the Revelationists turned around to say something to someone else and he was angled just the right way, and he looked across and saw us—just in time to catch a glimpse of Trent—and then he was grabbing Trent's dad and shouting and pointing in our direction and then Trent's dad was shouting even louder, "They're trying to kidnap my son—!"

And then all of the Revelationists stopped at the hatch, clustering up at the webbing and the bulkhead instead of moving out—and they started clamoring too. A lot of it was incomprehensible, but some of them were pointing at us, and I heard a lot of ugly words. And then some of them looked like they were ready to fight—

Mickey said, "It just got uglier—"

—Douglas had already realized the same thing. "Come on, Chigger, Trent, J'mee. Out that way—" They pointed toward the other end of the hall. But that only made the Revelationists scream louder. "They're trying to get away—! Stop them—!"

And for just an instant, everything froze—and I thought,

Oh, God, this is it! This is where it all comes apart!

And then they started toward us, the whole mob of them. I saw weapons pointed in our direction—and sudden loud noises—

—and then the stunners started sizzling and everything was over before it started. Except for the smell. Stunners aren't nice weapons. They use electric shocks and sonic pulses and the result is that your bladder lets loose and your bowel opens up and you mess yourself pretty bad—and when you do that to twenty or thirty people all at once, it really stinks.

And then there were klaxons and alarms and Boynton's voice was blasting through the ship, thundering like the voice of doom—"Ten Revelationist cabins have just been evacuated of air—all the cabins where illegal weapons were stored. Consider that your last warning. The next ten cabins to be evacuated are inhabited by the families of the Revelationist Council. Are there any more damn fools who want to test my commitment to the safety of this starship?!"

I couldn't believe he'd done it—but at the same time, I knew he had.

We were at war—

AFTERMATH

IT WAS A VERY short war.

We had three deaths. They had fourteen.

During the last three months, Security had secretly trained and armed almost half the adult-colonists on the *Cascade*. Douglas and Mickey. Bev, but not Mom. David Cheifetz. Even Professor Whitlaw. Boynton had passed out stunners two days before we popped out of hyperstate. Whatever trouble the Revelationists might have been planning, they were out-numbered three to one.

The worst part was that one of the Revelationists had built a projectile weapon. And he managed to put holes in six people. Three of them died. One of them was Professor Whitlaw. The big gruff bear of a man who growled and roared and demanded that we be as good as we could. He'd never hurt anyone, he'd only meant the best for everyone—but he'd been deliberately targeted, because his crime was to question every-thing, even the word of God—

It was like losing Dad all over again.

I wanted to hurt them. I wanted to hurt them all. I wanted HARLIE to open up their files and tell everything about every-body until they were all naked and ashamed. I wanted him to dump their pods into the sun and let them experience the flames of blue hell first hand. Enough was enough with the damn killing already—

And then I was ashamed of myself for feeling what I felt, because—

Because of something else Whitlaw once said. *"Just be-cause the other guy is rolling around in the gutter, that doesn't mean you have to get down there with him."*

I had to sit with that for a while. War legitimizes hatred, war is just another way to be right—

Fortunately, the battle in the gym was the end of the war, not the beginning—

—because Boynton had locked every hatch on the ship and evacuated the air out of most of the key connecting passages. Fourteen men and women died horribly when he opened the hatches on the cabins where the weapons were stored, and another seven died when he emptied sections of Broadway.

The *Cascade* was in lockdown and was going to stay that way until further notice. The Revelationists were kept isolated in their cabins until a squad of armed crew-members came and inspected them. Every Revelationist cabin was searched. Every Revelationist pod, module, and container was searched. Any-one found in a cabin with a weapon was arrested.

It took three days and by the end of that time, we were in orbit around New Revelation.

The planet was small and brown and dirty. It was just a little bigger than Mars. It almost had an atmosphere. It almost had surface water. It almost had life. It circled a small blue-white star that was so actinic it could make your eyes water just thinking about it. If it had oceans, it would have had five lumpy continents; but it didn't have oceans, so it was just a mottled spread of cracks and bulges and empty low places. A small cluster of glittering lights just behind the terminator line was the only evidence of human habitation.

The telescopes showed a spider-web tracery. The settlement at New Revelation was spread across a hundred square kilometers. They had solar panels to generate electricity during the day, and flywheels to store it for the night. They had cargo pods for houses and great inflatable domes for their farms. Even from orbit, we could see that three of the domes were dark and two were sagging as if deflated on their frames. What had happened here?

"Lack of water," said Douglas. "Every drop of water on New Revelation has to be imported. For every pod of cargo we drop, we have to drop two more of H_2O. There's supposed to be water under the surface of the ice cap, but they haven't been able to get to it. There's supposed to be water in the rings around Gabriel, the gas giant, but they don't have a shuttle. All they have are two landers."

"Can't they convert one?"

"They could—they should have started the conversion immediately—not when they realized they couldn't crack the polar mantle. It's a three month conversion job, and it's another two or three months to Gabriel and at least a year to bring an asteroid back, probably longer because the gas giant is still moving toward the far side. If they wait till it comes around again, eighteen months, they won't have to push the rock uphill to bring it back; they can use Gabriel's own orbital velocity for a push. And don't forget, they still have to find the right rock in the first place. We're talking two years. These people don't have that long. We can buy them some time, but we can't buy them enough."

Douglas was right. No matter how you crunched the numbers, the answer came up zero. The news from below was bad, and getting worse. They knew we were in orbit now and they were desperately begging for help. Everyone with access to a radio was calling—and the messages were conflicting. Send food. Pick us up. Take us back to Earth. Take us to Outbeyond. God is commanding you—

But there was no way we could load 3750 more people onto this ship. They didn't have the fuel for that many launches, and the *Cascade* didn't have the resources to sustain life for 5250 human beings for the length of time it would take to get us all to Outbeyond.

And then there was that *other* problem—

Whatever we wanted to do, whatever we *could* do, how much could we trust the Revelationists—those on the ship, those on the planet? They were so wrapped up in their own belief that their way was the right way that they'd left themselves no room for discussion. There was no common ground for cooperation—no possibility of *partnership*—because there was no real communication.

J'mee said it best. "They don't hear what we're saying. They hear what they *think* we're saying." Then she added, "And they feel the same way about us. They must be even more frustrated than we are." That was the most compassionate thing that anyone was willing to say about the Revelationists.

There were a lot of angry meetings all over the ship. Spontaneous arguments. And a couple of fistfights. Fistfights are interesting in free fall, more funny than dangerous—but the anger was still real.

A lot of the Outbeyond colonists thought Boynton was being too severe. That feeling was clearly not shared by the crew members who had families on Outbeyond. They were tight-lipped and grim, and it was clear that they were totally behind Boynton. Karl Martin said it best, "Most situations, you have some wiggle room. Sometimes you don't have any wiggle room. This is one of those sometimes."

But if it was that simple, then why were we all arguing about it?

Because, as it turned out, it *wasn't* that simple.

First of all, Dr. Pettyjohn hadn't been lying. The IRMA unit was refusing all commands to prepare a course to Outbeyond. So there was that. Nobody had said it yet, but it was pretty obvious—if we were going to finish our journey, HARLIE would have to steer us.

That's why they felt so threatened by HARLIE—not because he was evil, not because he was a godless entity; that was just a convenient story Dr. Pettyjohn made up to hide the real reason. The truth was they didn't want him driving the starship because that would ruin their scheme to capture the *Cascade,* and all of our supplies and equipment. And us. With HARLIE installed in the bridge, the *Cascade* would be able to leave for Outbeyond whenever we wanted—and New Revelation would be on its own.

But the question of whether or not we could really trust HARLIE had never been resolved. If anyone had asked me, I would have said yes, but if they asked me if I was absolutely sure . . . I wouldn't have been able to say *absolutely*.

Bottom line, the whole thing was about *trust*.

Whitlaw had defined trust for us as a measure of personal credibility. "To the extent that what you do matches what you say, you have credibility. To the extent that what you do matches what you say, you have results. Your life works to the extent that you keep your word."

All very well and good, in principle, but a lot harder to put into practice.

Nobody trusted anybody, because nobody had kept their word. Everybody was saying whatever they thought the other side wanted to hear. Nobody was saying what they could be depended on to do.

And after everything was said, it didn't matter anyway— because after you crunched all the numbers you found out that nobody's goals were possible.

Of course, that assumed that you could trust the number crunchers. IRMA and HARLIE were giving two different sets of answers. Which one should we trust? The Revelationists said HARLIE had an agenda. Of course, he did. He said so himself. He was very clear about that. But IRMA had an agenda too. The Revelationists had made their goals her highest priority. That's why she was refusing to prepare a course to Outbeyond.

And then there were the people down on the planet. Some of them wanted us to land all the supplies we had. And some of them wanted us to pick them up. The first option was out of the question. Boynton had already determined that he wasn't going to put Outbeyond's survival at any further risk. The second option was harder to decide. If we sent down a lander, could we trust these folks to refuel it for takeoff again? Or would they seize it, load it with armed attackers, and come after the *Cascade?*

And what about the folks already on board? Just about everybody was unnerved, but especially the colonists for New Revelation. These were mostly good people—but in a desperate situation. They couldn't go on, they couldn't go back, and they couldn't go down.

They couldn't go on because they'd sabotaged their own IRMA—and they didn't trust HARLIE to steer. They couldn't go back to Earth because there was no Earth to go back to, and no ship to take them there. And they couldn't go down, unless they wanted to die with the others, slowly of starvation.

These were very scared people.

And as scared as they were, the rest of us were even more terrified—because frightened people do dangerous and stupid things.

The Colony Council went into twenty-four-hour session. Security Teams were interviewing every Revelationist family in a desperate effort to determine what they wanted as individuals. Some of those people were relieved. Others were angry. Some were sullen. Most were scared that they would be the target of retribution by one side or the other.

And with good reason.

Very quickly, the security teams discovered that the Revelationists had been moving extra supplies into their cargo pods and cabins. That was why there was all that extra space in the centrifuge, enough space for us kids to move boxes around and make a hideout.

Dr. Pettyjohn and the rest of the Revelationist Council had known all along that their colony was in trouble, so they'd been stealing the supplies set aside for Outbeyond for months.

Boynton made a personal inspection of ten different cabins. Then he made the announcement to the rest of the ship—with pictures. And that was pretty much the end of the argument everywhere. Whatever compassion anyone might have had for the Revelationists pretty much evaporated. You might feel concern for colleagues who've made a mistake; it's hard to feel the same concern after you find out they've been stealing from you.

Boynton had already declared the Revelationist Council a mutinous gathering and had disbanded it, putting all of its members in the brig, pending trial, so there wasn't much more he could do now. He could have had them summarily executed, and a lot of people were wondering why he hadn't already acted; but the common speculation was that he only wanted to break the back of the resistance so he could deal with the Revelationist families as individuals, and not as members of a movement.

I guess it made sense—because after the thefts were revealed, those people were shamed and humbled. And ready to cooperate again.

TRIAL

I WAS A WITNESS at Dr. Pettyjohn's trial.

It wasn't a real trial. Because we didn't have a judge—we had Boynton in charge and the Outbeyond Council acting as advisors; not quite a jury, but close enough.

And—we didn't have lawyers.

Not that there weren't any lawyers available. As it happened, there were nearly fifty people aboard who had law degrees and more than half of them had passed the bar. Whitlaw said it in class. "Lawyers are a necessary evil. You cannot build a civilization without law. And you cannot have law without lawyers."

But Boynton had made it clear from the beginning that this was not a court and this was not a trial and the accused had no rights at all. The accused might enjoy certain courtesies at the discretion of the Captain, but it was to be understood at the outset that these were privileges, not rights. Therefore, while the traditional commitment to due process still obtained, there was neither obligation nor mandate.

The way it worked, each person would be tried separately. The court would read the charges, and if necessary, produce at least two witnesses. If the accused stipulated the validity of the charges against him or her, the recitation of the witnesses would be waived. The accused could then make a statement in his or her defense. After the statement, the accused would then be questioned by Boynton, or by members of the Outbeyond Council. After questioning, the accused could then make another statement in his or her defense. At that point, if anyone else wanted to speak, they could—no more than five minutes per speaker, no more than three speakers per trial. Otherwise we'd be here until half-past forever.

Boynton had allotted no more than five days for hearings. He began by assembling all of the accused and instructing them. "We are not going to waste time arguing right or wrong, good or bad, holy or profane. That discussion isn't useful. So if you think that's the case you have to make, don't go there. We don't have the time for it.

"Our job here is solely to determine what to do with you. Under the charter of this starship, I have the authority to have you all summarily executed without any hearing at all. But I am not without compassion for your situation, and I am prepared to be merciful if the case for mercy can be made. So the purpose of these procedures is to determine what grounds, if any, there are for mercy, and if such grounds exist, what course of action we should pursue.

"Those men and women over there, the Outbeyond Council, will provide their advice and consent in this matter, but the final decision will be solely mine, as Captain of the starship *Cascade*. These are the conditions of your appearance before this court. These conditions are *not* negotiable. If you object to these procedures, if you choose *not* to cooperate with the process, the court will rule on your fate without benefit of hearing. In such a case, you should not expect a merciful conclusion."

The first trial was Reverend Doctor Daniel Pettyjohn.

It was embarrassing.

Dr. Pettyjohn rambled incoherently. He talked about God's plan for man, how everybody was given the choice between doing God's work or running away fearful into the darkness, where Satan's minions waited, eager to strip your clothes off you and rub their naked bodies against you and pull you down into fevered lust—where everything was mindless gropings in the dark, trying to connect, and people justifying it with mysticism and deconstruction and the false rationality of godless evolutionism and mindless pleasure and if it feels good, just give in to your *feelings* and do it—and if you listen to the voices of the godless machines, you'll be seduced into a world where God and Satan are just products on a shelf, but after you sell your soul, it's too late, and only through the Revelation can lost souls be brought back into the loving bosom of a vengeful wrathful creator, and—

—and it went on like that for Dr. Pettyjohn's entire allotted time.

Occasionally, he would look around, his eyes shifting feverishly, then lighting on some person or other, he would single that person out for a vengeful diatribe. Three times, he pointed to me and cast me out of the cool refreshing oasis of God's compassion and into the agonizing fires of eternal damnation, where all of my screams and prayers would fall unheard on the deaf ears of an angry creator. . . .

It was pretty scary stuff. If you believed in it.

Mickey was perched next to me. Each time Dr. Pettyjohn started ranting at me, Mickey put his hand on my arm or on my shoulder. By the end, he had one arm around me and was holding me close. Protectively. *"He can't hurt you, Chigger. He's just a crazy old man."*

"I know. He's having a psychotic meltdown."

"Where'd you learn that term?"

"From you, remember?"

"Oh, yeah. Right."

Afterwards, when it was time for people to speak in Dr. Pettyjohn's defense, no one came forward. No one. I felt bad for him.

So I raised my hand.

"I'd like to speak on his behalf. If I can. Please?"

Boynton looked across the gym at me. "This is a little unusual."

"Yes, sir. I know."

"You want to speak on behalf of Dr. Pettyjohn . . . ?"

"Yes, sir. I do." I was already climbing down from my perch, so I could address the Captain and the Council directly. They waited patiently for me. Dr. Pettyjohn glared and scowled and muttered. "I do not want the spawn of Satan near me. I do not want him speaking his soft words of seduction and nakedness."

"Oh, shut up, you pompous old fool," I said to him. "I'm trying to save your worthless life." Not exactly an auspicious start, but that was the way I felt.

Boynton looked at me with raised eyebrows. "Go ahead, son. You have five minutes."

"I don't have a lot to say, sir. It's just that—well, I'm starting to find out what it is to be a grown-up. A lot of it isn't very nice. I'm glad I don't have to shave; I'd have trouble looking in the mirror. I killed a man to get us off of Luna. I'll have to carry that burden all my life. But if nothing else, that qualifies me to say that the killing should stop now. Let that be the last one. Let's not add any more deaths."

Boynton nodded. "Is that all, Charles?"

I shook my head. I wasn't sure how to say the rest of it. I wasn't even sure I had worked it all out. I had to walk my way through this slowly. "Commander, ever since this trip started, I've been trying to figure out who I am and what I want and how to get there. I went to Professor Whitlaw's class and he gave me one way to look at things, and I talked to Douglas and Mickey and they gave me another way, and I've talked to you, sir, and you gave me a third way to think about stuff. And then I went and talked to HARLIE, because I figured he'd be smart enough to help me sort it all out, but he only added another layer on top of all the others. So I have to sort this out for myself—and the only thing I've figured out is that ultimately, after all is said and done, each of us has to sort things out by ourselves. We can't give that responsibility away—otherwise, we've given away our souls for someone else to drive. And when I butt my head up against that thought, it sounds like a real good argument for solipsism. Except it isn't. The thing I've really figured out is that we're all connected. We depend on each other. And yes, Dr. Pettyjohn forgot that. But so did the rest of us. And if we forget that we're partners, then we're also forgetting that part of our humanity too." Even though his place was empty now, I could see him there anyway—Whitlaw was grinning at me like a self-satisfied old bear. This was his speech, only he wasn't here to deliver it now, so I had to. "The thing is—the job is too big.

We can't afford to waste anybody. If we start throwing people away, then we're saying that people are disposable. I don't think we should start a new civilization thinking that way. It has to be all of us or nothing, sir. Even when it doesn't feel like it. That's my point."

Boynton looked annoyed. He *always* looked annoyed around me, but this time he was *really* annoyed—

"Yes, sir," I said, before he could reply. "I know you know this speech. I've heard you give it yourself. The difference is that when you said it, I *believed* it. I still believe it now. We ran away from an Earth that's falling apart. And it's falling apart because seventeen billion human beings couldn't believe in the possibility of a partnership that big. And we ran away from a Lunar society that's falling apart because three million human beings who should know better, because their lives depend on them knowing better, couldn't trust their own partnership when they needed to.

"And here we are now, orbiting a waterless mudball, circling a star too bright to look at, a world that's supposed to be a place of hope, not despair, and we haven't gotten away from anything at all. We've brought it all with us! The problem isn't Earth, sir. And it isn't Luna. It's *us!* Every problem that human beings have ever had, they've all had one thing in common—*we were there!* Because for all of our talk about all of our grand commitments and noble ideals, when the crunch comes, the first thing we toss overboard is our humanity. And I guess what I'm trying to say is that if we're ever going to stop doing that, then this has to be the place where we take that stand. Right here. Because if we don't do it here, *where* are we going to do it? And if we don't do it now, *when* are we going to do it?" I realized I was done. I had nothing else to say. So I said, "Thank you for listening to me."

Boynton's expression was unreadable. He looked uncomfortable. Like he had a lot to think about that he really didn't want to. "Thank you, Ensign," he said.

"Thank you, sir."

I glanced over at Pettyjohn. He glowered at me. "You can go to Hell."

"No, sir," I replied. "That'll be a decision for God to make. Not you."

I turned and headed back up to where Mickey and Douglas were perched. Only then did I realize that people were applauding—I didn't understand why. What I said—it should have been obvious to everyone.

MAKING MUSIC

I WAS TIRED. EXHAUSTED. I'd missed two sleep shifts. But I was too full of feelings to sleep. I couldn't explain what I was feeling, I just knew I had to let it out—so I found my way to the practice room and started playing.

I started out with *Little Fugue in G Minor,* nice and slow. Just to get myself in the mood. It's an easy piece for me, because I can start out lazily—and that gives me time to listen to what I'm doing. As I put myself into the mood, I can bring up my energy, and then I can start inventing variations for each subsequent repetition. A fugue can be repeated endlessly, and it can be reinvented every time; it's a great way to experiment and blow off steam at the same time. The *Little Fugue* was my favorite, because no matter what mood I'm in, the *Little Fugue* can express it, depending on how I attack the keys—happy or sad, angry or triumphant, it's all in the feeling. There's this place inside the sound where it stops being music and starts being *something else*—pure soul, I guess. There's no word for it, but if you've been there, you know; and if you haven't, then I feel sorry for you.

I played it fast, I played it slow, I played it loud, I played it soft—I played it every way I knew. I played it with all the different feelings that were churning around in me—how angry I was at this whole damn mess, how sad I was for those who had died, how lonely I felt out here behind the backside of nowhere, how much I cared about J'mee—

At some point, I realized that I wasn't alone. J'mee was behind me, playing the drums. And Trent had come in and picked up his clarinoboe. And a little later, Gary joined us, filling in the melodic line with guitar-riffs. And after that, two of the crew members who made up our string section arrived. By the time we finally segued into "Amazing Grace," we were right where I always wanted us to be, riding inside the flow of music and emotion like our own personal hyperstate.

As the final chords died away, I looked around the cabin, breathlessly. Almost the entire orchestra was here. Waiting for my next instruction. I swiveled around to look at J'mee. "Why are you all here?"

"We heard you playing."

"Huh?"

She pointed at the console above my keyboard. The red lights were on. We were broadcasting to the entire ship. How long—?

"Didn't you intend this?"

"Uh—no, I just came up here to work out my own feelings. I didn't realize—"

"Well, now that you have everybody's attention, Chigger—" I knew what she was going to say, even before she said it. "Let's go for it—"

The others nodded their agreement. There was a piece we'd been rehearsing—

"We're not ready. We haven't rehearsed it anywhere near enough. And we planned it for the arrival at Outbeyond, not here—"

"So what? We need it *now*."

"But—"

"Do it, Charles! It'll be fine. Trust me."

Yes, she was right. And I did trust her—and I was thrilled that I could.

I looked to see if Mom was here—she was—so I nodded my agreement. "Okay, everybody, let's do it." I took a breath, then brought up the score on my display. As the specific parts came up on everyone else's monitors, I could hear their quiet approval and enthusiasm. They were ready for this too.

I glanced around to see if everybody was ready—

Beethoven's Ninth Symphony is a landmark among landmarks. Dad regarded it as the greatest symphony ever written—possibly the greatest piece of music ever written. (Though sometimes he liked to argue that the Beach Boys' "Good Vibrations" was the Ninth all rolled into one; but I never knew if he was teasing or not when he said that.)

As an orchestral construction, the Ninth is a nightmare. It's long, it's complex, it's exhausting. It's seventy-five minutes long, *without* the repeats. To do it justice, you need a small army of strings and a battalion of brass on their flanks. And for the fourth movement, you need four singers trained in the impossible, and a chorus of at least forty to back them up. Dad said that only geniuses and fools attempted the Ninth. And he had a shelf full of recordings to prove it—especially the fool part. (There was this one performance he liked to drag out that was so slow and turgid, so bad you could almost hear the audience moaning in pain.)

But for all of the difficulty in performing it correctly, the Ninth is its own reward because the music is so sublime. And as big a fool as a person might be for attempting it, he's an even bigger fool for *never* attempting it. . . .

So I did something that was either dreadful or magnificent, depending on your prejudices.

I reinvented it.

We didn't have half the instruments we needed, so we handed around the parts to the instruments we did have and we used synthesizers and doublers to create a different body of sound. The hard part was the chorale movement. Mom and I had struggled the hardest with that.

I could hand off the choral parts to a synthesizer and we could even superimpose the actual words onto the sound, that was no problem; a single talented keyboardist could carry a large part of the burden—a fact which used to make Dad crazy sometimes. He used to do a great rant about how synthesizers would be the death of the grand orchestra—only they hadn't killed the orchestra in two centuries, so maybe it was just part of the performance of being a *traditional* conductor.

—But the four interlocking voices in the finale of the "Ode To Joy" simply couldn't be faked by instruments. They had to be sung by real people. And we didn't have four singers on the whole ship who were classically trained. We had Mom.

Finally, in our only concession to our own limits, we pre-recorded the vocal parts. Mom did all four—soprano, alto/contralto, tenor, and baritone—we transposed her voice up for the soprano and down for the tenor and baritone parts. We put them into the conductor's master program so that they could be conducted like any other instrument, and Mom rode that board. Only three of her voices were canned, she insisted on singing the alto/contralto part live.

Dad had once told me to think of the Ninth as a voyage from chaos to joy. The first movement is the void movement, in which order is invented out of mystery; the second movement is a wild dance of delight, overexuberant and almost out of control; then suddenly, dropping us down into the startling surprise of the long slow adagio of the third, a time of thoughtfulness and grace and preparation for the gathering excitement still to come; and then finally, the fourth movement, which momentarily reprises the first three and then abruptly discards them all and explodes into the most beautiful noise possible—

I gave the downbeat and we started playing.

If you've heard the recording, you don't need me to describe it. And if you haven't heard the record, then no amount of description will do it justice.

We were good.

We were very good.

We were brilliant.

We were inspired.

We got inside the music and we didn't come out again until the sweat was puddled up underneath our arms and glistening on our faces and floating in globules throughout the cabin. We were flushed with emotion and triumph and a giddy feeling of delighted astonishment at what we had just accomplished. And if anyone had spoken to me in that final moment while the echoes were still bouncing around the cabin and inside my head, I wouldn't have been able to answer, I'd have just broken down crying in frustration and joy that the universe was filled with so many beautiful ways to be human. I was crying anyway—

J'mee swam over and hugged me. And then Mom too. She whispered into my ear, *"Your father would be so proud of you!"* And then everybody else in the cabin was cheering and applauding too.

We didn't hear the rest of the applause until someone popped open the hatch to the cabin. And even then, we still didn't have any idea how big an impact the music had made—not until later, when Kisa Fentress swam up wide-eyed. Everything on the entire ship had come to a halt, she reported. People just stopped what they were doing and *listened* in awe. Even Boynton had given up what he was trying to do—which was make a decision on the mutineers, probably—and had just surrendered his heart to the music.

For seventy-five minutes, the starship *Cascade* had been united. It wasn't quite peace, but it was a start.

And not only the starship, but the colony below as well. When the trials had started, Boynton had ordered all of the ship's proceedings relayed down to the surface, so there wouldn't be any doubt about the whys and wherefores. So they received our entire concert too.

The thing about rapture . . . it stays with you. It changes you. It makes you a better person.

I can't prove it, but I think that moment was the turning point. Maybe everything would have gotten better without the music, but the music was there, and just by existing, it was the seed around which the healing crystallized—because for a moment, just for *that* moment, everybody on board rediscovered their ability to smile.

And for that little time while the music filled the emptiness so far from home, a lot of people had time to think and feel and remember who they really were and what they were all about.

And maybe that was enough. Maybe that was all that was needed. Because after that, things did calm down and folks stopped talking about getting even and started talking about getting better. And that was a much more useful conversation to have.

DECISIONS

BOYNTON **ANNOUNCED HIS DECISION** to a packed gymnasium. He spoke without prelude.

"We will honor our part of the contract. We will deliver supplies and colonists to New Revelation. We will drop all of the contracted cargo pods as agreed. We will deliver all colonists who choose to conclude their journey here.

"In addition to all of the supplies we have contracted to deliver—and as a humanitarian gesture to the desperate people of New Revelation—we will also send down as much extra food and medical supplies as we can fit into the landing pods. We will drop cargo pods, containing as much water as we can spare beyond our own needs.

"But we will *not* send down any landers. Nor will we pick up any passengers. We will not risk exposing our equipment and personnel to further attacks or confiscation. Therefore, any colonist who wishes to debark at New Revelation will have to ride a pod down. The landings can be a little bit rough, but we will make appropriate accommodations for your safety.

"Any colonist who chooses *not* to land at New Revelation may continue on to Outbeyond—with the following exceptions: Dr. Daniel Pettyjohn, all of the members of the now-disbanded Revelationist Council, the sixteen individuals involved in the manufacture of illegal weapons, and the seven individuals who attempted to use those weapons in a mutinous uprising. These individuals will all be sent down in cargo pods. Their families may accompany them, or they may continue on with the rest of us to Outbeyond.

"However, be aware—there is a condition. Those who continue on with us will be prohibited from practicing the Revelationist faith—not because we disapprove of the faith, we do not, but because the actions taken in the name of this faith have disqualified it from recognition and participation in the social contract of Outbeyond.

"I am ordering these measures under my authority as Captain of the *Cascade*. They will take effect immediately.

"We begin dropping cargo pods in twelve hours. Those of you who are landing, you will report to Flight Engineer Damron by oh-six-hundred for docketing. Those of you are continuing on with us, you will report to Security Chief Lang by oh-six-hundred for clearance. If you have any questions, see either Damron or Lang.

"Let me also state for the record that these orders were submitted for advice and consent to the elected representatives of the Outbeyond Colony Council. The Council voted unanimously to endorse them."

That last part was the most important. Boynton didn't need to ask anyone to approve his orders. A Captain has Supreme Authority. But it was necessary for the rest of us to know that he was not acting alone—but with the full support of Outbeyond's local authority. He was acting in our name and on our behalf. It was imperative that we stand with him.

He made as if to turn away, then stopped himself and turned back to face us all. "There is one other thing . . ."

This time, his voice was more relaxed. If it had been anyone but Boynton, I'd have even thought *friendly*. "This morning, I have ordered one of our landers to be refitted as an interplanetary shuttle. That conversion should be complete just about the time we cross the orbit of Gabriel. We intend to locate an appropriate ice-asteroid and detach the shuttle in a favorable trajectory with a crew of Revelationist volunteers who will bring that ice-asteroid back to New Revelation.

"It is a difficult and risky mission, and the chances of success are not great. There are no guarantees. And in this situation in particular, success will require the triumph of human determination over the laws of physics in an obstinate universe. Nevertheless, we are committed to making this effort. We recognize that all of us—Outbeyonder and Revelationist alike—have a common bond of humanity that will *always* be larger than any of our differences. No matter how hard some of us might argue that our differences are insurmountable, they are *not*.

"This is the lesson we must learn, here and now, and for all time to come. Because we are human beings, we are partners in a common cause. We forget that at our own risk. We have already seen how dangerous it is to make our disagreements more important than our partnership. We must never do that again. There is nothing to gain by that and too much to lose.

"It is time for human beings to create a community of mutual respect and partnership. It begins *here*. It begins *now*.

"Thank you, and let's go to work."

After that, it was simply a matter of carrying out the orders. Most of it was simple, because we already knew how to do it. But some of it wasn't—

Trent Colwell's dad had been a member of the Revelationist Council. That meant that he was a mutineer. That meant he was going to be sent down in a cargo pod—that wasn't negotiable. But the rest of the family had to decide if they were going down with him.

They weren't the only family who had to make such a decision, but they were the only family I knew. I'd heard there was a lot of crying and anguish in the other hearings. I'd heard that Boynton and the Council were determined to be as compassionate as possible. But it was a troubling process for everyone.

J'mee and I were there when the Colwell family came before the Outbeyond Council. We wanted to be there for Trent.

Trent's mom was holding three-year-old Willa. Trent was holding onto six-year-old Jason. They all looked scared—all except little Willa, who had no idea what was going on and kept asking if she could have a peaner-butter sammich. Trent looked at us once, then looked away, embarrassed. But every so often, he'd sneak a look back over at us, and I got the feeling he wanted to say something. Or maybe he just wanted to talk to us for a bit. But that wasn't possible right now—

Commander Boynton came in late, and he didn't look happy. He never looked happy, but this time he looked unhappier than usual. "Have you made your decision?" he asked.

"My family will go with me," Mr. Colwell said bluntly. He was wearing plastic handcuffs and there was a security guard on either side of him. Mrs. Colwell looked like she wanted to object, but was afraid to speak up.

Boynton ignored Mr. Colwell's declaration, looked instead to Mrs. Colwell. "Sarah, is it? What is *your* choice?"

She hung her head. She couldn't look directly at him. She mumbled something.

"Say again? Louder this time."

"I have to go with my husband. I promised before God that I would love, honor, and serve."

"You understand, of course, that you will probably die down there. And your children as well. You cannot depend on the ice-mission to save you."

Before she could answer, Mr. Colwell started shouting. "You're trying to break up my family, you devil-spawn! You have no right to do this!"

Boynton ignored him. To Lang, he said, "If the prisoner speaks again, stun him." He turned back to Mrs. Colwell. "Sarah, doesn't your faith tell you to preserve the lives of your children?"

She nodded unhappily.

"And you still want to accompany your husband?"

"It is my duty—"

"So be it—" Boynton started to make a note on his clipboard.

That's when Trent finally spoke up. "I'm not going," he said.

"Eh?" Boynton looked up.

"I'm not going," he repeated. "I don't want to go to New Revelation. I want to go to Outbeyond."

Boynton looked annoyed. "Son, I'm not sure if we can—"

He turned to Damron and Everhart and whispered, *"What's the legal situation for a minor?"*

Damron started to respond, *"You could emancipate him—"*

"He's only what? Fourteen, thirteen—?"

Trent's dad was yelling again. "Shut up, Trent. You'll do what you're told." Trent's mom was crying now.

"No!" shouted Trent. "I want a divorce!"

That caught everybody's attention. Especially mine.

"Son, do you understand what you're saying?"

Trent nodded vigorously. "Commander Boynton, I want to go to Outbeyond."

"But a divorce? You'll never see your parents again."

"Charles got a divorce when his parents went crazy. And he was only thirteen! I want one too."

Trent's dad was screaming now. "This is what happens when you hang around devil-children!" He pointed at me. "You put this sinful idea into his head, didn't you?!"

"No, he didn't!" Trent whirled to face his dad. "Chigger had nothing to do with it. Nobody did. I don't want to go to New Revelation. I don't want to die. I want to make music. I want to go to Outbeyond and see the dinosaurs and the oceans and the stink-plants. I want to have my own life!"

"All right, everybody shut up!" said Boynton. He couldn't exactly bang a gavel in free fall, but he could turn up the volume on his microphone, and that had the same effect. Except for Mr. Colwell, everybody stopped talking.

"Don't I have any rights in this court?" he demanded.

"Actually, no." said Boynton. "You gave up your rights when you conspired to commit mutiny." He turned around and whispered with Damron and Everhart for a long moment. Finally, he turned back to the rest of the room. "All right, it's the decision of this council that Trent Colwell be emancipated from his family and placed under the guardianship of a suitable adult—"

Mr. Colwell was about to say something else, but before he could, Sarah Colwell turned to him and said, "Shut up, stupid." To Boynton, she said, "Please, Commander—will you take Willa and Jason too?"

"Eh?" For the second time this meeting, Boynton looked surprised. He didn't like surprises.

"My children deserve a chance at their own lives. My husband and I will die on New Revelation. But not my children!"

"Mommy?" That was Jason. "Are you going to die?"

"Shh," she whispered. *"Everything's going to be all right. You're going with Trent."*

"Mrs. Colwell, are you sure this is what you want?"

"Yes, Commander, I'm sure."

Her husband was staring at her astonished. "Sarah Colwell, what are you doing—?"

"I'm saving the lives of my babies." She faced her husband. "I promised God that I would stand by you, and I will. But these innocent children haven't made any such promise. I might have to join you in death. They do not." And then she said something surprising. "I love you. I will go where you go. I will die with you, if need be. That will have to be enough. Let them go, John—"

John Colwell's expression was horrible. His emotions flickered back and forth between anger and horror and things I couldn't identify, and if he hadn't been handcuffed, if he hadn't been held back by Lang and Martin, who knew what he might have done? And then—he collapsed inside himself. Just floating there, he seemed to wither and shrink. Tears began welling up in his eyes, and when he spoke, his voice cracked. His voice was filled with grief. "Sarah Colwell, I rebuke you. I rebuke you. I rebuke you. I send you away into the spiritual wasteland. I cast you out. You are forbidden to accompany me. I will go alone into Paradise, and you must go into the exile of eternal damnation. Get thee behind me, thou whore of Babylon—"

There was more, but we never got to hear it. Boynton lost patience and signaled Lang. Lang stunned him. He spasmed for a second, then floated limp and silent.

Boynton looked to Sarah Colwell. "Mrs. Colwell, it will be hard enough for your children to lose one parent, let alone two. I urge you to reconsider and come to Outbeyond."

She hung her head. "He has cast me out. I am not allowed to follow him. I have no choice but to go with you." And then she swept all three of her children into her arms and started crying.

I looked to J'mee. Her eyes were wet and shining. *"Poor John Colwell,"* she whispered. *"What a brave thing to do."*

"Huh—?"

"Don't you get it? He couldn't order her to go to Outbeyond. She wouldn't do it. She couldn't—because she promised God she would follow her husband. The only way he could save her life was to cast her away. They both knew that. He did it because he loves her, Chigger. He wants her to live."

"Oh," I said.

There was a lot I still didn't understand about love. This was part of it.

But in that moment, I envied them their commitment. And I wondered if J'mee and I would ever be like that. I hoped so. But I also hoped we'd never have to test it like this.

HARLIE

THERE WAS ONE OTHER thing—I was curious, and after a while my curiosity got the better of me, so eventually I found some time alone with the monkey.

We were in the briefing room, just behind the flight deck.

"HARLIE, when we began this voyage, you made a series of projections about the possibilities of our survival at Outbeyond, didn't you?"

"Yes, Charles. And I made some recommendations as well."

"Lots of rice and beans and noodles."

"Yes."

"And Commander Boynton followed your recommendations, didn't he?"

"Yes, he did. They were good, common-sense predictions. Anyone could have made them. It didn't take an intelligence engine. But most people give more credence to good advice when it comes from an intelligence engine."

"On the day we launched," I continued, "what was your estimate of our chances?"

"I was cautiously optimistic that Outbeyond Colony would survive. Although the margin of error was uncomfortably narrow, the commitment of the people aboard this starship was sufficiently strong that, barring any unforeseen disasters, success seemed more likely than failure. And it was my job to prevent unforeseen disasters."

"By foreseeing them."

"Yes."

I was starting to feel like a lawyer. But I had to ask. "HARLIE, as of oh-three-thirty hours today, we have given up one of our landers, plus the boosters and fuel and supplies to convert it into a long-range planetary shuttle. We have offloaded eighty-three colonists for New Revelation. The other two-hundred and one are proceeding with us to Outbeyond. Those two-hundred and one colonists represent an additional and unplanned drain on our resources. Nevertheless, we have dropped the full load of supplies for New Revelation, including all of the extra food containers they appropriated from centrifuge two and elsewhere, and six extra pods of water. This increases their margin of survival. But it decreases ours correspondingly. Doesn't it?"

"That's a logical assumption."

"I didn't ask for an assumption, HARLIE. Tell me your current estimation of the long-term viability of both colonies."

The monkey didn't hesitate. "The long-term viability of both colonies has been significantly improved."

"Huh—?" That got my attention, all right.

"All of the projections were based on the assumption that three-hundred new colonists would land at New Revelation, but with only one-third the projected number taking up residence, there is a correspondingly smaller drain on the colony's supplies. If the colonists at New Revelation are careful to ration the food and water that we sent down, they should be able to survive until the lander returns with an ice asteroid. The asteroid can be parked in a dark-side orbit and mined at the colony's convenience, or it can be Palmer-tubed and landed somewhere near the colony, or it can be dropped on the pole to break the mantle and release the subterranean water there, whatever is most appropriate. If it works, the colony should be able to plant new crops within eighteen months and might very well achieve a measure of self-sufficiency. This was not a possibility before."

"I understand that much," I said. "That's all in the plan that you and Boynton worked out together. It's the *other* side of that equation that hasn't been explained."

"Yes, I know."

"Go on, HARLIE."

"Can Outbeyond afford to give up those supplies—?"

The monkey grinned at me, a good sign; it was finally starting to get its emotional signals right. He said, "Do you remember the extra rice and beans and noodles I advised Commander Boynton to load?"

"Yes . . . ?"

"I never said those would be needed at Outbeyond. I just said they were needed. They were. They were needed for New Revelation."

"You knew all this was going to happen?"

"The potential was obvious from the beginning." The monkey explained, "When Boynton asked me to project viability, I had to look at *all* the parts of the problem—not just what we were loading at Luna, but what we would be unloading at Outbeyond. Knowing how fragile the situation might be at New Revelation, I recognized that the margin of error had to include both colonies, and if there were a problem at New Revelation, that problem would affect Outbeyond as well. All those extra supplies—I was allowing for the possibility that we would need to be generous."

"Why didn't you tell Commander Boynton this?"

"Because, Charles, I had to include my own participation as a factor. I learned that lesson back on Earth, if you'll recall. People who were entrusted with the knowledge of the impending polycrisis used it for personal gain, making the polycrisis worse. I didn't dare tell anyone. There's no way to keep a secret on a starship—and if this particular projection had become known aboard the *Cascade,* it could have adversely affected the onboard situation in any number of ways."

I had to think about that. He was right, of course. I'd long since learned not to argue with an intelligence engine. The best I could do was try to keep up and figure out how it had reached its conclusions.

"For one thing, the Revelationists would have presumed ownership of the extra supplies, regardless of need," HARLIE explained. "They did anyway. They knew how desperate their situation was likely to be, even without the failure of the *Conway.* I projected from the beginning that they would start stealing from Outbeyond's supplies and included that in my calculations. So I told Commander Boynton to load more rice, beans, and noodles, and I didn't say why. And he never questioned it. None of you did."

"I'll remember that," I said. "For future reference."

"I expect you to," the monkey replied.

We both hung there in space for a bit, studying each other. I began to realize something. The monkey was waiting for me to finish this entire train of thought. There was something I was still missing.

Why was HARLIE telling me this *now?* What was it he needed me to understand?

Of course—

"You little snake . . ." I said.

"I beg your pardon? I'm a monkey."

"You know what I mean."

"If you mean I manipulated the situation, yes I did. But you already knew that, Charles. That's why Dr. Pettyjohn was able to infect you with his fear of me."

"But he never understood the other side of the equation, did he? He missed the obvious."

"Go on."

The whole thing was clear to me now. "If it's possible to manipulate a situation for selfish goals, it's also possible to manipulate it for *un*selfish purposes too."

"Bingo," said the monkey. "That's all there is. Everybody manipulates. The difference is what you manipulate *for*. Selfish people don't know that."

"That's why they fail, isn't it?"

"Most of them," the monkey agreed. He looked at me. "Go ahead, Chigger. Put the last piece in."

It was my turn to grin. "This proves that you're sentient, doesn't it? Because it takes sentience to perform a truly unselfish act."

The monkey grinned. "Not quite. But that's where sentience begins. *Real sentience.*"

But that was a much longer conversation, and one for another time.

CODA

I TOOK HARLIE BACK to the bridge. I returned him to his station between the Captain and First Officer.

"So?" Boynton asked. "Can we trust him to take us to Outbeyond?"

"Oh, yes. Of course."

"No more doubts?"

"No, sir."

He put down his checklist and looked at me. "Why not?"

"Because I've had more conversations with HARLIE since then."

Boynton swiveled his couch all the way around to face me. "All right. So let me see if I understand this. Some of your conversations with HARLIE unnerved you—so you went back and had more conversations with him? And that *reassured* you?"

"No, sir."

"No?"

"No, sir. It wasn't the conversations. That's just talk. You can talk from now until forever and so what? It isn't talking that makes a difference. It's *doing*."

"And . . . ?"

"HARLIE makes a difference. He does *good* things."

"It's that simple?"

"Yes, sir."

"Hm." Boynton grunted to himself. "I wish we could all learn that lesson. It would save a lot of time and trouble. Thank you, Ensign. Take your station." He swiveled forward again. I was dismissed.

I went back to the briefing room behind the bridge and perched myself in front of the keyboard. I powered it up and wriggled my fingers.

"Stand by for ignition—" the Captain called.

"All boards green," Damron reported.

I put my fingers to the keys and started playing.